PASSION IN THE ARMS OF A DANGEROUS WOMAN

As yet he could not understand the miracle by which the cool and lovely Angelita had come to yield herself to him, and was sure that she must be slowly aroused if the embrace of love were to mean more to her than simply pain.

But when his hands had touched her body in a caress, he soon found a naked houri in his arms, eagerly matching his own desire with an even greater one.

Books by Frank G. Slaughter

Published by POCKET BOOKS

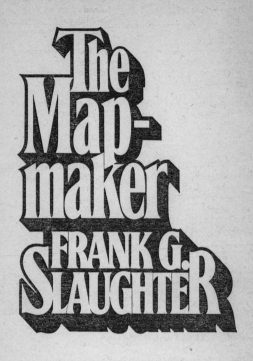

The Map-maker

FRANK G. SLAUGHTER

A KANGAROO BOOK
PUBLISHED BY POCKET BOOKS NEW YORK

POCKET BOOKS, a Simon & Schuster division of
GULF & WESTERN CORPORATION
1230 Avenue of the Americas, New York, N.Y. 10020

ISBN: 0-671-81192-4

First Pocket Books printing March, 1978

Trademarks registered in the United States and other countries.

Printed in the U.S.A.

Author's Preface

I am by no means the first to be convinced that no sharp line can be drawn separating fiction from history. *The Mapmaker* is a novel, and yet real history is an integral part of every page. Andrea Bianco, the mapmaker of this story, actually lived, as did Fra Mauro, Bartholomeu di Perestrello, Prince Henry of Portugal, a Norse shipmaster called Vallarte, a Venetian galley captain named Alvise de Cadamosto, the geographer Jahuda Cresques, and many others who appear in the succeeding pages. Some fifty years before the epic voyage of Christopher Columbus, Andrea Bianco drew one of the first maps of the world. Upon it appear several islands with an amazing resemblance to Cuba, Jamaica, one of the Bahamas, and at least the southern part of Florida. The Bianco map, in turn, seems to have been patterned after the "Nautical Chart of 1424," the original of which is now in the James Ford Bell Collection at the University of Minnesota.

At least five hundred years before Columbus, Arab seamen were making routine voyages across the Indian Ocean, covering many thousands of miles and making amazingly exact landfalls upon the ports of India. For navigation they used a device called the Al-Kemal. Whether or not, as many believe, Phoenician sailors saw the shores of America centuries before Christ will, of course, never be known, although much evidence has been accumulated to show that this is true. Whatever knowledge of the world existed prior to the fifteenth century—and it was considerable—the first real breakthrough in Atlantic exploration occurred early in that century.

It was then that Prince Henry of Portugal, immortalized much later as "The Navigator," gathered on the promontory of Sagres 'at the southern tip of that country many of the foremost mapmakers, navigators, astronomers, mathematicians, shipbuilders, and sailing masters of the day. From this treasure house of knowledge came inspiration for the Portuguese voyages of exploration leading to the circumnavigation of Africa, the discovery of a water route to India by Vasco da Gama, and in all probability the stimulus that sent Christopher Columbus sailing westward some fifty years later.

Against this background I have chosen to set my story. To acknowledge the hundreds of references consulted in developing an authentic picture of this exciting period of history would, of course, be impossible. I do owe a particular debt to Messrs. Simon & Schuster for permission to use the songs of the gromets from Samuel Eliot Morison's superb biography of Columbus, *Admiral of the Ocean Sea*, as well as other valuable facts concerning ships and sailing in the fifteenth century. *Conquest by Man* by Paul Herrmann (Harper & Brothers), "Fourteenth Century Discovery of America by Antonio Zeno" by W. H. Hobbs (*Scientific Monthly*, Vol. 72), *A History of Marine Navigation* by Per Collinder (St. Martin's), and the brochure *Antillia and America* from the University of Minnesota describing the "Nautical Chart of 1424" have been especially valuable, along with many other books of reference.

My greatest debt goes, however, to the chief actor in this drama, Andrea Bianco . . . THE MAPMAKER.

Frank G. Slaughter
NOVEMBER 2, 1956

Contents

BOOK ONE
The Learned One
1

BOOK TWO
The Al-Kemal
57

BOOK THREE
Land of Wealth
117

BOOK FOUR
Voyage to Antillia
177

BOOK FIVE
The Hand of Satan
235

BOOK ONE

The Learned One

I

E<small>L HAKIM—LEARNED ONE—THE OTHER SLAVES CALLED</small>
him, because at night, when they were allowed to rest for
a few hours upon the rowers' benches and lie looking up
at the skies, he would sometimes talk of the fabulous lands
that lay to the east. When El Hakim spoke of the heavens
and how, by using the stars, a man could guide a great
ship across the boundless ocean to the Spice Islands, the
distant realm of India, and as far east as the domain of the
great Khan and the Island of Cipangu, the spell of his
words gripped them as nothing else could. Then even galley
slaves could forget for a while the agony of pulling long
oars in the heat of the midday sun, with the whips of the
overseers always ready to fall upon the naked backs of any
who faltered. Only a few of the wretched dregs of human-
ity huddling on the rowers' benches actually believed the
tales of the tall man with the deep-set burning eyes and
the black beard, but none jeered him. They knew the
strength of the Learned One—did these slaves of Hamet-
el-Baku, the scourge of Barbary—and had no wish to
arouse his anger.

More than once El Hakim's oar had taken over the pull
for another so that Abdul, the overseer, did not notice the
faltering, thus saving a sore back from the whip or perhaps
a slave from death. The lash was the only cure the slave
drivers knew for weakness, idleness, or even sickness. If an
oarsman slumped at his handle, he was whipped until unconscious. Then a piece of bread soaked in wine was thrust
between his lips, and if this failed to revive him, his body
was unleashed from the long chain that bound him to the
bench and dumped overboard.

It was truly said that death was the only escape from the
galleys, death at the oars or by capture in battle between
the corsairs and the ships that plied the narrow passage
between Sicily and the mainland of Africa. Nor did capture often improve the lot of the galley slaves, since it only
meant exchanging one hard taskmaster for another,
whether Christian or Moslem.

Today the slaves at the oars were not pressed, for the

3

big lateen sail was taut and full before the single mast and the sleek brigantino sped across the great rollers like a sea bird about to take flight. To the north the dark mountainous outline of the island of Sicily rose on the horizon, helping to form the narrow passage between the islands and the mainland of Africa dividing the Mediterranean here into two parts, as a girdle cinches the waist of a buxom maid.

Through this channel all shipping between Genoa, Florence, the cities of Spain and Portugal, and the far coasts of England and France must sail on the way to Venice, the ports of Greece, or the distant storied cities of Constantinople and Trebizond unless they chose the route of caution through the Stretto di Messina to the north.

It was a choice preying ground, this area dominated by Hamet-el-Baku and his fleet of brigantinos. Actually they spent almost as much time battling other contenders for it as they did attacking Christian shipping, but so rich were the prizes that even the continual fighting among themselves was well worth the trouble. After all, what was the loss of an occasional fighting man, a few galley slaves, or even an entire brigantino in battle, when the return from a single captured merchant ship and its cargo could make a captain rich in a single day?

Smaller and lighter than the Venetian galleys—which alone were free from attack because of the tribute paid annually to the corsairs by the shipowners of Venice—the pirate brigantino had but one mast and no castle on the prow. It was equipped instead with a huge iron ram projecting beyond the bowsprit for crashing through the sides of a vessel. Eighteen banks of oars with three men to each gave the sleek vessel the utmost in mobility. The hundred-odd fighting men jamming the poop and the narrow waist of the ship between the benches of the rowers made it a formidable opponent in the swift strikes by which the corsairs stunned and held their prey.

More than half of the sixty galley slaves were Christians, the rest having been hired in Tunis, Algiers, Tehran, or El Araish at ten ducats a trip, whether or not a prize was taken. The soldiers were partly volunteers or levents, mostly Turks but some *Kuroghler* or natives, in this case Ottoman Janissaries. Their number was limited to roughly twice the roster of galley slaves by the size of the ship, but they could be counted upon to fight at the command

of their own aga, since they were not paid unless a prize
was taken.

While the sails furnished motive power and the slaves
were able to rest—often their only chance for as much as
twenty hours on a stretch—one from each pair of oars had
been freed of his bonds to bring jars of the mixture of
vinegar, oil, and water that served as a drink for them
and the moistened biscuit or rusk that furnished their food.
On the center catwalk, where half the fighting men sat, and
on the poop the soldiers were regaling themselves with
wine bought with gold from their own purses.

El Hakim's position was at the after oar, near the huge
steering sweeps hanging from the stern on both sides of the
ship. He had been unshackled to bring food and drink to
the others and while he sat drinking the sharp-flavored
brew and munching bread his eyes were roving the sea
ahead for some sign of a ship that might be able to fight
against the swift brigantino and thus, by some miracle,
effect the release of the slaves. He had hoped for such a
miracle so many times that the faint possibility of succor
seemed hardly worth the trouble, yet he kept on, knowing
that the moment when he gave up hoping would mark the
beginning of the end, leaving him like the others who
slumped hopelessly over the long oars, with only a loin-
cloth to protect their bodies from the wind and sun.

The rowers' benches had two steps and the slaves were
chained loosely to them by one ankle. When rowing, they
climbed the steps, following the rotation of the oar as the
ship moved forward. When the long blade bit into the
water, the rowers stepped backward in unison, with a
brusque jerk and a muscle-straining pull that could jar a
man's teeth, until he learned to clench them for greater
effort and to keep back a cry of pain at the lash of the
overseer's whip. This was the body blow of the galley
slaves, far more powerful than the simple backward thrust
of an oarsman. The palms and buttocks of the slaves had
long ago become as hard as sharkskin, and they were rarely
allowed to wash for fear of splitting the callosities.

Over and over again, this maneuver was repeated when
the brigantino was driven at full speed, hour after hour
with no relief. Chained to the timbers of the ship itself,
the half-naked and nearly starved wretches sometimes
spent twenty years of their lives—if they were unlucky
enough to live that long—in the same ship.

For an artist the body of El Hakim would have made a perfect model. Not so much as an ounce of extra flesh could be found upon him as he sat waiting for the chain to be secured, the sinews rippling beneath his skin like those of a graceful jungle cat ready to spring upon its prey. Even in repose a tense alertness and a quick intelligence distinguished him from the other slaves, who slumped upon the oars, pictures of hopelessness and resignation to their fates.

"A ship!" came a sudden cry from the lookout clinging to the masthead above the sail.

Instantly the whole picture on the brigantino changed. The jars in which the water and food had been stored were quickly put away. Soldiers looked to their weapons, and, in spaces below the rowers' benches, gunners blew upon slow-burning matches and looked to the squat bombards that could smash an iron ball through the hull of a wooden ship almost at the water line, or loaded slender falconettes, which could rake the deck of a victim with jagged fragments of metal and small stones.

In the excitement of raising a possible prey, the overseer who was locking the fetters failed to secure El Hakim. The Learned One quickly crouched down with the others, leaving the long chain that ordinarily attached him to the bench lying close beside him as if it were secured, while a sudden excitement sang in his heart. After five years of torture and toil, this might be the day he had been waiting for and the mere promise of it filled him with a quick exultation. Crouching at the oar, he prayed silently that the distant ship would not turn out to be a Venetian galley, for then the corsair must let it pass unharmed.

"Slaves, to your oars!" Hamet-el-Baku commanded from where he stood on the small afterdeck. The overseers repeated the order, laying the whips across the bare backs of the oarsmen to make certain of instant obedience. While the rais in charge of the rowers chanted the rhythm, the slaves threw themselves against the oars to escape further lashing, and the swift brigantino literally lifted her skirts like a fleeing maiden and ran across the water.

This was hard rowing, for the rhythm was twice as fast as when the great lateen sail was not pulling with them. A false move here, a foot slipping on benches that were always wet with sweat and the excretions of the slaves, who did not move sometimes for a whole day, could snarl a whole bank of the long oars in hopeless confusion. The overseers prowled the central catwalk, stepping between the fighting men crouched there and the bent backs of the gunners kneeling beside their weapons, ready to bring the cruel lash of the whip down upon any sunburned body that showed signs of faltering.

Like the others, El Hakim crouched over his oar and concentrated upon the task of pulling. He took fully half the load of his own oar upon himself with his strong muscles and back, so there would be no faltering to call the attention of the overseer to the fact that his fetters had been left unsecured. Occasionally, when he rose to lift the end of the huge oar and engage the blade in the water, he was able to glance in the direction toward which the brigantino was moving so swiftly.

At first he could make out only the outline of a ship ahead, but as the two vessels came closer together, he was soon able to distinguish the pattern of its sails and the shape of its hull. The first quick evaluation brought no satisfaction; the other ship seemed small, smaller than many of the victims Hamet-el-Baku had successfully attacked in the past. As it came nearer, however, sailing bravely on, although its master must undoubtedly have seen the attacking brigantino, El Hakim's hopes began to rise. For there was something about the outlines of the caravel—he recognized it as such immediately—that told him this was no ordinary merchant ship crammed with cargo but poorly defended.

Her lines were much trimmer than most vessels in the Mediterranean and there was almost a rakish tilt to her three masts. She was moving fast, too. Having crowded on all sail with the intention of trying to outrun the brigantino she was already swinging into a course that would bring her close to the looming headlands of Sicily where the pursuer would be afraid to follow for fear of being trapped.

With all canvas flying, the caravel had a small square foresail on the foremast, a square mainsail and topsail on the main, with a lateen on the mizzen. In the freshening breeze she made a beautiful sight, and a murmur of admiration arose from the attacking vessel. The galley slave had no time for anything save the long sweeps that drove the pirate craft on in pursuit, but El Hakim still managed every now and then to catch a glimpse of the caravel and

her beauty filled him with a savage sense of exaltation—
and hope.

The converging courses of the two vessels—the other
seeking to escape and the swift brigantino speeding to in-
tercept—brought them steadily closer together. The
caravel's strategy was obviously to outrun the attacker
and reach the safety of one of the ports along the south
shore of Sicily. Equally apparent was Hamet-el-Baku's
intention to ram the larger vessel in mid-flight and thus
bring her up short, so the fierce levents and Janissaries,
eagerly testing the edges of their curved scimitars, could
take her in one swift boarding action.

Faster grew the rhythm chanted by the rais in charge
of the galley slaves and the poor wretches threw themselves
into a frenzied effort while the whips fell across their
straining backs without letup. The distance between the
two vessels was decreasing rapidly and El Hakim glimpsed
the bustle of preparations for the coming battle taking
place on the decks of the caravel. One man seemed to be
directing it, a tall red-bearded fellow wearing armor, but
the force available for the defense of the ship was obviously pitifully small compared to the close-packed ranks
of the fighting men waiting tensely upon the brigantino.

Only a rapidly narrowing space of open water separated
the two ships now. In the waist between the rowers'
benches the gunners had already charged the short squat
bombards and were blowing upon slow-burning matches.
An arrow from the caravel, driven from a long bow,
buzzed like an angry hornet and one of the levents near
El Hakim coughed and died with a three-foot length of
shaft through his breast. Realizing that their own bodies
had no protection at all from the arrows, some of the
slaves faltered in their rhythm, but the whips of the overseers cut through the air to paint a pattern of scarlet upon
straining brown backs.

El Hakim never let his pull upon the oar slacken, but
his alert eyes returned to the caravel at every opportunity.
Hamet-el-Baku was an old hand at this sort of warfare.
At the first arrow he had ordered the fighting men to
raise their shields, thus forming a temporary barrier to
protect the galley slaves and themselves. Now, ignoring
the arrows that were falling all around him and the whir-
ring of arbalest bolts, the Moorish captain was calmly directing the helmsmen who handled the long steering

sweeps—one on either side of the stern—extending almost vertically downward into the water. The caravel was steered by a rudder; El Hakim could see the great wooden tiller with its after end mortised into the rudder post. But, like many pirate leaders, Hamet-el-Baku preferred the older method of steering with two vertical sweeps, one on either side.

Slowly the prow of the corsair began to swing as one of the steersmen threw his weight upon his sweep; soon the course of the pursuer was centered upon an empty space of ocean ahead. Watching the two vessels, El Hakim could see that the Moorish captain had shrewdly chosen to ram the larger ship just aft the prow, where the force of the impact would damage her least. Such a valuable prize would sell for a high price in the markets, and with the obviously puny number of her defenders, there was no point in crippling the caravel more than just enough for the fighting men to swarm up across a bridge of oars on the port side of the brigantino and attain the decks of the doomed vessel. Once boarded by such a superior force, her fate would be settled in moments.

A sudden shout from his own ship directed El Hakim's quick glance to the caravel and he saw two brawny steersmen straining at the great bar of the tiller. The bow of the large vessel was swinging around, revealing that the red-haired man directing the caravel's defense had decided to employ the daring tactic of ramming the brigantino full amidships. With the banked oars on both sides, such a maneuver could fatally cripple the attacker in a matter of seconds.

Hamet-el-Baku was too skilled at this sort of thing to be taken by surprise, however. He spoke sharply to his steersmen and they in turn strained against the handles of the big sweeps, seeking to put the brigantino on a more parallel course that would still enable him to choose the place of contact. Watching the prow of the swift corsair start to swing, El Hakim realized that he must act now, if ever, for the chance which had left him unfettered might never come again.

As he bent forward upon the oar, he reached down with his right hand and seized the long chain lying loose on the bench beside him. Then he straightened up and in the same movement released his grip upon the oar. The strength of his strong-muscled limbs carried him in a tremendous flying leap to the edge of the small platform upon which the steersmen stood, with Hamet-el-Baku himself just behind and between them, where his commands could be heard and instantly obeyed.

El Hakim was weaponless, but as he swung the long chain in a wide circle, using both hands and all of his strength, a fierce joy of combat welled up within him. The heavy ring by which the fetters normally were secured to the rowing bench struck one of the steersmen across the temple, splitting his skull. His body tumbled from the platform and hung over the low railing around the deck for a moment, then dropped into the sea. So great was the astonishment of those around him that El Hakim was also able to butt the other steersman in the belly with his head and send him tumbling overboard, even while he prepared to swing the chain once more as a weapon against the corsair captain.

Hamet-el-Baku was an experienced fighter however. Drawing his curved sword, he launched a brutal cut at the galley slave's unprotected back, a cut that would have ended El Hakim's revolt and his life simultaneously had the blade touched him. But the Learned One was fighting for his life, too, and as the Moor slashed at him, he swung the chain again. It struck the sword, knocking it to the deck and, in the same motion, El Hakim grappled with Hamet-el-Baku upon the small afterdeck. Meanwhile the brigantino, with no hand now upon the steering sweeps, yawed wildly and lost way.

Even so, the day might have been saved for the Moors had any one of the crew recovered from his astonishment quickly enough to seize the steering oars while the captain and El Hakim wrestled for advantage. But the spectacle of an unarmed galley slave daring to attack his master was so utterly foreign to their experience that for an instant everything else was forgotten. And that instant, while the brigantino was momentarily out of control, turned the tide of battle.

Hamet-el-Baku was a strong and wily antagonist, but the knowledge that at any moment one of the subcaptains standing only a few paces away would recover his senses and sink a dagger into his back gave El Hakim the strength of desperation. With a quick twist of his body— a trick he'd learned from the huge-bellied wrestlers of Cipangu—he managed to fling the heavy body of Hamet-el-Baku through the air as a farmer would toss a sack of grain. The captain landed with a crash in the midst of the galley slaves only a moment before the caravel struck the Moorish vessel.

El Hakim was thrown to the deck by the force of the impact. Lying there, momentarily stunned, he saw the tall bows of the caravel tower above him as it sheared along the port side of the stricken brigantino, smashing oars and crushing bulwarks down to the water line. Above the crash of the timbers rose the agonized screaming of galley slaves whose bodies were being torn by the flailing, splintered ends of the oars and the shouting of the agas, seeking to marshal the fighting men, many of whom had been tossed into the sea in full armor to sink like stones.

Looking up at the deck of the caravel as he struggled to his feet, El Hakim found himself staring into the fiercely happy face of the tall, red-haired man who was directing its defense. He wore a conical-shaped helmet with a jutting face protector and carried on his left arm a round shield with a spike in the middle. A short-sword was in his right hand.

"The fire!" shouted the red-haired warrior exultantly. "Loose the fire."

Something hissed through the air and struck the narrow catwalk of the brigantino. Without sound, it exploded into a dozen licking tentacles of flame that ran about like small eager serpents. New screams of agony from the stricken men told Hakim what had happened before the voice of a Janissary cried, "The fire! The fire of the Greeks! Allah has deserted us."

Flames were already licking at the wooden benches and the catwalk, while globules of the liquid fire being poured down upon the doomed brigantino from the deck of the caravel dripped into the hull and set up new islands of flame deep within its bowels. A mixture containing principally pitch, sulphur, and lime, the "Greek fire" was a fiendish weapon which, once ignited, could not be extinguished by water, yielding only to sand or earth, neither of which the brigantino carried. The big lateen sail, flapping furiously upon its mast in a fresh breeze, caught fire now, and the roar of its flames added a devil's melody to the scene.

Unhurt except for a few bruises from the jarring crash to the deck at the moment of impact, the tall slave stood with the chain in his hands and laughed, leaning back and guffawing while those who a moment before had despised and flogged him now scampered furiously about in an attempt to save their puny lives, or leaped overboard to escape the flames. Meanwhile the grinding crash of ship against ship continued as the caravel crunched its way along the bulwarks of the corsair, crumpling heavy wooden beams like pieces of parchment.

Standing there laughing like a maniac, El Hakim could see the crew of the caravel moving past him as they looked over the rail, their eyes wide at the scene of destruction taking place before them and the seeming presence of a madman in its midst. Then the realization that the caravel was about to swing away brought him back to his senses like a dash of cold water in his face. He must leave the brigantino quickly, he realized, if he would carry through the plan that had taken form in his mind the moment before he had leaped from his position at the oar and attacked the steersmen. And in truth, he had no choice, for Hamet-el-Baku was already shouting to one of the agas to throw him a sword.

Moving to the side of the steering platform, with the chain that was still attached to his ankle thrown over his shoulder, El Hakim searched the side of the caravel for a trailing rope or chain by which to pull himself aboard. A bellow sounded above him and he looked up to see the red-bearded man tossing a line toward him. When the bight at the end snaked through the air and fell across his shoulders he seized it, instinctively thrusting his arm through the loop so it settled about his body beneath the armpits. The next instant he was jerked from the deck of the brigantino by the forward motion of the other vessel and flung through the air to crash against the side of the caravel just above the water line.

El Hakim had tensed himself for the impact, but the blow almost stunned him nevertheless. As he clutched the line with both hands, the chain attached to his ankle flailed about and the heavy iron ring at the end struck his head. Just then the rope suddenly lost its tautness and, no longer supported, he dropped into the boiling wake of the caravel. The turbulent water promptly seized him as if with a giant hand and smashed his body against the hull once more.

Flailing out instinctively against the water that poured

over his head, even as waves of blackness swept over him from the beating he was taking when the line attached both to his body and the caravel flung him repeatedly against the hull, El Hakim plummeted into the depths, dragged down by the weight of the chain still attached to his ankle. His lungs fought frantically for air, but there was no staying that headlong plunge into the sea. He knew a moment of panic, then mercifully—nothing.

II

Vaguely, as through a cloud, the man called El Hakim saw light. The impact of it upon his eyeballs brought dark clouds of pain and blackness swirling in again and he closed his eyes to shut away the light. When he opened them again a face slowly materialized, a round face with a red button of a nose, kindly eyes, and a tonsured head. The pain from the light made El Hakim shut his eyes tight for a moment and, when he looked again, the monkish countenance had, miraculously enough, become that of a lovely young woman with dark hair and eyes, full red lips, and healthy pink cheeks.

Nothing like either the monk or the girl seemed possible in the light of any recent experience that he remembered and, when she continued to watch him a little anxiously, he wondered momentarily if indeed he had died there in the depths of the sea beside the caravel and this was one of the houris whom every devout Moslem believed would greet him upon his entry into Paradise. On more than one occasion he had pretended to espouse the Moslem faith—as an expedient to save his skin. Now it seemed best to pretend still, just in case he had somehow reached the Paradise of the True Believer.

"*Allahu akbar!*" he murmured. "There is no god but Allah and Mohammed is his prophet."

"He is speaking in the Moorish tongue!" the girl cried. She used a Portuguese dialect, which no houri would use to one of the faithful, Spaniards and Portuguese being hated more, if possible, by the sons of Allah than Shaitan himself. "I am sure he's a Moor, now, little brother," she added.

The monkish face swam once again into El Hakim's

rapidly clearing senses. "God be praised," the plump friar said. "We have saved him from both a watery grave and the bonds of heathenism." Then he added, "But still I think he's a European, madonna. Perhaps he was captured long ago and the sun has burned him so he looks like a Moor."

"He can't be more than forty," the girl protested. "Look how well-muscled he is, and his beard and hair are not gray at all."

El Hakim lay still and listened, reveling in the pleasure of hearing a Christian tongue spoken again after eight long years, five of them in the galleys. He was quite certain now that this was no heavenly paradise, although he was young enough—fully ten years less than the girl's estimate—to feel that this houri, who was beginning to be more and more substantial as his vision cleared, might contribute much to an earthly one.

"If he is not of our own people, why did he come to our aid when the corsairs attacked us?" the friar asked.

"Perhaps he thought to escape that way."

"A Moor would not escape to a Christian ship." Then the Franciscan added dryly, "Most of them know that the process of converting a heathen to our faith is rather painful."

"We'll wait until he wakes up then," the girl decided. "I had a Moorish nurse when I was a child and I speak a little of their language. Perhaps I can talk to him."

"At least you can give him our thanks," the friar agreed. "Eric says he saved us all by knocking the steersmen of the galley overboard at just the right moment. So, slave or not, we should be grateful to him."

"What will we do with him?"

"He was pulling an oar on a corsair galley," the friar pointed out. "All pirates are under sentence of death, but I think the infante might be generous and reduce his sentence to perpetual slavery, since he helped us escape from the corsair."

"Whose slave would he be then?"

"This is your father's ship; naturally he would belong to him."

"I'll make Father give him to me as a bodyguard," she said excitedly. "He can wear a turban and a fine robe with baggy trousers and boots like the Moorish soldiers and a curved scimitar at his belt."

"As your spiritual adviser I should reprimand you for your false pride, Dona Leonor," the friar warned, although not very seriously.

"But you won't," she said confidently. "I will speak to Father about it now."

El Hakim heard light footsteps cross the enclosure where he was lying—he had already recognized it as the aftercastle of the caravel—also called the *toldilla*—and a door close. Gingerly he opened his eyes again and found the round face of the friar reguarding him thoughtfully.

"So you have decided to join the ranks of the living," the Franciscan said briskly in Portuguese. "Here, have some wine." He poured out a cup and lifted El Hakim's head so he could drink. The movement set his senses to swimming again, but the wine warmed his body, driving away the chill from his ducking in the sea.

"Allah is good," El Hakim whispered in the Moorish tongue. "His are the kingdoms of heaven and earth. He knoweth all things, verily we are gods and to him shall we return."

"Speak a Christian tongue, if you can," the priest admonished him. "It will go better with you, even though you are a Moor."

El Hakim decided to try the same Portuguese dialect the girl had used. Many Moors spoke Spanish—Islam having so recently controlled that land—and using a dialect would not appear unusual in case he decided to keep on being a Moslem for a while.

"What place is this?" he asked.

"You are aboard the caravel *Santa Paula,* belonging to Dom Bartholomeu di Perestrello, in the service of the Infante Henrique of Portugal. Dom Bartholomeu has been serving as the prince's envoy to the Holy Father in Rome."

El Hakim digested this information in silence. In Moslem lands the name of Prince Henrique of Portugal was well known—and hated—as leader of the successful attack upon the Moorish citadel of Ceuta at the western end of the Mediterranean some twenty years before.

Ceuta until then had been the main bastion of the Moors, from which they had hoped one day to launch an attack across the narrow watery mouth of the Mediterranean—known since ancient times as the Pillars of Hercules—and regain their former rich prize of Spain. In the bazaars and slave marts of the cities of Tunis, Algiers, Tripoli, Tetwan, and El Araish, the continual questing southward along the African coast by Prince Henry's ships had been recognized as a threat of the booming trade in African slaves, exotic woods, and other valuable items that kept the caravan trails busy throughout the interior of the vast continent of Africa.

"How was I saved from the waters?" El Hakim asked.

"The line you were holding slipped from the captain's hands, but luckily one of the seamen snubbed it around a spar. You had thrust your arms through it, so they hauled you aboard like a drowned rat."

Just then the door banged open and the red-haired man who had thrown the line from the deck of the caravel came in, bringing a gust of salt air with him.

"Hallo, Fra Mauro," he boomed. "Dona Leonor tells me our prize has regained his senses."

There was no doubting the big man's nationality. Centuries before, a group of Vikings—tall, blond- or red-bearded giants, whose swift vessels sailed the northern seas almost since time began—had entered the Mediterranean and settled as far east as Sicily. Their descendants were all over Italy now, but this one was obviously no mixed blood. That red beard and massive body could belong only to a native of the northern climes. His Portuguese, too, was colored with a strong accent and the short-sword he'd worn during the brief battle still hung from his belt.

"He has returned to the land of the living at last," said the Franciscan. "But seems reluctant to tell much about himself."

"Does he speak the language of Portugal?"

"Enough to understand it—and to be understood."

"Well, whoever you are," the Viking said to El Hakim, "we owe you our lives. That galley was outwitting us until you came to our aid."

"The debt was paid," El Hakim said in Portuguese, "when you lifted me from the water."

"And a heavy catch you were, my friend." The Viking laughed. "Your weight and those chains you wore jerked the line from my hands, but we snubbed it around the yardarm and lifted you from the sea as we would haul in the anchor." He slapped the priest affectionately on the back. "Care for him well, good Fra Mauro. The fair Leonor is busy persuading her father to keep him as a slave. We must not let her be disappointed."

"I will pray for his speedy recovery from the ducking you gave him," Fra Mauro said.

"And I will invoke the power of the old Norse gods," the red-haired man promised with a grin. "With all the deities working in his favor, he is sure to do well."

"If Allah wills," added El Hakim piously. "It is in his hands."

Fra Mauro snorted and poured a generous portion of wine into the cup and handed it to the prostrate man. "Drink deeply," he advised. "Perhaps it will loosen your tongue." His eyes twinkled. "Or do you still wish to keep up the pretense of being a Moor?"

El Hakim drank deeply as he was bidden and felt the rich wine warm his gullet all the way down to the loin-cloth that was still his only garment. His head was clearing rapidly and his thoughts were busy trying to decide just how much he should reveal to the priest about his real identity.

"Why do you think I am not a Moor?" he asked.

"Your skin is brown, but from the sun, not Moorish blood. You speak the Portuguese dialect of the Spanish tongue, but not as Moors do; your speech is that of an educated man and your eyes show intelligence. If I were guessing, I would name you an Italian, and educated. The Moslem galleys are manned by many Christian slaves who fell upon evil days while at sea and were captured by the corsairs. If you are one of these, you would logically have tried to escape, but not if you are a Moslem."

El Hakim saw that there was no point in trying to hoodwink the Franciscan. "I am a Christian like yourself, little brother," he admitted, lapsing into Italian. "Nearly eight years ago the ship on which I was journeying to Trebizond was captured by a Moslem brigantino and I was sold as a slave."

"And your name?"

El Hakim hesitated only a moment. "Andrea Bianco."

The priest's eyes widened. "What was your profession before you were captured?" he asked eagerly. "And where did you live?"

"I am a mapmaker. And a citizen of Venice."

III

The rotund priest stared at the bronzed man, his eyes dancing with excitement. *"Benedicamus!"* he cried. "It is a miracle—a true miracle."

"Other men have come back from the galleys."

"But not Andrea Bianco, the mapmaker of Venice. *Sancta Maria!"* He crossed himself hastily. "It is unbelievable."

"You have heard of me then?"

"Heard of you? Did you not draw a map of the world in 1436?"

"Yes."

"I was a lay brother then, working in the convent of the Camaldolese fathers outside Venice, at the trade of mapmaker. When I entered the service of Prince Henry I found that he had copies of your maps at Lagos."

"Eccolo!" Andrea exclaimed. "I remember sending a portfolio to him eight years ago."

"They have served us as a guide ever since and have been widely copied all around the Mediterranean," the friar assured him. "Few finer maps have ever been drawn than those of Andrea Bianco."

"Do you refer to Andrea Bianco in that way because you don't believe me?"

Fra Mauro shook his head. "In the holy orders we assume that every man is telling the truth, my son, until he has proved otherwise. The facts of your identity are not for me to decide; we will leave that up to Dom Bartholomeu di Perestrello."

"And if he decides I am not what I claim?"

The Franciscan shrugged. "The slaves of Dom Bartholomeu are kindly treated. You will be much better off than you were as a galley slave on a vessel of Islam."

"I did not save this ship and the lives of all of you to be enslaved again," Andrea Bianco said angrily.

"Dom Bartholomeu is honest and fair. You can be sure any decision he makes will be a just one."

"Who is the girl?"

"Dona Leonor, his elder daughter." The friar changed

the subject. "How did you happen to be captured by the Moors?"

"I was a passenger on a galley bound for Trebizond and Constantinople. We were attacked by a Turk off Ras el Milh."

Fra Mauro frowned. "Venetian ships are exempt from attack by paying a bribe to the pirates."

"This was a renegade vessel from the Turkish coast."

"And you were sent to the galleys?"

"Not immediately. A man named Ibn Iberanakh bought me in the market of Constantinople because I could read and write and speak several languages. He made me his clerk and treated me well. We journeyed east in the next few years as far as the Island of Cipangu."

"Cipangu! No white man has been there, not even the Polo brothers!"

Andrea Bianco smiled. "I was not a white man, remember, but the slave of a Turkish merchant."

"How did you reach the Island of Cipangu?" Fra Mauro asked eagerly.

"On a ship—the Chinese call it a junk—from the port of Cambaluc."

"Did you return from China by land?"

"No. We visited the Spice Islands and then we sailed along the coast of India and westward with the monsoons to the Red Sea. At Jidda we debarked and my master made the pilgrimage to Mecca. Then we traveled in caravans to Alexandria."

The priest's eyes were shining with excitement. "These are things no other white man has done," he cried. Then his face sobered. "You will have trouble convincing Mestre Jacomé of this and perhaps Dom Bartholomeu."

"Is that Jacomé of Majorca, the famous mapmaker and navigator?"

"The same."

"Is he on this ship?"

The Franciscan shook his head. "Mestre Jacomé lives at Villa do Infante, the town Prince Henry has built at Sagres. Keep on with your story," he begged. "It is at least diverting, whether or not you are telling the truth."

"I am telling the truth," Andrea Bianco assured him, a little shortly. "If Dom Bartholomeu does not choose to believe me, there are plenty of people in Venice who will swear to my identity."

The door burst open and Dona Leonor came in like a fresh spring breeze. Her eyes were bright with excitement and her cheeks were pink. In a simple gown that enhanced the youthful grace of her slender body and with her hair piled upon her head in a mass of dark ringlets, she was a picture of healthy beauty.

"Father says the slave is mine until Prince Henry decides what to do with him," she announced excitedly. Then she realized that Andrea was looking at her and blushed. "Oh, he is awake."

"He claims not to be a Moor at all," the friar said, "and I am sure he speaks the truth—at least that far."

She frowned. "What do you mean?"

"He also claims to be Andrea Bianco, the mapmaker of Venice."

Dona Leonor's eyes came back to Andrea again, but there was a look of displeasure in them now. "Andrea Bianco was lost at sea several years ago," she said severely. "How dare you try to steal his name?"

"I steal nothing that is not my own," Andrea snapped. "In good time I will prove it."

"With more lies?" she demanded haughtily. "You take much upon you, Senhor whoever-you-are, for a slave. We will see what my father says about that." She turned and left the cabin, carrying her head high.

"If I were faced with the job of proving my identity to save myself from slavery," Fra Mauro observed caustically, "I would not go about angering people who wish to treat me kindly."

Andrea Bianco shrugged. "She is young, only a child."

"If you think that, my son, your judgment has been warped by the whips of Islam. Leonor di Perestrello is twenty years old, runs her father's household with an iron hand, and is every inch a woman."

"Is that any reason why I should be happy to be her slave?" Andrea demanded. "Remember, I have been one for eight years." He swung his legs from the bunk to the floor and sat up. "No, little brother. I do not believe that God in His mercy has freed me from the Moors only to make me a slave of Christians. As soon as we get to Venice I will prove my identity to the satisfaction of everyone."

"The resurrection of our Lord changed the history of the whole world," Fra Mauro observed philosophically.

"Who can say what effect the resurrection of Andrea Bianco—if you are he—will have?"

Dona Leonor returned a few moments later. With her was a slender elderly man with the clean-cut features, olive skin, and graying hair of an Andalusian aristocrat. "He claims to be the mapmaker, Andrea Bianco, Father," Dona Leonor cried indignantly. "The one who was lost at sea. That proves he is an impostor."

Dom Bartholomeu turned to Andrea. "What is your story?" he asked courteously.

"My name is really Andrea Bianco. I have a family in Venice; they will identify me."

"Obviously you are not a Moor," Dom Bartholomeu said thoughtfully. "And you have had some education. As to whether or not you are Andrea Bianco, we will be in Venice by the day after tomorrow. If your family identifies you, senhor, you are free—with our blessing."

Even Andrea's crusty mood toward the girl for naming him an impostor melted in the face of Dom Bartholomeu's sincerity and fairness. "I agree to that, sir—gladly," he said.

"He has traveled throughout the East, Your Excellency," Fra Mauro said eagerly. "I am sure the infante would like to hear of his travels."

Dom Bartholomeu smiled. "A famous mapmaker such as Andrea Bianco would undoubtedly be welcomed by our prince whenever he may choose to visit us."

IV

Standing at the rail of the caravel, Andrea watched the crew under the direction of Eric Vallarte, the Viking captain, warp the trim vessel toward the docks near the Piazza di San Marco. It was a clear day, and beyond the Campanile and the domes of the city the low line of the Alps was plainly visible. Before him, from the elevated foredeck of the caravel, the beauty of Venice stretched away in a seemingly endless pattern of lovely buildings, for even the slums of their city—the Venetians stoutly claimed—were more beautiful than the finer districts of the others.

Looking at the city where he had been born and spent

his early life, Andrea felt his throat fill and his eyes momentarily grow moist with emotion. Fra Mauro had obtained some garments for him from one of the sailors, but the cheap, ill-cut fabrics could not hide his erect carriage and the strength of his tall body. His well-muscled thighs threatened to burst the seams of the cheap woolen hose that covered them, and the sturdy tunic of rough stuff was tight across his chest.

The thrill of coming home had already made him forget any deficiencies in his apparel, however. All that could be quickly remedied in the expensive shops lining one side of the piazza before La Giacometta where he had been in the habit of buying his clothes. He fancied that he could hear, even at this distance, the deep-throated clamor of voices raised in the babble of commercial trading on the world-famed Rialto of Venice, the clink of golden ducats upon the tables of the money-changers—always an important part of any commercial city—and the tapping of the small hammers of the goldsmiths.

"*A-oe! Sia Stali!*" The gondoliers shouted their warning cries as they sent the swift single-oared craft scudding about over the canals and the lagoons. As always in Venice, everyone seemed happy and gay. With good reason indeed was the city known the world over as the Serenissima—most serene—the wealthiest and most beautiful metropolis in the world and the link, commercially and artistically, between the European West and the oriental East. Even in a time of approaching crisis, with the Eastern trade threatened by the swift rise of the Ottoman Turks, Venice was unchanged and without panic.

The caravel was being slowly warped to its berth at the Fondaco where huge warehouses faced the quays, ready to swallow up cargoes brought by incoming shipping and disgorge goods to be loaded for the return voyages. A little way up the canal stood a line of smaller vessels, boats that brought the daily supply of food, wine, and even water necessary for the subjects of the Serenissima to live.

Fra Mauro came along the deck and stopped beside Andrea. "Too bad you couldn't have sent word ahead of you," he said. "A man returning from the dead after eight years should have some sort of a delegation waiting to greet him."

Andrea smiled. "I'd rather surprise them."

"Them?"

"My father was very old when I left, he may have died during these eight years. But I have a brother, Giovanni, a half brother Mattei—and Angelita."

"Your sister?"

"No, my betrothed, Madonna Angelita di Fontana."

"I know a Di Fontana family," the Franciscan said. "They are associated with the banking and commercial house of the Medici."

"It is the same." The plump friar's words loosed a flood of memories and hopes Andrea had not dared let enter his mind during the long years in the galleys. With no prospect of escape, he had rigidly kept all thought of Angelita from his mind, for to worry about what he had lost was to court madness. Now everything was changed. A new life lay before him, not simply a return to the old, for the Andrea Bianco of today was a far different man from the one who had bid his betrothed good-by eight years ago.

Angelita of the stately grace and slow smile, always composed and always elegant, had been a fit mate indeed for a man whose fortunes were on the rise with his fame as a maker of maps and the established business bequeathed to him by his father in the profitable trade with Constantinople, Trebizond, and the cities of the Orient. It had been a logical match in every respect. The noble family of the Medici was already beginning to develop banking houses and commercial interests wherever Christians had settled, even trading with the Norselands and Arab slave dealers who followed the great trails of Africa. And although the Biancos were not of noble blood, they were highly respected and admired in Venice, influential with the Council of Ten. The name was well known among the shipping firms that carried on an immensely valuable trade in spices such as cinnamon, cubeb, ginger, nutmeg, or the fiery red galingale, and gems, exotic woods, and fine fabrics like brocade, velour, velvet and silk from the fabulous lands to the east.

Altogether, Andrea Bianco had been a happy man when he had sailed from Venice one fine day eight years before, bound for Trebizond on the Black Sea and a valuable cargo of spices to be sold at a profit in the marts of the Mediterranean cities. Actually he had been far more interested in the navigation of the swift galley on which he was traveling than in the profit to be made from its cargo.

And in Venice he had spent more time drawing maps and recording the position of the stars on celestial charts than enjoying the beauty and grace of Madonna Angelita, his betrothed.

Dom Bartholomeu and his daughter were standing at the bow of the ship, the highest point from which they could look down upon the activity of the waterfront. The girl made a lovely picture, with her slender and graceful figure, her eyes bright with excitement and her lips parted, as if she wished to drink in all the beauty and charm of the fabled city.

"Control yourself, Leonor," her father said fondly. "It is just another city."

"This is Venice, Father! *E'fantastico!*" They were speaking in the Portuguese dialect with which Andrea was familiar.

Senhor di Perestrello laughed. "We will have trouble with her, Fra Mauro," he called to the Franciscan. "You are familiar with Venice, so I am going to place her in your care."

Just then the prow of the vessel nudged against the dock, and in the excitement the conversation went no farther. Everyone was busy for the next several hours, mooring the caravel to the quay, arranging for the cargo to be unloaded, and getting the passengers ashore. Feeling that he was under some obligation to the shipowner for saving his life, Andrea busied himself helping with the many things that had to be done. He even carried the baggage of Dom Bartholomeu and Dona Leonor to a gondola that whisked them all quickly to the palace of Signor Martello, the commercial representative of Prince Henry in Venice, where they were to be quartered during their stay.

It was after dark before Andrea was able to set out through the familiar streets of Venice toward his old home, with some coins that Fra Mauro had lent him jingling in his purse. In spite of the high prevalence of thieves, he was unarmed, trusting to his size and the strength gained from years at the oars to even the balance in case he were attacked.

Perhaps it was too early for thieves to be abroad, or they were intimidated by his obvious self-assurance—in either case he was not molested as he made his way to the familiar house on the Via delle Galeazze. Pausing for a moment before the elaborate façade, he noted that the Bianco fortunes must be on the rise, for the *palazzo* had been freshly refurbished. The moldy growth which accumulated on walls in the damp climate of the Adriatic had recently been scraped away and the whole covered with a fresh coat of paint.

With his hand upraised to knock, Andrea changed his mind and made his way around the house to the small enclosed terrace of a piazza that fronted upon the canal. The garden was empty, although lamps were burning in the house. Andrea's eyebrows lifted at the sight of a sumptuously upholstered private gondola moored beside the stone quay forming one bank of the canal. Someone in the family had luxurious tastes these days, he thought. Even with the relative prosperity they had known before his sailing for Trebizond, the Biancos had possessed nothing so fine as this.

An enclosed summerhouse stood at the water's edge, and as memories of the past stimulated by the familiar surroundings began to flood his mind, he moved to it and opened the door. The single room was furnished with a couch and a table just as he remembered. As a boy he'd often slept there, awakening in the middle of the night from a dream of far-off places to listen to the wash of the canal upon the stones and the cries of the gulls in the dawn as they searched for refuse along the quays. Now he entered and closed the door, feeling the remembered warmth of the darkness envelop him. As if by the hands of one of the genii in which the Moors with whom he'd lived believed so implicitly, Andrea found himself carried back eight years to the night before he had sailed to Trebizond. He and Angelita had been betrothed only a few days before his departure and had been busy attending a round of gay parties and suppers in their honor. On this particular night they had returned from a supper by gondola and were standing on the quay beside the summerhouse, listening to the splash of the boat's single oar as it grew fainter in the distance.

The dinner had been very gay and both of them had drunk a great deal of wine, making the night seem warmer than it really was—and more romantic. Andrea's pulse had quickened when he realized that only a single light burned in the house and that old Dimas Andrede, the

Bianco chamberlain, would be asleep in his room, where only the devil's own clatter would arouse him.

The door of the summerhouse had been open, he remembered now, as his pulses began to stir again, and the darkness heavy with the fragrance of the roses that twined along its walls. Angelita had made no protest when he had drawn her toward the open doorway. They had kissed only once before, when he had slipped the betrothal ring, a square-cut emerald that had been his mother's, upon her finger.

There had been little of passion, on his part at least, in that first kiss. To him Angelita had always seemed like a goddess, remote, unattainable, to be worshiped from afar, her cool loveliness setting her apart from all other women he had known. And that night, in spite of the excitement beginning to race in his veins, he'd found time to marvel at his own temerity in drawing her inside the summerhouse and her own yielding when she had come into his arms in the fragrant darkness.

"Carissima mia," he had breathed. "How I am going to miss you."

"I shall miss you, too, Andrea." Her voice was low and throaty in the darkness, a thrilling note he'd never heard in it before.

She had made no resistance when he drew her closer. Her body, which he had thought so cool and distant, was warm and vibrant with life and with something that seemed like desire, yet which he could not possibly believe was such a base emotion. For a moment this hint of yielding in her shocked him and he almost pushed her away, but the softness and the nearness of her in his arms had already stirred him deeply.

When his mouth found hers in the darkness, her lips were eager and parted, and she clung to him, pressing herself against him as if she never wanted him to go away. He could feel the hurried throb of her heart against his and the matching rhythm released a surge of desire against which neither of them had any strength.

She had made no resistance when he had carried her to the couch, the imminence of their parting had broken down her reserve, he was sure. In the grip of the surging passion that swept them together, he still had enough control to approach her gently, even a little timorously. As yet he could not understand the miracle by which the cool and lovely Angelita had come to yield herself to him, and was sure that she must be slowly aroused if the embrace of love were to mean more to her than simply an ordeal of pain. But when his hands had touched her body in a caress, he soon found a naked houri in his arms, eagerly matching his own desire with an even greater one.

It had been dawn before they left the summerhouse, after a night of bliss incalculable. He had sailed a few hours later in a happy daze, already dreaming of his return and the long years he would spend with Angelita. Once the swift nightmare of attack and capture, enslavement and torture, had begun, however, he had resolutely shut away all memory of her and that night in the summerhouse from his mind, knowing that memories like those could drive a slave mad, when no prospect of regaining them seemed even remotely possible. But now he had returned and Angelita would be waiting for him as soon as she knew he was in Venice; perhaps at this very moment she was in his father's house, for the families had always been close.

Leaving the summerhouse, Andrea hurried over to the *palazzo* itself, eager with the thought that he might even hold his beloved in his arms this very night. The door of the *terrazzo* was unlocked and he let himself into the main room downstairs. The room itself was familiar, especially the paintings of his father and mother hanging over the broad mantle over the fireplace. But the furnishings and draperies were far more luxurious than anything he remembered and he decided that his brother Giovanni must have prospered indeed during the years of his imprisonment, as evidenced by all this finery and the private gondola bobbing at the quay.

Moving softly so as not to disturb anyone in the upper chambers of the house, he sought the small library to one side where his father had always kept the account books and the maps from which Andrea himself had early gained the love for mapmaking and travel which had taken him on that unfortunate voyage to Trebizond. The door was ajar and a lamp was burning inside. Thinking that Giovanni must be working there, he pushed it open silently so as not to disturb the man writing at the desk.

"Giovanni," Andrea said in a whisper.

The man at the desk went rigid and slowly turned his head.

"Mattei!" Andrea exclaimed. "Where is Giovanni?"

His half brother stared up at him, his face slowly draining of color. "What do you want?" he whispered hoarsely. "If it is gold, I have but little here——"

Andrea stepped farther into the room. "I want no gold, Mattei. Don't you know me?"

"The voice—but it could not be."

"I am Andrea—in the flesh."

Mattei recoiled. "You are dead. Why do you haunt me?"

Andrea grinned and came closer. As if fearing he would be attacked, Mattei quickly shoved his chair back and his hand dropped to a slender dagger hanging from the corded belt of his tunic. The handle of the dagger was jeweled and chased with gold and his garments were of rich velvet—the kind worn by the wealthier merchants.

"Touch me, Mattei," Andrea begged, holding out his hands to show that he carried no weapons. "You will see that I am no spirit."

Gingerly the other man reached out a trembling hand and touched Andrea's arm, but he still seemed unable to believe the evidence of his senses.

"Is my father dead?" Andrea asked.

"Y-yes. A—a few months after you di—after you were lost."

"And Giovanni?" As the next older brother, Giovanni would have suceeded to the direction of the Bianco fortunes.

"Alas, he, too, died of the plague," Mattei said and added hastily, "may God rest his soul."

This was a grievous blow, for Andrea had been very fond of his brother. Giovanni had been boisterous, cheerful, and full of love for life, while Andrea had always tended to be more serious and scholarly. But there had always been a strong bond of affection between them nevertheless.

Mattei was trembling and sweat had broken out in great droplets on his pale forehead. With shaking fingers he poured himself a glass of wine from an exquisitely cut flask on the taboret and gulped it down.

Mattei's reception disturbed Andrea. His half brother would naturally be surprised at his literally returning from the dead, but Mattei's reaction seemed to be more than surprise. Of one thing he could be sure; there was no gladness at his return. But then he had expected none from Mattei.

The other man seemed to realize now that his behavior might seem strange, for he made a rather poor attempt to put a better face on his reception. "Sit down, Andrea," he urged, "and tell me what happened to you."

Andrea sat upon a richly cushioned couch. "The story is not long. The ship I sailed on from Venice was captured by a Turkish brigantino and I was sold as a slave. Eventually I wound up in the galleys of Hamet-el-Baku."

"The galley and all on it were reported lost," Mattei told him. "The Jews who owned it were very much disturbed about the loss, but they could do nothing against the renegade who attacked you."

Andrea shrugged. "I might as well have been lost, too, until Hamet-el-Baku attacked a caravel belonging to Dom Bartholomeu di Perestrello of Portugal a few days ago. In the battle I managed to escape and was picked up by the Portuguese."

"Do the people of the caravel know who you are?" Mattei asked quickly.

"They think I am a Moorish slave named El Hakim pretending to be Andrea Bianco, but I assured Signor di Perestrello that my family would identify me."

Had he been watching Mattei's face, Andrea would have noticed a calculating gleam appear in his half brother's eyes, but his attention was drawn to the painting of a lovely woman hanging from the wall of the cabinet. He recognized her at once. It was Angelita as he remembered her—except for that last night before he had sailed—cool, lovely, poised, and unchanged, unless she had become more beautiful. For a long moment, he feasted his eyes upon her, then turned back to Mattei.

"How is Angelita?"

"In excellent health," Mattei hastened to say, "and——"

"Still lovely, I can see that. This portrait has been done since I left."

"It was painted by Iacopo Bellini a few years ago." Mattei took a deep breath. "It is hard for me to have to tell you this, Andrea, but, after all, you are officially dead. A Mass for your soul was even said in the Cathedral of St. Mark."

Andrea grinned. "That should make up for the times I've had to praise Mohammed to save my skin."

"After you were thought to be dead——" Mattei stopped and seemed to have trouble going on. Andrea looked at him keenly. Something was wrong, he was sure now, badly wrong. Mattei's whole manner could have no other meaning.

"What are you trying to tell me?" he asked.

The other man took a deep breath and blurted out, "After you were declared dead, Andrea, and a decent interval of mourning had passed, Angelita and I were married."

Andrea stared at him incredulously. "Angelita married? To you?"

Mattei flushed. Both Giovanni and Andrea had been rather contemptuous of their half brother as children. While their own mother had been of a noble house, their father's second wife was a virago who had ruled the *palazzo* with an iron hand, hating her stepsons because they were fine and strong, while her own puny offspring was querulous and inclined to pettishness.

"We found we loved each other, and you were dead," Mattei said. "Besides, you yourself recognized that a union with the Medici house was good for the business."

"First my betrothed and then my fortune! You were always quick to seize an opportunity, Mattei."

"Somebody had to look after the business when you went sailing away to Trebizond. You were always inclined to be more of a romantic than a merchant, Andrea."

Suddenly the library threatened to stifle Andrea, pressing in upon him like the sides of a coffin. "Where is Angelita now?" he demanded, getting to his feet and covering the length of the room in three long strides.

"With her father in Chioggia. He is ill and they sent a carriage for her."

"I want to see her."

"Naturally. But don't forget that you are legally dead and Angelita is married to me."

"Then I'll become legally alive." It wasn't that simple though, he knew. He loved Angelita still; the sight of her portrait here brought back the memories of that night in the summerhouse, brought them back in an overwhelming flood. How could a man or a woman love as they had loved and ever forget? The thought that, during the years he had been away, Mattei had claimed the bliss he had known for only those few short hours before sailing tortured him almost beyond bearing.

"Something must be done," Mattei agreed. "I will talk

to the lawyers. Meanwhile, perhaps it would be just as well if it isn't generally known yet that you have returned."

"*Corpo di Cristo*," Andrea swore. "Am I to be hidden like some madman the family is ashamed of?"

Mattei was regaining his composure rapidly, once he recovered from the initial shock of finding that Andrea had seemingly returned from the dead. "Our fortunes are closely tied to the Medicis in Florence now," he explained. "I have been able to make an excellent connection with them and they might not look with favor on any sudden change. Besides, this will be a shock to Angelita. We must prepare her for it."

That much Andrea could understand. "I can see your point, particularly about Angelita," he admitted.

"No breath of scandal has ever attached itself to the Bianco name. We must go very slowly."

Andrea went to the window and stared out, but there was only darkness outside, the same blackness that had seized his spirits. This whole affair had not turned out at all as he had planned. In fact, the savor of it now was turning to ashes in his mouth. And yet when he thought of Angelita and the eagerness of her body in his arms, he could not still a sudden rush of excitement and desire—or of anger that Mattei of the spindleshanks and beetle brows had usurped his place in her embrace.

As to how Angelita would take his sudden appearance from the dead, he had not yet considered. But he was certain of one thing: she could no longer feel bound to Mattei now, not even by the bonds of marriage. During that one night in the summerhouse she had been his, utterly and completely, and no vows recited later with anyone could change it.

"What do you want me to do?" he asked finally.

Mattei frowned. "Did the Portuguese ship dock at the Fondaco?"

"Yes. I came here from the *palazzo* of Signor Martello, who represents Prince Henry of Portugal here in Venice."

Mattei's face cleared. "Could you stay tonight with the retinue of this Signor di Perestrello?"

"They think I am a slave," Andrea snorted, "the personal servant of his daughter."

"Surely a few more days of such deception can do no one any harm," Mattei urged reasonably. "Meanwhile I

will talk to Messer Donato, our lawyer, and prepare
Angelita for the shock of knowing you are alive."

"It is not what I'd planned," Andrea grumbled. "But I
suppose I can stand it for a few more days."

Mattei was affable, now that he was going to have his
own way—too affable, if Andrea had stopped to think
about it. "You'll need some money to buy clothes and
visit a barber," he suggested. "Let me get a purse for
you."

"It will be pleasant to dress decently again. And to
have my hair and beard trimmed." Andrea grinned wryly.
"Make it a generous purse, Mattei—after all, you seem to
have done well with my money. For five years I've had
nothing but stale bread and rusk to eat and vinegar
mixed with oil and water to drink."

"The money is upstairs, I'll have to get it," Mattei said.
"Drink some wine while I'm gone. We have much to
make up to you, Andrea."

Andrea prowled the cabinet restlessly while Mattei
was gone. When his half brother did not return immediately, he opened the cupboard where he remembered
storing his maps. They were still there in a portfolio, dust-
covered and dry, just as he had put them away more than
eight years ago.

Looking through the maps idly at first, Andrea quickly
found himself absorbed in them, as he had always been
before. The lure of faraway places, strange islands, and
storied lands was as great as ever, even though he had
visited many of them, perhaps more in fact than any
man alive at the moment.

Mattei returned after a rather prolonged absence, but
Andrea did not notice the passage of time. As always he
had been caught up by the lure of the maps.

"Sorry to be so long." Mattei carried a fat purse in his
hands. "I think you will find this sufficient for your
needs."

Andrea took the purse and hung it from his girdle. "Be
sure to let me know as soon as you've arranged things,"
he cautioned the smaller man.

"The very moment," Mattei assured him.

As Andrea made his way through the darkened streets
toward the Palazzo Martello, his mind was in a ferment.
He'd given no thought to any complications from his sudden reappearance after eight years, but he could see now

that there was logic in Mattei's reaction. As to the question of his half brother's marriage to Angelita, he supposed the Papal Legate could arrange an annulment. It was unthinkable that she would remain married to another man now that he was alive and well.

As for the business, he might even be content to let the shipping firm of Bianco go on as it was; Mattei seemed to have done well enough in the past. That would leave plenty of time for Andrea's maps and his charts of the heavens, perhaps even a chance to put into effect some of the improvements in navigation he'd learned from the Arabs on the long voyage westward from China and India with the monsoons. It would be interesting to visit Prince Henry of Portugal, too, as Fra Mauro had suggested—perhaps on his wedding trip—and talk with the famous men who served the Portuguese nobleman.

Lost in thought, Andrea did not realize he was being followed until the sound of a furtive footfall upon the cobblestoned street behind him penetrated his bemused senses. The sound made him instantly alert and no doubt saved his life.

He was traversing a particularly dark area where a short and narrow street paralleled a canal, a route he'd taken at least a thousand times before in daylight, but which, he realized now, was the worst possible one he could have chosen in the darkness. By blocking both ends of the street the victim could be bottled up, with no escape except by way of the canal, which would also provide a handy repository for the body after the murder and robbery had been accomplished. And that just this was the plan of his still unseen attackers became clear when he heard the second furtive scrape of a footstep, this time upon the stones ahead.

The first foray came from the darkness behind him. Even as he turned to meet it, he sensed rather than felt the simultaneous attack of the man who must have gone on ahead, traveling in a circle to reach the other end of the street and block any escape in that direction. Grappling with the first assailant, a bulky fellow whose breath reeked of garlic and sour wine, Andrea felt the sudden hot stab of the second one's dagger through the fleshy part of his shoulder and the warm ooze of blood upon his skin beneath his rough tunic.

Years of toil at the oars had given Andrea a swiftness

of movement and co-ordination which the assailants could have no way of knowing in advance. Even as he felt the blade penetrate his flesh, he was twisting away from the first attacker, a maneuver which also prevented the dagger from penetrating deeply. His great muscles strained as he lifted the man whose knife had found his shoulder and swung the body like a bludgeon, hurling the other assailant back. At the height of the swing Andrea released his grip and the footpad shot through the air, bowling over his partner before he crashed to the rough cobblestones of the street.

Though knocked sprawling, the remaining thug managed to roll across the cobblestones in the darkness, away from Andrea's grappling hands. Moments later he had gained his feet and scampered away into the darkness, giving up the battle. The man on the cobblestones did not stir when Andrea turned him over with his foot. His head lolled on his neck like a broken doll's, sure sign that the force of striking the stone paving had broken his neck.

Andrea wasted no time over the dead man. He could feel blood running down his body inside his tunic and knew that he must find some sort of medical attention quickly. Clamping his hand over the wounded shoulder to control the bleeding by pressure, Andrea hurried toward the Palazzo Martello. His own blood was warm between his fingers and the pressure sent an exquisite stab of pain through his shoulder as he squeezed the wound, but he hurried on, hoping that, like many friars. Fra Mauro would know enough of medicine to be able to dress the shallow cut in his shoulder.

He felt no sorrow for the thief who had met death in plying his trade; that was one of the hazards of the profession. Tomorrow the *polizia* would find the dead body and probably recognize it as a known thief, which would be the end of the affair.

Fra Mauro was awake in the room he and Andrea shared at the *palazzo* of Signor Martello. Dona Leonor was with him, however; she had been giving the priest an account of tonight's dinner before going to bed. When she saw Andrea stagger through the doorway, the blood drained from her cheeks. Nor could he blame her, for his tunic was bloody and so was his right hand where he held it against his wounded shoulder in order to control the bleeding.

"El Hakim!" she exclaimed. "What happened?"

"I was attacked." He sank to a stool, panting. "Two men—thieves—tried to kill me on the street."

"Don't you see that he is hurt, little brother?" Dona Leonor called to Fra Mauro who was staring at Andrea in horror. "Bring water and strips of cloth for bandaging."

"I can take care of myself, madonna," Andrea protested. "You'll ruin your dress."

"Maria Sanctissima," she cried. "Would you have me stand here idle while you bleed to death? Help me get this tunic off your shoulder. I have often dressed wounds for the fishermen at Villa do Infante."

She pulled aside the tunic, exposing the wound made by the sharp blade of the dagger. The pressure Andrea had applied immediately after the wounding had already stopped most of the bleeding.

"It is only a shallow cut," she said. "A snug bandage will take care of it."

Fra Mauro hurried into the room, carrying a basin of water and several pieces of cloth. He and Dona Leonor busied themselves washing the wound and applying a stout bandage to it. The girl left then for her own chamber and the friar gave Andrea a cup of wine. "Now, what is this all about?" he demanded.

"The thieves were after my purse." Andrea lifted up the leather purse Mattei had given him and saw that the drawstring had come open during the fight. At least a third of the coins were gone. *"Eccolo!"* he added philosophically. "I was lucky to exchange a few gold ducats for my life. The wound will soon heal and then I will be as good as new."

"Why would they attack you? After all, you're not dressed like a man who would be carrying much gold."

Andrea shrugged. "They were common thieves. Venice has always been full of them. I forgot to watch for them."

Fra Mauro busied himself emptying the basin and putting away the remainder of the cloth they had used in binding the wound. "Did you say one of them circled ahead of you?" he asked.

"Yes. Why?"

"Doesn't that sound as if they knew where you were going?"

"Vediamo! It could be! But who would know my identity? Or where I was staying?"

Fra Mauro shrugged. "As you say, who would know? Will this affect your being able to prove your identity?"

"That is all arranged," Andrea assured him. "Mattei is to send for me when everything is ready. It will all be settled soon."

"Let us hope so," the friar said. "Now you had better get to bed. Coming back from the dead and getting stabbed is enough excitement for one day."

"*Eccolo!*" Andrea said happily as he stretched out on a pallet. "Mattei has done well with the business, little brother. I suspect that we are rich."

V

The morning was bright and clear, but not so the temper of Dona Leonor di Perestrello. When she found Andrea in Fra Mauro's quarters after the morning meal her cheeks were flushed with anger and her eyes shot sparks.

"Last night I was concerned because you were injured, Hakim," she said severely. "But after I thought about it I became angry at you for being so foolish. Why did you leave here after dark?"

"To visit my family."

She stamped her foot angrily. "Must you tell lies?"

"It is the truth."

She shook her head. "You'll have to make up a better story than that."

"Give me a few more days, madonna, and I will prove my identity."

"If someone tries to stick a dagger into you every time you go about, you'll have no need to prove anything," she said. "All Christians hate the Moors, it's a wonder you weren't killed last night."

"El Hakim is a match for any robber," Andrea assured her, "even if Andrea Bianco is not."

"Don't be so sure of that," she flared. "A sword or a dagger can strike down any man."

"The Beautiful One speaks words of wisdom," Andrea said in Arabic and saw by the flush in her cheeks that she understood the words.

"What about your wound?" she asked, changing the

subject, but apparently somewhat mollified by the compliment.

"It was nothing. A mere scratch."

"Are you sure it doesn't need caring for by a physician?"

"It is healing already," he told her. "I hardly feel any pain at all."

"See that he gets plenty of meat," she advised Fra Mauro. "It helps healing." Then she turned back to Andrea. "I am going to visit the shops this morning so I will see about buying you some more clothes."

"I am your slave," Andrea teased her in Arabic, enjoying the flush that came to her cheeks. Now that he was about to claim Angelita once more, he was too happy even to resent her taking charge of him.

When the girl was gone, Fra Mauro wiped his sweating face with his sleeve. *"Maria Sanctissima,"* he said fervently. "That one is a handful, no less. You will have a hard time convincing her that you are really Andrea Bianco."

"Not with Mattei and Angelita to vouch for me."

"When will that be?"

"Soon. Mattei wants to keep up the masquerade for a few more days for business reasons."

The priest shook his head doubtfully. "I don't like this. When a man returns from the dead, he should be welcomed—not hidden away."

"Mattei is only trying to avoid any complications with the Medici," Andrea explained. "He's afraid of losing their favor. Besides, he married my betrothed and she is sure to want an annulment now so she can marry me."

"Eccolo! You do not lack self-confidence, my son."

Andrea looked at the friar in surprise, for his tone was caustic. "Do you doubt that she will?"

"Your half brother has been married to her for several years, I imagine," the Franciscan pointed out. "The marriage was made in good faith when you had been declared dead officially. She may be quite satisfied with it."

"I wonder if I have any rights under Venetian law then?" Andrea exclaimed. "After all, I was declared dead and a Mass was said for my soul." He struck his forehead with his palm. "So that was why Mattei wanted time to talk to his lawyer."

"It would be much more convenient for him if you remained dead."

A light was beginning to dawn in Andrea's mind. "That's what you meant, wasn't it? When you suggested that the robbers might have been following me for a particular purpose?"

"I had nothing to go on," Fra Mauro hastened to say. "It just came into my mind."

"Fool that I was for not letting it come into mine." The pieces of the puzzle were falling into place neatly. "Mattei took a long time just to get the purse for me, but I was studying some maps and didn't notice. No doubt he was arranging then for me to be followed."

"You are leaping to conclusions," Fra Mauro warned. "Wise men know that is dangerous."

"Wise men don't let themselves be hoodwinked," Andrea said savagely, getting to his feet. "What did you do with the tunic I took off last night?"

"The servants took it to be washed. Why?"

"I'm going to see Mattei. Just by looking into those shifty eyes of his I can tell whether or not he had anything to do with this affair. Quick, little brother. Get me a robe or a shirt."

"But your wound——"

"Am I to let a mere scratch keep me from demanding my rights? If Mattei set those ruffians on me last night, it means he has something to hide, something he doesn't want me to know. Which is all the more reason why I should know it."

"I'll see what I can do," Fra Mauro promised. "But I may have to go to the ship. Eric Vallarte is as big as you are; his clothes might fit you."

"Hurry then," Andrea urged. "I have no time to lose."

"After eight years as a dead man, you can take a few hours for the resurrection," Fra Mauro said tartly. "Compose yourself and think this thing through while I am gone."

"I'll think it through with my hands around Mattei's throat," Andrea said grimly. "If he is guilty——"

"If he is guilty, he is entitled to a hearing like anyone else," the Franciscan reminded him.

"I'll give him a chance to speak—while I'm choking the truth from him. Now, get you gone, little brother, and hurry back with some clothes."

Fra Mauro was away only a few minutes, however, not even time to leave the *palazzo*. He came back hurriedly, his round face pale. "The *polizia* are outside," he said. "They demand the custody of a Moorish slave called El Hakim."

"Did they see you?"

"No. I overheard them talking to Signor di Perestrello."

"Then I may have time to escape."

"Why? Are you guilty of a crime?"

Andrea stopped short. "You are right! Why should I run when I am guilty of no crime? They probably want to ask me something about the attack last night."

"How would they know your name?"

"They could have traced me here by the blood I lost. One of the servants must have given it to them."

Just then Dom Bartholomeu appeared at the door of the room, his face grave. "The *polizia* are here," he said. "They have a warrant for the arrest of El Hakim."

A burly guard pushed his way into the room, elbowing Di Perestrello aside. "This must be the Moor," he said. "He fits the description we were given."

"What do you want with him?" Fra Mauro demanded.

"I have a warrant for his arrest."

"On what charge?"

"Robbery and murder." The guard stepped forward quickly and, before Andrea realized his intention, jerked loose the purse that still hung from his girdle. Loosening the string that closed it, he poured the golden ducats out ino his open palm and studied them.

"Hah!" he cried. "The coins are marked like the others. Bind him and take him to the prison," he ordered two other guards who stood behind him. "We make short shrift of thieves and murderers in Venice—especially Moors."

VI

On the Riva Degli Schiavoni, near the Ponte della Paglia at the end of the Molo, stood the Carceri, as the public prison of Venice was named. The apartments of the Signori di Notte, the heads of the Venetian police, faced upon the street, so the building did not look like a prison at first glance, with its rustic arches supporting Doric columns on pedestals, which in turn held up a fine cornice with consoles in the frieze. The upper rooms were used as a gaol. Their grated windows let the prisoners gaze out upon the church of San Giorgio Magiore, with the great lagoon beyond.

Andrea was confined in one of these. Through the window he could plainly hear the shouts of *"Sia Stali!"* and *"A-oel!"* as the gondoliers guided their swift craft through the maze of traffic on the broad lagoon. Actually he was in the midst of the city's busy life, yet shut away from it as effectively as if he were in a dungeon.

Although a day and a night had elapsed since his arrival, he had not yet been arraigned or given any opportunity to defend himself. When a turnkey appeared at the door and unlocked it toward midmorning he looked up eagerly, hoping that someone had come to rescue him from this ridiculous and unjust plight. Angelita, he was sure, would hurry to his aid as soon as she learned he was in prison. If she were given a choice between Mattei and himself, he did not doubt for a moment that she would forsake his sickly half brother and come to free him with open arms.

But it was Dona Leonor di Perestrello who stood outside with Fra Mauro.

"Madonna Leonor," Andrea said quickly. "You should not have come here."

She lifted her head proudly and he found time to think that he had never appreciated before how lovely she was, in her innocence and youth. "That is what Father said, but you *did* save our lives, Hakim. I could not let you rot here in a cell without offering to help."

"I have yet to face my accuser," he told her. "When I do, my innocence will be established quickly."

"Do you know who brought charges against you?"

"My half brother, Mattei, I'm sure."

She shook her head hopelessly. "If you would tell us the truth, we might be able to help you."

"I have told it, madonna."

"But if you are what you claim, surely someone in Venice would identify you. The real Andrea Bianco must have had some friends."

"Eight years away is a long time, and shut up here,

I can see no one except you and the good friar." Then his face brightened. "But you could help me."

"How?" the Franciscan asked. "We will do what we can."

"Angelita would come, if she knew I was here."

"Angelita?" Dona Leonor repeated, frowning. "Who is she?"

"My betrothed. That is, she was my betrothed; she is married to Mattei now."

"What makes you think she would identify you as Andrea Bianco when you claim that your own brother and her husband betrayed you?"

"She will, as soon as she knows I'm alive," Andrea said confidently. "If you really want to help me, madonna, go to Chioggia; Angelita is with her father there. It is only a few miles outside Venice. Ask for the villa of Signor Gregorio di Fontana and for Signora Angelita Bianco. Tell her that I swear by—by the summerhouse at my father's *palazzo*—that I still love her, and that she must come here and identify me at once. If you tell her that, she will know I am alive and come here."

Dona Leonor looked uncertain. She was obviously impressed by his sincerity and the ring of truth in his voice.

"I ask only this one thing of you, in return for saving your life on the caravel," Andrea added.

"I will go today," the girl promised then. "Fra Mauro can accompany me."

"Will you send me word what she says?" Andrea asked eagerly.

Dona Leonor nodded. "We must go now, Father will be angry when he knows."

When they were gone Andrea took up the restless pacing of the cell, his mind afire with impatience and eagerness to see Angelita again. That she would hesitate even a moment never occurred to him. After what they had been to each other she could certainly rush into his arms as soon as she learned he was alive, wherever he might be.

The long day passed without word from either Angelita or Dona Leonor, however; when night fell, a feeling of depression dampened his hopes. He slept fitfully through the night and when the stamp of heavy feet sounded outside his cell early the next morning he ran to the door, sure that Angelita had come at last.

Instead, two guards with halberds stood in the corridor while the turnkey unlocked the cell. They hustled Andrea out without paying attention to his questions, jerking him along by the manacles upon his wrists. On the way they talked to each other in Italian, quite ignoring him, in the apparent belief that a Moor could not understand them.

"This one will lose his head quickly enough," the first guard said. "Only the certainly guilty are tried by the *Inquisitori di Dieci.*"

The words chilled Andrea's bones. Even though he had been away from Venice for eight years, he knew the meaning of the title. A "Judge of the Ten," was a special prosecutor assigned to a case on orders of the Council of Ten that ruled the city, because that case for some reason needed particular attention without publicity. Usually this meant a trial in private to serve the purposes of some member of the council or a close friend, and a quick sentencing so the victim could be summarily executed without notice, or sent to the galleys, a fate hardly less severe.

"As well sign his death warrant without even arraigning him then," the second guard agreed. "After all, the evidence is clear. The marked coins found on him prove he was a robber, and I saw the body of the man he killed. This one must be strong; the fellow's neck was broken the way I would wring a chicken's gullet."

Shortly Andrea was ushered by the guards into a brightly lit chamber, which he judged to be one of the smaller courtrooms. He blinked at the bright sunlight pouring through a tall mullioned window and looked before him. Dom Bartholomeu di Perestrello and Dona Leonor sat to one side with Fra Mauro on a bench. On the other side of the room was a polished table upon which some documents lay. Behind it sat the judge in whose hands alone lay the decision of guilt or innocence, life or death.

The inquisitor was a slender man with graying temples and a severe expression, certainly not a visage in which one would expect to see any hint of mercy. Except for a clerk at the end of the table and two guards by the door, there was no one else in the room. Andrea's purse lay before the judge, with several golden ducats spilled out on the polished surface. Even at this distance he could see the identifying marks scratched upon the surface of the coins.

The inquisitor picked up a sheet of paper and glanced at it, then looked at the three visitors. "Signor di Perestrello," he said courteously. "Is it true that the accused was a galley slave on a Moorish corsair and that you captured him during an attack upon your caravel?"

"He was instrumental in saving us from being taken by a pirate brigantino, Signor Santorini," the Portuguese envoy said. "Somehow he freed himself from the bench to which he had been shackled and attacked the helmsmen of the enemy ship, putting it out of control for a few moments. In that time, our ship managed to ram the brigantino and disable it."

"You were fortunate," the judge said dryly. "We of Venice pay tribute to the Moors and so travel freely on the seas. Many another ship has been taken and all Christians aboard it killed or enslaved."

"That is why we feel particularly indebted to El Hakim," Di Perestrello explained. "He caught a rope thrown by our captain when we rammed the Moorish vessel, and was hauled on board nearly unconscious. All of us owe our lives to him."

"I can understand your interest and your gratitude," the judge agreed. "That is why I acceded to your request this morning, although ordinarily no one is allowed to be present at affairs such as this." He turned to Andrea and there was no sign of sympathy or tolerance in his face now. "Nevertheless, this man has committed the crimes of robbery and murder and cannot go unpunished, whatever he may have done for so distinguished a person as yourself, Signor di Perestrello."

"Your Excellency." Dona Leonor spoke in spite of her father's warning frown. "What if El Hakim should be innocent of the crimes?"

The judge smiled tolerantly. "He was recognized robbing the house of a respected gentleman of Venice, madonna. The coins he stole were marked; some were found at the place of the murder, the rest in his purse when he was arrested. There is no question of his guilt."

The pattern was taking shape now and with it, Andrea realized, the verdict of the court. Mattei had worked cleverly and swiftly, intending for him to be executed before his real identity could be established. There was only one possible chance to escape the fate that seemed inevitable. If he told the truth fully and completely and somehow was able to make the judge believe his story, he might be saved.

"Unfortunately I speak no words of the Moorish tongue," Signor Santorini said. "So it will be impossible to question him."

"El Hakim speaks Portuguese," Dona Leonor volunteered. "He is very intelligent."

The judge's eyebrows rose. "At least he has an eloquent —and lovely—advocate, madonna."

Dona Leonor blushed, but before she could speak again, Andrea Bianco took up his own defense. "Your Excellency need not trouble himself about questioning me," he said smoothly in cultured Italian, albeit a little rusty from disuse. "I am a native of Venice by birth."

The judge looked startled. "You, a Moor? There are few such in Venice." Then his eyes narrowed. "Lying will not save you, scoundrel. You could have learned Italian from a Christian galley slave among those captured by your people. The fact that you can speak the language proves nothing."

"As a citizen of Venice am I not entitled to be heard fairly and judged according to the truth, Excellency?"

"You will be heard fairly, even though you are not a citizen of Venice," Signor Santorini assured him. "That is every man's right under our laws. And be assured that you will be judged according to the truth."

"I ask only that," Andrea said quietly.

"Do you deny that you visited the home of Signor Mattei Bianco last night, entering the house by a door on the *terrazzo* facing the canal?"

"I did visit the Palazzo Bianco on the Via delle Galeazze last night," Andrea admitted. "And I talked with Signor Mattei Bianco."

"Ha! Then you cannot deny that you left the house with a purse full of gold coins."

"I do not deny it," Andrea said. "Signor Mattei gave me the coins and let me out of the house himself."

The judge leaned forward, a frosty light in his eyes. "Continue please," he begged on a sarcastic note. "You are condemning yourself quite effectively with your lies. What happened then?"

"I was on my way back to the Palazzo Martello where I was staying with the party of Signor di Perestrello when I realized that I was being followed. Two thieves set upon

me in the darkness near the Via delle Scuoli and tried to
kill me—for my purse, I supposed then. Although stabbed
in the shoulder, I managed to beat them off, and when I
threw one of them to the stones his neck was broken.
Some of the coins from my purse were spilled out there,
but I didn't discover that until I got safely back."

"We found the coins with the body of the man
you killed."

"Who was he?" Andrea asked.

"Girolamo Bellini, a servant of Signor Mattei Bianco.
For your information, the coins in the purse you stole were
freshly minted and have been identified by Signor Bianco."

"Why does not Mattei Bianco accuse me himself then?"
Andrea demanded. "Is he afraid of the truth?"

The judge brought his fist down upon the table with a
crash. "The truth, El Hakim, or El Shaitan—whatever
your name is—what is the truth?"

"The truth is what I have told you," Andrea said, but
he knew already that his effort was wasted. As one of the
dreaded *Inquisitori di Dieci*, Signor Santorini's word was
law in this court and his decisions beyond any appeal. He
had obviously made up his mind well before the so-called
trial opened, or, what was more likely, it had been skillfully made up for him.

Mattei had played his cards well, Andrea realized, and
with his usual thoroughness. And he, by being fool enough
to believe his scheming half brother even for a moment,
had helped. The delay last night when Mattei went for the
purse could only have been to give him time to mark the
freshly minted coins so they could be identified and serve
as evidence of theft in case he was not killed immediately
and the affair came to the attention of the *polizia*.

Not that Mattei had intended for him to be taken alive,
Andrea was sure. The two men had followed him on his
half brother's orders, knowing that he was on his way to
the *palazzo* of the Portuguese commercial envoy. Their instructions must have been to take him unawares and kill
him with the first thrust. But they had not reckoned on
the strength and agility generated by five years at the
oars of the pirate galley, or the acuteness of perception
that came from living constantly within the length of an
overseer's whip.

It was like Mattei, Andrea thought grimly, to leave
nothing to chance. The first attempt having failed, he had

then played his second card by having him arrested for murder and convicted at a farce of a hearing like this, without a chance to defend himself. It was also an indication of how far Mattei had risen in the world that he could wield enough influence in Venice to have the case tried in secret by one of the specal *Inquisitori*.

Whether or not Signor Santorini had already been bribed to see that he would be judged guilty, Andrea had no way of knowing, but he suspected that Mattei had also taken that additional precaution. In any event, the result would be the same. He, Andrea, would be truly, as well as legally, dead, probably before the day was over. And Mattei would be free to enjoy not only the benefits of the Bianco family wealth, the use of which he'd already had these past years, but Angelita as well.

"Have you any proof of this remarkable tale you have been telling?" Santorini inquired acidly.

"Order my brother to face me and I will wring the truth from him," Andrea suggested.

"So now you have a brother?" The inquisitor leaned back in his chair and shook with laughter. *"Per Bacco!* You are a droll fellow! It will be a pity to hang such an accomplished liar. Pray, who is this brother of yours?"

"Mattei Bianco. We are half brothers, with the same father."

The laughter suddenly left Santorini's face. "I knew Signor Gaetano Bianco," he said. "He was an upright and honest man. How dare you claim to be his bastard?"

It was Andrea's turn to be angry. He took a quick step toward the table, but one of the guards seized him by the wrist manacles he wore and jerked him back. "I am not a bastard," he shouted. "My name is as good as yours."

"And pray who are you?" Signor Santorini inquired.

Andrea controlled his anger with a great effort. Whatever else happened—and he did not have much doubt as to what it would be—he was resolved not to be baited further. "I am Andrea Bianco," he said proudly. "The eldest son of Gaetano Bianco."

Santorini stared at him thoughtfully and for a moment Andrea dared to hope that at last the judge was inclined to believe something he had said. Then the clerk who had been making notes of the proceedings reached out and touched the inquisitor's sleeve. They conferred in whispers for a moment and Santorini turned back to Andrea, his face set in an angry scowl once more.

"I am reminded of something I had forgotten," he said. "Signor Andrea Bianco was lost with all those aboard a galley during a voyage to the East ten years ago."

"Eight years ago," Andrea corrected gravely. "The galley was attacked by a Turkish renegade and captured. I was sold into slavery and traveled for three years with a merchant of Alexandria as his clerk. Later I was bought as a galley slave by a Moorish corsair captain called Hamet-el-Baku and was pulling an oar on the brigantino of Hamet-el-Baku when he attacked the caravel bringing Signor di Perestrello and his party to Venice."

"Andrea Bianco is legally dead," Santorini interrupted. "The galley was lost with all aboard; it is not possible that only he would have survived."

"All things are possible to God," Andrea reminded him. "Why I was saved I do not know, but I can assure you that I was. How else would I know these things?"

"You might have learned them from the real Andrea Bianco before his death."

"That would mean he did survive the attack upon the galley," Andrea pointed out quickly.

Santorini stroked his chin thoughtfully, then his face cleared. "Fortunately we have a way of proving your identity, if you are what you claim. Bring in the chamberlain of Signor Mattei Bianco," he ordered the guard and turned back to Andrea. "This man was with Signor Gaetano for many years. If you are Andrea Bianco as you claim, your father's chamberlain will recognize you at once."

The guard brought in an older man dressed in the familiar livery of the Bianco family. Andrea recognized him as Dimas Andrede, who had been his father's chamberlain or butler. If anyone would identify him immediately, it would be Dimas.

The old chamberlain shuffled forward without meeting Andrea's eyes. Before the table behind which the judge sat, he stopped and bowed deeply. "Your Signory sent for me?" he mumbled.

"Give your full name, your place of residence, and your occupation." Santorini instructed him.

"I am Dimas Andrede, chamberlain to Signor Mattei Bianco. I reside at the Palazzo Bianco in the Via delle Galeazze."

"How long have you been with the Bianco family, Dimas?"

"Thirty years, Your Excellency."

"Will you tell us what happened at the Palazzo Bianco last night?"

"A thief entered, sir, a Moor. He tried to blackmail Signor Mattei by claiming to be Signor Andrea, his older brother who was lost at sea."

"Did you see the stranger?"

"Y—yes, but not very clearly."

"Did he look like Signor Andrea Bianco?"

"This man was a Moor. He told Signor Mattei that in the Moorish lands he is known as El Hakim."

Santorini shot a triumphant glance at the prisoner and went on with his questions. "What happened then?"

"The Moor stole a purse of gold and escaped, but Signor Mattei sent two of the servants after him to try and get it back. They were following him, but he turned on them in the darkness and killed one. The other is here, as Your Signory ordered."

"You knew Signor Andrea Bianco well, I believe, Dimas?"

"Yes, sir."

"Could you identify him if you saw him now?"

The chamberlain hesitated momentarily. "I—I think so. Yes, I'm sure I could."

"Turn and face the man standing beside you and tell me whether you ever saw him before."

Dimas turned slowly, but did not speak.

"Do you know this man, Dimas?" the judge prompted.

"He—he is the thief who visited the Palazzo Bianco last night," the old chamberlain quavered.

"Is he Andrea Bianco?"

"Signor Andrea is dead."

Seeing the sickly fear in the old man's eyes, Andrea knew why the chamberlain was telling this structure of lies. It could only mean that pressure had been put on Dimas, probably the threat of losing his position and going hungry after all these years, or perhaps even losing his life.

"Thank you," Santorini said. "You have told us everything we needed to know. You may go."

The chamberlain was already at the door when Andrea

said impulsively. "Do not feel badly, Dimas. I understand and forgive you."

The old man half turned and the light of gratitude in his eyes was pitiful to see. Santorini did not notice it, however, for he was conferring with the clerk. As the door closed behind the chamberlain, the judge looked up. "What do you say now, Ser Liar?" he demanded of Andrea. "Do you still claim to be someone you are not?"

"I am Andrea Bianco," Andrea said stoutly. "I have told you only the truth."

Santorini shrugged. "You are a persistent rogue, at least, We have one more witness. Let the man Vittorio Panimo be brought in."

A man came in, his eyes darting nervously around the room. When he saw Andrea standing before the table he drew away a little and approached it from the side.

"Your name?" Santorini asked.

"Vittorio, Vittorio Panimo."

"You are employed by Signor Mattei Bianco?"

"Yes, Your Signory. As a gondolier."

"Did you follow a thief from the Palazzo Bianco last night?"

"Y-yes, sir."

"Why did you follow him?"

"He had stolen some gold. Signor Mattei ordered me to go after him with one of the footmen and get the purse back."

"What happened then?"

"The Moor must have heard us. He waited for us in a dark street; we did not know he was there until he attacked us. He broke Bellini's neck while I tried to battle with him. I saw that he would kill me too, so I ran away."

"Would you recognize this Moor if you saw him now?"

"I—I think so."

"Turn and look at the man standing there beside the table. Then tell me whether or not he is the one you grappled with last night, the man who murdered Girolamo Bellini."

The groom studied Andrea warily.

"Is he the man?" Santorini demanded.

"Y-yes," the groom said. "He is the one that killed Girolamo."

"Thank you. You may go."

"El Hakim," Santorini said solemnly. "You have been

heard and fairly tried. I must admit that you are a clever rogue, but in spite of the web of lies you spun so well, the testimony of Dimas Andrede and the groom who just left will hang you. Face the table and hear your sentence."

"Signor Santorini," Bartholomeu di Perestrello said courteously. "May I speak first?"

"Of course."

"You are about to sentence the man called Hakim to death, or to the galleys, I believe?"

"His crime justifies the death penalty."

"I have no wish to interfere with the orderly process of justice," the Portuguese envoy said. "But this man saved my life and that of the others with me on our ship, so we feel an interest in him and particularly in the salvation of his immortal soul. Do you not think that—being a heathen—he should be given an opportunity to embrace our faith?"

"Of course," Santorini said. "It is very thoughtful of you to consider it, signor. I will sentence him to the galleys for a year. In that way he will have an opportunity to learn of the mercies of Christ and perhaps to see the error of his ways before he is finally executed."

"Fra Mauro tells me that El Hakim is a skilled mapmaker and has traveled in distant lands," Di Perestrello continued. "My prince, Dom Henrique, is anxious to find such men to assist with a project now under way to map the world and thus help discover new lands where those who have no knowledge of our Lord and Savior can be brought to them."

The judge shrugged. "Venice and Portugal are rivals in commerce, signor. Why should we help your prince gain an advantage over us?"

Dom Bartholomeu did not have an immediate answer, but Dona Leonor spoke up quickly, and Andrea was sure that her father's intervention in his behalf had been at her instigation. "If the Turks attack the West, Your Excellency," she pointed out, "we will need all the information about their country and their strength that we can get. It would be a pity for Hakim to be executed before all he knows can be put on maps and set down in writing against the day when the Turks do attack."

"You have a strong argument there, madonna," Santorini admitted. "The Council of Ten is much concerned over the Turkish threat."

"Make him a slave in Prince Henry's service then," she urged. "Fra Mauro will instruct him in the mysteries of Holy Church so that his immortal soul will be saved. And the prince's mapmakers will be able to use whatever information he can give them to help defeat the Turks and the Moors."

Santorini hesitated. "As you say," he agreed. "It would be a good thing for what knowledge the condemned possesses about the Turks and the Moors to be made known to Christians."

"He will surely not dare to cause trouble if he is reprieved from a sentence of death," she urged.

Santorini's face cleared. "If he does, your prince can execute him at once. I will agree to your request, madonna." He turned to Andrea. "El Hakim, you are sentenced to perpetual slavery in the care of Signor di Perestrello and in the service of Prince Henry of Portugal. But remember! One false move on your part will lead to your death."

Andrea restrained his anger at the injustice of the trial. As to the sentence, he fully realized how close he had been to death and that he had been spared only because of the presence of Dom Bartholomeu and his daughter, and particularly Dona Leonor's skilled arguments in his behalf. It was certainly the better part of wisdom not to stir up Santorini any further by protesting his innocence, he decided, and to accept as gracefully as he could what might be considered his good luck in escaping death.

"The prisoner will remain in his cell until your ship is ready to sail," Santorini told Di Perestrello. "We cannot have a murderer loose upon the streets of Venice—even to please your prince."

"We gladly agree to that," Dom Bartholomeu assured him. "You may rest assured that your sentence will be strictly carried out."

VII

Andrea Bianco stood in the bows of the caravel *Santa Paula* and watched the sky line of Venice fade slowly in the afternoon sunlight. His torso glistened with sweat, for he had pulled one of the long sweeps while the trim vessel was being warped from its dock almost in the center of the city and rowed out into the open harbor by the crew. The sails had been set a few minutes before and now they bellied out, taut and full in the evening breeze, while the caravel quickly gathered speed.

Andrea's wrists were manacled together, as were his ankles, but the chains were light and gave him room to move about. The departure had been made a little before sunset so the caravel could clear the port and run down the eastern coast of Italy during the night, lying to in some convenient harbor shortly after dawn, and resuming her progress again the next evening.

Most ships in this area—save the Venetians who were immune because they paid tribute to the corsairs—followed this policy of sailing by night and resting by day wherever the waters were charted well enough for night sailing to be safe. Eric Vallarte, the red-haired Norse shipmaster, had chosen this course of procedure on the return voyage, rather than risk another brush with a corsair that might not turn out so well for them. Now he came up to where Andrea stood in the bows, treading the deck lightly for so large a man and balancing himself easily against the slight roll of the vessel.

"You pulled well on the oars, Hakim," the shipmaster said in his villainous Spanish.

"Five years in the galleys make a man strong—or kill him," Andrea assured him. "You must know what it is to pull an oar for hours at a stretch. The men of the North often sail on long ocean voyages."

"What do you know of the men of the North? Were you ever there?"

"It has been my good fortune to travel only as far west as Sardegna," Andrea admitted. "But the grandfather of a friend of mine sailed to Thule many years ago and then on to the island your people call the Green Land."

"By Woden!" Eric exclaimed. "Only in tales that old women tell to children nowadays is there any mention of the Green Land. This is a passing strange thing."

"In the country of the great Khans and Cipangu I heard talk of land still farther east of those countries," Andrea said. "It was my ambition one day to sail the unknown seas." He lifted his manacled hands. "But now——"

"You may still sail them, Hakim," a familiar voice said

close by. It was Dona Leonor and he turned to bow gravely to her.

"As a slave pulling an oar perhaps, madonna? I had hoped for a better fate."

Just then a call came for Eric Vallarte from the after-deck and he moved away, leaving them alone in the gathering twilight. "Are you not afraid to be here alone with a murderer, madonna?" Andrea asked.

"You killed that man in a fair fight, didn't you?"

He shook his head. "No. It was not really fair."

"But you said——"

"Girolamo Bellini had a dagger, while I was unarmed. And there were two of them. But perhaps the odds were really even after all. They had no way of knowing what strength a man gains from five years at the oars of a Moorish galley."

"But you did try to kill you."

He nodded. "On someone else's orders."

"Do you still persist in claiming to be Andrea Bianco?"

He shrugged. "Andrea Bianco is dead, madonna. It may be simpler not to bring him to life a second time, since he fared so badly in his first resurrection."

"Who are you, Hakim? Obviously you are not really a Moor."

"No," he said gravely. "I am not a Moor."

"Dimas Andrede must have known the real Andrea Bianco well. What reason would he have to lie?"

"You are young, madonna, and you have been tenderly reared. It is better that you have as little knowledge as possible of the evil that lies in some men."

"But that old man did not seem evil."

"Dimas lied for a reason that has swayed honest men before him—to keep from starving and perhaps from losing his life."

"But your story is so fantastic, Hakim. I can believe you killed that man in a fair fight—perhaps because I am grateful to you for saving us from the corsairs. But that you are Andrea Bianco——" She shook her head.

He remembered then that he had not had an opportunity to ask her about Angelita. "You did not go to Chioggia after all, did you?"

"I went—and I saw Senhora Angelita Bianco."

"You saw her?" he asked eagerly. "What did she say?"

Dona Leonor raised her eyes to his. "She said that

Andrea Bianco was dead and that her husband had described to her the man who claimed to be Andrea Bianco and he was an impostor."

"An impostor?" He could not believe that Angelita, too, had turned against him. "Did you tell her what I said —that I loved her?"

"Yes."

"And that I swore by the summerhouse of my father's *palazzo?*"

"I—I forgot that part. Did it make so much difference?"

He shook his head slowly. "Not any more. Thank you, madonna, for going to Chioggia." And yet he could not help feeling a sense of joy even through his disappointment. For had Angelita heard that he'd sworn by the summerhouse which meant so much to both of them, she would have known it was really he who had sent the message and would surely have come to help him.

"She is very beautiful. Andrea Bianco must have loved her very much," Dona Leonor said thoughtfully. Then she added, as if speaking to herself, "If I loved a man and he was lost at sea, I would carry his memory enshrined in my heart forever and never look at another."

"You are young, madonna——"

She stamped her foot angrily. "I am old enough to know what is right and what is wrong, Sir Slave——" She stopped and put her hand to her mouth in horror. "Forgive me, Hakim. I spoke in anger."

"Yet you spoke the truth. I am a slave—and under sentence of death as well, if I do not act as a slave should."

She shivered. "I thought to have you sentenced only as a slave to Prince Henry, not to have you condemned to death."

"If you and your father had not intervened, I would already have been executed, so I owe you both my life." He looked at her keenly. "It was you who actually caused me to be released, madonna. Why did you do it?"

"I—I'm not sure," she admitted.

"Isn't it because in your heart you believe I am really Andrea Bianco?"

"I think I was beginning to believe it," she admitted. "Until I talked with Senhora Angelita, and old Dimas testified against you. Now"—she lifted her arms and let them drop—"I can't help believing that if Andrea Bianco were really alive, his beloved would have known it in her heart. She would not have looked at another, but remained confident that our Blessed Lord would bring him back some day."

"Few women are as constant as yourself, I am afraid, madonna," he said gravely. "Fortunate indeed will be the man to whom you give your love."

BOOK TWO
The Al-Kemal

I

On the low headland at the southwestern tip of Portugal where the Atlantic and the Mediterranean meet —named the sacred promontory, or Sagres, since the time of the Romans—Prince Henry of Portugal had built a town called Villa do Infante. The village was only a few miles from the port city of Lagos, which stood a little way east of the promotory and hence in somewhat more sheltered waters. The name of the Infante Henrique was already widely known before Andrea Bianco had sailed on the ill-fated voyage to Trebizond. During the days it took the *Santa Paula* to travel to Lagos, he learned more from Fra Mauro about the voyages of exploration which had been carried out by tiny Portugal from this point.

Under the infante's father, Dom João, Portugal had begun to emerge definitely as a nation in her own right. She had repelled the latest in a series of invasions from Castile, anxious to return what was still regarded as only another rebellious Spanish province to the realm of Spain. And with an instinct for seafaring which only Prince Henry among his sons seemed to have inherited, Dom João had laid the foundations of a great navy and begun conquests over the seas. Under his rule voyages had been made westward and southward to what Phoenician sailors had called—perhaps two thousand years before—the Fortunate Isles. Later visitors had named them the Canary Islands because of the large numbers of dogs found there, from the Latin word for dog, *canis.*

Prince Henry himself had first trod the stage of history in an attack led by three princes of Portugal upon the Moorish stronghold of Ceuta, across the narrow straits forming the entrance to the Mediterranean called, since the history of man, the "Pillars of Hercules." Ceuta had fallen in 1415 to the considerable glory of the three infantes—especially Prince Henry. Duarte, Pedro, and Henrique were knighted by their father, Dom João, on the spot, and the latter was given the task of governing and defending this important seaport.

Perhaps in order to be near his charge of Ceuta, or

because even now the sacred promontory known as Sagres, jutting into the meeting place of two oceans, had already come to symbolize to him the great mysteries to be explored in what was called then the Western Sea, Prince Henry had chosen to take his seat there. His father had created him Governor of Algarve, the name of this southern province, as well as Duke of Viseu, and upon this spot he had lived ever since.

The town of Villa do Infante was small, consisting of only a few houses, an observatory, a meeting place for the experts employed by Prince Henry, a chapel, and the prince's own modest residence. But whatever it lacked in size, it made up in the quality of its population and the high level of intelligence present. Here, over the years, the beloved prince had gathered many of the foremost mapmakers, geographers, navigators, astronomers, mathematicians, and thinkers of the world, many of them refugees from the dread Inquisition of nearby Spain.

Nor was there a dearth of more practical folk for the task the infante had embarked upon, that of exploring, mapping, and conquering the vast land bulge of the continent of Africa to the south. At the port of Lagos nearby lived a full complement of skilled shipwrights and workers in wood and metal, forgers and fabricators, builders of caravels and *barcas,* sailmakers and fitters, rope workers and coopers, men whose whole lives were taken up with building and equipping ships upon which more venturesome souls sailed the seas.

Fortunately, too, there was no lack of daring seamen at Lagos, men like Eric Vallarte, the redheaded giant from the Norseland. Son of a line of explorers whose voyaging had carried them westward to Thule and to the storied Green Land—even as far west, some said, as a mysterious "Wine Land" where one Eric, surnamed The Red, and his son Lief had filled their boat with luscious fruit in a few hours—Vallarte was a skilled shipmaster.

Also at Lagos were such doughty Portuguese captains as João Gonçalves Zarco and Tristão Vaz Teixeria, who had sailed in clumsy *barcas*—ancestors of the swift caravels such as the one on which Andrea Bianco came to Lagos—to rediscover and later colonize the Fortunate Isles. No less glorious had been the feats of Gil Eannes de Azurarra, first to round the grim projecting headline of

Cape Bojador on the coast of Africa to the south. This promontory, with its shoals extending many miles out to sea, had defied explorers for centuries, protecting sailors— it was rumored—from seas that hissed and boiled with the tropic heat, monsters that could crush a ship with mighty jaws, and even an edge to the earth, over which both ships and men would fall to certain destruction.

Be it said, however, that few thinking men in Portugal —or anywhere else for that matter—shared his belief in a flat earth with an edge. Certainly no such idea was common to those gathered at Villa do Infante, all of whom knew well what the ancient Greeks had decided long ago, namely, that the world was as round as an apple. Furthermore, it was generally agreed that the quadrilateral mass of land and enclosed seas making up the known habitable land—extending as far east as the Island of Cipangu beyond the domain of the Khans, called China, as well as westward to the fabled islands of Antillia, St. Brendan, and the Hand of Satan in the Western Sea—somehow floated upon the surface of the waters covering the globe.

The most recent step in the daring program of exploration begun by Prince Henry had been accomplished by two men only a few years before. Antom Gonçalves and Uno Tristram had sailed far to the south along the coast of Africa, landing and capturing some dark-skinned men who came naked to the shore to greet them, and carrying their prizes triumphantly back to Portugal in chains.

The discoveries of Antom Gonçalves and Uno Tristram had moved Prince Henry to send Bartholomeu di Perestrello as an envoy to Rome to request of the Holy Father that the treasures of the Church be opened and funds provided to send ships and crews southward to fight and capture the infidels. By doing so, he argued, the immortal souls of the enemy would be brought into contact with the knowledge of the true God and His Blessed Son, thus achieving salvation. That in the process the bodies of the captives would be sold into slavery at a considerable profit to those who had snatched them from home and family was only natural. Such things were common and accepted as wholly right.

Prince Henry had prudently appended a request to his petition that the lands to be discovered also be granted unto him. This was a necessary precaution, since ships of England, France, and the great maritime trading cities of Genoa, Florence, and Venice were also anxious to make gains in this direction. Thereby they hoped to offset the considerable drop in profit from the trade in spices, precious woods and stones, fine silks, and other luxuries from the distant East. These had been sharply curtailed lately because of the failure of the Ottoman Turks to behave in a gentlemanly fashion.

That Senhor di Perestrello's mission had been successful was proved by the imposing official paper which he shortly delivered to his prince and which was read in the chapel at Villa do Infante. In it the Holy Father, Eugenius IV, answered Prince Henry's appeal with "great joy" and went on to say that:

> As it has now been notified to us by our beloved son Henry, Duke of Viseu, Master of the Order of Christ, that trusting firmly in the aid of God, for the confusion of the Moors and enemies of Christ in those lands that they have desolated and for the exaltation of the Catholic faith—and because that knights and brethren of the said Order of Christ against the said Moors and other enemies of the faith have waged war with the grace of God under the banner of the said Order—and to the extent that they may bestir themselves to the said war with greater fervor, we do to each and all of us engaged in the said war, by Apostolic Authority and by these letters, grant full remission of all those sins of which they shall be truly penitent at heart and of which they have made confession by their mouth. And whoever breaks, contradicts, or acts against the letter of this mandate, let him lie under the curse of the Almighty God and of the Apostles Peter and Paul.

To this fulsome praise of Prince Henry and his followers was added a somewhat more tangible reward by the Infante Dom Pedro, then regent of the kingdom, in giving to the Infante Henrique a charter granting him the entire fifth of the profits from all such exploring and trading ventures in new lands which would ordinarily appertain to the Crown.

The regent furthermore ruled that, since Prince Henry had carried out the whole plan of discovery resulting in the appearance of men and women with velvety black skins in the slave markets of Portugal, no one should be allowed to sail for these ports without the license and express command of the Governor of Algarve and Duke of Viseu.

Nor was the daring of Prince Henry's captains in rounding dreaded Cape Bojador and sailing southward along the coast of Africa any hollow victory. Since the days of the early caliphs hundreds of years before, the African trade had belonged to Islam and had been under their strict control. For untold centuries caravans had crossed the vast desert sands south of Morocco and the Atlas Mountains to sell their pepper, slaves, gold dust, and precious woods in Ceuta and other Moslem centers. To break this monopoly after seven hundred years was a consummation devoutly to be desired, not only for the lofty purpose of cleaving the simple black people from Islam, but also the more practical purpose of bringing a vast wealth into Portugal itself.

Small wonder then that there was rejoicing and dancing in the streets when the decision of the Pope was read in Lagos and nearby Villa do Infante. Senhor di Perestrello and his lovely daughter, along with Eric Vallarte and Fra Mauro, were idolized for a day by the townspeople and showered with gifts and every good thing. If, in the excitement, few noticed a tall slave with a magnificent body and a sun-darkened skin among the retinue of Senhor di Perestrello, it was because, of late, slaves had become very common in Lagos where the ships from Africa docked to market their valuable cargoes.

After his years with the Moslems, even so small a town as Villa do Infante and the somewhat larger port city of Lagos were a delight to Andrea Bianco. As a slave he was assigned to the retinue of Dom Bartholomeu until such a time as Prince Henry made a final disposition of his case. He quickly learned that his new master was one of the wealthiest men in this part of Portugal, as well as a trusted intimate of Prince Henry. The prince himself had departed for Lisbon immediately after their arrival, on matters of state, and did not return for several weeks.

The exploring activities of Prince Henry and his captains had been somewhat in abeyance for several years because of political difficulties in the kingdom of Portugal. The early death of King Duarte, who succeeded to Dom João's throne, had stunned the kingdom. Even more of a shock was the King's will, leaving Queen Leonor—for whom Bartholomeu di Perestrello's elder daughter had been named—sole regent of the realm for his minor sons.

When the people protested violently against placing an alien woman upon the throne, Pedro, the second son of Dom João, had finally taken over the reins of the regency. But there was no love lost between him and the Queen, who deemed herself a woman scorned. In the resulting eruption Prince Henry had been called upon again and again to intervene as peacemaker, a role he assumed as a duty but certainly not as a pleasure. Since royal affairs took so much of his time, little was left for personal supervision of the activities at Villa do Infante and Lagos that had been his whole life. And as a result, not much exploration had been accomplished since the daring voyage of João Zarco and Tristão Vaz Teixeria.

As for Andrea Bianco, he found it convenient for the moment to bide his time and see what would happen. Actually he had little choice, since if he made what Senhor di Perestrello or his agents considered any attempt to escape, he could be killed on the spot legally because of the sentence of death imposed by the court at Venice.

At the moment, however, Andrea felt no inclination to escape. Villa do Infante was something new in his experience, a whole community devoted solely to intellectual pursuits, the nightly observations when the skies were not obscured by clouds, and the huge room where patient mapmakers worked under the direction of Jahuda Cresques, known here as Mestre Jacomé. To Andrea the town had a fascination far greater than any place he had ever known.

A son of that same Abraham Cresques who had drawn the first really complete map of the world since the time of Ptolemy, the Greek geographer who had lived something like a century and a half after the birth of Christ, Mestre Jacomé had been brought from Mallorca by Prince Henry and given everything he needed for his work. To his presence, like butterflies to a lamp, had been drawn many of the leading men of the world in the fields of navigation, mathematics, astronomy, charting, geography and other intellectual pursuits.

As for Dona Leonor, Andrea came in almost daily contact with her, since she was mistress of Dom Bartholomeu's household. The other daughter, Filippa, was much younger than Dona Leonor, having been merely a baby when their mother died a few years before. Even though she treated him with strict impartiality, as she did the other household slaves, Andrea could not help admiring the efficiency with which Dona Leonor ran the establishment, or escape the realization that the entire household, including Fra Mauro, worshiped her.

Even his slight contact with Dona Leonor had impressed Andrea with the extent of her education in a day when women usually did not even know how to read and write. Much of this, he saw quickly, was due to the presence of Fra Mauro, who—in addition to being the spiritual adviser of Dom Bartholomeu's household—also tutored Dona Leonor in other fields. This he had done so well that she could hold her own with the mathematicians and navigators who gathered to talk with the portly friar. But had he not been working with an eager and alert mind, Andrea realized, the Franciscan's efforts would have been for nought.

The most important man in Villa do Infante—after Prince Henry—was unquestionably Mestre Jacomé. A small, bent man, who wore the flat velveteen cap of a devout Jew on a somewhat overlarge head, he ruled the students of what amounted to a small university with an iron hand. His deep-set penetrating eyes betrayed the sharp intelligence behind them, and a vast amount of knowledge was stored up within the egg-bald skull, along with, Andrea discovered, a crusty temper.

Mestre Jacomé often visited Fra Mauro. One night when Andrea came to bring the wine and cakes that the rotund friar often shared with him before retiring, he found the visitor there.

"Sit down, Andrea," Fra Mauro said kindly. "I want my friend, Mestre Jacomé, to know you."

The Jew looked up at the tall slave with those keen eyes of his. "The good friar tells me you claim to have journeyed to Cipangu, Hakim," he said.

Andrea eased himself to a stool and poured a cup of wine before he answered. His fetters had been removed, since here on the isolated promontory of Sagres there was little opportunity for slaves to escape. Besides, Fra Mauro treated him as an equal and he naturally assumed the other would, too.

"Yes, your honor," he said courteously. "I have."

"Do not think to curry favor by giving me underserved titles," Mestre Jacomé said sharply.

Andrea shrugged. "I was saluting you as a mapmaker—in which trade you certainly deserve honor."

"What do you know of mapmaking?"

Andrea glanced at Fra Mauro, but the Franciscan shook his head, indicating that he had told Mestre Jacomé nothing about him as yet.

"I have traveled far," Andrea said then, "and studied the charts by which men sail to and from India and China using the monsoons. And I know the tricks of the corsairs."

"Obviously you are a braggart as well," Mestre Jacomé said caustically. "Much talk often hides little knowledge."

"Have it as you wish, master," Andrea said quietly. "You questioned me and I answered you."

"What more did you learn in your voyaging than was told by Messer Marco Polo? Or perhaps you have read his book and made up a pack of lies from it to impress honest people."

"I have read Messer Polo's book," Andrea admitted. "But I have also seen sights not witnessed by him and traveled in lands he did not visit."

"Name some of them."

"On the Island of Cipangu I wrestled with strong men of that land. And I saw snow upon a mountain that burns inside with a fire which has never been quenched."

"What else?"

"Their soldiers fight with great broadswords and wear armor made from tough withes."

"Did they tell you how far the Island of Cipangu extends to the east? Or speak of other lands beyond it?"

Andrea was suddenly wary, for the old Jew's words had given him an inspiration, a hint of how the things he had learned in his travels might be put to a useful purpose in furthering his own interests. If Jahuda Cresques sought such information, then others might be willing to pay for it. Perhaps Prince Henry himself could even be maneuvered into giving him the reward in which he was most interested at the moment, his freedom from slavery.

"Go on," Mestre Jacomé ordered testily. "Answer my question."

"I have suffered much since that journey," Andrea

temporized. "Let me think and see if I can remember whether the men of Cipangu spoke of those things you mention."

Mestre Jacomé's eyes narrowed and Andrea saw that he had not fooled this shrewd old Jew. "Have you put a price upon your knowledge?" he demanded.

"Everything has its price, master."

"What is yours?"

Andrea shrugged. "I cannot decide until I have a chance to see what my knowledge is worth."

"You are an impudent rogue," Mestre Jacomé snapped. "The whip could loosen your tongue."

"I am a slave—through no fault of my own, sir," Andrea said quietly. "But you would learn nothing with the whip, unless I wanted to tell you. Besides, Dom Bartholomeu is a just man. He would not have a man whipped when no crime has been committed."

Mestre Jacomé turned to Fra Mauro. "Obviously this man is a charlatan," he said. "I doubt if he has ever done more than pull a galley oar and listen to travelers' tales."

The friar had been watching Andrea during this interchange, a thoughtful look upon his face. Now he spoke. "What is the meaning of this, my son?" he asked. "Mestre Jacomé is my friend, and a famous navigator and maker of maps."

"I have information which could be of great value to him and to the infante. Obviously I would be a fool not to better my lot by selling my knowledge if I can."

"I'll wager you can tell us nothing we do not know already," Mestre Jacomé said.

Andrea smiled. "Until I talked to you, good master, I did not realize just how much the things I have learned these past eight years might really be worth. Now I am beginning to have some idea of their value and you may be certain that I shall not put a cheap price upon them." He stood up. "May I have your permission to go, little brother?"

Fra Mauro nodded. *"Va bene,* my son. I hope you are doing the right thing."

Andrea grinned. "Sometimes a man can only do what seems best for him, and hope that it is also right. *Pax vobiscum,* good Master Cresques."

II

It was the custom of Senhor Bartholomeu di Perestrello, just after the family had breakfasted each morning, to listen to requests or complaints from members of his household and slaves, settling differences and assigning the tasks of the day, as recommended by Dona Leonor. On the morning after his interchange with Mestre Jacomé, Andrea presented himself before Senhor Bartholomeu and his daughter. He waited patiently until the other slaves had been given their assignments.

Dona Leonor read from a list she had written down. "Hakim, you will cut wood this morning in the wood-yard," she announced. "And this afternoon you will accompany me to the market to carry the baskets."

Andrea bowed his head in acknowledgment but did not move away.

"What is it?" she asked. "Do you wish other work?"

"I have a request to make of Dom Bartholomeu."

"We will listen to what you have to say, Hakim, as we do all the slaves," Senhor di Perestrello told him. "What is it you wish?"

"I would buy my freedom."

Dona Leonor's eyes opened wide. "Buy your freedom? With what?"

"With information concerning the far-distant places of the world, and the routes by which they can be reached."

"You are a slave," Dona Leonor said a little sharply. "Whatever you possess belongs to your master."

"You are wrong, madonna. My body can be enslaved, but not my mind."

Her color rose. "Impudent rogue. Is this another of your tricks?"

"I am offering my knowledge of maps and shipping routes, perhaps more, in return for my freedom," Andrea explained. "If you do not think them valuable, others may."

"Is this the way you reward us for saving you from the executioner?" Dona Leonor demanded hotly. "I promised Signor Santorini that what you could tell us would be useful."

68

"I think we are even on that score, madonna," he said quietly. "Senhor Vallarte has acknowledged that if I had not crippled the Moorish galley, you would be a slave in Islam now."

She paled a little at that and pressed her lip between her teeth. "There is much right in what you say, Hakim," Senhor di Perestrello spoke. "But neither I nor my daughter are qualified to judge the value of any knowledge you may possess."

"Have I leave to petition the infante then?" Andrea asked. Since leaving Fra Mauro and Mestre Jacomé the night before, he had spent much time in thought. And the more he had considered, the more convinced he was that he should not be content merely with asking for freedom in return for revealing what he knew about the little-known Eastern part of the world and the tricks of Arab navigators in particular. It was a daring game, but if he played his cards well, Andrea Bianco might once again achieve a place of honor in the world—especially among men of learning such as those gathered here at Villa do Infante. And to him that was very important indeed.

"What do you think, daughter?" Dom Bartholomeu asked.

"Hakim was right in reminding me of our obligation to him," she admitted. "And I was at fault in threatening him with the whips. If Prince Henry agrees that the information he has is worth his freedom, I think he should have it."

"Thank you, madonna," Andrea said quietly. "I was sure you would be just and fair."

Dona Leonor held her head high. "You may go now. There is still work to be done."

Fra Mauro stopped by the woodyard later in the morning, where Andrea was splitting billets for the ovens. He was stripped to the waist and the bright sun shone on his torso as he leaned upon the ax. *"Buon giorno, frater,"* he greeted the portly friar in Italian.

"Benedicamus," Fra Mauro said. "You look uncommonly happy for a slave."

"I may not be one much longer. Dom Bartholomeu is going to ask the infante to hear what I have learned about the world in my travels. If His Highness thinks the information is of enough value to be worth my freedom, I shall have it."

"You're playing for high stakes."

"The highest. It was bad enough being a slave of the Moors. But to be a slave of white men, my equals, is many times worse for a man with pride. I will do anything to be free of that."

"Some of the best minds in the world are gathered here at Villa do Infante," the Franciscan reminded him. "Little knowledge exists that is not already known to some of them and therefore at our prince's command."

"Thank you for the warning, little brother." Andrea looked at the friar intently for a moment before he spoke again. "Can they tell him a simple and sure way to guide a ship home from any part of the earth?"

"No one has such knowledge," Fra Mauro exclaimed. "Not even the prince's finest navigators."

"Then I shall certainly be free," Andrea said joyously. "Free—and more besides."

"More?"

"What I can tell your prince about the countries to the east and the maps I shall draw for him will surely earn me my freedom. The rest will be my fortune."

"Which will be?"

"Andrea Bianco was a respected mapmaker of Venice, an equal of gentlemen and scholars everywhere. I would have that position again."

"God grant that you gain your wish," the Franciscan said. "But you were wrong in antagonizing Mestre Jacomé last night. He is very intelligent and has great influence with the infante."

"Would he go so far as to persuade Prince Henry not to hear me?"

The friar shook his head. "The infante is eager for news about other lands, particularly facts about India and China that might help him find a new route to those countries. He will surely examine you as soon as he returns, but I would advise you to tell him all and throw yourself upon his mercy."

"Knowledge of distant places and the ways of getting there and back are the only possessions I have of any value," Andrea said firmly. "I alone will set the price upon them."

"Many people come to the infante claiming to have

information of value," the friar warned. "Some even tried to get gold in advance. That is why Mestre Jacomé was so suspicious of you."

"I will tell only the truth. You can be sure of that."

"Let us hope it turns out well then. The infante usually examines those who claim to have special knowledge publicly. It is like a court, with Mestre Jacomé as the inquisitor."

"What can I lose? A freedom I haven't had for eight years?"

"Your head—conceivably."

Andrea grinned and slapped the Franciscan on the back. "What use is a head to a slave anyway, little brother? He needs only a strong back, and the galleys gave me that."

III

Andrea's examination by Prince Henry came on the day following the infante's return to the village. He had arrived at Lagos from Lisbon the day before, on a Venetian galley. A fiesta and ball was planned for that evening by the townspeople of Villa do Infante celebrating the return of their liege lord, and the town was bustling with preparations when Andrea and Fra Mauro went to the assembly hall that morning.

The building was almost filled with men, most of them wearing the long robe of the scholar. Mestre Jacomé occupied a place at a table upon the elevated dais at the front of the room. Prince Henry sat beside him and the table was covered with maps and other papers. Senhor Bartholomeu di Perestrello occupied one of the front seats.

Tall and broad-shouldered, the Infante Henrique looked more like an Englishman than a Spaniard or a Portuguese, a lineage handed down to him from his mother's side of the family. Dom João's Queen had been a daughter of John of Gaunt and the good qualities of that doughty Englishman were bequeathed by her to their sons, particularly Prince Henry. His hair was almost blond and his craggy face was lit with an inner serenity and honesty that was apparent in his fine eyes.

The Governor of Algarve wore a plain black tunic and hose. His only adornment was a chain ending in a medallion hanging from his neck. Nothing about him or his apparel was in the least ostentatious, yet he radiated an air of regal authority and sincerity. Andrea found himself liking the man whose slave he was, on sight, and steeled himself against the nobleman's obvious charm, lest it cause him to deviate from his avowed intention to demand the greatest possible return for his knowledge of navigation and geography.

When his name was called Andrea dropped to one knee before the dais and bowed his head.

"You may rise," Prince Henry told him kindly.

From this man he would receive justice, Andrea decided, justice and perhaps mercy, if he conducted himself so as to deserve it—but nothing more.

"You are called El Hakim, I believe," Prince Henry said.

"I was called that by the Moors, Your Highness, because of my knowledge of navigation and astronomy."

There was a stir of interest from the onlookers. "Where did you learn these things?" Prince Henry asked.

"In Venice. I also studied in Padua, at the university."

"A Moor in Padua?" the prince exclaimed. "How did this happen?"

"I am not a Moor, milord. My name is Andrea Bianco, a citizen of Venice by birth, as was my father before me."

Andrea was facing the infante and so did not see a tall man at the back of the room who stood up to get a better look at him.

"Obviously he is a charlatan, milord," Mestre Jacomé exclaimed angrily. "We are wasting your time."

"We will determine in good time whether or not that is true," Prince Henry said mildly, and turned back to Andrea. "How did it come about that you were a slave of the Moors?"

"In the year 1437," Andrea said, "after finishing my first map of the world, I set sail on a Venetian galley for the Black Sea and the city of Trebizond. The galley was attacked by a corsair and all aboard were killed or taken prisoner."

Mestre Jacomé spoke briefly to the prince in low tones.

The infante nodded and inquired, "Was this a Venetian ship?"

"Yes, milord."

Prince Henry's expression was more severe. "It is well known that Venetian ships are not attacked by the Moors. I have just come from Lisbon on a Venetian galley. The captain tells me they pay tribute to the corsairs so their vessels will not be harmed."

"That is true, sir," Andrea admitted. "This one was a renegade Turk. Besides, I have reason to believe there could have been collusion."

Prince Henry gave him a startled look. "What do you mean?"

"I think this particular pirate had been notified when the galley would sail, so he could attack it."

"This is a serious charge," Mestre Jacomé interposed. "Who would have reason to do this?"

"My half brother Mattei," Andrea said. "In Venice a few weeks ago he had me set upon by two assassins and then had me imprisoned and sentenced to death because I killed one of the attackers in a fair fight."

"This is a strange story indeed," the infante observed. "And hard to believe, unless you are indeed Andrea Bianco. Can you give us further proof of your identity?"

"None save my knowledge of maps and the stars and the science of guiding ships at sea."

"Many possess that knowledge. You could have gathered it anywhere."

"I have no other proof at the moment," Andrea admitted reluctantly. It seemed that his cause was lost even before it had begun.

Mestre Jacomé spoke. "If Your Highness will permit, I think I have a means of proving that this man is not Andrea Bianco as he claims."

"Proceed," Prince Henry told him.

The old mapmaker took some sheets of parchment from the pile on the table before him and spread one of them out. "This is one of an atlas of maps drawn by the real Andrea Bianco," he explained. "With it I propose to determine whether or not this man is an impostor."

"I am ready," Andrea said quietly.

"Describe for me the atlas of Andrea Bianco."

"If your atlas is complete," Andrea told him confidently, "it should contain ten maps, two of which are charts of the world. I drew it between 1434 and 1436. Copies were made in Venice and signed by me a few months before I left on the voyage to Trebizond."

"You are correct as to the number," Mestre Jacomé admitted. "But you could have seen the atlas somewhere, since more than one copy was made."

"True," Andrea admitted. "But I can also tell you how the maps came into the hands of Prince Henry. They were sent to him on my orders."

"I remember receiving this particular atlas directly from Venice," the infante admitted. "With a letter from Senhor Bianco himself."

"The writing on the letter was in my own hand," Andrea said quickly. "You could compare it with my writing now."

"Unfortunately that is impossible." Prince Henry seemed genuinely sorry. "The letter was lost."

"Tell me something of the two world maps," Mestre Jacomé ordered.

After nearly ten years, three of them spent in another part of the world, it was not easy to remember details. "One was copied from Ptolemy," he said. "It is a graduated map of the world. The other is a circular map of the world which I drew myself."

Prince Henry leaned forward eagerly. "What is shown west of Africa upon your map?"

"The Fortunate Isles and the islands called Açores," said Andrea promptly. "Also the island of Antillia far to the west."

Prince Henry leaned back, a satisfied look on his face, but Mestre Jacomé said sharply, "All mapmakers know of the Fortunate Isles. They were rediscovered by ships sent out by our illustrious prince here and so were the Açores. Many maps show the island of Antillia to the west, too. You have proved nothing so far except that you have seen the atlas of Andrea Bianco and have a good memory. In fact," he added triumphantly, "the maps themselves were probably drawn from an earlier set made by a countryman of mine from the island of Mallorca."

Andrea smiled, for he was on solid ground now. "Many illustrious mapmakers have come from Mallorca, Senhor Cresques, including your father, Abraham. But none have earned a reputation more glorious than that of Raimundo Lull. My map was indeed drawn from his and I also studied his *Ars Magna Generalis et Ultima,* including the dissertation headed 'De Questionibus Navigationis.' "

Mestre Jacomé was obviously startled and Andrea decided now to play his trump card. "If you will look in the upper corner on one of the map sheets in the atlas, you will find a *toleta de marteloio* and with it a short direction, the *raxon de marteloio.*"

A buzz of whispered conversation rose from the onlookers while Mestre Jacomé leafed through the sheets. Finally he lifted one from the pile and moved it across the table so the prince could see.

"The word *marteloio* is not familiar to us," Prince Henry said.

"It means strokes with a hammer," Andrea explained. "On many ships, the turns of the glass are marked by tapping upon a bell. What is written on the chart there is a table for reckoning distance during the hour."

Mestre Jacomé's and the prince's heads were close together above the chart. The audience was tense, sensing that the climax of the scene was about to be reached.

"You can see that the *toleta de marteloio* is in two divisions," Andrea continued, "each in three columns. The first and fourth give deviations from the course while tacking, and enable a navigator to reckon his correct distance sailed, even when beating into the wind. The writing also contains directions for using the *raxon de marteloio.*"

Prince Henry and Mestre Jacomé conferred in whispers for a moment. Then the old man drew a blank sheet of paper from the pile on the table and took up a quill lying beside him. "Come up to the table and write your name," he directed. "We will compare it with the signature of Andrea Bianco here on one of the maps."

Andrea wrote his name on the sheet in a firm and legible hand, like the skilled draftsman that he was. Prince Henry and Mestre Jacomé pored over it for a moment, referring to the map sheet they had been examining. Finally the prince looked up.

"The signatures resemble each other closely," he said, "so closely as to imply, at least, that they were written by the same man. But Mestre Jacomé reminds me that anyone who knows as much about the real Andrea Bianco as you do must also have studied his handwriting. Yours is a story to confound even the tellers of tales, Hakim, or whoever you are. I am tempted to believe you, but I must remember that you are under a sentence of death in Venice." He stopped and then added, evidently with reluctance, "Therefore, I must ask for more proof than you have given us."

"I have no other proof," Andrea admitted, "save my oath upon the Holy Scriptures and my hope of salvation."

The oath of a man convicted of murder was not enough, Andrea knew. He had failed when he had almost won, defeated by the very thing he had hoped would win his case, the essential honesty and sincerity of Prince Henry. That same honesty and sincerity would not let the infante make the final decision which would give him his freedom upon evidence that was not wholly uncontrovertible.

"Your Highness!" A new voice spoke from the back of the chamber. Andrea turned and saw a tall man, whose face seemed vaguely familiar, standing there.

"Yes, Senhor Cadamosto," Prince Henry said.

"I knew the real Andrea Bianco very slightly in Venice," the man addressed as Cadamosto said. "If I could examine El Hakim somewhat more closely, I might be able to settle this difficulty."

"By all means come forward," Prince Henry said, and turned to the audience. "This gentleman is Senhor Alvise de Cadamosto, master of the Venetian galley on which I sailed from Lisbon."

Cadamosto advanced to the dais and subjected Andrea Bianco to a thorough scrutiny for perhaps a full minute. Finally his face cleared. "The beard confused me for a moment," he explained. "I am sure now that this gentleman is indeed Andrea Bianco as he claims."

A babble of voices broke out among the onlookers at this dramatic turn of events. Andrea gripped the hand of his benefactor. "I cannot repay you now, Signor Cadamosto," he said fervently. "But someday you will assuredly be rewarded as you deserve."

Prince Henry was smiling, too. "I am happy to welcome such a distinguished traveler and mapmaker as Andrea Bianco to Sagres," he said, giving Andrea his hand.

"Then I am no longer a slave?"

"With the permission of Senhor di Perestrello?"

Dom Bartholomeu smiled. "You are free, Senhor Bianco, free to do as you wish. May I be the second to congratulate you?"

"A word of warning, senhor," the prince said. "Dom

Bartholomeu and Fra Mauro have informed me about the circumstances surrounding your being sentenced to perpetual slavery by the judge in Venice. To me the evidence now seems clear that you were falsely accused and sentenced, so I will remit the sentence as far as my own country is concerned. But I must warn you that the Venetian court might not agree."

"I have no plans to return to Venice soon, milord," Andrea said happily. "You can be assured of that—and my eternal gratitude."

IV

There was considerable confusion while many of the men crowded forward to shake Andrea's hand and congratulate him upon escaping from the Moorish galleys and regaining his true identity. Many bore names well known in the world of mapmaking and navigation, ship designing and construction, and the related fields of mathematics, astronomy, and geography.

Finally Prince Henry called the gathering to order again and the onlookers took their seats. Andrea sat beside Fra Mauro now on one of the front seats of the audience chamber, no longer a condemned criminal.

"Very rarely indeed do we have among us one who has traveled so widely as you, Senhor Bianco," the infante said. "I hope you will not mind telling us something of what you saw in your journeys."

Andrea rose to his feet. "I shall be glad to speak of my travels, milord, and to answer questions about them." Then he added with a wry smile, "Especially now that Mestre Jacomé seems convinced I am not an impostor and a scoundrel."

A roar of laughter came from the audience and the old mapmaker gave one of his rare smiles. "A Jew rarely accepts any coin as genuine until he tests it between his teeth," he observed. "I am as glad as everyone else to welcome you to Sagres, Senhor Bianco."

"I have already told you that I was captured by a renegade Turk and sold into slavery at Constantinople," Andrea began. "A merchant named Ibn Iberanakh purchased me there and made me his clerk on a trip to China, buying spices, precious woods and fine silks to be sold in Alexandria."

The story of Marco Polo and his trip to the court of Kublai Khan several hundred years before had been widely distributed through Europe and almost everyone capable of reading or being read to was familiar with it. But travelers who had visited the far-distant lands of the Khans in recent years were few enough, since the Turks had drawn a curtain of curved steel across the western gateway to the Orient.

"What route did you follow?" Prince Henry asked.

"On the trip eastward we traveled overland, as did the Polos on their way to China, by way of Baghdad, Hormuz, and Kashgar. From there we turned south to Yarkand, Khotan, and Charchan in the land of the yellow men. At Campchu we joined one of their caravans returning home by way of the river called Hwang Ho in the province of Cathay. Thus we came to Chandu and then to Cambaluc. From there we sailed for the Island of Cipangu with a mission from the governor of that city to trade in silk-worms."

The audience was listening intently, their faces alive with interest. These were men who thought in terms of the whole world instead of only the small sections of it portrayed on the Mediterranean maps. Some were ship-masters who had already pushed back the frontiers of geographical knowledge by sailing down the west coast of Africa beyond Cape Bojador into unknown seas where men before them had been afraid to go. For them the far places of the earth had a lure more potent than for ordinary men.

"In Cipangu," Prince Henry prompted, "did you see any maps or charts showing the location and size of the island?"

Andrea shook his head. "The people of that island are unlearned, milord. They are fierce warriors but not sailors; few even dare to cross the narrow sea to China."

"Did they speak of other islands to the east of them?"

"No, milord. The men of Cipangu know little of navigation and nothing of the mapmaker's art. On some of the Spice Islands I saw maps made from thin strips of bamboo sewed together with shells attached indicating the location of islands, but the people of Cipangu do not even have such simple charts as these."

"What of China?"

"The men of China have developed the seafaring arts even more than in our own land—except the daring navigators who sail for Your Highness. In the town of Sin-Kalan I saw large vessels carrying as many as ten sails. The ships were very heavy and their hulls were made of three thicknesses of plank. They carried oars as large as an ordinary ship's mast, with as many as fifteen men to each oar. The ships are rowed by men standing in two groups, facing each other with thick ropes attached to the oars on which they pull alternately. Some of these vessels have as many as four decks."

"All these things were mentioned by the traveler Ibn Babuta over a hundred years ago," Mestre Jacomé broke in with some impatience. "He described these large ships but said they never dared to venture out of sight of land."

"So some people claim," Andrea admitted. "But in Sin-Kalan I heard a strange story that some five hundred years after the birth of our Blessed Lord—nearly a thousand years ago—a monk named Hoei-Sin journeyed far to the east. He sailed beyond the Island of Cipangu and was out of sight of land for many days. At last he came to a land which he thought was an island. He called it Fu-Sang because of a peculiar tree that grew there. Its sprouts were like the bamboo and could be eaten, and its fruit was in the form of a pear, but as red as blood itself."

He paused and looked around at his audience. Every face, including Prince Henry's and Mestre Jacomé's, was lifted to him now, intent upon his every word.

"From the bark of the Fu-Sang tree—the monk wrote —the people of this Eastern land prepared a cloth like linen which they used for clothing. They had no weapons and made no wars, nor built fortifications of any kind. Nor did they prize silver and gold as we do, or even copper, and the earth there contained no iron. They used stags as beasts of burden and made butter from the milk of the hind. It was a fair land, according to the monk Hoei-Sin, where the people were friendly and the sun was always warm."

"How far east did this monk sail to reach it?" Mestre Jacomé asked.

"I was not told that, but it was many days over a quiet sea with a fair wind."

"If Ptolemy is to be believed," said Prince Henry

thoughtfully, "the earth is not so large around as that. The monk could have reached the shores of Europe by sailing eastward from Cipangu without having to go a very great distance."

"If Ptolemy is to be believed—yes," Andrea agreed.

Mestre Jacomé shot him a quick glance. "Ptolemy's ideas concerning the world have been accepted by most mapmakers and geographers for a thousand years, Senhor Bianco."

"I suspect that any knowledge not improved upon in a thousand years was faulty in the beginning, sir," Andrea observed. There was a round of laughter, and he waited for it to subside. "Ptolemy also said that the seas in the region of the equinoctial line are boiling constantly from the heat of the sun. If that is true, the water should get noticeably warmer as you go south, warm enough to make the occupants of a ship uncomfortable long before the equinoctial line is reached. Did your captains find any such thing?"

"No."

"If Ptolemy was wrong in that, then, he could be wrong in other things."

"Do you have any further proof that he was in error?" Prince Henry inquired.

"I think so," Andrea said confidently. "In Alexandria, before my master died, I read some Arabic translations from the writings of the old Greek geographers. One book in particular mentioned that a Greek named Eratosthenes had measured the size of the world about two hundred years before the birth of our Blessed Lord."

Prince Henry leaned forward, a growing excitement in his eyes. "We have found some mention of this," he said. "Was the method used by Eratosthenes described?"

"Yes. According to the account I read, he learned from a traveler that at the time of the summer solstice in the month of June the sun shone directly into the bottom of a well in the city of Syene in Egypt. Eratosthenes took this to mean that the sun was directly overhead in the city at the time of the summer solstice. He also believed that Alexandria and Syene were on a direct line from north to south, passing through the poles of the earth. In drawing my own maps I discovered that this was not true, but Eratosthenes was near enough for the error not to make very much difference in his calculations."

Andrea paused again and looked over his audience. At

the sight of so many rapt faces staring eagerly up at him he could not repress a thrill of satisfaction and pride. For this he had gambled that very morning and won at least the first thing he sought—his freedom.

"Eratosthenes erected a pole in the yard of the museum at Alexandria," he continued. "He used it as a gnomon to measure the angle of the sun's shadow there on the day of the summer solstice. Thus he could tell how far the sun was from being directly overhead in Alexandria on the same day when he already knew it was directly overhead in Syene. By measuring the angle of the sun's shadow and using the principles of Euclidean geometry, he was able to establish that the angle included between Syene on the south, the center of the earth, and Alexandria to the north was the fiftieth part of a circle. He knew the distance between Alexandria and Syene and was thus able to calculate the circumference of the earth to be about twenty-five thousand miles as we know it."

An exciting buzz of whispers rose from the men gathered there. Prince Henry smiled and even Mestre Jacomé looked happy. "What do you think of his conclusions?" he inquired.

"Fortunately I happened to be in Alexandria at the time of the summer solstice, so I set up a crude gnomon, using the principle of the sun's shadow disk to determine its elevation."

"Would you tell us your results?"

"My figures agree very closely with those of Eratosthenes," Andrea said. "I calculated the earth's circumference at a few hundred miles less, but not enough to be of any real significance."

"What would you say of the globe envisioned by Ptolemy then?"

"It must be nearly a third smaller than the world actually is," Andrea said positively.

Prince Henry glanced quickly at Mestre Jacomé and leaned forward. No one could mistake the eagerness in his manner. "You have traveled perhaps farther on the surface of the world than any living man, Senhor Bianco," he said. "In the light of your travels and your calculations, which would be the nearest way to India and the Spice Islands, westward around the globe or eastward?"

"Eastward," Andrea said promptly. "The distance to the west would be at least twice as far."

The prince relaxed in his chair, a smile upon his face. "Well said," he agreed. "Here at Sagres we have already arrived at a similar conclusion from our own calculations."

"Since you believe the distance is shorter to India by the east than westward around the globe of the world, Senhor Bianco," Mestre Jácomé said, "how would you reach that land?"

"The land and water route is obviously the shortest," Andrea said. "I came here from India fairly directly, by three connecting routes. By sea we traveled from China to the Red Sea and on to Alexandria. By land I came from Alexandria to Tunis as a slave of the Moors. And again by water as a slave of Senhor di Perestrello from where the corsair I was on attacked the caravel *Santa Paula*. But that route is closed now by the Turks."

"How would you reach India then?"

"By the southeastward route around Africa and across the Indian Sea, unless the distance around Africa is much more than I think it to be."

"Are you sure you could sail around Africa, senhor?" Prince Henry asked. "Many mapmakers believe there is no passage to the south and that the Indian Sea is closed by land."

Andrea smiled. "They cannot have traveled much in the East then, milord. The Arabs have known for a thousand years or more that ships could sail around Africa."

"Are you sure of this?"

"My first master was an intelligent man, well educated and intensely interested in geography. I often heard him and other Moors say that Phoenician ships sailed around Africa more than fifteen hundred years ago."

"And the country of Prester John? Do you know anything of that?"

Andrea shook his head. "I have heard of Prester John, milord, but that is all." The story of a ruler believed to be monarch of a Christian land somewhere to the east, probably on the coast of Africa, cropped up in every discussion of Africa and the lands of the Far East. Legend had it that Prester John was one of the richest monarchs in the world, with seventy-two kings paying homage to him, an enlightened Christian bastion against the flood of Islam still surging westward in spite of the expulsion of the Moors from Spain. The kingdom of Prester John, reports said further, was troubled by neither war nor greed, because there was no ownership of private property and therefore no poverty.

Prince Henry was obviously disappointed by his answer. "I was hoping you could bring us real news of this Christian ruler," he admitted.

"You hear tales of Prester John everywhere in the Eastern lands," Andrea told him. "But I met no one who had actually seen him or had visited his kingdom."

"Truly, Senhor Bianco," the infante said admiringly, "you have been fortunate in having adventures beyond the lot of most mortals."

"I would count myself even more fortunate, milord, if you would make me a part of this company of gentlemen here and let me draw new maps showing the things I have discovered."

"It is our custom to enlist anyone temporarily who seems to bring some talent of value to us," the infante said warmly. "If he fulfills that promise, we admit him permanently to the company. Mestre Jacomé will assign you a place among our mapmakers."

"With your permission," Andrea said, "I would work also in another field."

"So? What is it?"

"The navigation of ships, milord. I believe I can adapt certain things I learned from the shipmasters of the Eastern Sea so as to enable a mariner to return unerringly to his home port from any part of the world."

A murmur of amazement rose from the crowd. Mestre Jacomé leaned over and whispered earnestly in Prince Henry's ear for a moment. The infante nodded and stood up, indicating that the assembly was terminated. "Mestre Jacomé will see that you are given every help," he assured Andrea. "We shall expect to hear more of this in the near future."

Fra Mauro was waiting at the door of the assembly hall, his round face beaming. "I am happy that you are free, my son," the Franciscan said. "Happier than I can tell you."

"*Eccolo!*" Andrea exclaimed. "After five years my wrists and ankles will feel naked without bonds."

"Mestre Jacomé asked me to bring you to his quarters," Fra Mauro told him. "He is having a light meal served us there."

Andrea was too happy today to object to anything. With

the portly friar, he made his way to a small house near the center of the village and there found the old map-maker directing servants as they prepared a meal of black bread, cold meats, and barley beer. They sat down to the table and ate for a while in silence. When finally his ap-petite was satisfied Andrea took a deep draft of the beer and leaned back in his chair.

"*Vediamo!* Good master," he said with a grin. "You questioned me like a true inquisitor this morning."

"And you answered like an honest man, an unusual enough experience for an inquisitor. But don't get puffed up, young man. Much of what you told us today we al-ready know. What impressed the prince most about you was the way you verified the calculations of Eratosthenes. Most people would have accepted them without question, just as many mapmakers accept the principles laid down by Ptolemy. Here at Sagres we have a general rule to ac-cept nothing until we are able to prove it ourselves."

"If I had so little to tell you of importance," Andrea said, "why did you bring me here to continue the discus-sion?"

The older man shot him a keen look. "You are a direct one, and I admire that in a man." Then he changed the subject. "What evidence do you have to support your be-lief that your half brother arranged for your galley to be attacked eight years ago?"

"No real evidence," Andrea admitted. "But the cap-tain of the corsair asked for me by name. He was about to kill me when the rais in charge of his galley slaves pointed out that I would bring a good price in the slave market."

"That could mean something," Mestre Jacomé admitted, "or nothing. The captain of your galley no doubt had a list of the passengers and the name Bianco could have been familiar to the pirate."

"He had recently visited Venice, too. I heard the crew speaking of it. If Mattei wanted to get rid of me and take control of our shipping interests, that was the logical way to do it."

"Was the vessel you traveled on one of your own gal-leys?"

"No." He stopped, then went on excitedly. "I remember now. Mattei suggested that I take a galley bound for Trebizond, and even arranged for my passage. I had planned to go only to Constantinople, but I was eager to go on to Trebizond when I heard this galley was sailing that far. It belonged to a firm of Jewish merchants in Venice. Mattei must have planned the whole thing."

"The evidence is certainly suggestive," Mestre Jacomé admitted.

Andrea clenched and unclenched strong, brown hands. "Someday I will get his throat between these two hands. Then I will learn the truth. You can depend on that."

"This method of navigation you spoke of. What is it?"

Andrea grinned. "That I intend to tell no one, good master—without pay."

"The infante might pay you for it if I tell him it is valuable."

"Someone will pay me," Andrea said confidently. "Perhaps even Venice herself."

"Venice! Why?"

"The prosperity of the Serenissima depends upon trade with India and with China, and the Turks now threaten to cut that off entirely. Already it has become very costly to pay tribute on goods from the East demanded in Trebizond, Constantinople, Antioch, and by the corsairs along the Moorish coast. When the goods finally reach Venice, the profit has been eaten up before the galleys can even unload. The merchants must come to terms with the Turks and lose even more of the profit, or find a way to the Indies by water, which means sailing around Africa."

"The same thing applies to Florence and Genoa," Fra Mauro pointed out.

"All three cities are in the same fix," Andrea agreed. "Whichever discovers a new route to India and China that the Turks cannot block will quickly become the richest city in the world and control the Mediterranean as well. With that prize at stake, men will risk great sums."

"That can also be said of Portugal," Mestre Jacomé reminded him, "except that we are a poorer country than the others."

"True. But your prince has already started voyages in that direction. He can hardly afford to let anyone else get ahead of him now."

"Granted that this secret of navigation may be all you claim," Mestre Jacomé said, "you are asking Prince Henry to buy a horse without examining the teeth. After all, our own navigators are skilled men. We have improved both the quadrant and the astrolabe."

"My method is simpler to use than either of them."

"Even the cross-staff invented by Levi Ben Gershon."

Andrea was quite familiar with the *balestilla,* or Jacob's staff, used by navigators for more than a century to measure the angle of the sun or the North Star above the horizon. It consisted of a shaft upon which was a slotted vertical crossbar set at right angles. With the instrument pointing at the North Star or the sun, the vertical crossbar could be moved backward and forward in front of the eye until the two ends just filled the distance between the horizon and what was being observed. It was a simple matter then to measure the angle formed by the crosspiece and the end of the shaft nearest the eye, and thus compute the angle of elevation of the star or occasionally the sun above the horizon.

The heavy metal astrolabe and its offspring, the quadrant, were fairly accurate, but presented certain disadvantages when used on a ship in motion. Particularly during a storm, it was difficult to measure with them the angles of elevation of the North Star, the method by which ships were navigated then throughout the world.

Although not quite so accurate, the Jacob's staff was considerably easier to use for measuring the angle of Polaris in the hands of an experienced navigator with good sea legs. But all the presently used methods of navigation, Andrea knew very well, had the disadvantage of requiring a number of adjustments. To make these upon a ship rolling in a storm, while obtaining only an occasional glimpse of the North Star, was not always an easy matter. A second method of determining latitude using the sun's height was very rarely carried out, and most shipmasters did not know how to do it.

"My method is simpler to use than the Jacob's staff," Andrea assured Mestre Jacomé confidently. "And more accurate. Besides," he added, "your sailors would fear long voyages less if they possessed a simple method of finding their way home."

Mestre Jacomé sipped his wine thoughtfully for a moment before he spoke again. "A man in Florence named Toscanelli claims the Indies can be reached by sailing westward," he said. "What do you think of that?"

"It is possible—if no mass of land exists in the Western

Sea. And particularly if the ship stopped for water and supplies at the island of Antillia."

"Do you believe that island exists?"

"That or another. I am sure some mass of land lies between Europe and the Indies, but I don't know just how large it is."

The old mapmaker shot him a keen glance. "Is this another of your surmises, Senhor Bianco?"

Andrea had no doubt that anything he told Mestre Jacomé would be reported faithfully to Prince Henry, but could see no reason why he shouldn't reveal his conviction that an inhabited land did indeed lie to the west of Europe. In fact, that knowledge might well make the infante even more eager to give him the status in the colony he desired and perhaps utilize his navigational device—rewarding him liberally in the process.

"You know of the Viking voyages to Thule and the Green Land, don't you?" he asked.

"Of course. Bishops from the Green Land paid homage to Rome for several hundred years."

"Then you must know, too, of the voyage made by Eric the Red and his son Leif to what they called the Wine Land?"

"Eric Vallarte has been able to get accounts of them for us from his own people," Mestre Jacomé confirmed.

"I'll wager you know nothing of the voyage made by the brothers Zeno of Venice, though. Or the map one of them drew."

"I would wager that I've seen every map of the Western Sea ever drawn," Mestre Jacomé said. "But I never heard of any such."

"It is hidden in the strongboxes of the Zeno family in Venice," Andrea explained. "I saw it once, by accident, years ago. But I remember the outline well."

"Could you reproduce it?"

"I think so—if it is worth my while."

"Your price?"

"That, too, must be determined."

Mestre Jacomé flushed. "You go far for a man who was a slave only a few hours ago, Senhor Bianco."

Andrea smiled. "But think how far I have come in just the few hours since I ceased to be a slave."

V

When he left Mestre Jacomé's home Andrea turned his
steps toward the low promontory of Sagres that jutted into
the ocean nearby and gave the cape upon which the village stood its name. A path wound over the dunes as far
as the point of the promontory. Beyond this there was no
going on, unless one descended to the beach and waded
into the sea.

The day was warm, with only a light breeze, and the
roar of the breakers upon the sands was muted. It was a
sound Andrea loved and he settled himself upon the top-
most dune, with his back against a stunted tree, content to
listen and think. Behind him the people of the village were
busy preparing for the fiesta that evening, a gay and festive
occasion in which everyone would participate. The sound
of their voices floated to him occasionally across the rolling dunes.

Andrea planned to attend the fiesta later, but for the
moment he needed time to consider the course upon which
he had embarked that morning and the direction in which
it might take him. For such contemplation he could have
chosen no better background than the broad sweep of the
ocean extending to the western horizon and the rhythmic
chant of the rollers sweeping in to break upon the beach.

For the first time now, with the endless breadth of the
sea before him, he felt really free. As free—he realized
with a sudden thrill—as the sea birds swooping in great
arcs over the waves, darting here and there to seize a fish
in taloned claws and rise with their silvery gray gleaming
in the sunlight. Like one of those birds, he could go where
he wished, save within the confines of Venice. And except
for Angelita, there was nothing to draw him back there
now.

Sitting there he found himself reviewing in his mind
what Mestre Jacomé had said concerning the geographer
Toscanelli and his belief that the Indies could be reached
best by sailing westward. If the world were no more than
eighteen thousand miles around—as the Greek geographer Ptolemy and many mapmakers had believed—
then it would indeed be more sensible to sail boldly west-

ward to reach the Indies, rather than to make the long circle around Africa as Prince Henry's ships were trying to do, with no knowledge of what might lie in the vast regions of that mysterious southern land.

Of the African continent's rough shape mapmakers had gained a general idea from caravan drivers and black slaves brought by the Moors from its steaming depths and sold at the ports of Europe. The western branch of the Nile was said to lie there, a great stream flowing to the Western Sea from a source far to the south of the cities of Egypt, and a route by which, conceivably, ships might be able one day to sail across Africa itself.

Tales were even told of great empires deep within the continent to the south, with fabulously rich mines of gold and silver, besides the lure of spices, valuable woods and other items of a richness almost incalculable. However vague geographers were about the shape and extent of Africa, none questioned the riches it contained, or that they could and should be wrested from the hands of Islam by Christians.

But Ptolemy could not be right, Andrea assured himself as he drew patterns idly in the sand with a stick. By his own calculations the world was larger than the Greek geographer had maintained, at least a third larger. And if the westward voyage of the Zeno brothers and that of the monk Hoei-Sin from the East were to be believed, a considerable body of land must lie somewhere to the west between Europe and the Indies, a region more substantial than Antillia and the other fabled islands shown on Andrea's own map of the world.

Of Antillia's actual existence he had no doubt. Its presence was accepted by all the mapmakers he knew, which meant that somewhere in the distant past men from Europe must have seen such an island. In fact, to Andrea's mind it was fully as substantial as the now thoroughly authenticated Green Land and Wine Land of the Norsemen.

Villages had been built in the Green Land, he knew, bishops consecrated, and regular voyages carried out to and from the Norse kingdoms for hundreds of years. Nor did the accounts of the voyages of Eric the Red and his Leif seem to make the existence of the Wine Land any less substantial. They had described a fair and warm country southwest of the Green Land where fruit grew in profusion, inhabited by a savage people who went naked most of the time and resisted strenuously any attempt to usurp their country.

Engrossed in his thoughts, Andrea did not notice footfalls upon the sand behind him until a discreet cough brought him to his feet. He whirled to face the intruder, hands extended ready to defend himself, since he carried no weapon. Then he recognized the other man and his hands dropped to his sides.

It was Alvise de Cadamosto, the Venetian ship captain who had identified him that morning.

"A thousand pardons, Signor Bianco," Cadamosto said in Italian. "I did not mean to startle you."

Andrea smiled. "I still remember the slave drivers' whips vividly enough to move quickly at the slightest sound, Signor Cadamosto."

"In an hour I leave for Lagos to join my ship," the galley master explained. "I wanted to speak to you before I left and Fra Mauro told me you came this way."

"I looked for you after the audience this morning," Andrea told him. "But so many people were coming up to speak to me that I didn't get a chance to think you properly."

"It was nothing." Cadamosto's lean face was warmed by a smile. "Have you decided what you are going to do?"

"It will take me a little while to convince myself that I am really free," Andrea admitted. "Besides, I am interested very much in what is going on here at Villa do Infante."

"I can easily understand that. The infante has invited me to join the company, if only as a shipmaster."

"Are you going to accept?"

"First I must return to Venice; meanwhile, I will think it over. My ship is owned by the house of the Medici. They have interests in many places and trade with all large ports." He gave Andrea a keen look. "A man can go far in the service of the Medici; a place with them is not lightly to be cast aside."

"Why are you telling me this?"

"The method of navigation of which you spoke this morning interests me. Its possessor might conceivably become master of the seas."

"Possibly," Andrea conceded, wondering just where this conversation was leading.

"When I reach Florence on my way to Venice," Cadamosto continued, "I will naturally report to my employers that you possess this new thing. Word of it is sure to reach your half brother Mattei in Venice."

"I owe no obligation to him," Andrea said sharply. "He tried to have me killed on a trumped-up charge of murder."

"Signor Mattei rarely lets anything stand in his way," Cadamosto agreed. "But now that you possess such valuable knowledge to the firm with which he is associated, he might be brought to see the error of his ways and arrange for the charges against you in Venice to be stricken from the record."

It was an exciting thought, and it led to another even more so. "Would you do something for me, since you are going to Venice?" Andrea asked.

"Of course, signor. Anything you wish."

"Signora Angelita—my half brother's wife—was my betrothed. Tell her that I am alive—and that I love her still."

The Venetian's eyes gleamed. "Ah! A romance! Be sure I will tell the lady—and no one else." Cadamosto held out his hand. *"A rivederci,* signor. This new method of navigation could be the beginning of a great future for you, if it does what you claim."

"It does," Andrea assured him. "You can take my oath upon it."

"Then guard it well. The trade of the Indies is so valuable, now that the Turks are cutting us off from it, that many men would willingly kill to obtain your secret —or see that it does not fall into the hands of their business enemies. As a galley captain for the Medici, I must tell them what I have heard." He grinned. "And because the telling will no doubt mean gold in my purse. But be warned, Signor Bianco. Do not sell what you possess cheaply, and guard the secret with your life until you do sell it. That same life could be a price you must pay for knowing more than other men."

VI

The fiesta in honor of Prince Henry's return was already in full sway when Andrea left the room in Signor di Perestrello's home that he shared with Fra Mauro, now that he was no longer a slave. Eric Vallarte, being about his size, had provided him with a decent suit of clothes until such a time as garments of his own could be tailored.

The suit was of black, both tunic and hose, and, the night being warm, he needed no cloak. A flat velvet cap such as scholars wore sat on his head. His black hair was trimmed and curled, as was his black beard, but he wore no jewelry, since he possessed none. Even masked, as was everyone on this night of fiesta, however, he stood out from the crowd because of his splendid physique and erect carriage.

All of Villa do Infante and most of Lagos, it seemed, had turned out for this joyful occasion. The subjects of Prince Henry had every reason to be happy, for their lord was kind and generous, paying well those who served him. Even the lowliest hewer of timbers for the caravels that were always being built in the yards at Lagos had plenty to eat and enough left to buy a bottle of wine occasionally.

Tonight the prince's chamberlain had sent casks of wine to be opened for the fiesta and, with the rich dishes prepared by the women of the town plus a whole ox—also donated by the infante—which had been roasting for the past twelve hours, there was food aplenty for everyone.

Colored lanterns had been strung all around the village square. *Lança-se-confetti* and *serpentine* were everywhere, and the buildings were decorated with colored streamers that floated in the evening breeze. All the people were masked and many wore fancy costumes. Dragons, harlequins, jesters, swaggering soldiers, and buxom peasant maids mixed with great ladies in powdered wigs and expensive dresses, and richly garbed gentlemen.

Andrea dined well on roast beef, washing it down with good red wine. A sparkling-eyed maid gave him a pastry and, giggling, accepted a kiss in payment. A vast sense of satisfaction and comfort began to spread through him as he moved toward the plaza where the musicians were tuning up for the dancing.

He looked for Dona Leonor, intending to thank her, too, for her father's generosity in giving him his freedom that morning when Prince Henry had finally accepted his claim to being the real Andrea Bianco. But there were so many graceful young women with dark hair and laughing eyes behind masks tonight that he was soon hopelessly lost as far as identifying her was concerned. When a slender girl in the dress of a milkmaid seized his hands and pulled him toward the dancers, he did not resist.

The music had a stimulating rhythm and Andrea found himself throwing off any reserve left from his years of slavery. He joined in the exuberance of the dancers when they formed a ring and changed partners to the call of the musicians. The night was warm, the wine flowing freely, and the end of one of the dancing periods found him with a dark-haired girl who danced with the grace of a frolicking doe. A lacy mask covered her whole face, exposing only a pair of dark eyes.

"May I offer you some refreshment, senhorita?" he asked gallantly. "I have sampled that cask of wine over there in the shadows and can guarantee its flavor."

She took his arm and they threaded their way through the crowd. He dared to hope that she really was Dona Leonor, but could not be sure. The wine cask was in the shadows and as he filled a pair of goblets and handed her one, the girl's eyes met his over the cups. They sparkled with mischief and he found himself wondering just what would happen if he lifted the lacy mask she wore and kissed the red lips beneath it.

Suddenly daring, he suited action to fancy and put his arm around the girl's waist. She did not resist when he drew her deeper into the shadows nor did she make any objection when he took the goblet and set it down, and turned to take her in his arms. When he lifted the mask and found a pair of red lips that were as eager as his own, he was certain that this could not possibly be Dona Leonor. For he already knew her well enough to be sure that she would not thus casually yield a kiss, even under the guise of a mask.

"Que galanteria!" an indignant voice, which he recog-

nized at once, cried behind him. "So the slave is aping his betters."

Andrea released the girl, who giggled and promptly scuttled away into the darkness, leaving him to face a furious Dona Leonor.

"I am no longer a slave, madonna," he said, angry at being thus caught in *flagrante delicto,* as it were. "Or were you not told?"

"Who gave you your freedom?"

"The infante—and your father."

"Does that give you the right to kiss any girl who is fool enough to let you?" she asked hotly.

"Are you angry because you lost a slave, madonna? Or because I kissed a girl?"

She drew herself up. "Being free, you are no longer under any obligation to either me or my father. You can kiss anyone you wish."

She was always lovely and even more so when angry. The kiss she had interrupted had been a spur-of-the-moment affair, nothing more, compounded of the night, the fiesta, the wine, and an even headier feeling of being free. But to kiss the girl who faced him—the very idea was enough to stir a man to action.

"I will tell you the truth, madonna," he said impulsively. "When I kissed her, I thought she was you."

He saw her go rigid. The next moment she stepped quickly forward and slapped him hard on the face. The act startled him, but not so much that he failed to seize her wrists before she could jerk away.

"I am a free man now, *madonna mia,*" he said angrily. "Free as you said to kiss anyone I please—even you."

Before she had time to fend him off he pulled her toward him and pressed his lips to hers. Startled, she lay in his arms for a moment with her mouth soft beneath his. Then he felt her stiffen and a sudden sting of pain shot through his lip as her teeth sank into it in a vicious bite. He pushed her away roughly and then put his hand to his mouth, from which blood was already beginning to fall in little droplets.

"You little devil!" he gasped.

She was staring at him wide-eyed and he saw in the faint light of the moon that her face was marble pale. She swayed a little, he could not know whether from the shock of his kiss or from indignation. Momentarily there was a strange look of unbelief in her eyes, almost of fear, and he thought she was going to faint.

"My blood will not poison you," he growled, pulling a handkerchief from his sleeve and pressing it to his lips. "If that is what is troubling you."

She gave a little strangled cry then—almost a sob—and, turning, ran away into the darkness. Andrea remained where he was for a few moments, holding the handkerchief pressed against his lip until the bleeding stopped. Then, without crossing the square where the dancing was now in active progress, he made his way around it and back to Dom Bartholomeu's house.

Fra Mauro was preparing for bed when he entered. "You cut an uncommonly handsome figure tonight, my friend," he said admiringly. "I am surprised that you would leave the fiesta so early."

Andrea shrugged. "It had no more interest for me."

The Franciscan looked at his mouth. "Have you been fighting?"

Involuntarily Andrea raised his fingers to his mouth, then lowered them and went on undressing without answering.

"How did you get the cut in your lip?" Fra Mauro asked again.

"A girl bit me," Andrea said savagely.

"Really——"

"It was Dona Leonor if you must know. I kissed her and she bit me."

"You should have known better," the friar said sharply. "Dona Leonor is not one to be pawed by everyone."

"I know that now," Andrea admitted. "I guess I knew it before." Then he grinned. "But she is a creature of spirit all right."

"She is a fine woman, with more integrity in her little finger than most girls have in their whole body!"

Andrea laughed. "In his arms in a dark place, a man wants something besides integrity, little brother. Other things are more essential at such a time, and our *bella* Leonor has all of them."

Fra Mauro changed the subject. "Dom Alfonso Lancarote was asking about you tonight."

"I don't know him."

"For several months he has been wanting to make a

voyage of exploration to the south, but Prince Henry is reluctant to give permission."

"Why—if he is going to explore the African coast?"

"I think the real trouble is the infante thinks Dom Alfonso wishes to sail mainly in search of slaves."

"What's wrong with that?"

"You have been a slave, my son. You should know the answer."

Andrea frowned as he removed his tunic. He had never thought of Negro slaves, and the Moors who had labored with him at the oars, as having the same feelings and sensitivities, the same love for freedom, that actuated him.

"Is it not a good thing to bring the blacks and other heathen to the knowledge of our Blessed Lord and the means of salvation?" he inquired.

"Undoubtedly," Fra Mauro agreed. "I personally have used that very argument in favor of Dom Alfonso and his proposed expedition. Prince Henry is moved by it, but he thinks finding an eastward passage to India is more important. Besides, he feels that if ships seek only slaves, they will not be likely to sail beyond the first place where they find them."

"Why are Prince Henry and Senhor Lancarote so convinced that they will be able to capture many slaves on the African coast?"

"Several years ago, in the year 1441," the Franciscan explained, "Antão Gonçalves and Nuno Tristão in two caravels went to the Rio d'Oro, south of Cape Bojador. Gonçalves landed and followed the tracks of camels inland. He captured ten Bedouins, including a chief named Adahu. The chief had traveled far and wide in the central part of Africa. He said that at a city called Tombouctou on a great river he had seen as many as three hundred camels laden with gold dust from lands to the south."

"*Dios!* What a prize that would be. Did he tell where the mines are located?"

Fra Mauro shook his head. "According to Adahu the gold is bartered for salt from the blacks of Guinea at the edge of the great desert. Those who barter never see each other's faces. They leave the salt in piles in a place they know of and when enough salt is left, one day it is gone and a pile of gold is left instead. In that way the transaction is completed, nor is anyone ever cheated."

"What happens to the gold?"

"It is taken by caravan to the city of Tombouctou and on to Tunis and Tripoli. Eventually, I suppose, some of it reaches Alexandria."

"Did he say where the desert ends?"

"According to Adahu it extends as far as Guinea, where the blacks live in a country so rich and green that a man can hardly make his way through it. They use the rivers for roads and travel in long slender boats dug from logs. The waters are filled with giant serpents that have skins like armor and jaws that can snap a man's leg in two."

Andrea smiled. "I saw those on the Nile; the Egyptians call them crocodiles."

"Prince Henry is anxious to find the river on which this city of Tombouctou is located," Fra Mauro continued. "He believes it may be the western branch of the Nile that leads to the kingdom of Prester John."

"Why not send an expedition there? It should be profitable."

"If profit were the only consideration, I am sure he would," the friar agreed. "After all Prince Henry gets one fifth of everything gained on such a voyage."

"Why does Senhor Lancarote hesitate—with four fifths for himself?"

"The sailors are afraid to go very far south along the coast."

"Why?" After the distances Andrea had traveled over water along the coasts of China and India and across the broad eastern ocean to the Red Sea, the distances involved here were nothing.

"On his last voyage, Antão Gonçalves went as far south as a headland called Cape Blanco," Fra Mauro said. "He saw there the bleached bones of many animals and some men, and word has gotten around that no fresh water can be found in that region. The sailors fear that if a ship sails farther south, it cannot come back."

"Would they go with him if they knew a certain way of getting back?"

"Dom Alfonso evidently thinks so, for he was asking about that device of yours."

"Hah!" Andrea exclaimed. "He will have to pay a high price for it."

"Are you going to offer it to him?"

Andrea grinned. "I learned to dicker from the Arabs,

little brother. They are even smarter at it than Jews. Senhor Lancarote must come to me."

"You dare much."

"But look what daring has already gained me. First my freedom and now a chance to get rich. *Vediamo!* I am beginning to think Andrea Bianco is the luckiest man alive."

VII

The very next morning a messenger came, begging Andrea to wait upon Dom Alfonso Lancarote at his home in Lagos. The shipowner's house proved to be one of the most luxurious in Lagos. Andrea was ushered into a paneled sitting room whose furnishings showed evidence of both good taste and wealth. Nor was he kept waiting long before a hawk-faced man with jet black hair, piercing eyes, and a swarthy skin entered.

"Senhor Bianco," Lancarote said affably. "How kind of you to come."

"Um prazer, senhor," Andrea said with equal urbanity.

"Some wine? It is from the island of Pôrto Santo and very pleasant."

Andrea accepted a cup of wine and drank deeply. *"Excellente,"* he approved. "A wine like this should make even the expense of discovery worth while."

Lancarote shot him a keen glance. "I'm sorry I did not get to hear the story of your travels yesterday, senhor," he said. "They tell me it was very interesting."

"I would hardly recommend going under exactly the same circumstances I did," Andrea told him. "But it gave me a chance to see a part of the world the Turks no longer let Europeans visit."

"All the more reason why we must quickly find a water route to the Indies."

"And explore the coast of Africa." Andrea kept a casual note in his voice.

"The riches of the land have hardly been tapped," Dom Alfonso agreed. "You have perhaps heard that I plan a voyage to explore the coast of Africa below Cape Blanco."

"Word of it has come to me," Andrea admitted. By nature he was not addicted to this sort of fencing with words, but in this case it seemed best to let the other man reveal his intentions first.

"Perhaps you would be interested in making such a voyage, senhor," Dom Alfonso suggested casually.

"I am not a shipmaster."

"Lagos has more than enough shipmasters. I had in mind that it might be interesting to you as a mapmaker —or a navigator."

Andrea lifted his eyebrows. "I would welcome such an opportunity," he conceded. "Provided, of course, it offered enough profit for me."

Dom Alfonso looked a little startled. "Profit, senhor?"

"You must have heard from your friends who were in the assembly yesterday about my new instrument for navigation."

"It was mentioned to me," Lancarote admitted.

"When word gets around that I can guide a ship directly home from any part of the earth. I am certain to get many offers to sail as a navigator. Naturally, I must choose whichever one looks the most promising to me."

"You are very direct, senhor."

"It is my way," Andrea said firmly. "The only way to avoid misunderstanding and controversy."

"Perhaps you are right." The Portuguese put slender fingers together to form a little tent beneath his chin. "Have you arrived at a figure concerning what profit you might hope to derive from such a voyage?"

"Only a tentative one," Andrea admitted. "I had planned to listen to whatever offer you might feel you could make."

Again it was Dom Alfonso's turn to be startled. "How could you be so confident that I would make an offer?"

Andrea shrugged. "I have something you need very badly in order to persuade crews to sail with you into unknown waters, Senhor Lancarote. There is a market for everything, if you can only find a buyer."

"How much do you want for the instrument?"

"Not the instrument," Andrea corrected. "That I have no intentions of selling."

"What then?"

"My services as navigator for your fleet—plus the assurance that I can guide you safely home."

Dom Alfonso got to his feet and went to the window. His sallow cheeks were flushed and he was obviously not pleased with the turn the interview had taken. Expecting to dicker with a former slave who could easily be browbeaten into giving up his secret for a pittance, he found himself faced instead by an opponent whose coolness and keenness for a bargain exceeded even his own.

"What guarantee would I have that you can do what you claim?" the shipowner demanded. "No one has seen this device of yours."

"And no one will, until I am ready to reveal it," Andrea assured him. "But if I am not able to do what I claim, I would hardly risk my own life on one of your ships."

"Name your price then," Dom Alfonso said almost wearily, and Andrea knew the battle of wits was over.

"A hundredth part of the profits from this voyage," Andrea said.

Dom Alfonso looked relieved. He had evidently expected a more exorbitant demand.

"And a hundredth part of the next voyage if I travel with you and am successful on the first one."

"Done," the Portuguese said, and held out his hand. "You will not regret this, Senhor Bianco, I can assure you."

"I am sure I will not," Andrea agreed. "Will you have a notary draw up the agreement or shall I?"

"I had thought the word of gentlemen was sufficient," Dom Alfonso said a little stiffly, "but my notary will draw up an agreement at once, if you insist."

"Thank you, senhor. When do we sail?"

"In about a month. The ships will have to be provisioned and a crew signed on for the voyage."

"I will be ready," Andrea promised. "Of course I shall have to live until then," he added pointedly.

Dom Alfonso laughed. "You are a gambler, Senhor Bianco, I think we shall get along very well. How large a purse do you need as an advance against your share of the returns from the voyage?"

"Whatever you consider reasonable," Andrea assured him urbanely.

He left Dom Alfonso's house shortly afterward, with a fat purse hanging from his belt. Neither he nor the shipowner had broached the subject of the real reason for the voyage, the capture of black slaves to be sold in the markets here at Lagos and at Lisbon, the capital, some hundred-odd miles to the north.

Andrea had declined Dom Alfonso's offer to send him back to Villa do Infante by carriage, preferring to remain awhile in Lagos and study the activities of the seaport city. And in truth, he saw as he strolled along the waterfront, they were activities to gladden the eyes of anyone interested in the sea and in seafaring. Men were busy in the shipyards, hewing frames for the swift caravels for which Portugal was already becoming famous, and fitting heavy planking to the skeletonlike ribs of a large vessel already under construction.

Until the early part of the century Mediterranean ships had been built only for navigating that enclosed body of water or for the short run to England, Scotland, and the coastal seaports of France and Holland. Rarely was it necessary to journey out of sight of land, and at most a week's voyage might elapse between ports where supplies could be replenished and casks filled again with sweet water.

When the mariners of Prince Henry had begun to voyage far out to sea in order to round treacherous Cape Bojador with its shoals and remain away from port for weeks, a new type of vessel had been needed. This had to be large enough to carry a supply of stores, sufficiently seaworthy to deal with ocean gales, suited also for running before a steady trade wind, and yet able to sail fairly close-hauled in order to beat a way back home in the face of adverse winds.

When oars had begun to be dispensed with in favor of the considerably greater efficiency of sails alone, flexibility in handling ships had been obtained by using a full lateen rig with a large triangular sail. As the vessels increased in size, a second canvas had to be added and square sails were often placed on both masts. This maneuver, however, diminished sharply the ability of such vessels to sail close-hauled. And when a lateen was used instead of the square sail on the aftermast—also called the mizzenmast —the ship became difficult to steer because the whole sail area was too far aft. A balance had been effected by stepping a third mast in front of the mainmast with a square sail. This arrangement, plus cleaner lines and a general improvement in ship construction, had led to the swift caravels of Prince Henry's day, with three masts, the fore and main square-rigged and the mizzen bearing a fore and aft sail.

The caravel took its name from "carvel," a word describing the way the ribs of the vessel were planked, that is, with smooth joints between the planks instead of the lapboard style formerly in vogue. Actually it was based on a Mediterranean vessel called the *tarida*, modified to suit the conditions prevalent upon the Atlantic. The new ships had a high, square forecastle to break oncoming seas and a high tapered poop providing much-needed storage space. A modification of these ships called the "carrack" was broader and deeper and therefore more seaworthy and capable of remaining away from port for a longer period.

Andrea found Eric Vallarte watching the progress of construction upon a particularly beautiful specimen of the caravel-carrack type of vessel on the waterfront at Lagos. The Norseman greeted him warmly.

"Ho, Senhor Bianco!" he said. "How does it feel to be without chains?"

"Like a soul released from hell," Andrea said soberly. "What is this you are building?"

"A new type of caravel. You can see that it is larger and of a deeper bosom than our little *Santa Paula*."

"She should be able to sail far, if not quite so fast as the smaller ship," Andrea said admiringly.

Vallarte lowered his voice. "As far as Antillia perhaps? Or the Wine Land?"

Andrea gave him a startled look. "Why do you say that?"

Eric shrugged. "My ancestors discovered the Wine Land. Naturally I'm curious to see it."

"But Prince Henry seeks a water route to India around the southern tip of Africa."

"If there is such a thing."

"Do you doubt it?"

Vallarte shrugged. "I am a sailor, not a mapmaker, or even a geographer. We Vikings rarely make the mistake of taking anything for granted. If there is a way around Africa, I think the infante's ships will find it. But what then?"

"With the monsoons it is simple to sail from the east coast of Africa to India or China and back again."

"You have been there, so you must know," Vallarte admitted. "But suppose Africa extends below the bottom of the world, as many people believe? Then it is better to steer straight west and look for a passage between the

Green Land and the Wine Land, or somewhere else. We seek a way around Africa to the East, yes." He pointed to the west and the long curving line of the horizon. "But we also look to see what is out there."

Andrea regarded him speculatively. "I suspect that you are not so simple as you would have me believe, Eric Vallarte," he said. "The whole world knows the direction in which Prince Henry's captains sail. Is this voyage to be kept a secret?"

The red-bearded man's eyes twinkled. "Why should it be a secret when Senhor Bartholomeu di Perestrello goes out to colonize islands known as the Açores in the name of the infante? If the merchants of Genoa, France, and Venice suspect that we seek a western route to the Indies, we will not deny it. Let them be as confused as they wish to be."

"Meanwhile the African fleet searches for the shorter route?"

Vallarte shrugged. "The African fleet is always searching. After all, Catholics count it a good thing to bring the Moors and the blacks your religion, even if they must wear chains."

"Is this vessel to take Dom Bartholomeu to the Açores?"

Eric Vallarte nodded. "With his family and some colonists. If it develops that Africa is larger than Mestre Jacomé and the others believe and we must sail west to reach the Indies, provision will have to be made for taking on new supplies and repairing ships in the Açores, as we do now at Madeira on the African voyages. It is the sort of venture that Dom Bartholomeu is well able to head." The Norseman grinned. "And the presence of the beautiful Dona Leonor will not make it any the less attractive for me. Are you with us?"

Andrea shook his head. "Dom Alfonso Lancarote employed me this morning as navigator for a fleet exploring the coast of Africa beyond Cape Blanco."

"By the beard of Woden!" Vallarte exploded. "He lost no time, did he? Last night the infante mentioned to me that he was considering asking you to navigate this ship to the Açores."

"Dom Alfonso is paying me a hundredth of the profit from any cargo the ships bring home," Andrea said proudly. "And a hundredth of the next voyage."

Vallarte whistled. "It is a goodly sum, considering the prices the blacks bring. But I did not think you would sail with him."

"What is to keep me from making my fortune while I can?" Andrea demanded. "Would Prince Henry pay me as much for a voyage to the Açores?"

Vallarte shook his head. "There will be little profit on this trip, unless we find something no one else has seen on these islands."

"Then I would be a fool not to go with Dom Alfonso."

"That is one way of looking at it."

"Is there any other?"

"For you, maybe not, although you know what it means to be a slave. But we of the North have never worn chains and we like not the idea of any man being other than free. I will take the voyage to the Açores, my friend." He put his hand on Andrea's shoulder. "But I wish you well and a safe return. In fact, we may still be here when you get back. We are building this one strong. It may travel in seas no man of Europe has ever seen before."

VIII

As Andrea had predicted, the news that he was familiar with a method of navigation used by the Arabs—who were known to sail thousands of miles beyond sight of land across the Eastern seas, yet find their way unerringly homeward—created new interest in the expedition of Dom Alfonso Lancarote. No more trouble was experienced in finding a crew; men signed on every day, and a full complement was quickly obtained for the five ships.

At the invitation of Bartholomeu di Perestrello, Andrea continued to live at his home, sharing his old room with Fra Mauro. He saw Dona Leonor only occasionally, usually at mealtimes.

Ever since the night of the fiesta when he had kissed her, she had treated him with a lofty coolness which he had not known how to break. Nor had he tried, realizing that whether or not she chose to like him was her own right. And yet, a man would have been made of stone not to admire the clean lovely lines of her profile as she sat at the table with her father and her younger sister, Filippa, or the slender grace of her body when she left the room at the end of the meal and passed the place where he sat.

He had little time to think of Angelita now, or of his revenge upon Mattei, for he had volunteered to help supervise the final rush of loading supplies into the ships of Dom Alfonso Lancarote's fleet, in order to expedite their departure before the onset of bad weather with the coming of the summer heat. This was the first step on the road back for Andrea Bianco, and with characteristic intensity, he concentrated upon it alone. With the money from this voyage and the next, he could begin to think about establishing his innocence of the crimes for which he had been convicted in Venice. After that he would deal with Mattei —and take Angelita for himself.

Andrea had seen little of Prince Henry, since the Governor of Algarve had been busy with affairs connected with the regency. He was surprised one warm day when he looked up and saw the prince standing near where he was working in the shelter of a shed, counting bags of onions being loaded into the hold of one of Dom Alfonso's caravels. He dropped to one knee, but Prince Henry said warmly, "Rise, Senhor Bianco. I work here as you do."

"It is a work to gladden the heart of one who loves the sea, milord," Andrea said. "I have learned more about ships these past weeks than I thought remained yet to be known."

Prince Henry looked southward toward the faint blue line of the African coast. "There is much yet to be learned, and so little time to learn it. Sometimes I find myself discouraged."

"If you are speaking of the water route to the Indies, I am sure it is there."

The infante nodded. "It must be. Sometimes I wish life had cast me in the role of a sea captain. What a thrill it will be for whoever finally does round the southern tip of Africa to see only an ocean between him and the Indies." He turned back to Andrea. "You have visited those lands, senhor. Will the discovery of a new route be worth what we may have to suffer in the loss of men and ships?"

"And money?"

"I count that as of no importance, if we can reach the kingdom of Prester John." The sweep of Prince Henry's hand took in the vast bulk of Africa to the south. "The black men of Guinea—and even the Moors—do not know our Blessed Savior; I would bring word of Him to all. Then with Prester John as my ally, we can open up that continent for white men to settle and find room to live decently, not penned up like cattle in cities with their filth and disease."

"It is a noble prospect. With only one weakness."

"What is that?"

"Your plans must be carried out by men, milord. And men are frail vessels to pour your hopes into."

Prince Henry shook his head. "You are wrong there, Senhor Andrea. They are frail, yes, but only man, below God, is capable of the lofty ideals and ambitions needed for such a project."

"Then we of Villa do Infante are lucky to have an example in yourself," Andrea said sincerely.

The nobleman smiled. "I do what I can. But as you say, all of us are at best frail vessels, so I have no choice except to use the ambitions of men for riches in order to further a greater purpose."

Andrea gave him a startled look, for the prince had put into a few words what seemed to be the whole purpose of the voyage upon which he was shortly to embark.

"Fortunately," the infante continued, "hope for riches often leads men to venture farther than mere love for discovery, or even the desire to propagate our holy faith."

"If you know that much," Andrea said wryly, "you must know that I, too, am embarking on this venture largely for profit."

"For profit, yes. Nor do I blame you, since fortune has treated you rather badly. But as to the word 'largely,' I have my doubts. More than most men, you have the true discoverer's spirit, Senhor Bianco."

"I am not worthy, milord——"

"But you are, even if you do hope to fill your purse at the same time." The prince's eyes were twinkling. "Besides, who knows what new confidence this secret method of navigation you possess will give to other men, once you have demonstrated its value on a long voyage such as Dom Alfonso contemplates?

"Each new landmark we reach is one step farther toward the Indies and linking up with Prester John," he continued. "A man from Guinea among the slaves brought back from another voyage told me of a great river to the south, whose mouth is marked by tall palms. I believe it may be the western Nile; perhaps you may even see it on this voyage. Who can say that it does not lead directly by water to the kingdom of Prester John, Senhor Andrea? If it does, we can join hands and ring the forces of Islam with Christian steel."

"It is a great dream."

"What is a great dream but many small dreams fitted into a pattern? As the shipbuilder fits the planking together to make the hull of this caravel?"

"It takes a great man to dream great dreams, milord."

The infante shook his head. "Don't tell me you were not dreaming them when you learned your secret of navigation from the Arab shipmasters. Or when you set up a gnomon in Alexandria—even though you were a slave— and confirmed Eratosthenes' measurements of the world. We can go far together, you and I."

"I fear that I will not serve you well by selling my knowledge to a slaver," Andrea protested.

"You will if you lead the ships of Dom Alfonso to the western Nile."

"And if I do not?"

"You will at least have tried your method of navigation and there will be other voyages."

"I haven't forgotten that I owe all this to you, milord," Andrea said gratefully.

Prince Henry's smile was like a friendly hand on his shoulder. "You can reward me by seeing that Dom Alfonso reaches the land of Guinea. Go with God, my friend."

IX

Andrea's presence and the assurance of being able to return safely home seemed to be the good omens needed for Dom Alfonso Lancarote's adventure of alleged exploration. The ships were quickly loaded by eager hands and in less than a month after his entering into the agreement with Dom Alfonso, they were ready to sail.

But before sailing, Andrea had a task to accomplish. He spoke to Fra Mauro of it during the morning meal on his last day at Villa do Infante. "Will you speak to Dona Leonor for me, little brother?" he asked. "I want you and her to meet me tonight on the promontory of Sagres."

The Franciscan gave him a startled look. "If you are bidding a lady farewell, why have me present?"

"There is no romance in this meeting; I have something to show you both."

"She may not come unless you tell me more of your purpose," the Franciscan warned.

"Tell her it is a matter of extreme importance that may concern her own life and that of her family."

Fra Mauro looked at him keenly. "I never saw you more serious, my son."

"Tell Dona Leonor that and she may come tonight."

"I think she will," Fra Mauro agreed. "Not necessarily for herself but for the others."

It was a clear starlit night and the moon was rising over the rolling sand cliffs of Sagres when Andrea made his way along the path leading to the promontory. The point projected well out into the ocean, and when he stood at its furthermost tip he was almost surrounded by water, with fully a two-thirds circle of the horizon visible in the moon-light around him.

He selected a spot at the very tip of the promontory, allowing a clear view of that section of the horizon which was visible. To the north the star called Polaris gleamed in the sky, a solitary beacon for the mariners since the beginning of time.

The beach was deserted now, although a few hours ago it had been alive with people when the fishing fleet put out to sea an hour before sunset on its nightly foray. Far out on the water he could see the lights of the boats bobbing up and down on the long rollers that came sweeping in from the west.

Andrea had often helped with the daily ritual of launching the fishing fleet, always a time of great excite-ment in the village. Nearly everyone turned out for it, not just to watch, but to help if needed. Old women, chil-dren, everyone hurried down to the beach at the blast of a shell horn, wading into the surf to shove the sturdy craft past the breaker line where long sweeps could propel them into quieter water.

A few hours from now, at dawn, there would be even more excitement when the little vessels with their high-peaked lateen sails—their Moorish ancestry showing in every line—came rushing in to seek shelter on the beach, deep-laden with the night's catch. Then a line of people would seize the long ropes and haul the fishing boats from the surf to their daytime berths on the beach over large logs placed as rollers. The larger vessels were hauled out by oxen driven by shouting boys.

Sturdy craft indeed were required to withstand the daily launching and hauling out, well planked and strong ribbed. Lateen-rigged, with high prows and sterns— the mark of the Moors who had occupied this tip of Portugal across from Africa until only a little over a century ago—the boats were drawn up on the beach during the day in orderly rows.

Even when the fishing boats were at rest upon the sands, huge glaring eyes painted on their sleek prows looked always toward the vague blur of the African coast to the south, as if wary of the time when dark-skinned men waiting there might again attempt to seize this province of Algarve, a sun-drenched land of flowers, green pastures, almond trees, and white cottages, that had seemed truly an earthly paradise to the men of Islam after the hot desert sands.

For a moment Andrea could not help feeling an acute nostaglia at the thought of leaving the picturesque little town of Villa do Infante, which he had come to love. A peculiar peacefulness characterized this place where men devoted most of their time to the pursuit of knowledge, a feeling far different from the bustle of shipbuilding and fitting out that characterized Lagos only a few miles away. He had enjoyed here the comradeship and stimulation of contact with alert and learned minds, able to give and take in a discussion joyously.

The sound of voices from the landward end of the point brought Andrea's attention back to the present. The solid form of Fra Mauro appeared, climbing along the path, followed by a slender graceful figure that could only be Dona Leonor. Calling to them, Andrea went down the path to help them up to the rounded top of the dune cliff upon which he had been standing.

"Thank you for coming, madonna," he told the girl as she came out on the tip of the promontory.

"You said it was important for myself and my family," she reminded him.

"You may be sure I did not mislead you. I want you and Fra Mauro to know the secret of my method of navigation."

"Why would you reveal it to us?" she asked, startled.

"I may not come back from this voyage, madonna; seafaring is always a hazardous business. Something as valuable as this must not be lost."

He saw her eyes upon him in the moonlight, but could not tell just what was her reaction.

"No conditions are attached," he assured her. "If I do not return in a reasonable time, you and Fra Mauro are to reveal the secret to Prince Henry."

"How do you know we will not sell it ourselves?"

"I know you," he said simply. "And I know the good friar here. Neither of you would betray my trust. Besides," he added, "I have another reason for wanting you to know it. Eric Vallarte tells me that Dom Bartholomeu is taking all of you on a voyage of colonization to the Açores. You might need the device, either to get there or to come back—possibly both."

"How could it help us to get there?" Fra Mauro asked. "You said once it was for showing the way back to port."

"My device will guide a ship completely around the world along any circle of latitude drawn on its surface with the North Star as a center," Andrea explained. "Once you have visited the place or somewhere on the same parallel of latitude, and made certain preparations with the instrument, it can never fail."

"Travelers to the Açores have already determined that the islands lie on a circle of latitude touching Portugal about halfway between Lisbon and Sagres," Fra Mauro said. "Are you saying you can set it at that point and guide yourself to the Açores without having to visit there first?"

Andrea smiled. "Wait and see. I think you will be surprised."

"If your device is everything you say it is," Dona Leonor observed, "traveling on the ocean will be almost as simple as following a road on land."

"You forget one thing," he objected.

"What is that?"

"The longitude—what most shipmasters call the East-West height. That is still an unsolved problem."

"But at least, with this device of yours, you can tell whether or not you are on the right path."

"Exactly—but not how far you have gone. That still

has to be discovered by counting the hours and estimating the speed of the boat—as navigators do now—unless an eclipse of the moon occurs just when you want it to happen, which isn't very likely."

"What is this magical instrument of yours?" Dona Leonor asked. "I cannot wait to know more about it."

Andrea drew two small objects from inside his tunic and held them up to the moonlight. "These are not magic," he assured her, "but the simplest means of navigation yet devised—and the best."

X

"I see only two small pieces of wood." Dona Leonor's disappointment showed in her voice. "Surely those things couldn't guide a ship across the ocean."

Andrea handed her one of the blocks. "Indian mariners call this the 'Al-Kemal,' meaning 'the consummation' or 'the guiding line.' " He held up one of the wooden plates to the brilliance of the moonlight. "As you can see, it is really only a small rectangle of wood, not even as large as my hand. I made these two from what I remembered of one I saw an Arab sea captain use, but size makes no particular difference—as I will show you in a moment. To the center of the wooden plate you can see that a piece of string is attached."

"Surely that thing is too simple to be of any value," Dona Leonor insisted.

"Not so fast, madonna," Andrea warned. "The simplest things are often much the best, as Fra Mauro will agree. Use of the Al-Kemal depends on at least one thing in this turbulent world of ours that seems to be constant, the height of the North Star called Polaris above the horizon. For any given point on the earth, it never changes enough to affect the use of my method. The Phoenicians knew this long before our Blessed Lord was born."

"I know that from any point on the circle of latitude you spoke of drawing around the earth, the North Star should have the same angle measured by the eye," she admitted.

"Fra Mauro has been teaching you the principles of

geometry," Andrea observed. "With a means of measuring the angle made by the Pole Star—which is the same as measuring its height above the horizon—a shipmaster can guide himself along any given circle of latitude in the part of the world where the star is visible."

"But surely an angle cannot be measured with that little piece of wood."

"I cannot actually measure it," he admitted. "But I can so arrange the Al-Kemal that it will tell at any time in the future just when I am located on the particular circle of latitude from which I started. And this is true no matter what part of the world I am located in, as long as a fixed star like Polaris can be seen."

"It still looks impossible."

"Face the North Star," he instructed her, pointing to where it hung in the sky, "and hold the Al-Kemal out from your face in your left hand. Do you see where I have cut a notch in one side of it?"

"Yes."

"The side with the notch must always be up when you are using the device."

"What about the string?"

"That will come later. For the moment just let it hang. Now, hold the plate in your left hand between you and the star so that the bottom edge is exactly level with the horizon."

She had some difficulty adjusting the small wooden plate and he stood behind her, reaching around her shoulder to move her arm up and down until the bottom edge of the plate was level with the horizon.

"Notice now that Polaris is blotted out by the plate," he instructed her. "Which means that you are holding it too close to your eye. Move the Al-Kemal away from you slowly, making a smaller angle between its upper and lower edges and your eye, but being careful always to keep the bottom edge level with the horizon."

While he steadied her hand, she moved it back and forth, until the star was just visible through the notch in the upper edge of the plate. "Now," he said triumphantly, "the angle between your eye and the top and bottom of the plate is exactly the same as the angle your eye makes with the horizon and Polaris."

"I can see that," Dona Leonor agreed. "When I look under the plate my line of sight travels straight on to the horizon. And when I look through the notch in the upper edge, it travels directly over the plate to the North Star."

She did not seem conscious that she was practically in his arms when he reached around her shoulder to steady her hand.

"All we have to do now," Andrea continued, "is to be sure that we can measure exactly this same angle again by using the Al-Kemal and Polaris. The way we do that is simple."

Dona Leonor laughed. "To you everything seems simple, but to me it is unbelievably complicated."

"Pick up the string attached to the wooden plate," Andrea directed, "and draw it between the fingers of your right hand until you can just touch your nose with the string held tight and without moving the Al-Kemal."

She obeyed and held the string taut, drawing her fingers back along it until they just touched her nose.

"Hold it at that point," Andrea directed. "We will tie a knot there."

"Why do you do that?" Fra Mauro asked while Andrea deftly tied the knot at exactly the place on the string where it had touched Dona Leonor's nose.

"The knot becomes the apex of a triangle with the Al-Kemal as its base," she cried. "Then if I hold the knot to my nose and look at Polaris along one side and at the horizon along the other, I can always tell whether or not I am on the same parallel of latitude as Sagres here, even though I were on the other side of the earth.'"

"You are worthy to be called a navigator, madonna," Andrea told her. "Now, I will give you a problem in navigation. Suppose you were at sea and looked at the North Star with the Al-Kemal and found it above the upper edge. What would you do?"

She frowned for a moment, then her face brightened. "It would mean I was north of the latitude circle that would take me back home. So I would set a course to the south."

"Suppose the star is below the edge of the plate?"

"I would sail north until it was exactly visible in the notch," she said eagerly. "Then I could turn directly west and almost reach the Açores."

"You could do better than that," he said and held up the other Al-Kemal. "I journeyed last week up the coast to a point where I think the latitude of the Açores—from maps showing those islands—touches Portugal. There I took an observation of Polaris and made this knot in the cord." He touched one of the two knots. "The other is for Lagos, to bring you straight home in case anything should go wrong."

For a moment she did not speak. When she did her voice was soft. "Why would you go to such trouble?"

"If your father's ship had not been attacked by Hamet-el-Baku, I would still be pulling the oars of a Moslem galley. As it is, I am myself again and likely to become rich when this voyage to Africa and one other is completed."

"But you still have not been cleared in Venice."

"I will be," he assured her confidently. "That will come later."

"It may come sooner than you think, my son." They had forgotten Fra Mauro for the moment. "Mestre Jacomé has written to the firm of Jewish shipowners in Venice whose galley was lost when you were taken prisoner by the Turks. He laid before them the facts of the case as you presented them to Prince Henry and the assembly here. Before you return from this voyage, your name may have already been cleared."

"That is all the more reason why I will need the Al-Kemal to speed me safely back to Lagos and Villa do Infante," Andrea said happily. "Do you think you understand its use fully, little brother? I wanted you both to know of it."

"You have made it so clear that a child could guide a ship home, if he knew how to find the North Star," Fra Mauro assured him.

"How will you use it on the African voyage?" Dona Leonor asked.

"I plan to knot the cord as we sail south," Andrea explained. "Then when we return, I need only refer to the various knots to know where we are. Shipmasters in the Indian Ocean have been sailing thousands of miles that way for centuries, making landfalls with great exactness. In fact the Phoenicians must have used some such method, probably by holding a hand between the eye and the North Star and seeing how many fingers were covered by the angle it makes."

As the three of them walked back across the dunes toward the sleeping town of Villa do Infante, Dona Leonor was more like her old self than she had been since the night of the fiesta. She willingly took his hand to help herself over a rough spot. And once, when her foot caught upon a root growing across the path, he had to catch her in his arms momentarily to keep her from falling. Walking slowly and talking together, neither of them noticed that Fra Mauro had gone on ahead. When they came to the edge of the town, they saw his pudgy figure already entering Dom Bartholomeu's house.

The moon was still shining brightly, bathing the quiet village in a silvery radiance. The warm night air was heavy with the scent of blooming flowers when they entered the enclosed court of Dom Bartholomeu's villa by a rustic gate, and they stopped by mutual—if unspoken—consent in the shadow of an arbor beside the well that furnished water for the household.

"I am glad you decided we could be friends, madonna," Andrea said. "If I could do it and still tell the truth, I would apologize for kissing you that night at the fiesta."

"And why would it not be the truth, senhor?"

"Would any man be telling the truth if he said he was sorry for kissing a beautiful woman?"

"Once you said I was only a child."

"That was before I really knew you and realized how fine you are—or what an excellent mind you have."

Her laugh rang out then, full and rich. "Is it my mind you are admiring, senhor? I thought you more gallant."

He took her hands in his and she did not resist.

"Gallantry is easy when you mean none of it, madonna. I was paying you a real compliment—from my heart."

"And I took it as such," she said gravely. "I want you to know my prayers for a safe return will go with you."

"No more than your prayers, madonna? You would pray for anyone, even if you only felt sorry for them."

"What else would you have me give?"

"A token of your favor and trust, perhaps, such as knights wear into battle."

"I have nothing," she said quickly. And then in a lower tone, "save this." Before he realized what she was doing, she had risen upon her toes and kissed him lightly upon the lips, like the touch of a fragrant flower petal. *"Vaya con Dios,"* she said softly. Then drawing her hands from his before he could move to take her in his arms, she was gone into the house.

For a long moment after she had left, Andrea remained beside the flowery arbor. He was oddly moved by the feeling of comradeship, intimacy, and trust that had risen between them, moved more actually than he liked to admit even to himself. Until tonight he had thought of her as no more than a graceful lovely girl. But the lips of a woman had touched his just now, and very much the body of a woman had been in his arms for a moment twice tonight. The first was while he had taught her to use the Al-Kemal, the second when she'd tripped upon the root back there on the path.

With an effort he conjured up the memory of Angelita, as if to remind himself that hers was a prior claim upon his affections and his allegiance. Between the two, a man would have a hard time making a choice, he thought, perhaps because they were both so entirely different.

Angelita, in his arms, had been a creature of fiery passion and abandonment, a true houri such as the Moslems looked for in Paradise. Dona Leonor's beauty was a far more fragile thing, and yet, he sensed somehow, a stronger one. Just as the fiber of her being was stronger, so the thrill of her yielding—and that would only be, he was sure, to a husband she loved deeply—would be a hundred times more complete and rewarding.

As he went to the room he shared with Fra Mauro, Andrea found himself remembering something he had said to Dona Leonor when they had stood together on the deck of the caravel *Santa Paula* and watched the sky line of Venice recede into the dusk.

"Few women are as constant as yourself, I am afraid, madonna," he had told her then. "But fortunate indeed will be the man to whom you give your love."

That night he had been moved only by gratitude to the girl for the part she had played in saving his life. But he knew now that his words had been far more surely true than he could have thought then.

BOOK THREE

Land of Wealth

I

LATE IN APRIL THE FLEET OF DOM ALFONSO LANcarote set sail from Lagos for the African coast. A week later the burning peak of volcanic Tenerife was visible upon the southern horizon long before the rest of the Fortunate Isles could be seen. Pausing only one day at the port of San Sebastián on the island of Gomera to take on fresh food and water, the fleet headed southward with a good wind at their backs over a smooth and sunlit sea.

As navigator, Andrea traveled on the *Santa Clara,* largest caravel in the fleet and the flagship of Dom Alfonso. His position gave him no special privileges, however. Like all of the company except Lancarote and his two aides, he slept on deck, storing his few possessions and instruments in a small chest in the hold of the vessel. The Al-Kemal he carried in a canvas belt strapped about his waist, mindful of Cadamosto's warning against thieves.

The only cabin space on the caravel was contained in the *toldilla,* as the aftercastle was called. It was barely large enough for Dom Alfonso and his two *fidalgo* aides, João Gonçalves and Gil Vicente. Gonçalves was a pleasant young man from Lagos and Gil Vicente a relative of Lancarote's from Florence, who had arrived a few days before sailing time and asked to accompany them.

Prince Henry had wisely insisted upon the keeping of accurate navigational records by captains who sailed the ships in his service. Because observations aboard ship with the instruments available were at best only partially satisfactory, he also required that careful records be made on shore at every landfall. The results of previous voyages had thus been incorporated into some excellent maps showing the African coast in detail as far as Arguim Island, a little south of the outthrust headland of Cape Blanco. In addition, using information obtained from the Bedouin chief, Adahu, several years before—as well as from blacks among the slaves brought back from previous ventures—the mapmakers had been able to arrive at an approximate idea of the general contour of the African coast line for a considerable distance to the south.

From various sources it was known that the country of the blacks or Guinea—sometimes called the "Land of Wealth"—lay south of the burning deserts forming the interior. The northern boundary of Guinea was said to be the great river of which Fra Mauro had spoken to Andrea. This the geographers at Villa do Infante believed to be a western branch of the Nile and a possible water route to the kingdom of Prester John. Black slaves captured in the region of Cape Blanco had revealed that the river was called Sanaga and that its mouth could be distinguished from far at sea by a cluster of tall palms on the shore.

No one in Prince Henry's service had ventured that far south yet, but from information which Mestre Jacomé had patched together for him, Andrea was able to make a tentative knot in the cord of the Al-Kemal, based on the known distance covered to the Canary Islands and the estimated distance to the river Sanaga. This, he figured, would take them almost directly to the mouth of the river, even in bad weather.

Of the nautical instruments available for Andrea's use in addition to the Al-Kemal, the astrolabe—or "sea ring" —was the oldest. In the simplest form it was merely a flat circle of metal that hung vertically from a hook attached to the edge. Fixed to the center of the circle so it could pivot was a small metal ruler or sighting arm. When in use the astrolabe was held aloft with the cross diameter parallel to the horizon, a position it assumed automatically when held by the hook. By sighting along the movable pointer in the direction of the sun or the North Star, the angle of either above the horizon could be measured.

Simple in theory, the astrolabe was difficult to use except on a very quiet day, because the swinging movement of the instrument made accurate observations unlikely. The quadrant, in reality only a quarter of a circle of the astrolabe and theoretically less cumbersome to use, was still but poorly accurate under most circumstances.

The compass, sometimes called the "Genoese Needle," had been in wide use for several hundred years and in more primitive forms for much longer than that. It gave an excellent means of determining north, but did not enable a navigator to plot his position on the sea with relation to any known latitude or longitude. Some mariners had already begun to suspect, too, that the compass did not always point exactly north at every spot in the world. As yet, however, no accurate records of any deviation had been made.

For keeping time, Andrea's ship—like all others of that day—used a half-hour glass called the *ampolleta*. Made of two bottles with their mouths fused together, it contained enough sand to run through the narrow opening in just thirty minutes. The glass itself was quite accurate but had to be turned exactly every half hour by the gromet, or ship's boy, on watch. Each time the *ampolleta* was turned on many ships, the passage of the half-hour period was marked by striking a small bell. Unfortunately the gromet didn't always turn the glass exactly when it was empty—or turned it too soon—so errors in time could easily creep in.

Two other methods of keeping time were available. At exactly noon each day, the shadow of a small staff, or gnomon, erected upon the compass card fell along the compass needle and the *ampolleta* could be turned up then to begin another twenty-four-hour period.

A second method involved the use of the stars, particularly the mariner's infallible beacon—when he could use it—Polaris. Finding the North Star in the sky was no problem, since the ancients had long ago pointed out that the two end stars, the Guards, of the dipper-shaped constellation—called variously Charles's Wain, the Big Dipper, the Great Bear and Ursa Major—always pointed to it. Even more exactly, the distance between the Guards and Polaris was known to be six times that between the two Guards themselves.

Both Ursa Major and Ursa Minor, the smaller constellation of which the North Star itself was the brightest member, were known to rotate around Polaris in a few minutes less than the space of a day and a night. Mariners had long ago discovered how to tell time from this rotation, and most of them carried an instrument called a night disk for this purpose.

A small circle of metal graduated into 360 degrees with two pointers and a hole in the center, the night disk was not difficult to use. First the North Star was sighted through the center hole, then one pointer was allowed to hang vertically downward and the other moved until it pointed at the Guards—if Ursa Major were being used—or at a bright star called Kochab in the case of Ursa Minor. Using the pointer readings, plus scales and a calendar, the exact time at that particular moment could be calculated.

An even more important use of the time estimation from the stars lay in the determination of longitude—or the East-West height as it was called by mariners of the day. For that purpose, simultaneous observation of an eclipse of the moon was needed and, since none was expected for several months according to the lunar calendar, Andrea did not trouble himself with it. Besides, they had only to sail directly east from any point on their expected course to touch the African coast, so an estimation of the longitude would have been useful only to provide more exact data for the mapmakers back at Villa do Infante.

All these things were Andrea Bianco's province as chief navigator for the fleet of five ships under the command of Dom Alfonso Lancarote. The captain of the *Santa Clara* was Ugo Tremolina, a Genoese of long experience with the sea. Andrea early made friends with the taciturn Italian and from him learned many practical things about the estimation of distance traveled and the handling of ships at sea.

Dom Alfonso had hinted several times that he would like to know more about Andrea's method of navigation, but he skillfully parried any questions. His observations with the Al-Kemal were made in the middle of the night, when the rest of the company was asleep except the watch. He was careful to keep those on duty from seeing the Al-Kemal and, when he had finished observing the North Star, always replaced the small wooden plate with its attached cord in the canvas belt he wore about his body.

That his belongings stored in the hold had been searched several times while he was asleep, Andrea discovered shortly after leaving Gomera, but this did not surprise him. A new instrument for navigation such as he possessed naturally aroused the curiosity as well as the cupidity of many people Actually, considering its value, almost anyone on board would likely be interested in getting his hands upon the Al-Kemal.

Each day Andrea marked on his map the position where he thought they were. As he was doing this one morning, Dom Alfonso approached and looked over his shoulder.

"You have us making good progress, Senhor Bianco," the shipowner said amiably.

"Thank the wind for that, senhor. The shipmasters at Lagos told me we could expect it at our backs steadily in these latitudes—when sailing south or southeast."

"Coming back is the problem, not the voyage southward," Lancarote agreed. "How far do you place us from Cape Blanco?"

Andrea made rapid mental calculations. "Roughly ten days' sail, if the wind and the weather hold."

Lancarote looked up at the sails and then at the foam scudding past the caravel on the surface of the water. The five ships were spread out on the ocean, their white sails forming a geometric pattern that was vastly reassuring to anyone with a mariner's instinct for orderliness and method.

"With fine weather such as this, I believe I could guide you almost directly to the river the blacks call Sanaga," Andrea added. "The people of Guinea are worth far more as slaves than those north of the river and we would be exploring new country, too, as the infante wishes us to do."

"You may well be right," Lancarote admitted. "But there are other things to be considered. You have probably noticed that our fleet carries more than the usual number of men-at-arms?"

"I thought you were only being extra cautious."

"We have a deeper purpose, senhor. On one of the last voyages to the region of Arguim and Tiber Islands my close friend and companion, Gonçalo de Sintra, was foully murdered by the Moors. It is our intention to punish these people for daring to attack a ship of our prince. In the process we shall no doubt gain not a few slaves and perhaps some honor may accrue to the knights who engage in battle."

"What possible honor could come from fighting savages?" Andrea exclaimed. "They use only crude lances and primitive bows and arrows."

Alfonso Lancarote stiffened. "Obviously you are not familiar with the laws of chivalry, Senhor Bianco. A true night may obtain honor in any combat where he comports himself bravely and honorably."

Andrea shrugged. "I am a mariner and a mapmaker, not a soldier, senhor. If you say there is honor in killing savages who are only defending their homes, I will respect your opinion. But don't ask me to join you."

Lancarote eyed him with a flush of anger in his cheeks. "You are dangerously frank, Senhor Bianco."

Andrea's gaze did not falter in the face of the other man's anger. "Venetians are a strange people," he said evenly. "We believe in the right of men to think as they please, although we do not always defend that right as it should be defended."

Lancarote kept up his hard stare for a moment, but when Andrea's gaze did not waver he shrugged his shoulders. "Since you are not a knight, Senhor Bianco, no honor can be gained by pursuing a quarrel. I am sure I do not need to remind you that your employment on this voyage is as a navigator. Leave the policy making and the strategy to me."

"Gladly," Andrea said. "I am content with my instruments and my maps."

II

The balmy weather and the brisk wind continued. Only rarely was it necessary to make any change in the set of the sails. After his encounter with Lancarote over the honor to be gained by forays against savages such as inhabited this coast of Africa, Andrea found himself left much alone by the gentlemen of the shipowner's retinue. This, in truth, displeased him not at all. Instead, he cultivated Captain Ugo, a taciturn man who knew his business well.

However skilled he was in navigation and mapmaking, Andrea knew there was still much he could learn about running a ship, things acquired only by a long apprenticeship and experience at sea. And since Captain Ugo was glad to find someone aboard who spoke Italian, the two hit it off very well. Wise in interpreting the many signs by which an experienced sea captain could judge his speed and his relative positions, Ugo Tremolina convinced

Andrea that they were actually making better speed than he had calculated.

Andrea's nightly observations of the Pole Star with the Al-Kemal were becoming steadily more difficult, for the mariner's beacon dropped lower in the sky each night as they sped southward toward the region of the equinoctial line. Before the line was reached—Andrea had been informed by Arab navigators in the East—the Pole Star disappeared entirely below the horizon. Then there appeared a constellation set in the southern skies in the form of a cross or—more fancifully—a chariot. This southern star group, they had assured him, was a constant and reassuring beacon, although not a very accurate one for navigation, since no table or other information existed concerning it, as was the case with Polaris.

Andrea had calculated, through information acquired on previous voyages and landfalls made by other captains, roughly the distance on the cord of the Al-Kemal that would indicate the latitude of Cape Blanco. When one night he was able to touch that particular knot in the cord with his nose while the wooden plate of the Al-Kemal exactly filled the space between Polaris and the horizon, he realized with a thrill that it was in his power to do something few ship captains had yet been able to do, sail directly to a predetermined spot on an as yet invisible coast line.

It was after midnight and Andrea had the foredeck to himself. With the bow of the ship narrowing to a point in front, and the canvas of the foresail forming a barrier behind, this small, secluded spot was not visible to the men on watch. Most of them were lounging on the deck in the small circle of light cast by the binnacle lamp, some playing games, some napping. On the whole ship, in fact, only a few people were awake besides the man at the tiller and the officer on duty on the afterdeck, where he could watch the compass course in case the steersman relaxed his vigilance.

In order to be absolutely certain of his observation, Andrea decided to take one final sight with the Al-Kemal before going back to his pallet on the broad hatch cover amidships, protected from the wind by the longboat that was carried always on deck while they were under way. Intent upon his observations, he did not hear a soft footfall on the deck just behind him, or see a dark figure whose head was covered with a crude mask of black cloth duck beneath the bottom edge of the foresail. The first warning that he was not alone came when the visitor's foot struck the base of the mast and let out a muffled curse. Dropping the Al-Kemal into the open front of his shirt, Andrea turned quickly, but not in time to escape completely the force of the bludgeon aimed at his head.

Dazed momentarily by the blow, he instinctively rolled away from it and came perilously close to falling over the rail into the sea. But his assailant evidently had no desire for that to happen, at least not at the moment. Still half stunned, Andrea felt a hand grip him by the shoulder and fling him back from the rail, so that his body struck against the foremast in the narrow triangular space.

"Thief! Thief!" he managed to shout as he felt the assailant's hands searching his body rapidly, even while he slid down the mast to the deck and, momentarily, lost his senses.

"Senhor Bianco! What happened to you?" Andrea saw the gaping faces around him and recognized Dom Gil Vicente, the *fidalgo* aide of Dom Alfonso Lancarote, bending over him anxiously. Actually only dazed by the blow on his head, he quickly recovered his wits and his first move was to press his hand against his chest and feel the reassuring presence of the Al-Kemal inside his shirt. Having discovered that it was safe, he decided to feign ignorance in an attempt to discover the identity of the attacker.

"Are you all right, senhor?" Gil Vicente was supporting him with an arm around his body. One of the onlookers held a lamp and Andrea saw now that the whole watch, along with some others of the crew who had been sleeping on deck, were gathered around him.

"Must have slipped and fallen," he mumbled.

"You shouted, 'Thief! Thief!,'" said a grizzled soldier named Martin Vasques, with whom Andrea had been friendly.

"I was dazed by the fall. Maybe I did shout something."

"I heard a thump and a cry as I was going across the deck for a drink of water," Gil Vicente told him. "When I got here, you were lying on your face at the foot of the mast."

"Must have run into it in the dark." Andrea grinned.

"Sorry to cause such a commotion; I'll go back and lie down awhile."

"I have some knowledge of physic, senhor," Gil Vicente offered. "Perhaps I should examine you for any injuries."

"Thank you, Senhor Vicente, but I've taken harder bumps than this one and survived." Andrea stopped to pass under the lower edge of the sail, and with the aid of Martin Vasques walked across the deck to his own pallet in the lee of the longboat. The old soldier went to the water cask and came back carrying a pannikin of water mixed with wine.

"Drink this," he commanded. "It will help clear your head."

Andrea drank gratefully. "You are a poor liar, Senhor Bianco," the soldier said as he stowed the pannikin away.

"Why do you say that?"

Martin Vasques took a billet of wood from beneath his loose tunic. It was as large as a man's wrist and half as long as his arm. "Either you have the toughest skull on earth, or our Blessed Mother watches over you. I picked this out of the scuppers on the foredeck while everybody was looking at you."

Andrea examined the club; it was a formidable weapon. "I was warned in time, so I only got a glancing blow. But why would anybody attack me?"

"You are an honest man, Senhor Bianco; that is always a handicap when dealing with scoundrels. Not a man aboard this ship but knows that you make secret observations with your navigational device late at night. If this thing is all you say it is, whoever owns it will be a rich man."

"And his country the leading maritime power," Andrea agreed soberly.

"So it would be worth any man's while to get it from you."

"Provided he knows how to use it."

"Someone skilled in such matters could probably learn. Besides, many countries would pay well to have it destroyed so Portugal cannot use it."

"You think whoever tried tonight will attack again then?"

"As sure as the sun will rise. You are in grave danger, my friend, but I will do what I can to protect you."

"Thank you, Martin," Andrea said warmly. "Do you have any idea who it could have been?"

"We all ran that way in the dark when you called out. He could easily have mixed with us and nobody would have been the wiser."

"Then there's only one way to identify him," Andrea said. "By making him try again."

"A trap which you will bait with yourself." Martin Vasques grinned. "It is something only a brave man would think of. *Vaya con Dios,* senhor."

III

Andrea waited upon Dom Alfonso Lancarote the next morning early. "My calculations show us to be on the latitude of Cape Blanco," he reported. "If you will order the course set due east, we should raise the African coast in no more than two days."

Lancarote's eyes brightened. "This is good news indeed, Senhor Bianco. I thought we were several days' sail to the north."

"I have faith in my observations, senhor."

"What does Captain Tremolina say?"

"He agrees."

"Then change the course by all means. And God grant you are right."

The order was given and passed by trumpet across the water to the other ships. The seamen scrambled aloft to set the sails, and the trim caravel swung around until her prow pointed due east.

The going was not quite so easy now, since they were quartering across the wind. After the first twelve hours Andrea stayed in the prow most of the time watching for a sign of the coast ahead. Near dawn on the second day, the roar of breakers could be heard distinctly and Captain Ugo ordered the *Santa Clara* hove to until dawn, when a more thorough survey of the coast line could be made. There had been no repetition of the attack upon Andrea, perhaps because he was on his guard now and did not sleep without Martin Vasques nearby.

Dawn showed them the long dark line of the African coast dead ahead. Only a little to the south loomed the almost white sand cliffs of a projecting headland. This, one of the ship's crew who had been on a previous voyage led by Antão Gonçalves, positively identified as Cape Blanco.

In his happiness at making a direct landfall on the white cape without the usual searching that went on when a ship sought a place previously visited, Dom Alfonso seemed to have recovered from his pique against Andrea. He congratulated the navigator hugely and in his honor a feast was held on board with much wine to drink. Since Lancarote did not want to warn the Moors in this region of their presence by making a landing at Cape Blanco, they sailed on southward, and late the next afternoon saw upon the port side a large island, which the same crewman identified as Arguim.

They approached Arguim Island cautiously, for it was here that Gonçalo de Sintra had lost his life a few years before when the Moors had descended upon him in large numbers as he led a fighting party ashore to try and take captives. In all, more than a dozen Portuguese had been killed in that short but bloody encounter. The caravels were almost ready to drop anchor in a bay sheltered in the lee of the island, when a dozen small boats suddenly shot out from behind a point and sped toward the mainland, separated from the island here by only a narrow neck of water.

It was the first time Andrea had seen any natives of this part of the African coast. The boats appeared to have been dug from large logs, a method of construction which, he had been told, was characteristic of most craft in this area. But what startled him was the strange manner of propulsion. The men in the boats were quite naked and they straddled the gunwales of their flimsy-looking craft with one leg over the side. These they used exactly as more civilized people did a paddle, the combined propulsive power of eight black limbs sending the small craft scudding toward the shore like nothing so much as a huge bug with eight legs on either side walking on the water.

"Sangre di Cristo!" Alfonso Lancarote exclaimed. "Now the Moors will be warned and perhaps run away. Then we will take no slaves."

"When would you attack?" Andrea inquired.

"In the morning. But now that they are warned, they

may seek to keep us from landing, and our crossbowmen will have to kill some. That means less slaves, too."

"Why not give the appearance of sailing southward then?" Andrea suggested. "The map shows an island nearby called the Ilha das Garças, the Isle of Herons. I see many herons flying from the next island south of here; that might be it."

"Are we to run away from poorly armed blacks?" Dom Alfonso asked stiffly.

"That's what I hope the Moors will think," Andrea said. "If so, they will not flee and you can land your men on the shore of the mainland at dawn tomorrow with small boats to cut off those who remain on the island."

"Por Dios!" Dom Alfonso exclaimed. "You are a clever man, senhor."

Andrea grinned. "Clever at saving my own skin, at least. I didn't come this far to lose my life on a foreign beach. Besides, I am a shareholder in this expedition."

Only about an hour of daylight remained as they worked busily, moving the caravels toward the island Andrea had pointed out. The distance was only a little more than a mile, and as they approached, clouds of graceful, white birds rose and swarmed about the ship. They were so tame that the men easily knocked them to the decks and wrung their long, slender necks without recourse to guns, and a pile of white bodies soon lay on the planking. Fortunately, many tall trees grew on the Ilha das Garças and they were able to anchor the caravels on the far side of it without being visible from Arguim Island.

IV

The company of the *Santa Clara* feasted that night on herons' flesh and eggs which some of the men gathered on shore. On orders from Dom Alfonso they were quiet, for sound traveled well over water, and he did not wish to warn the natives on Arguim Island or the mainland of their presence behind the protection of the Isle of Herons. Nor was there much tendency to merriment, for tomorrow would almost certainly be a day of battle and enough of their fellows had been killed on previous voyages by the Moors for them to know the danger they faced.

It was still dark when the fighting men who were to go ashore gathered on the deck of the *Santa Clara* the next morning. Because only one boat was carried aboard each of the caravels, the number who would make the foray ashore was limited to six from each of the ships, the capacity of the boat, making thirty men in all from the five vessels. In the darkness they could hear preparations going on aboard the other vessels, the clank of armor and occasionally a voice raised in a curse as its owner bumped into something or someone in the darkness.

Dom Alfonso Lancarote did not accompany the first group, but remained behind to lead the party attacking from the ships. The plan was to move the caravels to the anchorage at Arguim Island as soon as the sun rose, from which point the men aboard would launch an attack from the seaward side, pinning the enemy down between the two forces.

At his own request, Dom Gil Vicente headed the shore party from the *Santa Clara*. Andrea was surprised when the fiery young *fidalgo* from Florence chose him as one of those to make up the party, but he welcomed an opportunity to set foot on the African coast. The *fidalgos* and the soldiers wore cuirasses and morions of steel, but Andrea contented himself with a steel helmet to protect his head and a sword and dagger in case he was attacked.

Shortly before dawn they clambered over the side and slid down ropes to the boats waiting below. Then, with Andrea at the steering sweep and the others manning the oars, they began to feel, rather than see, their way toward the nearby shore. Around them the splash of oars and an occasional muttered curse indicated the locations of the other boats. Their orders were not to attack at once, but to outflank any Moorish settlements they could locate close to the shore by making a circle inland. Thus they would be able to cut off any retreat by the Moors on Argium Island when the main attack was launched from the caravels, besides preventing the bringing up of reinforcements.

The air was damp and warm, reeking with the droppings of herons nesting by the thousands on the nearby islands. A fairly dense cloud of vapor hugged the surface and Andrea found himself staring ahead eagerly into the semidarkness of dawn, seized already by the excitement of making a landing upon an alien shore and perhaps fighting for his life before he crossed the beach. As they skirted the shores of Arguim Island on the way to the mainland, they could hear voices raised in a foreign chatter from the Azanegue village and the braying of an ass now and then disturbed the breathless hush of early morning. From these Andrea judged that the Moors had fallen victim to his stratagem. Thinking that the great ships with the white wings, by which men seemed able to fly over the water, had sailed on, the savages were apparently ignorant of the impending attack.

Less than an hour after leaving the ship, a small inlet opened up before them and, calling in a low voice to the others to follow, Andrea guided the boat into it and grounded it upon a narrow, sandy beach where their presence would not be apparent to any natives who happened to be on the shore. The first rays of the sun were just breaking through when he stumbled from the boats and, crossing the narrow beach, began to move into the underbrush growing along the edge of the inlet.

Gil Vicente, as agent for Dom Alfonso, was leader of the expedition, but Andrea found himself wishing one of the more experienced and grizzled soldiers was in charge. As yet they had seen no sign of a native village in this area of the mainland, although those who had accompanied Gonçalo de Sintra on his ill-fated expedition to this very shore had spoken of one. The men soon began to pant and curse as they staggered through the sand, and the warmth of the rising sun quickly caused sweat to break out beneath the heavy armor, increasing their misery. They had brought ship's biscuit and a few bottles of water and wine, and before they had gone a half mile inland, Gil Vicente called a halt for rest and food.

The men threw themselves down gratefully on the sandy earth to rest. Partly because he wore no armor, but for the most part because of his splendid physique from recent service in the galleys, Andrea was not as tired as the others seemed to be. He swallowed a gulp of water and bit into a ship's biscuit, before approaching the shade of a stunted palm where the leaders were resting.

"Senhor Vicente," he said. "I would like to ask permission to go ahead a little way and examine the area we are approaching."

Gil Vicente bristled a little. He was very jealous of the small measure of authority given him as leader of the expedition and vain concerning the tribute to his fighting ability that it implied.

"Why you, Senhor Bianco?" he demanded. "You are not even a soldier."

Andrea grinned, refusing to be angered by this popinjay. "In the galleys a man learns to move silently," he said. "And to value his own skin."

"I forgot that you had been a slave," Vicente said condescendingly.

"The navigator gives good advice, your honor," Martin Vasques spoke up. "Give me leave and I will go with him. In the battle for Ceuta, the infante sent me and another ahead to spy out the lay of the land and thus saved his command from being cut to pieces by Moors hiding near the beach."

The shrewd reference to Prince Henry's action settled any doubt in the young officer's mind about the delegation of authority. "Go then, both of you," he agreed. "But see that you are back in no less than an hour. We will await you here."

Martin Vasques promptly shed his cuirass and fell in beside Andrea. "You lead, Excellency," he said as they left the resting place.

"Give me no titles," Andrea said with a grin. "I have no noble blood."

"You possess intelligence—which is worth more." The old soldier grinned. "Kill enough Moors here today and you may find yourself a knight tomorrow. Men have achieved it for less. Which way?"

"I think we should circle inland and see if the village mentioned by the other ships is still here. This area must be a rallying point for the Moors."

Moving slowly, for the underbrush was thick, they began to follow a wide circle and presently they came to the banks of a stream whose water was fresh.

"If we go upstream we will probably find the village," Andrea told Martin Vasques. "They probably located it near a source of fresh water."

The soldier nodded. "Lead on."

Andrea stepped into the water. The bottom was sandy and it was no more than knee-deep, forming by far the easiest path into the interior. The water was cool and fresh upon their legs as they waded along. Hardly had they gone a hundred paces, however, when Andrea stopped so suddenly that Martin Vasques bumped into him. Now that the splashing of their steps had ceased, he heard again the sound that had arrested him, the chatter of voices coming from somewhere ahead.

"Senhor Bianco," Martin Vasques whispered. "Do you see a path there on the left bank of the stream?"

Andrea saw it now and cursed himself silently for not being more closely on the watch. The sound of voices was growing louder, which could only mean that a group of people—how many he could not judge—were approaching along the path and would pass within a few yards of where they stood. Already it was too late to climb from the stream and hide in the underbrush along its banks.

"Lie down in the water close to the bank," Andrea said in a whisper. "The overhang will hide us."

Martin Vasques wasted no time in argument. In seconds he was stretched out in the water with only enough of his face above the surface to allow for breathing, his body pressed beneath the slight overhang of the bank. Andrea did the same. The coolness of the water upon their sweating bodies was something of a shock, and he fought to hold back a sneeze that would have betrayed them instantly. The sound of voices was quite loud now and apparently all male, which probably meant a war party from the village farther up the stream, on its way to the beach.

Andrea strained his ears, hoping the men might use one of the Moorish dialects with which he was familiar from his years as a galley slave of the Arabs farther to the east. A few of the words did sound familiar and he guessed that—with a co-operative subject—he might be able to make something of the tongue. But at the moment he learned nothing of value in their present situation. Unable to see the Moors from his position in the stream, Andrea could only estimate the number in the war party.

When the war party had passed, Andrea got up from the stream and helped Martin Vasques to his feet. Water cascaded from their clothing and sloshed in their boots, but they were too thankful for their narrow escape from danger to mind such minor discomforts.

"How many would you say there were?" he asked the old soldier.

"Fifty at least, most of them men."

"And therefore warriors."

Martin Vasques nodded soberly. "The *fidalgos* may

win much of their precious honor before this day is over.
I have battled these Moors before; they are devilish
fighters."

"Then we'd better hurry back and warn the others,"
Andrea said. "The caravels will soon be in a position to
attack the shore."

They found Gil Vicente and their comrades where they
had left them, lying in the shade of some stunted palms
that grew among the underbrush. Andrea gave a quick
account of their encounter with the Moors and how they
had hidden in the stream. "The path they took evidently
leads to the shore," he finished. "By following it, we can
come upon them from the rear as we had hoped."

Gil Vicente, it developed, had other ideas. "How far
upstream do you think this village is, Senhor Bianco?" he
demanded eagerly.

"Probably not far. What difference does that make?"

The youngster gave him a hard-faced look. "I give orders here—without questions from those who are not
even soldiers."

Andrea shrugged. "Senhor Lancarote will not like it if
he attacks from the ships as planned and you are not
there to cut off the rear."

"How better could we cut off the rear of the Moors than
by controlling the path?" Gil Vicente demanded impatiently. "We can take the village and have plenty of time
to reach the shore."

"It will probably be defended only by old men, women,
and children," Andrea protested, "and hardly worth the
trouble."

"We will avenge the death of Gonçalo de Sintra then,"
Gil Vicente cried, getting to his feet. "As brave a knight
as ever drew sword, I am told." He drew his sword. "Follow me, men!" With that he went lunging forward but
was slowed immediately by the soft sand.

"We will do well this day," grunted Martin Vasques
sarcastically. "But it may not be entirely for nothing at
that. There will surely be young maidens in the village
and they bring a good price as slaves." He grinned. "Especially when pregnant by white men. Then a buyer gets
two for the price of one and the lighter-skinned ones make
fine house servants."

V

They found the native village without difficulty by following the path along the banks of the stream. As Andrea had predicted, it was peopled largely by women, children, and old men. Nevertheless these managed to put up a good fight when the Portuguese attacked, using such paltry arms as were in their possession.

The *fidalgos* went into combat with lusty eagerness, shouting, "San Jorge!" "Portugal!" and "Santiago," while hacking away at any dark skin that resisted them. Andrea did not even draw his own sword but watched the carnage from the edge of the village, with a growing distaste.

He was thrown into it finally, whether he wanted to be or not, when a boy of perhaps twelve or thirteen years who had been protecting a younger girl with a lance ran toward where he was standing. Gil Vicente was in hot pursuit, brandishing his sword and shouting hoarsely. Something deep down inside Andrea made him do what he did then, an impulse he did not bother to identify.

The boy was sobbing as he backed toward where Andrea stood, jabbing with his spear to try and gain time for his sister to reach the woods surrounding the village where she would be safe. Obviously the youngster was fully resigned to giving his own life to save hers and was fighting only to gain time. When he was almost opposite Andrea, the Moorish boy stumbled and went down to his knees. Shouting "Santiago" as he leaped to attack, the *fidalgo* lifted his sword for the lethal thrust.

It was then that Andrea acted. Moving swiftly he was beside Gil Vicente before the weapon could descend and gripped his sword arm.

"Hold your sword, *fidalgo*," he said. "There is no honor in killing children."

"He—he cut with that lance," Gil Vicente shouted, and Andrea saw a shallow gash on his cheek.

"Go fight men, not children."

"I'll have you killed for this," Vicente cried, panting with rage.

"Not before I break your wrist and probably your

136

neck," Andrea told him grimly. The *fidalgo* struggled futilely, for Andrea held him pinned with the grip on his wrist as easily as he might have held a struggling child.

Glancing around, Andrea saw the boy and the girl disappearing into the trees. The carnage was rapidly slackening, too, and some of the soldiers had already started to bind those of the natives who had chosen the wiser path of non-resistance.

"Don't make a fool of yourself before the others," he urged Gil Vicente. "Promise not to attack me and I will release you."

The *fidalgo* was almost sobbing with rage, but in Andrea's grip he was helpless and—he evidently realized—ridiculous. "I—I promise," he gasped.

Andrea released him and stepped back quickly, not sure that Vicente would keep his promise. But the *fidalgo* was as good as his word. Still holding his sword aloft, he rushed back among the huts of the village, but all resistance was over now.

A half dozen men and a few children lay on the ground dying, the rest were being herded together by the soldiers, with their hands bound behind them. A dozen young women were in the group, some almost comely, for these Moors were not black like the natives farther south, but of varying shades from a rich cream to dark brown. One of the old soldiers was going from one to the other of the prostrate figures, mercifully putting the dying out of their misery with a quick thrust from his sword.

Although he had seen violence and bloodshed enough during the swift forays by the corsairs upon shipping and against each other, Andrea could not help being sickened by this needless butchery. The others seemed not to be disturbed by it, however. The *fidalgos* were laughing and shouting congratulations to each other at their feat of capturing nearly fifty slaves, with only a few scratches in return.

Only a short time was required to bind the Moors who were to be enslaved, tying their wrists and tethering them by their necks in a line with ropes of grass fiber and vines from the village. Soon the party was moving back toward the shore, making good time over the well-traveled path. They had not yet reached the beach when the boom of a bombard sounded, the agreed-upon signal that the caravels had reached the rendezvous and were ready to attack from the sea.

Leaving a few soldiers to guard the captives, Gil Vicente and the others hurried on in order not to miss the battle that was just now starting. But having no wish to witness another orgy of butchery, Andrea stayed behind with the slaves. They still came out on the beach across from Arguim Island in time to witness the fighting, however. And a scene of utter confusion it was indeed.

The natives on the island had chosen to flee toward the mainland and the safety of the interior as soon as the caravels appeared, not realizing that Gil Vicente and his band had already cut off any chance of retreat in that direction. Since the tide was low, they were able to wade across the narrow arm of the sea separating the island from the mainland. But even before they had all gained the beach, a bombard from Dom Alfonso's ship had boomed the signal for the attack, and the soldiers had come pouring over the sides of the caravels into the shallow water, making for the shore in pursuit.

Many of the Moorish warriors remained behind to guard the retreat of the women, children, and old people from the island. They were armed for the most part with crude lances and shields made from what Andrea learned later was elephant hide imported by caravans from the land of the Negroes to the south. Upon them, Gil Vicente and his men descended from the rear, shouting their battle cries, and the situation soon became hopeless for the natives. Sure, now, that people who were able to appear simultaneously from the woods as well as the ships could be nothing less than demons, the fear-crazed Moors sought only to flee.

Andrea and his group, with the captives from the village, emerged from the underbrush onto the beach just as Gil Vicente and his men attacked from one side and those from the caravels splashed ashore with swords, spears, and arbalests to enter the fray. Seized by terror, mothers abandoned children and husbands left wives. In the mad desire to escape, the Moorish warriors even attacked their own people when they got in the way, killing some and wounding more. Many rushed into the water and tried to swim, but Dom Alfonso's men, wading in the shallows as they debarked from the ships, quickly cut off escape.

Soon the water of the inlet was red with blood and dark-skinned bodies rolled in the wash upon the shore. Some mothers hid their children in the underbrush and a few even buried them in a muddy area to one side, hoping to escape detection. In the midst of this carnage the *fidalgos,* the soldiers, and the crews of the caravels methodically went about the business of cutting down any who did not appear to be candidates for a good price as slaves.

Watching the massacre while he guarded the slaves taken with the village, Andrea sought to explain to himself the change that had come over him in the past several hours. Violence was nothing unusual in his experience and he could remember no qualms whatever when he had killed Girolamo Bellini on the street beside the canal back in Venice. Nor had the bloodshed in the galleys ever affected him this way.

What he felt was not simply nausea, such as many people experienced at the sight of violence. Instead it was a sense of revulsion which he found even harder to understand because the capturing of slaves by Dom Alfonso and his men obviously meant wealth in his own pocket. Perhaps, he told himself, the trouble was that, having been a slave himself, he could not help feeling sympathy for the unfortunate Moors.

By the time Dom Alfonso finally waded ashore, in full armor, the group under Gil Vicente had finished killing those of the Moors who resisted and were busy rounding up any who had fled. The rest were herded together on the beach. Many of the blacks were sobbing and a number were wounded. All capacity to resist gone, they stood patiently like cattle, ringed in by soldiers with lances and drawn swords. Only two of the Portuguese had been killed, as far as Andrea was able to see, a cheap price to pay for more than a hundred slaves.

Gil Vicente was in the act of reporting to Dom Alfonso when Andrea's group led the captives they were guarding out upon the beach. The expedition's leader had been too handicapped by the weight of his armor and the soft sand to take much part in the fighting.

"This is a great day for us!" Lancarote cried when he saw the second group of captives. "And a great victory for our arms."

"I count a hundred and sixty-five in all," Martin

Vasques reported with a broad grin. "With a fair number of young women."

"God has indeed rewarded our zeal," Dom Alfonso said piously. "What higher gift could we bring our Blessed Lord than that of bringing the souls of these heathens to knowledge of our faith?" He turned to the soldiers and the *fidalgos*. "I would have you know that I am vastly pleased with what you have done, senhors. Our noble and brave comrade, Gonçalo de Sintra, has been well avenged this day, and a goodly cargo obtained for our ships besides."

A shout of approval went up from the men, but Andrea did not join it. His share from the sale of the slaves they had already taken would repay him well for his work so far, but he felt no satisfaction in the knowledge.

"Tonight we will feast and drink wine in honor of this great victory," Dom Alfonso continued. "We discovered pigs for roasting in the village on the island. They will furnish meat for the feast and tomorrow we will embark the slaves on board the ships and go in search of others."

Another cheer greeted this information. Andrea's services as a guard were no longer needed, so he started across the beach, intending to wade out to the *Santa Clara* and get his navigation instruments. He'd had no time yet for observations on the height of the noonday sun above the horizon, a method of navigation which Prince Henry and Mestre Jacomé were very anxious to study more fully.

Halfway across the open stretch of the beach to the water he heard a voice behind him ask contemptuously, "Are you running away, Senhor Bianco?"

It was Gil Vicente and when Andrea turned he saw the *fidalgo* standing only a few paces behind him, stiffly erect in cuirass and morion, with a sheathed sword at his side and a leather gauntlet in his hand. Fully realizing what was about to happen, Andrea still could hardly believe it. As far as he was concerned, the affair of that morning had been ended, but Vicente evidently planned to carry it further.

"Or are you too much of a coward to defend your honor?" the *fidalgo* added. Stepping forward, he slapped Andrea in the face with the leather gauntlet.

VI

Even the blacks were suddenly silent, sensing the import of this new drama, although they could not understand the words. Andrea's first impulse was to seize Gil Vicente in his bare hands and break him in two, as he would a stick, but he realized that such an action would not do here. With the formal challenge, the *fidalgo* had invoked the code of chivalry and, even though Andrea was not a knight nor aspired to be one, he must still follow the rules or be branded a coward and an outcast by the others.

"I am not afraid, senhor," Andrea said quietly. His gaze swept the circle of grave faces staring at him. "All of you are witnesses that I am the challenged one."

Dom Alfonso managed to break the spell that had gripped them all at this unexpected turn of events. "What is the meaning of this, senhors?" he asked.

"Senhor Bianco gave me offense early today in the attack upon the village," Gil Vicente said quickly before Andrea could speak. "I could not challenge him before, but now that the fighting is over, I insist upon the satisfaction of my honor through combat to the death."

Lancarote turned to Andrea. "What do you say, Senhor Bianco?" he inquired.

Andrea shrugged. "If Senhor Vicente chooses to take offense at any action of mine, it is his privilege."

Dom Alfonso shook his head slowly. "At a time like this we should be fighting the enemy; not among ourselves. I must beg you both to settle your differences in some other way."

"I will accept nothing but combat to the death," Gil Vicente said. Obviously he was confident that as a knight-to-be, his superior skill with weapons would give him victory.

"I shall be happy to give Senhor Vicente satisfaction if he demands it," Andrea said quietly.

"Then I have no choice," Dom Alfonso said reluctantly. "The affair will be settled this afternoon here on the beach, with sword and lan——"

"*Una momento, senhor.*"

Dom Alfonso looked at Andrea with surprise, for his

tone had been sharp and the admonition loud. "Yes, Senhor Bianco?"

"Senhor Vicente challenged me to a combat, as you all heard. I am neither a knight nor a soldier, nor do I desire to be either. He knows this and hopes to entice me into battle with weapons in whose use he is an expert." He grinned wryly. "Frankly, I have no wish to commit suicide here on the coast of Africa."

He saw a look of contempt begin to form in Dom Alfonso's eyes. "Then you wish to apologize and evade——"

"I evade nothing." Andrea's voice was like a whiplash. "Since Senhor Vicente has challenged me, I insist upon choosing the method of combat."

"Such is your right under the laws of chivalry," Dom Alfonso conceded.

"Then I will fight him with daggers alone and both of us stripped to the waist."

"A knight does not fight in such a manner," Gil Vicente snapped.

"Do you withdraw your challenge then?" Andrea demanded.

The color drained slowly from Gil Vicente's face. With daggers as weapons, the odds would be closer to even. Yet if he now withdrew the challenge or refused to fight, the tables would be turned and he would be branded the coward. "I will do combat with Senhor Bianco as he requires," he said stiffly. "Only give me a little time to rest from battle and refresh myself."

"You may have an hour," Dom Alfonso conceded. "The combat will take place here on the beach."

Martin Vasques volunteered to act as Andrea's second and he accepted the old soldier's services gratefully. They withdrew to one side, but when Martin brought a cup of wine Andrea refused it. "Wine never made anyone brave, my friend," he said. "I have a job to do that demands skill."

"It will require no skill to cut the throat of that strutting cock."

"I have no intention of killing him."

"*Dios!* Why not? He is only asking for it. And don't think he wouldn't have spitted you with the lance and enjoyed it."

"He is young. I will show him who is master and then grant him his life. It may make a man of him."

Martin Vasques shook his head. "You are a strange man, Senhor Bianco. Why did you stay aloof from the killing this morning?"

"Something inside me is revolted by the idea of killing helpless people," Andrea admitted. "Even if they are heathen."

"The priests tell us we are doing the Moors we capture a favor by saving their immortal souls."

Andrea shrugged. "I'll not argue religion with you, my friend. Or what is right or wrong for a man's soul. In the galleys I knew Turks and Moors who had more nobility than most Christians. And I have met scoundrels of all faiths everywhere."

VII

It was not yet noon when Andrea stepped into the wide circle made on the beach by the onlookers. Dom Alfonso had chosen a hard-packed area left dry by the receding tide, where the sand would not be soft and therefore likely to make a treacherous footing. Both men were stripped to the waist, and although some of the color burned into Andrea's body by the sun while he had been in the galley was now faded, his skin was still a rich brown compared to the pale white of Gil Vicente's torso.

Their weapons were identical daggers with metal guards, provided by Dom Alfonso. Now he brought them together in the middle of the circle. "I ask you both once again to compose your differences without battle," he said. "If you feel that it can be done."

"Senhor Vicente needs only to withdraw his challenge," Andrea said quietly. "I have nothing against him."

Gil Vicente was pale but he did not seize the way out. "That I cannot do and maintain my honor," he said firmly.

"Then I decree that honor will be satisfied by the bringing of first blood and the encounter terminated at once," Lancarote announced and extended his sword between the two men. "The contest will begin when I withdraw my sword and end when I call 'First blood.' Is that understood?"

Both parties nodded agreement and Dom Alfonso stepped back until only the tip of his sword was between them. Suddenly he lifted it and moved away a few paces, holding the drawn sword still in his hand.

Andrea watched the younger man warily. Trained to fight in the hope of attaining knighthood, as were all fiery young aspirants for that honor, Gil Vicente would be a worthy opponent, he knew. But there was less chance for skill to determine the outcome with a dagger no more than a foot long as a weapon, and he was counting on his greater strength to give him the advantage. Besides, it was no part of his intention to kill the other man.

They circled warily, each reluctant to make the first move. With their torsos bare, the smallest wound would show at once and Dom Alfonso, as he had promised, could stop the fight. Both were barefooted in order to give them a better footing upon the sand.

In the end it was Gil Vicente who could not stand the tension of circling and moved to attack. Andrea had been watching the younger man's eyes, however, and anticipated the *fidalgo's* lunge. He was able to meet the attack easily and neutralize it by catching his opponent's blade upon the metal guard of his own dagger. Thus linked wrist to wrist, they strained against each other for an advantage, while the watchers kept up a continual shouting, each encouraging the one upon whom he had wagered.

The two men's faces were hardly a foot apart, so Andrea was able to hear Vicente when he said in a terse whisper, "You won't escape me this time as you did on the ship."

Andrea knew now who had been responsible for the attack upon him that night aboard the *Santa Clara*. He had thought it odd at the time that Gil Vicente, who was supposed to have been sleeping in the *toldilla*, had been the first one to reach him. The answer, of course, was that Vicente had been there all the time, but Andrea's quick action in dropping the Al-Kemal inside the loose front of his tunic and shouting for help had foiled him. With the watch converging upon the foredeck where the brief struggle had taken place, Vicente had been left no choice except to pretend to be one of those responding to Andrea's cry.

For a long tense moment Andrea held Vicente pinioned. Then, with a quick shove, he threw his opponent back and disengaged the two daggers. So great was the difference in their strength that the *fidalgo* was thrown to the ground. A murmur arose from the spectators when Andrea stepped back and allowed the younger man to rise before resuming the fight.

He could easily have killed Vicente then, but he waited until his opponent was on his feet, panting and gripping the dagger firmly once more. Andrea moved in quickly then, twisting his body as the *fidalgo* stabbed downward. Warding off the blow easily with his own blade, he struck the slighter man with his shoulder, spinning him around and half stunning him.

The sickly fear of death showed in Gil Vicente's eyes as he realized that Andrea could kill him whenever he wished. To do so, however, was no part of Andrea's immediate purpose, for he had remembered that the *fidalgo* had come from Florence only a few days before sailing, claiming, as a kinsman of Dom Alfonso, the privilege of joining the expedition. And he was determined to discover whether there was any more sinister reason than the love of adventure for Vicente's decision to visit Lagos and join the fleet.

Once again Andrea held his opponent pinioned with their daggers locked. "You can save yourself by confessing," he said in a voice low enough so none of the others could hear. "I have no wish to kill you."

Gil Vicente hesitated only a moment. "I will confess," he agreed.

Andrea stepped back and lowered his guard to break off the engagement. Too late, however, he realized that Vicente's pretended capitulation had been only a trick to gain an advantage. Instead of breaking off combat, the younger man lunged forward, the dagger in his hand stabbing upward toward Andrea's unprotected belly.

Unable to parry the treacherous thrust, Andrea could only twist his body away from it. He felt a sudden blow against his buttock as he turned, but strangely enough none of the fiery stab of pain from what could easily be a fatal wound. Momentarily staggered by the blow, he watched incredulously the flash of sunlight upon the dagger guard as it flew from the younger man's hand. And at the same moment he realized what had happened.

The point of the dagger had struck, not yielding flesh as Gil Vicente had intended, but the thick callosity extending across Andrea's buttock, product of five years of falling back upon the rowers' bench in the teeth-jarring oar stroke of the galley slave. And the resistance of horn-hard skin had jarred the dagger from the *fidalgo's* fingers, causing it to bury itself to the hilt in the sand.

Gil Vicente lunged desperately for the dagger, but this time Andrea did not let him reach it. Turning his hand so that his fist, rather than the point, struck the other man, he gave him such a clout on the side of his head that Vicente went down upon his knees, half stunned. Kicking the dagger out of reach, Andrea seized the *fidalgo's* short beard and jerked him erect.

"Tell the truth," he ordered grimly. "Tell the truth or I'll slit your throat."

"It was I who tried to steal the navigational device on the ship," Gil Vicente squealed. "I challenged you today so I could kill you and take it from your body."

"Who sent you to Lagos?" Andrea demanded.

"Mattei Bianco! He was in Florence when Captain Cadamosto stopped there and told of your discovery. He paid me to come to Lagos and kill you for the secret."

"And when you learned I was sailing on this voyage you asked to join it so you could carry out your mission?" Andrea finished the confession.

"Yes, yes—— Don't kill me."

Andrea thrust the other man from him contemptuously. He had already forgotten him in fact, concerned with the more important realization that Mattei, having failed to have him killed in Venice, had struck again here at the other end of the Mediterranean. His half brother must be desperate indeed, and a desperate man would try again and again, so long as he and his intended victim were both alive.

Dom Alfonso came up in time to hear the confession and turn upon his kinsman savagely. "Dog," he snapped. "I should execute you here and now, but you will remain under arrest until we return to Lagos. The courts there can decide what to do with you." Then he turned to Andrea and bowed formally. "My apology for the cowardly act of my kinsman. Senhor Bianco. You may demand of me whatever satisfaction you desire."

"I've had more than enough fighting, senhor," Andrea assured him, "especially for a man who wants only peace."

Although he had foiled this particular attempt to kill him, Andrea did not delude himself that he would know much peace in the forseeable future. Mattei, perhaps more than anyone else, would be able to appreciate the almost

unbelievable advantage the Al-Kemal could give an un-
scrupulous person who possessed it. At the moment Mattei
could have no way of knowing that Gil Vicente had failed
in his mission, but upon their return to Lagos, news of
Andrea's presence there must soon come to the agents of
the Medici in Lisbon and eventually to Mattei in Venice.
From that day, Andrew knew, his life would be in danger
—until either he or Mattei were dead.

There was feasting and celebration on the beach that
night, as Dom Alfonso had promised, but Andrea stayed
only for a good meal of roast pig. His hunger for fresh
meat satisfied, he had himself rowed out to the *Santa
Clara* where it lay at anchor near Arguim Island. There
he brought out his navigating instruments and took from
its fine wooden case the astrolabe that Prince Henry had
given him to use on the voyage.

It was an Arabic instrument captured in the attack
upon Ceuta, he had been told, but the Moorish symbols
were familiar. With it, he carefully determined the angle
of the North Star above the horizon several times, aver-
aging his figures for accuracy and setting them down on a
rough map he was drawing of that region. On it he had
already indicated the location of Arguim Island, the Ilha
das Garças, and several others which had been visible
that afternoon from the beach.

He noted also in the account he was writing of the
voyage that—when the tide was low—the water was shallow enough for men to wade ashore from the island to the
mainland, and that there was a plenitude of food in
the form of fish, herons, and other birds, and eggs from
the island rookeries. Lastly he recorded the presence of
the animals called sea wolves whose sleek black pelts
were so prized in Portugal for warmth and for ornament-
ing the clothing of the rich. Tomorrow he intended to ask
Dom Alfonso for a boat and rowers with which to make
soundings around the island as a part of the rough sketch
he was making of the area. This information he planned
to incorporate later into a grand map of the African coast
line upon which he had worked back at Villa do Infante.

He was bending over the sketch, with a candle burning
beside him, when a voice said just behind him, "Senhor
Bianco."

Andrea turned quickly. It was Dom João Gonçalves,
the *fidalgo* aide of Dom Alfonso Lancarote.

"I—I apologize for disturbing you at your work, senhor," the younger man said. "But I wanted you to know I was never a friend of that cowardly Gil Vicente."

Andrea smiled. "To tell you the truth, I had already forgotten him." He pointed to the sketch. "I am busy drawing a map of this region. Prince Henry hopes to set up a colony someday on the shores of Africa as a base for further operations, and Arguim Island might well be the place. It has fresh water, plenty of food, and a good anchorage."

"Do you regard that sort of work as more important than bearing arms and achieving glory, senhor?"

"I find no fault with bearing arms," Andrea said. "But that sort of fame rarely outlasts him who achieves it."

"Does this?"

"Sometimes. Your prince is known to a few—mostly your people in Portugal—as one of the conquerors of Ceuta and a great knight. But his name is honored and respected throughout the world as the sponsor of these voyages of exploration. I am sure his fame in that sphere will long outlast the glory of his battles against the Moors."

"I never thought of it that way," Gonçalves admitted. "To me he is an ideal knight and the standard-bearer of our Christian faith in the battle against Islam."

"He is all that," Andrea agreed. "And I admire him very much. But our faith may yet be spread more widely by ships carrying goods for sale and by building trade cities in heathen lands than by any feat of arms."

"When you explain it, I can believe you, senhor," João Gonçalves admitted. "But one thing I cannot understand. Why did you let Gil Vicente live today?"

"What good would it have done me to kill him?"

"He challenged you and accused you of being a coward. And he tried to kill you."

"He did not succeed."

"You would have gained honor in killing one who so obviously deserved to die."

Andrea smiled. "Honor is not something to be worn on a man's sleeve, Senhor Gonçalves, like a lady's favor. It is a quality deep within a man, giving him humility and understanding and kindness—as well as bravery. Our prince possesses those qualities to a high degree, yet no one accuses him of being a coward because he is not quick to fight any man if he does not like the color of his skin or his eyes, the sound of his voice, or even the way he worships God."

"I never thought of it that way," Dom João admitted.

"If you had pulled the oars of a Moorish galley for years, as I did, you would know that a time can come when enough food to eat, a little vinegar and oil mixed with water to drink, and the strength to pull an oar so his back will not feel the lash of the overseer's whip means more to a man than even life itself. I almost went that far; only the desire for escape kept me from being utterly broken as others were. I can assure you there was little time to brood over honor then."

Gonçalves grinned wryly. "You make me feel like a child."

"It is good for a man to feel like a child," Andrea told him. "Remember our Blessed Lord said; *'Whosoever shall not receive the kingdom of God as a little child, he shall not enter therein.'* "

"Thank you, Senhor Bianco, for what you have taught me tonight," the *fidalgo* said gravely. "I will try to be the kind of knight you describe."

"I am sure you will be," Andrea told him warmly. "Like your prince."

Andrea worked at the sketch long after Gonçalves had gone. The sky was clear and with the moon shining so brightly, he found himself wishing for an eclipse in order to fix accurately the east-west location of Arguim Island. But no eclipse was on the calendar for several months, so that was out of the question. However, with his own records and those made by previous voyages of exploration along this coast, a considerable mass of information had been accumulated for the mapmakers and geographers back at Villa do Infante.

VIII

Using signs, plus what he had learned of the Moorish dialects while a slave of Hamet-el-Baku, Andrea questioned some of the captured Azanegues—as the tribe was called —the next morning. Only a few words of the local dialect were familiar to him, but by piecing what little he had learned together, he was able to give Dom Alfonso a good deal of information.

The Azanegues, he discovered, were a lower clan among the people of Islam, not to be compared with those of the Mediterranean coast and the great cities of Tunis, Alexandria, and other points where Moorish culture had been brought to a high degree. At best they seemed to be a lying and treacherous people who wore their black hair down to their shoulders and anointed their bodies with fish oil, giving them a rank and acrid odor. Farther inland, they said, some gold was found, but only rarely did any find its way to this part of Africa. Mostly it went to the city called Tombouctou and thence to Tunis and other Moorish cities where it was sold into Europe.

The Azanegue men went naked or wore at most a small apron over the loins. The women, whose skins were often a golden brown, as well as varying shades of black or lighter hues, were sometimes surprisingly beautiful. They wore small skirts around their waists and nothing else. Those possessing the longest breasts were considered the most beautiful, so it was the custom of mothers to bind the breasts of their daughters when they first began to swell with maidenhood in order to make them grow long.

As far as the neighboring countryside was concerned, Andrea was able to tell Dom Alfonso—after his conversation with the captured Azanegues—that several settlements existed on nearby islands and also farther inland on the mainland. Because of the difficulties of travel and the danger of being cut off, Lancarote decided to raid only the island villages. Gathering a body of men in the boats, he set off before noon for a two-day foray upon an island that lay to the south, where a large village was located.

Andrea was busy with a project of his own, an accurate determination of the sun's height above the horizon at noon. As soon as the others departed, he waded ashore with his astrolabe and other material. First he set up a lance as a gnomon on the white sand in order to mark the shadow cast by it in the bright sunlight and thus determine the exact time of noon when the sun was directly south, as marked by the needle of a small compass which he also brought ashore.

Because of the general lack of accuracy of the astrolabe, navigation by means of the sun's noon height was only rarely used by shipmasters. Prince Henry and Mestre Jacomé had asked him to take such observation whenever he could along the coast, however, because no expedition before this one had carried a fully qualified mapmaker and navigator. As always, the infante was anxious to accumulate any information which could be used later in the studies being made at Villa do Infante.

The natives captured the day before had been herded together in an improvised pen on Arguim Island, guarded by a group of soldiers. All day long the cries of the captives made the air hideous, disturbing the herons who flew about in great clouds. Some of these struck the masts of the caravels, dashing themselves to the deck, while the sailors on board the ships attacked the rest with lances, knocking down many to be plucked and preserved in brine for use later. All in all, the whole area was in a state of bedlam until the coming of night. Then the natives, resigning themselves apparently to their fate, began to grow quiet except for a low moaning that kept up constantly, rising and falling in volume as the hours passed. This sound, Andrea was to learn, was as much a part of a slave ship as the creak of its rigging and the groaning of its timbers.

Busy on the shore with his observations, Andrea still found time to wish for more knowledge in the field of living things so he could identify and describe the strange birds, fish, and other animals found here.

One group of large birds, he was told by the natives, were called *framengos*. Somewhat larger than herons, with long necks and thin feathers, their bills were so large and heavy that they seemed unable to support them, resting their heads against their legs or their feathers when standing in the water.

The party led by Dom Alfonso Lancarote returned late the second afternoon, bringing about fifty more slaves, mostly children. These were driven along the shore by half the soldiers acting as guards, while the others brought back the ship's longboats that had carried the raiding party.

With some two hundred captives—the largest number ever accumulated by any previous expedition, and that in a matter of only three days—Dom Alfonso was naturally overjoyed. The following day he called a conference of his captains and found them generally in favor of returning home at once with their prizes.

Finally he turned to Andrea. "Since you will share the profits from the voyage, you have a right to speak, Senhor Bianco. Do you not agree that we should return to Lagos?"

"That depends upon whether you are content with only a modest profit," Andrea told him.

Dom Alfonso frowned. "What do you mean?"

"Prince Henry hoped we would sail at least as far south as the river Sanaga and the land of Guinea. Having come this far, it seems a pity to go back without discovering any new land."

"Signor Bianco speaks well," Ugo Tremolina agreed. "The infante will surely reward us if we map the route to the land of the blacks."

"Moors sicken and die on long voyages," one of the captains objected. "We will be lucky to reach Lagos with two thirds of those we have now."

"Why not send some of the caravels back to Portugal with the slaves we have?" Andrea argued. "The rest can sail farther south. The blacks of Guinea are worth much more as slaves than the Moors, but even if we take no slaves from the land of Guinea on this voyage, it will be easier to reach on the next."

"Why do you say that, senhor?" The speaker was Captain Gomes Pires of the caravel *Santa Maria,* an alert and intelligent mariner.

"If we go as far as the river of palms that marks the boundary of the land of Guinea," Andrea explained, "I will make the necessary observations to locate exactly the parallel of latitude on which it lies. Then a ship can always sail directly to it as we did to this place, without having to search along the coast again."

"Are you entirely certain of being able to do this, Senhor Bianco?" Gomes Pires asked.

"I can return to any spot in the world, once I have been there," Andrea assured him, "unless it be below the equinoctial line. And even then I believe I could find it."

Alfonso Lancarote stroked his chin. "You argue well, Senhor Bianco," he admitted. "And the lure of greater profit from a cargo of blacks is great."

"Plus the praise of the infante," Andrea reminded him. "I have heard that he is very liberal in rewarding those who make important discoveries."

"We will take a vote on it," Dom Alfonso decided.

The vote split as Andrea thought it would. Three of the captains were for sailing directly back to Portugal. Gomes Pires and Ugo Tremolina, with Dom Alfonso, voted to go on. "We will load all the captives on the three caravels," Lancarote decided. "They can sail for Lagos as soon as they take on water and fresh food. The rest of us will make the journey south. Our fate is in your hands, Senhor Bianco," he added gravely. "Pray that your calculations are correct."

IX

Three days later the entire fleet weighed anchor. Off Arguim Island Dom Alfonso's caravel boomed a signal gun and the three who were returning to Portugal began a long tack to the west. Because the prevailing winds in this area blew almost continually southwestward, and the caravels could not sail into the wind, they would be forced to tack back and forth during most of the journey to Lagos.

Andrea set the course of the other two caravels boldly southward and a little west. According to the information Prince Henry had been able to obtain from captured Moors and blacks, such a course would parallel the coast line well out to sea and bring them eventually to the river Sanaga. They were soon out of sight of land, and with a brisk wind at their backs, the two vessels bowled along over a smooth sea.

They had taken on a quantity of fresh fish, herons, and sea wolves' flesh at Arguim Island, so the diet was much richer than the usual fare at sea. This consisted daily of one and one half pounds per man of the staple sea biscuit which all ships carried, a pound of beef or a half pound of pork, two and a half pints of water with a pint and a half of wine—plus oil, vinegar, and onions enough to season the food. On fast days cheese from a goodly store carried in the hold was substituted for the meat. And on the very few occasions when the wind lessened, the men fished with good success.

One thing troubled Andrea in these latitudes, the steady sinking of the North Star in the sky as they sailed southward. He had expected this, of course, but as it became lower each night, decreasing the angle between Polaris and the horizon when he held the Al-Kemal before his eyes, he realized that the accuracy of his navigation was also diminished.

The length of the cord of the Al-Kemal gradually increased, as he was forced to move the wooden plate farther and farther from his eye in order to fill exactly the angle between the North Star and the horizon. As yet, he had been able to identify no other constellation to use as a guide, but he was hoping that the group of stars variously described by the Arabs of the eastern sea as a crescent, a chariot, or a cross, would appear soon in the southern sky.

Four days south of Arguim Island Andrea ordered the course changed to a southeasterly direction at midnight and took up a position with Captain Ugo in the bows of the caravel to watch the sea ahead. Dawn broke with no sign, as yet, of land, and they breakfasted on ship's biscuit and wine, with a little cheese, it being Friday and a fast day. The morning was half gone when the lookout clinging to a perch near the top of the mainmast called down that he had spotted a dark barrier almost dead ahead which could be the coast line.

Dom Alfonso and the *fidalgos* who occupied the aftercastle burst from their quarters at the news, chattering eagerly.

"Do you see any tall trees?" Andrea called up to the lookout. "Or a break that could be the mouth of a river?"

"Nothing yet."

"Look to the south," Andrea ordered. "Are they visible in that direction?"

"Nothing. Wait! I see something in the water." The lookout's voice rose excitedly. "It looks like a broad, brown line drawn across the sea."

Immediately a babble of conversation arose on the deck. Captain Ugo glanced inquiringly at Andrea, who shook his head. "A ridge of land would hardly extend this far from shore," he said thoughtfully, "but it might be wise to shorten sail."

The captain shouted an order and as the sails on the main- and mizzenmasts were lowered, the speed of the caravel slowed rapidly. Gomes Pires on the *Santa Maria* saw the maneuver and imitated it. Both caravels moved slowly over the sea while Andrea, from a position in the bow, strained his eyes southward. He soon saw what the sailor had reported, a sharply demarcated brown stain apparently crossing the surface of the ocean ahead of them.

"It is a sign!" one of the sailors cried excitedly. "A warning from heaven for us to go no farther!" Others took up the cry and a babble of confused voices came from the deck, all of them tinged with fear.

Dom Alfonso's voice sounded above the babble of conversation. "Stop the ship, Captain," he ordered. "We have been warned by heaven against going farther!"

As the remaining sails were lowered, the trim caravel came almost to a stop. Andrea, however, had no intention of letting this strange thing go unexplained, after having come this far. "What we see must have some reasonable explanation," he assured Dom Alfonso. "Give me leave to lower the boat and I will investigate it without taking the caravel any closer."

Lancarote was reluctant, but Andrea insisted. "If anything happens to me," he said, "you can raise the sails and leave this place at once."

"The whole responsibility is yours," Dom Alfonso warned. "I will order no one to go with you."

Martin Vasques stepped forward. "I can pull an oar as well as fight."

"And I," said João Gonçalves, joining him.

Several other men volunteered now, and a full crew of six manned the boat when it was put over the side. A few hundred paces away, where the other caravel had also come to a halt, a second boat was being lowered.

With six strong men at the oars the longboat shot southward over the calm sea. As they approached the strange brown line, Andrea shipped his oar and stood upon the thwarts. He could see now that what they had discovered was actually the edge of a broad area of sea extending as far as they could see both to the east and the west as well as some distance southward. In this area the water was colored a muddy brown, but with no sign of land above the surface. The realization of what it was, with an explanation of its source, struck Andrea so suddenly that he laughed aloud in relief.

"It's mud," he shouted happily. "Mud carried to sea by the current of a great river. I have seen this at the mouth of the Nile near Alexandria."

"Then this must be the western Nile," João Gonçalves cried. *"Por Dios!* It is a rare thing to see."

They had drifted over the edge of the brown flood by now and Martin Vasques dipped his hand into the water and tasted it. *"Sangre di Cristo!!"* he exclaimed. "The water is sweet, not salt, and only a little muddy in taste."

"It must be the river Sanaga," Andrea agreed. "Perhaps even the western Nile, as Senhor Gonçalves says."

The boat from the second caravel had approached now and Andrea told Gomes Pires, who was at the steering oar, his explanation of this strange discovery.

"Then we have only to follow the brown stream eastward to reach the river mouth," Pires said at once. "It is like finding a road in the sea."

The news that they had discovered the mouth of a great river quickly dispelled the fears of Dom Alfonso and the others. The sails were again raised and the ships began to move eastward, staying well within the brown flood stretching before them. Soon they found further evidence that they were indeed breasting the current of a mighty river, although still several leagues from the shore. Not only were the caravels slowed by the current, as if a giant hand were holding them back, but bits of debris, branches of trees, and occasionally a whole log floated past.

Shortly after noon the lookout called down that he could distinguish what seemed to be the beginning of a break in the coast line ahead and a half hour later Andrea could identify two tall palms growing beside the opening, their tops like giant feather dusters against the sky.

As the caravels moved slowly toward the river mouth— sounding as they went, lest they pile up on a shoal made by the delta formed as the mud of countless centuries was poured by the great river into the sea—the outlines of a considerable forest on the cape marking the northern boundary of the river mouth could be seen. The two sentinel palms rose well above the others, just as they had been described to Prince Henry by the slaves from Guinea.

"Another miracle of navigation, Senhor Bianco," Dom Alfonso cried jubilantly. His fear of a few hours ago was assuaged by the prospect of obtaining a cargo of valuable blacks, as well as the favor of Prince Henry for their great discovery. "You have brought us to the western Nile and the gateway to the land of Prester John."

X

The coast in the neighborhood of Cape Blanco had been sandy and largely desert, but the south bank of the river Sanaga—if indeed this were it—was a towering wall of green as far as the eye could see. The north shore was somewhat less densely overgrown with vegetation; but even here it was far thicker than anything they had seen before on their voyage.

The river appeared to be almost a league in width, giving them some idea of the tremendous flood of water it poured into the sea. The tide had reached its ebb before they were inside the actual mouth of the river itself and as the direction of flow changed and the sea poured back into its channel, the caravels began to move more rapidly. Sand bars and shallow reefs extended well out into the sea at the northern border of the river mouth, and Andrea was sure the same was true of the southern border, which they could not see. Between these was an island, dividing the entrance into two parts.

Feeling their way with the incoming tide, the caravels were able to effect an entrance into the river itself, without going aground. Gingerly working their way shoreward from the main force of the current, they anchored in fairly deep water a hundred paces or so from the southern shore.

As yet, they had seen no sign of any human life in this area, although the region was obviously well qualified to maintain it, being of an amazing fertility. The trees and vines along the southern bank formed almost a solid wall of green extending much higher than the masts of the caravels, and the growth was only a little less heavy on the northern bank. Bright-colored flowers seemed literally to grow in the air, and a profusion of gaudy-colored birds flew about or perched on limbs overhanging the water, regarding them with solemn curiosity. On shore a great crashing and loud trumpeting occasionally sounded. They could not identify the cause, but Andrea thought it might be elephants, since the captured Azanegues had told him they were found in great numbers in this region.

Just before dusk a strange animal was seen swimming in the water. Its back, fully as broad as that of a large draft horse, was just awash. The head, too, was shaped like that of a horse, but was at least twice as broad, with great tusks fully two hands in length, resembling those of a boar. Martin Vasques named it a "horse-fish" and they were startled when the strange animal climbed from the water at a place where the bank was low and waddled into the forest on short legs fully as large as a man's thigh. With the coming of darkness, giant bats occasionally swooped low over the ships. Their wings were as wide as the spread of a man's arms and they made the night hideous with screeching cries.

The water was full of fish, many as large as a small boy; a baited hook dropped over the side was snapped up almost before it struck the water. The heat, which had been oppressive during the day, abated but little here on the river at night, shut in as they were by solid walls of green. Their clothing was soon soaked with sweat and even the rigging seemed to drip water.

Dom Alfonso wiped the sweat from his face with his sleeve as he stood with Andrea and Captain Ugo in the waist of the ship, waiting for some fish to be cooked over a fire of coals built in a pot filled with sand. "I like not this place you have brought us to, Senhor Bianco," he said. "It is too hot and I feel as if eyes were watching us from the shore."

They may be," Andrea agreed. "The blacks are hard to see at night, and even by day a man two paces inside that wall of green would be completely hidden."

A coughlike snort sounded beside the vessel. Seizing an oil lantern hanging from the mast, Andrea went to the low rail.

"Por Dios!" Dom Alfonso cried, pointing into the darkness. "What is that?"

A large evil-looking head with two round unblinking eyes was regarding them from the water. The animal— or fish—was able to hold its place against the swift current merely by undulating a long tail, for they saw it break the surface every now and then. Its long, thick body was almost black in color and appeared to be covered with scales like some kind of armor. Floating in the current beside the ship, the strange beast had a frightening quality as it regarded them with those brilliant eyes.

"I think I recognize that fellow," Andrea handed the light to Dom Alfonso. From the deck he picked up a bucket of scraps and entrails left after cleaning the fish for their supper, and moving back to the rail, emptied the bucket toward the strange beast. It lunged halfway out of the water to seize the entire contents of the bucket with a snap of its great jaws. So fierce-looking was the great mouth with its two rows of glossy teeth and the obvious power indicated by the snap of its jaws that Dom Alfonso recoiled from the rail and almost dropped the lantern.

"Mother of God!" he gasped. "What is it?"

"Only a crocodile," Andrea assured him. "I saw many of them in the Nile at Alexandria."

"Then this must really be the western Nile."

"If there is such a thing," Andrea agreed.

"Perhaps we could sail across Africa to the land of Prester John," Dom Alfonso suggested.

Andrea shook his head. "In Alexandria they say the Nile rises to the south in a region called the 'Mountains of the Moon.' If that is true, this river would be navigable only a part of the way. I imagine it has cataracts farther inland, as the eastern Nile does."

"I have heard learned men say a stream flows west from Paradise," Captain Ugo said. "Perhaps this could be it?"

Andrea grinned. "A paradise whose waters are filled with crocodiles, Captain? If a man fell in the river, those jaws could snap his body in half as easily as a headman's ax does its work."

"Prince Henry will certainly reward us for finding this great river," Dom Alfonso said. "So there is no reason why we cannot leave here soon."

"The blacks are said to have the only gold found in this part of the world," Andrea reminded him. "I, for one, would like to return to Lagos a rich man."

"How do you propose to get it?"

"We can sail upstream tomorrow when the tide sets in again. There should be a village near the banks of the river."

"The Moors said the men of Guinea poison their arrows with herbs," Dom Alfonso said doubtfully.

"We have armor. And your crossbowmen can kill them before they get in range."

"I must sleep on it," Lancarote said. "It is a great responsibility to take so many men where no white man has ever been before."

All night long the clamor of living things from the forest and the rush of the current, with its strange and fearful creatures, continued. The scream of birds from the trees, the sighing of the horse-fish, and the grunts of the giant crocodiles that infested the water mingled with the cries of the bats to turn the night into bedlam. And with the coming of dawn the river was blanketed in a white cloud or mist that was almost the consistency of cotton, through which a man could hardly see as far as he could reach. In fact, the two ships seemed to float in it, as if suspended in another world.

Their clothing soggy and their spirits even damper, the men of the *Santa Clara* huddled around the cooking pots and crunched sea biscuit and warmed-over fish while they waited for the morning sun to burn away the mist. Gradually the world around them grew lighter as the minutes passed, and soon the outline of the riverbanks began to take form. With the lifting of the fog it became like any other river, and their spirits rose a little.

"The tide will be settling in soon, sir," Captain Ugo told Lancarote. "We can start upriver then if you wish."

Dom Alfonso hesitated, but the desire for gold, and the honors Prince Henry would no doubt shower on him for exploring this newly discovered river at least a little way, finally overcame his fears of the unknown dangers it afforded. "We will move a little distance upstream," he decided, "and see what we discover."

With the incoming tide as the driving force and a rag of sail on the foremasts to help hold the course, the two caravels began to feel their way slowly upstream. The river did not narrow perceptibly as they progressed and the depth still remained the same, by which they judged that it must penetrate a considerable distance into the interior and might indeed be the western Nile.

It was almost noon when they swept round a bend and saw five Negroes, who were fishing from a canoe, staring at them in astonishment. The paralysis was only momentary, however, and before the caravels were near enough to call them, the blacks had seized paddles lying in the bottom of the canoe and, thrashing the water frantically, sent the light craft skimming over the surface toward the shore.

One of the crossbowmen seized his arbalest, but Dom Alfonso ordered him not to shoot. The blacks, paddling fiercely, quickly disappeared upstream and the caravels followed more slowly. Everyone was alert now and the arbalesters knelt beside the rail with their weapons ready in case of an attack.

Perhaps a half hour later they saw a clearing with many thatch huts on the south shore near where a tributary stream entered the main current. Anchoring well away from the village, out of arrow range, they waited for the next move by the natives. The village appeared to be deserted, but they judged this to be only temporary, the natives having fled when word was brought of the strange visitors in the great winged boats.

An hour or so later, several canoes put out from the tributary stream and approached the ships gingerly, paddling around them in a circle of ever-narrowing radius. The men were very black with short hair, and some appeared to have pieces of bone thrust through their ear lobes and noses as ornaments. Their bodies glistened with some sort of oil and they were large and well-muscled. From a vantage point upon the elevated foredeck of the caravel, Andrea could see spears and bows and arrows lying in the bottom of the canoes.

"The savages are armed and the weapons are probably poisoned," he warned Dom Alfonso, who had put on full armor to impress the natives if they came aboard. "I doubt if they will attack first though; they seem only curious."

A man taller than the others sat in the largest of the canoes. Unlike the rest, who were naked except for breechclouts, he was dressed in what appeared to be goatskin, made in the shape of a pair of breeches or pantaloons, and a shirt of some thinner material, which Andrea judged to be cotton, having already identified a few cotton trees growing along the banks of the river.

Gradually the canoes came nearer. When they were within earshot Dom Alfonso went to the rail where the Negroes could see him. Andrea stood behind him and called out to the blacks in several Moorish dialects. He was hoping some of the words would be understood by the natives, since the chief at least must have had some dealings with the Azanegues to the north or with the caravans who traded from the interior.

A sudden babble of voices broke out among the canoes, but the larger man, evidently the chief, silenced it with a sharp command. Then he called out in the same dialect, "Who are you?"

"White gods from beyond the sea," Andrea told him. "We come in peace."

The blacks held a conference, after which the chief spoke again. "Why do you come?"

"To visit your country and bring you gifts."

Apparently deciding to accept the white men at their word, the Negroes began to move closer.

"Keep your arms ready," Dom Alfonso warned those in the caravel a little nervously. "But make no move unless they do."

When the first canoe touched the side of the ship a line was tossed to the chief, who came up the side like a monkey climbing a tree and dropped to the deck. He was a magnificent-looking savage, with bright intelligent eyes. Others were climbing over the rail now and soon a dozen or more stood on the deck, studying the white men, their clothing and weapons, with wonder-filled eyes.

"We come in peace," Andrea repeated in the same Moorish dialect. "This is our leader, Dom Alfonso Lancarote."

The Negro leader frowned, apparently not understanding the meaning of the name.

"Chief!" Andrea repeated, pointing to Dom Alfonso. When that did not register, he tried the word for king.

The Negro chieftain nodded. "Budomel," he announced. "King of Jaloffs. We come in peace."

Dom Alfonso ordered gifts distributed, jewelry, bric-a-brac, and pieces of cloth over which the natives exclaimed in wonder. Apparently they were able to spin and weave the cotton grown upon the trees only into narrow strips of cloth, no more than a hand's breadth in width, for Budomel's shirt was sewn from such strips. The broad bolt of cloth from which Dom Alfonso cut the pieces for gifts seemed to excite their curiosity more than anything else.

"Are you Moors?" Budomel inquired. "Your skin is whiter than the Moors we know."

"We are Christians," Andrea told him. "From a land far away, the land of Portugal."

"Christians." Budomel tried the word but had trouble with it. "Portugal." Then he added, "Mohammed, prophet."

"They seem to follow the religion of Islam," Andrea told Dom Alfonso. "At least he knows of Mohammed."

Some of the blacks were examining the weapons of the white men, particularly the arbalests, which they seemed to recognize as having at least some resemblance to their own bows. The arrows they carried were made of slender wattles. They had no feathers, however, and were tipped with small spikes of iron stained a dark brown with what Andrea judged to be a poison.

Budomel pointed to one of the crossbows. "Does it shoot?" he asked, and Andrea relayed the message to Dom Alfonso.

"Garcia!" Dom Alfonso called to a soldier who was particularly skilled with the crossbow. "Give them an example of your skill."

Garcia stepped to the rail and looked for a target. A large bird was floating on the surface of the stream some twenty paces or so away. Setting the stock of his arbalest against the deck, he began to crank the gaffle, also known as the *crie* or *crane-quin*. With the use of stronger and stronger bows for arbalests, and now a curved band of steel itself, a man could no longer spring them at all by hand. Powerful devices were needed to bend the bow, and the gaffle was one of these, working on the principle of the rack and pinion, operating in a sort of gear case. With it a tremendous force could be placed behind the projectile.

With his weapon cocked and a steel bolt in the slotted stock, Garcia raised it to sight at the bird. The Negroes jumped at the sharp twang of the bow and cried out when the bird squawked and tried to rise from the water, only to fall back, obviously mortally wounded.

Dom Alfonso turned to Budomel, expecting him to be very much impressed by what he had seen. But the chief spoke sharply to one of his own men, who set an arrow into his bow and stepped to the rail. He called down to one of the blacks who had remained in the canoes and this man tossed overboard a piece of meat. When a fish as long as a man's arm rose to seize it, the bowman released his arrow, hardly appearing to put any force behind it at all.

The arrow struck the fish in the back, penetrating the flesh no more than the length of the point. Yet the fish gave only a few convulsive spasms before it turned to float, belly up and quite dead on the water. One of the Negroes in the canoe seized the arrow shaft as the fish floated by and tossed both to Budomel with a powerful overhand movement. The chief wrenched the arrow from the fish's back without effort and handed it to Dom Alfonso. Obviously the fish had died from the poison on the arrow and not from the small wound.

A murmur of astonishment went up from the white men. Nothing the blacks could have done would have demonstrated more effectively the dangers surrounding the two ships and their company here in a land never before explored by white men.

"Tell him we wish to buy gold and slaves," Dom Alfonso said hastily, "as soon as possible."

Andrea translated to Budomel, who listened carefully, then spoke in the Moorish dialect. "A war party is raiding a neighboring city now," Andrea translated. "He says there will be many slaves and he will sell them to you. But he has only a little gold."

"What does he wish in return?"

Andrea held a brief conversation with Budomel. "He says that you have many things he does not have. He will decide later what the slaves will cost you. But he does want a cuirass like yours and a hat of metal for his head."

Dom Alfonso ordered one of the soldiers to bring out a cuirass and helmet, which he gave to Budomel. The chief was much pleased with the gift and spoke at some length, making clear that he would be deeply offended if the white gods did not visit his village that evening and partake of a feast to show his appreciation. To this Dom Alfonso had little choice except to agree, especially with the memory of the way the fish had died fresh in their minds.

The blacks departed, Budomel proudly wearing the cuirass and helmet. When they were gone, Dom Alfonso wiped the sweat from his brow. "The chief seems a fine enough man," he said, somewhat doubtfully. "We should do well here, if we do not sicken from the heat."

Shortly before dark Dom Alfonso, the *fidalgos* of his

immediate retinue, Andrea Bianco, and half the soldiers, went ashore for the celebration Budomel had prepared for them. The captains remained on the ships and were cautioned to be on the alert, in case an attempt was made to capture the vessels and thus leave those on the shore helpless. The bombards were loaded and trained on the Negro village, as a further argument in case of trouble.

Budomel and his people appeared friendly enough, however. The village was composed of reed huts, forty or fifty of them grouped in the form of a circle and surrounded by a hedge that served also as a sort of palisade. Each of the houses had a private court, which likewise was enclosed with a hedge. The chief proudly presented six buxom black women as his wives. Each wife had several young girls as attendants who must also serve the chief as his fancy dictated, so he actually had a considerable harem. This was quite in accord with his religion, a debased form of the Islamic faith.

Budomel, they learned, was an important man, ruling over a half dozen such villages, each numbering about five hundred people. A group of nobles were always in attendance upon him. These owed none of their rank to wealth, which was communally owned in the person of the chief, holding rank and position only as advisers of the ruler.

Among his own people Budomel maintained a great haughtiness of manner, and commoners could approach him only with considerable ceremony. Between the entrance to his palace—if it could be called such—and the throne room were several enclosed courts. A petitioner, unless of very high rank, must progress from court to court until he reached the royal person, making obeisance as he entered each in turn.

When approaching the royal seat petitioners were obliged to go down on their knees, with their foreheads in the dirt, quite naked and throwing sand upon their backs to show their own unworthiness. Slowly then they could approach the King, still on their knees and rubbing their faces in the dirt, to a distance of two paces from the royal person. Here each made his petition and was summarily dealt with, usually in no more than a few words. As Martin Vasques observed wryly, God himself could not have demanded and received more reverence if He came to earth.

The actual feast brought no dish more exotic than goat's flesh roasted over open coals and eaten half raw. There was one plant or vegetable, which Andrea was told came from the fruit of a great tree that grew near the riverbank. He saw one of them later and estimated that it was at least twenty paces in circumference, although not very tall. From the bark of the tree the blacks obtained fibers which they twisted into strong cords that also burned with a hot flame. The fruit was gourdlike in shape, with a wry greenish taste, and they were told that the seeds, which were as large as walnuts, could be dried and eaten like nuts.

As the feast continued, the natives drank freely of a thick beer made, they said, from the seeds of still another plant. Andrea could learn nothing about the poison used on the arrows, save that it had no effect upon humans when the meat was cooked and eaten. Evidently the blacks considered the poison an important secret, for at the mention of it they suddenly became silent.

Budomel stated that the river arose many days' journey in the interior, but he did not think it was the western Nile. He traded with Arab caravans and had heard them speak of another and far greater river to the south, which was said to begin in a large lake. Nor did he know whether there was a water passage around Africa, since the blacks rarely went beyond the mouth of their own river in the canoes they used for transportation.

XI

A week after their arrival at the river Sanaga the effects of the heat were becoming more and more apparent as the white men sickened rapidly with an odd sort of a fever. They had no physician with either of the caravels, so Andrea and Dom Alfonso dosed the sick as best they could, but with little effect. When another three days passed and half the men were shaking and sweating with the agues of the strange fever, Andrea suggested to Dom Alfonso that they leave the country of Guinea and head for Lagos, hoping the sea air would drive out the strange malady. Lancarote, however, did not receive this suggestion with favor. "Budomel has promised to sell us a hundred black slaves," he objected. "Would you have us leave a fortune like that behind?"

"It's better than leaving half the crew here dead," Andrea warned.

The shipowner shrugged. "It is only a little fever from the heat. No one has died from it yet."

Andrea decided to appeal to the shipowner's fear for his own welfare. "Our medicines have no effect on this plague," he said. "It is a wonder you haven't succumbed to it yourself."

Reminded of a personal threat, Dom Alfonso's manner changed as Andrea had hoped it would. "I will speak to Budomel today," he promised. "Perhaps he has further news of the slaves."

Lancarote came back several hours later from a visit to the village. His face was beaming. "The chief had word of a victory over another village three days ago," he reported. "A hundred or more slaves will be here tomorrow. We can sail as soon as they are aboard."

"What pay has he decided to ask?"

"He says the Arab caravan drivers demand either gold or slaves for salt or other goods, so he insists on one or the other."

"We are low on salt," Andrea said. "I hope you have plenty of gold."

Lancarote smiled thinly. "Your job is to navigate the ship, Senhor Bianco. Let me worry about paying Budomel."

The slaves were brought aboard the next day, fifty to each vessel, men, women, and children with ebony black skins and the cowed look of those who have chosen servitude only in preference to death. The crews of the caravels had been busy since Dom Alfonso had learned of the coming of the slaves, filling casks with water and loading all the fresh food they could find room for on the ships. Budomel came aboard with the last batch of captives to receive his pay.

Dom Alfonso had not revealed his plan of payment, but Andrea could not help noting that all the soldiers not bedded by the fever were fully armed and alert. Lancarote himself was in full armor, as were the *fidalgos,* when he met Budomel on the deck.

The tide was setting out with a strong current and only one anchor held each of the caravels in the stream.

These were attached to ropes which could be cut quickly, letting the vessels sail for the mouth of the river and the open sea in a matter of moments. A dozen Negro warriors had come aboard with Budomel and as the last of the captives was brought over the side to be stowed below the deck, the *fidalgos* drew their swords and moved up beside the King's guards, as did the soldiers.

Martin Vasques came over to where Andrea was waiting to interpret during the bargaining. "This does not concern you, Senhor Andrea," he said in a whisper. "Take no part in it."

"Is there going to be trouble?"

"Perhaps. Dom Alfonso loves gold; he doesn't intend to pay it out."

"He already has a fortune in slaves here," Andrea protested. "Even after paying Budomel."

The old soldier grinned. "And a greater one, if he pays nothing."

Andrea surveyed the situation thoughtfully. At least fifty of the native canoes were floating on the current around the two vessels, with several warriors in each of them. If Budomel chose to fight, Dom Alfonso's plan to take the slaves without paying for them might prove difficult to put into effect without some loss of life on both sides.

"Senhor Bianco!" Lancarote called. "Come here and translate for me, please."

Andrea made his way to a position beside Dom Alfonso. One look at Budomel's wary eyes told him the leader of the blacks was quite cognizant of what was going on.

"Tell Budomel we are leaving today for our country and we thank him for treating us so well," Dom Alfonso directed.

Andrea translated rapidly. The black chief nodded to show that he understood, then spoke a few words.

"He is ready to be paid for the slaves," Andrea reported.

Dom Alfonso took up several bolts of cotton cloth and handed them to Budomel, who passed them to one of his retinue. He spoke rapidly and Andrea translated the words.

"Chief Budomel thanks you for the cloth. He says give him the gold and he will go."

"Tell him the metal in the cuirass and the morion I gave him is worth more than gold," Dom Alfonso ordered.

Andrea translated, repeating Dom Alfonso's words. A hot fire began to burn in Budomel's eyes, for the Negro was no fool and knew that the breastplate and helmet were really made of iron. He spoke so rapidly that Andrea had trouble translating. Even without translation, however, the import of what he said was obvious. The white men were thieves and were trying to steal the slaves.

Andrea answered without stopping to translate, for he was sure now that this type of insult was what Dom Alfonso wanted, giving him an excuse to seize Budomel and his warriors.

"What are you saying?" Dom Alfonso demanded suspiciously.

"I am trying to convince him of the worth of the morion and cuirass," Andrea said, and went on speaking to Budomel. "If you fight us, many of you will be killed, and we will still take the slaves."

He saw a look of calculation in Budomel's eyes but was not sure the black King would give in so easily. After a moment Budomel spoke a guttural command to his guard and they began to climb over the rail and descend the ropes leading down to the canoes. He spoke again and Andrea translated his words. "King Budomel says they will go now, but the next time you must bring gold."

Dom Alfonso nodded eagerly, pleased to be getting off so easily. "Tell him we will—and more cloth and armor for his nobles."

The guards had scrambled down the ropes to the waiting canoes now, and Captain Ugo passed the order to raise the anchor, with tackle slung for that purpose from the yardarm. In the hold of the ship the captives set up a sudden wailing as they realized the meaning of these preparations for departure.

Andrea was watching Budomel closely. The danger was not yet past, he was sure, for the glint in the black chief's eyes was certainly no token of submission. As the last of the guards dropped into a canoe, Budomel threw his leg over the rail. Poised there, he spat out a string of curses which Andrea did not even translate. Then seizing the rope he started to drop down to the waiting canoes.

Dom Alfonso moved quickly before Andrea could stop

him if he had tried. With a slash of his sword, he cut through the rope down which Budomel was sliding, and the Negro chief, still holding to the rope, dropped into the water like a stone, weighed down by the metal cuirass and morion he was wearing.

The crew of the *Santa Clara* had already loosened the anchor from the river mud and as the sails were rapidly hauled aloft, the ship began to move downstream with the ebbing tide. The caravel captained by Gomes Pires was also under way, both vessels smashing ruthlessly through the cordon of canoes still surrounding them.

"Get back, senhor." One of the soldiers pushed Andrea from the rail as he knelt beside it with his arbalest. "They are going to fight."

The blacks waiting in the remaining canoes started shouting angrily at this insult to their King. Arrows and spears were already beginning to drop upon the deck as the caravels got under way. A soldier went down with an arrow through his throat, clutching at the shaft even as his eyes bulged horribly and blood began to gurgle from his throat.

On the afterdeck a bombard crashed and the acrid smell of powder smoke made the men on the deck choke. The ball landed in a group of canoes, smashing one and setting up confusion among the others. On the other caravel a second cannon sounded, while the crossbowmen knelt beside the rail steadying their weapons to take aim and dropping the black figures standing up in the canoes with deadly accuracy.

Running to the stern, Andrea looked back to where he had last seen Budomel in time to watch the Guinea King being hauled from the water into a canoe by means of the rope to which he still clung. An arrow, oddly silent without feathers, stuck into the mast and quivered not six inches from Andrea's head. Without armor or weapons, he was a fair prey to the poisoned arrows, so he slipped within the open door of the aftercastle to watch the fight.

It did not last long. Terrified by the thunder of the bombards and the bolts from the arbalests that struck with deadly aim, the blacks were quickly left behind as the caravels gathered speed. Soon they were out of arrow shot and a giant cheer of victory went up from the decks of the ships at the realization that the battle was over.

Since his navigational talents were not needed until they were at sea—Captain Ugo being more capable than he of conning the caravel through the channel by which they had entered the river Sanaga—Andrea busied himself looking after the wounded. One man was dead, the one whose neck had been punctured by the arrow. Another had only a deep flesh wound, but already his body was beginning to jerk with the spasms of approaching death from the arrow poison. There were a few spear wounds, these weapons apparently not having been poisoned. Andrea bandaged them and inspected the blacks, who were packed into the hold so tightly that they barely had room to lie down upon each other. None of these seemed to be in any danger; those badly enough wounded for there to be any doubt whatsoever of survival had apparently been executed by Budomel before the captives were brought to the ship.

They were safely on their way home, having discovered a great river, a new land, and a way to obtain a valuable cargo—at no cost.

XII

By midafternoon the two caravels were clear of the African coast, with the land only a dimly outlined dark shape to the east. A little before sunset Dom Alfonso ordered the *Santa Clara* hove to, and, with Captain Ugo and Andrea, was rowed in a ship's boat to where the other caravel waited. Gomes Pires welcomed them over the side and they retired to the quarters of the captain in the aftercastle.

Pires' crew had fared even better than those aboard the *Santa Clara* during the brief battle. They had lost no men and suffered only a few minor wounds. Like Dom Alfonso, the captain was jubilant at acquiring a shipload of slaves so cheaply.

"Well, Senhor Bianco," he said, as they were served freshly roasted meat and ship's biscuits soaked in wine. "You brought us directly to our two landfalls so far. Can you do the same on the home voyage?"

It was a sobering question. Sailing southward down the African coast had not been much of a problem, for the wind had blown from their backs the greater part of the way. The return trip was a different matter, however.

Caravels sailed but indifferently against the wind, and the long voyage back was in reality hundreds of smaller ones, first west, then east, tacking to keep the ships at an angle to the wind and thus use its propulsive force without being driven backward.

"How long can you go without refilling the water casks?" Andrea asked.

"Perhaps four weeks. With fifty blacks in the hold besides our own crew, we could still be in grave trouble north of Cape Blanco."

"It seems we have two choices then," Andrea said. "One is to sail for Arguim Island and take on food and water there."

"We would be approaching a hostile shore," Gomes Pires warned. "The Azanegues there have no love for us."

"I am mindful of that," Andrea agreed. "And even if we succeeded in getting water and supplies at Arguim Island, there is still the run for the Fortunate Isles, with strong seas against us most of the way."

"A long voyage and a hard one," Captain Ugo agreed gravely. "Epecially with our ships laden heavily and people to water and feed."

"You spoke of another choice," Dom Alfonso said. "What is that?"

"I believe we can reach Lagos more quickly by sailing northwest," Andrea said.

"By way of the Indies?" Gomes Pires cried. "Surely you jest, senhor."

Andrea grinned. "I didn't have in mind going that far." He unrolled a chart he had brought with him from the *Santa Clara* and spread it out on the table. "This map covers the African coast as far as we have come," he explained. "I drew it from maps in the possession of Mestre Jacomé at Villa do Infante and sketched the rest." He put his fingers on a spot well out in the sea west of Portugal where several islands were indicated. "You will see I have drawn in here the location of the Açores which are said to lie about seven hundred leagues from Sagres and the coast of Portugal."

"Certainly you don't propose to visit the Açores on the way home," Dom Alfonso said heavily.

The others laughed, but not Andrea. "It may be advisable if we need food and water. I am not certain as yet."

"Explain yourself, please," Gomes Pires begged. "This sounds fantastic."

"Look closely at the map," Andrea instructed them. "You will see some tiny arrows which I have drawn representing the direction of the winds that prevail most of the time as reported by other voyagers and also as noted by me during this particular one. As you can see, the winds in the area where we are now blow almost directly southwest. In addition, I made observations of the ocean currents on our voyage to Cape Blanco from the Fortunate Isles. I believe a strong current sets in from that area paralleling the coast of Africa and moving southwestward."

"Maria Sanctissima," said the Genoese captain. "That explains why it is so difficult to sail back to Lagos. Not only must a ship go against the wind but also the current."

"Exactly," Andrea agreed. "Now look at the region of the Açores on this map. You can see by the arrows that the prevailing winds blow eastward. In fact, it would almost seem that they flow in a giant circle around a center somewhere in the sea to the west of us. I propose to use these known movements of the wind to bring us home much faster than has ever been done before."

"But suppose the ships are trapped by these winds?" Dom Alfonso protested. "We could be blown in an endless circle until we died of hunger and thirst."

"Not with vessels such as the infante builds," Andrea assured him. "Caravels like this do not sail well directly into the face of the wind; no ship as yet manages to do that. But with a good breeze on either quarter, they make good time."

"Santiago!" exclaimed Gomes Pires. "This is a daring thing you have in mind, Senhor Bianco, but I think a sensible one nevertheless."

"I still see nothing except this imaginary circle of winds Senhor Bianco talks about," Dom Alfonso admitted.

Andrea took a piece of parchment from the table, folding it so as to make a straight edge. "Look here, senhors," he said, laying the edge on the map they were discussing. "If we sail a little to the west of north from this point, we will soon cross the current from the Fortunate Isles and be free if it. The wind should be on our quarter continually and we should make excellent progress."

"How far would we sail in that direction?" Dom Alfonso asked. "I don't like this idea of going away from home to get home."

Gomes Pires laughed. "At sea a straight line is not always the shortest distance between two points, Senhor Lancarote."

"How far?" Dom Alfonso insisted.

"Until the winds blow toward the east," Andrea said. "Probably a little north of the latitude of the island of Madeira."

"How will you be able to tell when we reach the latitude of Madeira unless you go close enough to see it?"

"I will guarantee to locate it for you," Andrea told him confidently. "And the promontory of Sagres as well. There is no chance of our sailing farther north."

"And then?"

"Then we set a course to the east and home with the wind at our backs," Gomes Pires cried. "It is as easy as that."

"It is like this, Senhor Lancarote." Andrea could see that the Portuguese leader, being a landlubber, did not understand these things as quickly as did Gomes Pires. "We will actually be sailing along two legs of a right triangle. The hypotenuse is a direct line from here to Lagos and the shortest way, of course. But because of currents and winds, it is not the best or quickest way for us, so we will sail the other two legs."

"Suppose it does not work out as you say," Lancarote said doubtfully. "If we are overlong at sea, it will go bad with us."

"The Fortunate Isles and also Madeira will be only a few days' sail to the east at all times," Andrea assured him. "I can lead you to either of them without any difficulty."

"Is this the secret method you boasted of?" Gomes Pires asked. "That of locating any parallel of latitude you have visited before?"

"Yes."

"*Sangre di Cristo!* Such a thing will make sailing the seas as easy as riding across the country."

"Not quite." Andrea laughed. "We have still to find a practical way to measure the East-West height when there is no eclipse of the moon."

"You will do it," Pires assured him blithely. "I have the most sublime confidence in you as a navigator and a maker of maps, senhor."

"Then you approve of this idea, Senhor Pires?" Dom Alfonso asked.

"Wholeheartedly."

"And you, Senhor Tremolina?"

"I have confidence in Senhor Bianco," Captain Ugo said. "If he says he can guide me home by the quickest way, I know he will do what he says."

"Then we will follow your plan, Senhor Bianco," Dom Alfonso agreed. "God grant that you are right, or we will all die of hunger and thirst."

"You are making a wise decision, senhor," Gomes Pires told him. "We will undoubtedly be able to save many blacks who would be lost on the long voyage to Lagos."

"I am mindful of that," Dom Alfonso said and added piously, "surely our Blessed Lord will guide us quickly home so we may soon begin teaching these poor heathens the glory of God's word."

Andrea went with Gomes Pires to the stern, where one of the two compasses used in steering was set in its box in front of the steersman. The other was on the afterdeck. They conferred there for a few moments, agreeing upon the course both caravels would follow. Then he and Dom Alfonso and Captain Ugo were rowed back to the *Santa Clara,* whose lights were already beginning to wink into being with the swift falling of darkness in these latitudes. Once they were aboard and the boat had been hoisted onto the deck, the sails were set and the sleek ship moved through the water at a steadily increasing pace.

Far to the north the star Polaris began to wink into light as the darkness grew deeper. The prow of the vessel was pointing a little to the left of the beacon star now. It was somewhat on Andrea's right hand when he took an observation of its angle for his records before the ship began to roll with the long swells brought by the southwest wind that set their sails taut as drumheads.

He could not help feeling a sense of excitement at the thought of the change in the field of navigation and seafaring in general this new course-plotting method of his would make if it proved successful. Nor could he repress a sense of pride in the fact that, having already traveled farther east than any European in his knowledge, he had now sailed farther south than any had recorded doing since the days of the Phoenicians in the service of the navigator Hanno, some two thousand years before.

BOOK FOUR

Voyage to Antillia

I

THE SKIES WERE CLEAR AND THE SUN BRIGHT SOME three and a half weeks later when the *Santa Clara,* its ensign floating proudly in the breeze, sailed into the harbor of Lagos with the *Santa Maria* close behind it and prepared to moor at the quay. They had bowled along at a fast pace under clear skies most of the way, with the winds almost exactly as Andrea had predicted.

At the latitude of Madeira—whick Andrea had determined without difficulty by means of the Al-Kemal—the captains had conferred and decided to take on water and supplies, since both were running a little low, with nearly a hundred people on each ship drawing upon them. A few days' sail directly east had brought them to that beautiful island and their stores had been quickly replenished before sailing on to Lagos.

The captives arrived in much better condition than had been the experience of previous slave ships, which sometimes thrashed about for several months before making enough northing to reach the home port. As many as a third of the human cargo had sickened and died on some expeditions, but with a quick passage, sweet water in the casks, and fresh food, the two caravels suffered very little loss with their valuable cargo.

Packed like cattle below the decks, the blacks might have been a good deal worse off had Andrea not insisted that they be brought on deck for a part of each day while the quarters below decks were scrubbed out with salt water to remove the filth that accumulated so rapidly. Although jealous of any delegation of authority, Dom Alfonso made no objection to these measures, for he could see that the Negroes were far healthier under this sensible regimen. And a healthy black meant a better price in the slave market.

A number of young women were among the captives. These had fared better than the rest, as soon as they learned that a night in the aftercastle, where Dom Alfonso and two of the *fidalgo* officers were quartered, was worth extra food and wine, plus a chance to sleep on the floor when the almost nightly orgy was ended.

Dom Alfonso stood beside Andrea in the bow of the *Santa Clara* while it was being warped to a mooring at the quay of Lagos. Like the others, Andrea was examining the shipping moored in the harbor, but it was João Gonçalves who first voiced the news they were all seeking to learn.

"Por los entrados!" he exclaimed. "You and your methods of navigation have triumphed indeed, Senhor Bianco. The other caravels have not yet arrived."

Andrea was searching eagerly the small sea of faces uplifted in welcome to the decks of the caravel and the arriving heroes. Finally he saw the two he was seeking. Fra Mauro, plump and red-faced as ever, was squinting up, his tonsured head already red from the sun. Beside him stood the slight, but always graceful figure of Dona Leonor, the sunlight bright on her dark hair only partially hidden by a tall comb and lace mantilla.

Andrea felt his heart suddenly quicken at her loveliness. Busy as he had been since that evening on the sand cliffs of Sagres when he had shown her how to use the Al-Kemal and again in the garden after Fra Mauro had left them when she had kissed him, he'd had little time for any conscious thought of Leonor or loneliness for her. But now he realized how much he had really missed her slim grace and beauty and her quick penetrating mind.

Crowding out everything else, however, was the memory of her lips when she'd kissed him the night before he sailed. He could still remember the softness and freshness of her mouth upon his own, like the touch of a fragrant flower petal.

Could a man love two women, he wondered? Particularly two such utterly different people as Angelita and Dona Leonor?

It was a troubling thought, but this was no day to be troubled. In the joy of arrival and the welcome awaiting them, only one note of discord and unhappiness was apparent, the low animal-like moaning of the slaves shut away in the waist of the ship, a tragic obbligato which had never completely ceased since their departure from the river Sanaga.

Beside Dona Leonor and Fra Mauro stood Eric

Vallarte, his red head and broad shoulders towering above the crowd, just as the new caravel—whose building he had been supervising when Andrea had sailed—towered over other shipping in the harbor. Andrea saw at a glance that the vessel was almost ready for sailing; the workmen had obviously stopped halfway in the process of rigging the giant square sail on the mainmast to join the welcoming crowd. It would no doubt be departing soon, unless for some reason the plans of Senhor Bartholomeu had changed.

Farther on in the crowd, Andrea saw the almost gnome-like figure of Mestre Jacomé, his bright intelligent eyes watching the vessel as it was drawn to the mooring by lines thrown down from the caravel to the quay and seized upon by the crowd. He could already savor the pleasure that would be his when he told the old Jewish mapmaker and Prince Henry of the things he had learned: how to take a ship directly to a predetermined landfall over a thousand miles and more of ocean; and how, by using the winds and their prevailing direction of flow, to sail along the two legs of a right triangle and still come in ahead of another ship sailing the conventional route along the hypotenuse. What a fine debate it would be when he defended his conclusions before Mestre Jacomé and the assembly at Villa do Infante and revealed to them the new information he had gathered about the coast of Africa and the region of the Sanaga's mouth, the land of wealth that was Guinea.

With a slight jar the caravel came to rest against the quay and the sailors leaped ashore to lash the hawsers to stout pilings set up for that purpose. The gangplank was quickly secured and Dom Alfonso Lancarote, in full armor and flanked by his two *fidalgo* aides, marched down it amidst the cheers of the crowd. Andrea followed, pushing his way through the happy, laughing people to where Dona Leonor stood with Fra Mauro and Eric Vallarte.

"Madonna Leonor!" he cried, taking both her hands in his own. "Your face was the first I saw in the crowd."

He saw the rich color rise to her cheeks, but the look in her eyes was not the welcome he had expected. In fact, they were misty, as if she were holding back the tears.

"I thank God that you have returned safely, senhor," she said. Then drawing her hands suddenly from him, she turned and almost ran through the crowd.

Andrea stood looking after her with puzzled eyes, while Fra Mauro pumped his hand in welcome and Eric Vallarte gave him a clap on the back that set his teeth to chattering.

"Are you not happy to see your old friends, Senhor Andrea?" Eric demanded.

"Of course I'm happy," he cried, embracing them both. "And I'm happier still that you have not sailed, my Viking friend."

"Another two weeks and we will be gone," Eric told him. "The good friar here is worried about storms, but I tell him such a caravel as we have built this time need fear nothing but the wrath of God himself."

Eric moved on to greet Gomes Pires, whose ship was now moored to the quay. Andrea turned to Fra Mauro. "What happened to Dona Leonor, little brother?" he asked. "The night before I sailed we were good friends. Now she treats me as if I were a leper."

"The thing I have feared for a long time has happened," the friar said gently.

"She is not sick?"

"No. I never saw her in better health."

"What would keep her from being happy to see me back home safely then?"

"She is happy to see you, but the Leonor you once called a child is one no longer," the Franciscan said gravely. "She has fallen in love."

Andrea stared at him in astonishment. "Who is the man?" As far as he had known before he left, Leonor had selected no regular favorite among the young men of Lagos and Villa do Infante, although many admired and sought to court her.

"Can't you guess?"

"Make me no more riddles," Andrea admonished him. "What concern of mine is it if she is dewy-eyed over some strutting jay of a *fidalgo* who is not half good enough for her?"

"It is no strutting *fidalgo* she loves," Fra Mauro told him severely. "But a strutting bird of another sort—a mapmaker."

"A mapmaker?"

"Named Andrea Bianco. Although what she sees in you——"

Andrea seized him by the shoulders of the loose robe, suddenly more excited than he could account for. "Why should she love me?" he demanded. "Have I ever courted her?"

"Not intentionally perhaps."

"And I am ten years older than she."

Fra Mauro shrugged. "Eight would be a nearer figure, but for some reason that only makes a man more attractive to women, particularly a serious-minded girl like Leonor."

"Maria Sanctissima!" Andrea exclaimed not yet comprehending why the knowledge that Leonor loved him should create this tremendous excitement in his breast. He had felt nothing like this before, not even with Angelita in their most intimate moment. This was a great soaring happiness, a sensation of riding on a cloud and looking down at the world below, singing and shouting and cheering for no reason at all, save that he was loved—and, he suddenly realized, loved in return.

He started to go in search of Leonor, but Fra Mauro's grip on his sleeve held him back. "Where are you going?" the Franciscan demanded.

"To find Leonor—and tell her I love her."

"Not so fast," the friar said. "What of the woman in Venice? Do you love her still?"

"I—I don't know. What I feel for Leonor is something entirely different."

"Before you speak to her, you must be certain just how you feel about this other woman," the friar insisted. "Dona Leonor is too fine a girl to have her heart broken."

"You know I wouldn't hurt her," Andrea cried indignantly.

"That is why you must not speak of love to her until you are sure." Fra Mauro was very serious. "And until no other woman has any claim upon you."

"I love Leonor too much ever to make her unhappy," Andrea protested.

"And the other woman?"

He did not answer, for the memories had come flooding back: Angelita's sweet surrender there in the summerhouse before he had sailed for Trebizond, and the consuming flame of passion that had swept them off their feet, tearing away all reserve, all restraint. Even now he could not quell the sudden flame that began to burn deep within his body at the mere memory.

"Your body, at least, still longs for her," Fra Mauro said sadly. "First purge yourself of that desire before you speak to Dona Leonor of love."

II

The next few days were so busy that Andrea had no time to be alone with Leonor. Both ships' companies were greeted warmly by Prince Henry on the day of their arrival, and the following day Andrea appeared before the assembly at Villa do Infante and described the results of the voyage to the men gathered there. He was shrewdly questioned by Mestre Jacomé and some others, but stoutly defended his conclusions, particularly the method of sailing so as to take advantage of the prevailing winds, rather than simply in the direction one wished to go. When it was over, he felt certain that he had considerably improved his position in the eyes of Prince Henry and in the estimation of Mestre Jacomé

Only one aspect of the whole affair still rankled in his memory, the trick played on King Budomel at the river Sanaga. The constant moaning from the slave compound where the blacks had been placed awaiting the arrival of the other ships and the division of the spoils was a constant reminder. Andrea knew his share of the profits would be a substantial one, but even the thought of the money that would be his could not still the proddings of his conscience whenever he passed the slave compound and heard again the mournful wailing of captives.

Andrea sensed that Leonor was avoiding him, but made no attempt to see her until she made the first overture. Nor was his problem simplified by the news Mestre Jacomé gave him one evening while he sat in Fra Mauro's room with the Franciscan and the old mapmaker, drinking wine and talking of the land of Guinea.

"You may remember my promise to write to friends in Venice concerning the circumstances surrounding your being convicted of murder there," Mestre Jacomé said.

"Did you hear something?" Andrea asked eagerly.

"They are making progress; a letter came only a few days ago by a Venetian galley."

"Then my name is not yet cleared?" Andrea's disappointment showed in his face.

Mestre Jacomé shook his head. "To remove a charge of murder placed by so influential a person in Venice as Mattei Bianco is not easy. After all he has the resources of the Medici at his command and exercises considerable influence with the Council of Ten besides."

"I should have known my case was hopeless," Andrea said dejectedly. "Mattei is clever enough to cover his tracks well."

"Don't give up so easily," Mestre Jacomé admonished him. "My friends have obtained a statement from the footman, Vittorio Panimo, who testified against you. He has given a true account before a notary of what happened the night you were attacked, establishing the fact that you were defending yourself when the other man was killed."

"How did they manage that? Panimo swore in court that I stole the money and attacked them without provocation."

Mestre Jacomé smiled. "We Jews control many purse strings, Senhor Andrea. Money will open lips that are tightly closed, money and the reminder of certain—shall we say mistakes?—in one's past life that might be interesting to the police."

"Then with Panimo's testimony I should be able to prove my innocence."

"In time, and with enough money. My friends hope to get statements from your brother's chamberlain, too. They are investigating the loss of the galley now and when they have enough evidence to arrest Mattei Bianco, they believe Dimas Andrede will want to tell the truth—especially since then he need fear his master no longer."

"When will you know more?" Andrea asked impatiently.

"A galley from Venice is due to arrive here next week according to the captain of the one that brought this information. It is commanded by the man who identified you before the assembly when you first came here, Senhor Alvise de Cadamosto. I expect to have more letters then."

Although he was back at Villa do Infante after a successful voyage and much acclaimed as a navigator, Andrea still could not throw off a vague sense of guilt that had troubled him for weeks now. The source he was not able to identify, but it was there nevertheless, an unease that disturbed him even now when he should have been happy. Nor was it helped when he came upon Leonor on the beach one morning, watching the return of the fishing fleets and the clamor of the villagers as they hauled on the ropes to drag the graceful boats with the huge shining eyes painted on their prows upon the shore.

She had been pulling the ropes with the villagers. Her face was flushed and her breathing still quick, making an altogether lovely sight as she leaned against a tree to get her breath.

"Madonna," he said from just behind her, "I have been looking for you."

She stiffened and for a moment he thought she was going to run away. Then the tension went out of her body and she turned to face him. "I come to the beach several times a week to buy fish for the kitchen," she said.

"Then let me carry your purchases." He picked up the basket that stood beside her. "I remember carrying them when I was your slave."

"You have come a long way since then, senhor. Everyone is speaking of your daring and skill in navigating the fleet to Guinea and back."

"I would like to tell you about the voyage, madonna, if you will let me walk with you."

"Why not?" she asked lightly. "Are we not friends?"

"I hope we will always be friends, Leonor." Then he dared to add, "And perhaps—one day—more."

"Oh, what a fine fish!" she cried and went running down the beach to one of the boats. Andrea followed, not sure whether the sight of the fish had taken her mind off what he had said, or whether she had used it as an excuse to break away. He waited while she bargained shrewdly with the fisherman and filled the basket. When it was full they set out across the dunes to the village.

"You would have loved the river Sanaga," he told her. "The banks are like a bright green wall and the birds every color of the rainbow."

"Dom João Gonçalves told me of the 'horse-fish.'" Andrea could not stifle a flash of irritation at the young *fidalgo*, even though he had come to like him on the voyage. Gonçalves, he judged, was almost the same age as Leonor.

"You must have been seeing much of Senhor João."

Dona Leonor laughed. "I do not live in a convent, senhor. Young gentlemen come to call on me at times."

"Why have you been avoiding me then?"

"Avoiding?" She raised her eyebrows. "Why would you think that?"

"The last night before I left, you kissed me."

"Is it not the custom to kiss departing heroes good-by?" she asked demurely.

"Then it meant nothing to you?"

She did not answer, but changed the subject again. "Dom João told me of the fight with King Budomel. It must have been exciting."

"It was treachery," Andrea said shortly. "We took the slaves without paying for them after Budomel had treated us fairly."

"Sometimes I hear them at night, moaning in the compound." She shivered. "Why must we chain them like beasts? They are people like you and me."

"Fra Mauro would tell you we are saving their souls," he reminded her. "And that it is a good thing in the sight of God to make prisoners of them."

"Do you believe that?"

For a moment he did not answer; then he said slowly, "When I look at the blacks I remember a man who was chained for five years to a wooden bench and an oar. And then I wonder how you can save a man's soul by depriving him of his freedom."

"Then you must have felt it too," she said quickly. "The thing their moaning does to you. It makes you feel ashamed of your own people for keeping them shut up like that."

"I have felt it," he admitted, realizing now that she had identified the cause of his depression lately. "But what can I do?"

"People look up to you and admire you for what you have done." She turned to face him and spoke earnestly. "You have been a slave. If you tell them how wrong it is to lock up people like beasts, they might listen."

"Suppose I failed. What would I get for my pains—besides being laughed at?"

"You would know you had done right! That is worth something."

"It is worth much," he agreed soberly. "In fact, that might be the most important reason of all."

They were closer in that moment, he sensed, than at any time since the night on the dunes before he had sailed for the river Sanaga. Holding the basket between them, they walked back to the village while he told her of Cape Blanco and Arguim Island and the lush land of Guinea to which the river Sanaga was only a gateway.

III

The remainder of Dom Alfonso's fleet arrived at Lagos a few days later, no little chagrined at finding the two caravels there ahead of them. They counted themselves lucky to have lost no more than a fourth of the slaves with which they had set out from Arguim Island, having had a hard voyage and a long one.

The day after their arrival all the slaves were herded together on the beach before Lagos so the spoils could be divided among those who had participated in the expedition. Here occurred the most harrowing scene Andrea had ever experienced, one that was to have a tremendous influence upon his life.

Early that morning the slaves, blacks from the Guinea coast, Azanegues from Arguim Island, men, women, children, young girls already pregnant by the *fidalgos* and sailors of the expedition—in all, a group of some three hundred people—were herded together on the sands. Some were almost white, well proportioned, and even handsome. Others were of varied hues that characterize the mulatto. Those from the land of Guinea were so black that their skins looked almost like velvet.

Each member of the expedition who was to share in the spoils took up a position in a rough circle around the massed slaves, while buyers waited at one side for the sale that would follow the division. Prince Henry was there astride a tall white horse. His face was stern, as if he were steeling himself against any sorrow or pity for the blacks and the Moors.

The moaning of the captives increased in volume with

the realization that some new aspect of their fate was about to take place. Some kept their heads low, while tears streamed down their cheeks. Others sobbed and moaned, clinging to each other for reassurance that they were not summarily to be killed. A few raised their faces to heaven, crying out loudly in a tongue that none of the whites knew, as if begging help from God. Still others struck their faces and their bodies with their hands or threw themselves prostrate on the ground before their captors, mutely begging for mercy.

Dom Alfonso Lancarote was on horseback beside Prince Henry. "A fifth of all captives to the infante," he shouted to the men who were to superintend the division of the slaves. "And mind you, select stout men and pregnant young women. Let no one say our prince's share was not heaped up and running over."

The *fidalgos*, with the help of the soldiers and the crew of the vessels, went into the crowd, separating out the stoutest among the men and young women with strong bodies and wide loins that would fit them well for childbearing. In so doing, they often divided families, which caused the wailing to rise in volume. They paid no attention, however, ruthlessly pulling out the forty-odd slaves that constituted the prince's share.

With Prince Henry's quota taken care of, the share going to Dom Alfonso was now cut out of the milling herd of human flesh, each captive being jerked out of the group as his or her lot fell. Some of the women tried to run to their families, or go with their children. These the *fidalgos* dragged back, while the sailors acted as overseers, using long whips to discourage any who tried to escape separation from their loved ones.

Andrea was thoroughly sickened long before the time came to select his share of the four slaves assigned to him; two were obviously inferior, but he made no objection.

"Shall I keep yours in my slave pens for you, Senhor Bianco?" Dom Alfonso called to him. "Or will you sell them now?"

Andrea was watching Leonor, who stood at the edge of the crowd with Fra Mauro. She was watching the scene with horror-filled eyes and, perhaps because of his own sense of guilt, it seemed that her gaze was upon him alone. Perhaps because his own conscience was sorely troubled by what was going on, he could almost believe she was pleading silently with him to speak up in protest against this inhuman thing, as she had on the evening when he'd carried her basket back from the beach.

"You would at least know that you had done right," she'd said, and remembering her words now, as he watched the human cattle being herded about with whips, Andrea came to a decision he'd been evading ever since they arrived in Lagos.

"What say you, Senhor Bianco?" Lancarote asked a little impatiently.

Andrea spoke then, but not to Dom Alfonso. "Fra Mauro," he called. "Come over here, please."

The pudgy friar strode across the open space to where Andrea stood, his robe flapping in the breeze. "What do you wish, my son?" he asked.

"Take these slaves to the Franciscan convent," Andrea directed. "See that they are made legally free and instructed in our faith, so they may be sent back to tell their people of it."

Dom Alfonso spurred his horse over to where Andrea stood with the friar. His thin lips were white with fury. "You cannot give blacks their freedom," he snapped. "If you don't want them, they will be divided among the rest of us."

Andrea's voice was like a whiplash. "Our agreement was a hundredth part of the proceeds of this expedition as my share, senhor," he said. "You have already assigned these slaves to me, they are mine to do with as I please."

"Not to set free." Dom Alfonso turned to the *fidalgos*. "Take these people and put them with the others," he ordered. "Senhor Bianco has refused to accept them, so he gets nothing."

"A moment, Dom Alfonso." Prince Henry's voice stopped Andrea as he started forward angrily, fully intending to drag Lancarote from his horse. "By what law do you take away a man's property?"

Dom Alfonso whirled angrily. But at the stern look in the infante's eyes, he seemed to lose some of his assurance. "He has refused to accept his share," he spluttered.

"I did not refuse," Andrea said quickly. "I accepted the slaves assigned to me. They are now my property and I can free them if I wish. Nobody is the loser but myself."

"Senhor Bianco is within his rights," Prince Henry ruled.

"The law gives him the right to do anything he wishes with his property."

Dom Alfonso bit his lip in exasperation. "I will buy them then," he offered. "Surely Senhor Bianco is not such a fool as to spurn gold."

"The slaves are no longer mine," Andrea said. "I have already given them their freedom and the good brothers of St. Francis have charge of them now."

"So be it," said Prince Henry. "Proceed, please, Dom Alfonso."

To Andrea's surprise, he found Leonor at his side. Her eyes were shining and her cheeks were flushed with excitement.

"That was a wonderful thing you did," she cried. "I will help you and Fra Mauro take them to the convent."

Even the blacks sensed that some piece of good fortune had come to them, although they could have no real understanding of what had happened. They made no objection when Andrea, with the friar and Leonor, led them to the small Franciscan priory that stood between Villa do Infante and Lagos. There he explained to the prior his desire to have the Negroes instructed, not only in the Catholic faith, but also in other things which could be of use to their people on the river Sanaga. That Prince Henry would send them back home later, he did not doubt for a moment, remembering the way the infante had supported his legal right to free the slaves.

"I was proud of you today," Leonor said warmly as they were riding back to Villa do Infante in the carriage Dom Bartholomeu sent for them. "Very proud."

"And I, too," said Fra Mauro.

Andrea grinned wryly. "For a man who's just given away his entire fortune, I feel strangely good myself. Tomorrow when I empty my purse and find nothing comes out, I will probably kick myself for being a fool."

"God will reward you for seeing that His truth will be made known to the blacks," the friar assured him. "I am sure of that."

IV

The galley commanded by Alvise de Cadamosto arrived from Venice a few days later. The Venetian sought out Andrea as soon as he had paid his respects to the infante and handed him a letter. The hint of Angelita's perfume still lingered upon the thin parchment.

> *Andrea Carissimo* (she wrote),
> *Signor Cadamosto has brought me the wonderful news that you are still alive after all this time. I beg you to return at once to Venice and claim everything that is rightfully yours.*

Andrea could hardly doubt her meaning. Angelita had been his, in every sense of the word, before he had sailed. The words and the tone of the letter could only mean that she was willing to be his again.

> *It was a terrible thing Mattei did* (he read on), *but believe me you will forget all that, and the years you spent as a slave, when you are in my arms. Signor Cadamosto will be returning soon to Venice with his galley and I shall be heartbroken if you are not with him, carissimo mio. Let nothing stop you from flying to*
>
> > *Your beloved,*
> > *Angelita*

Andrea looked up from the letter to the smiling dark face of the Venetian shipmaster. "I am happy to be the bearer of good tidings, Signor Bianco," Cadamosto said.

"You know what this letter says then?"

"The Signora gave it to me with her own hands, sealed as it was when you opened it. But were the happiness I saw in her eyes there because of me, I would be literally transported with joy—as you are no doubt now."

"What about my brother Mattei?"

"Dona Angelita is related to the Medici, signor. When they learned the truth from her I imagine they took steps to boot him out."

"Has he been punished?"

"I left Venice before I could learn more. But Venetian justice is well known. The punishment will surely fit the crime."

Had he been less excited, Andrea might have paused to reflect upon the fact that—as he well knew—Venetian justice was often far from perfect. But he could think of nothing now except the promise in Angelita's letter. "It seems I need only to appear and petition the Council of Ten to have the sentence against me canceled?" he said happily.

"I have little knowledge of legal matters," Cadamosto admitted. "Still, if you put enough gold in the right places, almost anything can be accomplished."

Andrea's face sobered. "I possess only the clothes I stand in," he admitted.

"Surely after your great success on the voyage to Guinea, you can easily negotiate a loan."

"Prince Henry might let me have what I need." Andrea's face brightened. "Or Dom Bartholomeu."

"Then it is settled. I will call here for you on my return voyage from London."

"How long will that be?"

Cadamosto shrugged. "Depending upon the winds— perhaps a month."

"I should know what I am going to do by then," Andrea agreed.

Cadamosto clapped him on the back jovially. "With so beautiful a lady waiting for me in Venice, I know what my decision would be. And yours will be the same."

"By the way," Andrea said. "Do you know a Dom Gil Vicente, a kinsman of Dom Alfonso Lancarote's from Florence?"

Cadamosto shook his head. "I do not remember the name. Why?"

"He tried to kill me on the voyage to Guinea and steal my navigation secret."

"*Eccolo!* How did he know of it?"

"Vicente confessed that my brother Mattei was in Florence when you arrived—at the Medici establishment there. He read your report and the two of them conspired to destroy me and get the device."

Cadamosto's face was grave. "Signor Mattei was in Florence when I arrived, but I did not talk to him. I am sorry this occurred, Signor Bianco, very sorry indeed, but I warned you that I would have to report your discovery to my employers. Now it seems I was almost responsible for your death."

Andrea grinned. "You may have unwittingly done me a favor, Signor Cadamosto. The warning was sharp enough to make me more vigilant in the future. And you did a greater favor in bringing me this letter, so I am actually in your debt."

Cadamosto sailed that afternoon. The next day Andrea received a summons to the modest house that served the infante as a palace at Villa do Infante. Mestre Jacomé was there, in addition to the prince, with Eric Vallarte and Dom Bartholomeu di Perestrello. After the usual courteous greetings had been exchanged, Mestre Jacomé took charge.

"We have a matter of some importance to lay before you, Senhor Andrea," the old mapmaker said. "Since all of us are concerned with it, I took the liberty of inviting these other gentlemen to be present."

"Have you received more information from your friends in Venice?" Andrea asked quickly.

"They report progress. Everyone concerned agrees that it will be only a little time now until they have enough evidence to clear your name."

"Just yesterday I had a letter from someone in Venice," Andrea said. "It stated that the matter was already cleared up and my brother had been arrested."

Mestre Jacomé looked surprised. "My information said nothing of his arrest. Are you sure you are right, senhor?"

"It was from someone I—I consider fully trustworthy," Andrea said. "But I remember now that the letter only implied that he had been arrested. The person who wrote it urged me to return to Venice at once and clear my name."

"Do you plan to go?" Prince Henry asked.

Andrea grinned wryly. "I am penniless, milord, and gold will be necessary to pay for my passage and employ an advocate to draw up a petition to the Council of Ten."

"To say nothing of a little bribery along the way," Mestre Jacomé added dryly. "Such things are not accomplished without something to smooth the path, senhor."

"That, too, has worried me," Andrea admitted.

"I will be glad to ...
name," Prince Henry o...

"Thank you, milord," ...
cide to accompany Senhor ...
when his galley touches here ag...
cept your generosity. You may be ...
very moment I regain my rightful po...

"I have no doubt of that," the in...
propose to you... the rightness of something I ...
added, "Your generous act in fr... ...to
to sail soon for the Açores on a voyage of colonization. In
fact all plans had been made—until you returned from
the river Sanaga."

He paused for a moment, then continued. "Dom Alfonso
Lancarote is already planning a second voyage to Guinea
to seek another cargo of slaves and others will surely follow. In fact, Mestre Jacomé and I are convinced now that
the water route around Africa will only be found by ships
sailing for no other purpose than exploration. Others will
always be tempted to stop short of that goal, if they can
obtain a valuable cargo of slaves as easily as you did on
the river Sanaga."

"I had trouble persuading Dom Alfonso to sail beyond
Arguim Island after we captured the Moors. He only
agreed after I reminded him how much more the slaves
from Guinea are worth."

"Not that I blame Dom Alfonso, and the other shipmasters who sail in my service, for making a profit," Prince
Henry said. "After all, they put a great deal of money into
preparations for the voyages and are entitled to a just reward. But so long as the taking of slaves is a major consideration, I don't think our ships will sail as far southward as it is possible for them to go."

"I quite agree," Andrea said.

"Nor do I believe from what you have described that
the river Sanaga is the western Nile."

"King Budomel described to me a much larger river to
the south," Andrea told him. "It is said to arise in a large
lake."

"I propose to send the new caravel, captained by Senhor
Vallarte here, on a voyage wholly of exploration. He will
seek the mouth of the western Nile south of the river
Sanaga, of course, but his main purpose will be to try

...uthern tip of Africa—if a way ex-
And we all agree that only one man in
...qualified to navigate such an expedition. His
...Andrea Bianco."

Andrea was more moved by the simple statement than
he had been by any of the praise which had come to him
since his return to Villa do Infante. If Prince Henry and
Mestre Jacomé believed him capable of such ...ing to
meant that they reposed the highest confi...
And the confidence of men like this
be regarded lightly.

"The caravel is ready and can sail in a week," Mestre
Jacomé said. "You will not be delaying your return to
Venice more than a few months at the most if you go with
it."

"Meanwhile I will draw up all the facts concerning you
in a petition to the Holy Father in Rome," Prince Henry
added. "Your own petition to the Council of Ten in Venice
for restitution of your property and your fortunes there
will be tremendously enhanced by a request for special
consideration from the Vatican."

Andrea did not answer at once and Dom Bartholomeu
spoke, "You know, of course, Senhor Bianco," he said,
"that those who sail in the service of our prince are always
handsomely rewarded."

"Believe me, milord, and senhors," Andrea said, "I was
only marveling at my own good fortune since the first time
I saw a vessel in the service of Your Highness, and not
any question of reward. To serve you and to search for a
route to the Indies is reward enough."

"Then you accept?"

"Gladly, milord. You have honored me more than I can
tell you."

There was a round of pleased congratulations, after
which they got down to the details of the coming voyage.
"Mestre Jacomé and I have decided to concentrate entirely on the African coast for the time being," Prince
Henry explained. "That means we must make better use
of the Canary Islands as an intermediate base of operations. Fortunately I have persuaded our good right hand
here, Dom Bartholomeu, to become governor of our possessions there. He will sail with you in the new caravel
and as soon as possible establish sawmills, cut timbers for
the repair of ships, and arrange for other supplies. With

a base of operations as far south as the Fortunate Isles, our search for a water route to India should be much expedited."

"You may need another base farther south later," Andrea suggested. "Arguim Island would be an excellent situation."

"That will probably be our next project," the infante agreed. "Actually this voyage may well be one of the most important ever made, opening up a whole new world never before visited by white men."

With which sentiment Andrea found himself in hearty agreement, as he celebrated the new venture with Eric Vallarte that evening over a bottle of wine. Neither, of course, had any way of knowing just how prophetic Prince Henry's words really were, or how much each of them would be concerned.

V

On the first day of June the caravel *Infante Henrique* set sail from Lagos for the isle of Gomera in the Canary Islands, where Senhor Bartholomeu di Perestrello would take up his new duties as captain general. As the port of call for vessels sailing for the African coast, San Sebastián, the main town on the island, overlooked a fine roadstead at the mouth of a swift-flowing river. Here, according to Prince Henry's plan, Dom Bartholomeu was to establish lumber- and shipyards and superintend the laying up of food and other stores for ships calling there on voyages to and from the Guinea coast and the unexplored portions of the world to the south and east.

The route to the Canaries was thoroughly mapped, and the courses to be sailed in order to reach them clearly prescribed from the experience of previous voyages, so Andrea was not busy on the first leg of the trip. Dom Bartholomeu and Dona Leonor had the use of the aftercastle or *toldilla* to themselves. A partition separated it into two small cabins, affording a modicum of privacy. The rest of the company, including Andrea and Fra Mauro, slept on deck, as did the crew and Eric Vallarte, the shipmaster.

Andrea still followed the policy of making his observations of the North Star with the Al-Kemal in the early hours of the morning. On the second day out of Lagos he was surprised, as he perched against the rail to steady himself while he moved the Al-Kemal back and forth, to hear a light footfall behind him. He turned quickly, thinking that someone was trying to learn the secret, but found only Leonor standing there.

"Madonna," he said. "You should be asleep."

"I was restless. Will you let me study the stars with you so I can practice using the Al-Kemal you gave me?"

"Of course." He looked around quickly to make sure that no one on the deck was watching. As had been his practice on the voyage to Guinea, he was making his observations from the elevated foredeck of the ship. Hidden by the mainsail from the helmsmen and the watch who usually gathered around the binnacle where the great tiller that controlled the rudder came through a break in the afterdeck, there was little chance of his being closely observed here.

Dona Leonor turned aside momentarily and he saw her reach quickly into the bosom of her dress and draw out the small wooden plate with its attached cord. "I've kept it hidden," she told him, "as you told me to do."

"Do you remember how to find Polaris?"

She searched the northern sky with her eyes. "I can see the Great Bear and the 'pointers,'" she said in a whisper. "Yes, there it is." She held up the Al-Kemal in her left hand and moved it back and forth for a moment before fixing it. "That should be it," she said then. "Don't you think so?"

He stood behind her and looked over her shoulder. "The angle looks about right," he continued. "Now, if you wanted to return to this spot, all you would need to do is tie a knot in the string."

"Why do you suppose no one ever thought of such a simple thing before?"

"Perhaps because it is so simple. I imagine many people had noticed that a needle rubbed with loadstone would turn to the north before someone thought of using it to guide ships."

"Is it true that the people of China knew of the Genoese Needle a long time ago?"

"Perhaps for a thousand years," he agreed. "They always had a little carriage in their caravans. By watching the compass needle, a man inside it kept an arrow on top pointing to the south. The caravan leaders guided themselves across the plains by looking at the arrow."

"I wish I were a man!" she cried.

"Why would anyone as lovely as you want to be a man, madonna?"

"I would like to be the one to discover the route to India for the infante."

"Who wouldn't?"

She turned to face him. "Why don't you?"

Andrea was a little taken aback by the bluntness of her question. "Perhaps I may, in time."

"The time is now!" she cried. "I heard Fra Mauro and Mestre Jacomé talking the other day. Some shipmasters in Genoa and Florence are thinking of sailing westward around the world to India. If our prince's ships fail to find a route eastward around Africa soon, the others may reach India that way."

"Have no fear, madonna," he assured her. "The distance around the world is much greater than those people think. They are thinking in terms of the world described by Ptolemy. It is much smaller than the real one we are sailing tonight."

"But India does lie to the west, doesn't it?"

"Of course, since the earth is a sphere. But the way around Africa is certain to be shorter. Besides, there's some sort of a land barrier out there to the west, at least in the northern latitudes."

"Do you mean the voyages to the Green Land and the Wine Land?"

"Those—and others."

"Eric has told me about them. The Vikings were great heroes to sail so far from home."

The idea that she had spent more time with Eric than she had with him was not particularly palatable. "I could tell great tales if I wanted to," he said, a little stiffly.

"About the beautiful women of the East?" she teased. "It must have been very exciting."

"There is nothing exciting about being a slave, madonna."

"Forgive me," she said quickly and there was no lightness in her voice now. "You gave up a lot of gold when you freed your share of the slaves and didn't go with Dom

Alfonso on another voyage to Guinea. I know what it meant to you after being a slave."

"The most important thing to me right now is knowing I can return to Venice at the end of this voyage and clear my name," he said.

She turned to look back across the deck, where the crew on watch were shaking dice in a small circle of light cast on the deck by the binnacle lamp. "Then it is really true?" she said in a small voice.

"What?"

"That your brother is in prison. . . . And his wife will soon be free to marry you?"

He did not answer at once because he didn't know what to say. He could not deny the truth of what she had said, for that was substantially what Angelita had written. It did not occur to him that Leonor would naturally take his silence for confirmation, until she suddenly turned and, ducking under the mainsail, ran across the deck to the *toldilla* and her cabin.

"Madonna! Wait!" he called after her, but she either did not hear or did not want to. Before he could speak again, the door of the *toldilla* had slammed shut, leaving him to berate himself for not telling her why he was really going to Venice—namely to see Angelita again and prove that the attraction she had for him was something far different from the tender emotion he felt toward Leonor.

As Andrea crossed the deck to his pallet, Eric Vallarte rolled over and sat up, rubbing his eyes. Getting to his feet he went to the rail and dropped overboard one of the buckets on a long line by which water for washing was drawn up over the side. Pulling up a bucketful he emptied it over his head at the rail, stripping the water away from his hair and his red beard with strong sturdy fingers. The moonlight was almost as bright as day and Eric was a majestic figure against the background of the ship and the sea.

"Still determined to keep your navigation trick a secret?" the shipmaster asked.

Andrea flushed a little. He was fond of the Norseman, but Eric Vallarte's speech often had a directness, a penetrating quality that could make a man feel small by pricking his deepest conscience.

"Until my fortune is made," he agreed a little shortly.

"That will come soon enough to a fellow as handsome

as you are." Eric's eyes were fixed upon a cluster of
bubbles and foam thrust aside by the prow of the caravel.
His gaze followed them back until they passed the stern.
"We're making good time," he said then. "A little faster
than yesterday, if anything."

When it came to estimating the speed of the vessel,
judging by the passing of bits of foam or even small
pieces of wood thrown overboard, Andrea had long since
learned that any experienced sailor was far more accomplished than he. With the wind blowing steadily from one
source most of the time as it was now, and the ship rarely
requiring a change in the set of its sails or the course
followed by the steersman at the tiller, such calculations
were not difficult.

Under other conditions, however, particularly when
beating back and forth on alternate tacks against the
wind, the estimation of forward progress was far more
difficult and considerably less accurate. Then shipmasters
had to fall back upon traverse tables using the principles
of plane geometry and trigonometry in order to calculate,
from the direction and the speed of each tack, the actual
number of miles traveled in the direction they really
wanted the ship to go. Even there, however, some sort of
a sixth sense seemed to be more valuable to an experienced captain than anything else. More than once, when
working with the traverse tables, Andrea had seen his
calculations confirmed by canny ship captains like Eric
and Ugo Tremolina, who apparently judged position by
nothing more stable than the flight of a bird or the shape
of a cloud in the sky.

Sometimes, in fact, this mariner's sense was more re-
liable than the compass, for sailors had noted long ago
that in some regions the Genoese Needle did not point
directly to the North Star. Still another failing of the
compass was its tendency to lose the power of pointing
to the north at all. Fortunately this could be remedied
quickly by rubbing the metal needle with loadstone, a
black metal-bearing rock carried on board every ship,
along with a number of needles that had been rubbed
with it to give them the north-pointing property.

Shortly before dawn the watch who had been dozing
began to stir themselves while the gromet of the dawn
watch stood ready beside the *ampolleta*. When the last

grains of sand had run through, he turned it up while piping his customary dawn salute:

> *"Blessed be the light of day*
> *and the Holy Cross, we say;*
> *and the Lord of Veritie*
> *and the Holy Trinity.*
> *Blessed be the immortal soul*
> *and the Lord who keeps it whole.*
> *Blessed be the light of day*
> *and He who sends the night away."*

While the gromet next recited the Pater Noster and Ave Maria, the crew on watch, with Andrea, Eric Vallarte, and Fra Mauro, stood with heads bowed. Finally the boy added in his piping voice:

> *"God give us good days, good voyage, good passage to the ship, sir captain and master and good company, so let there be a good voyage; many good days may God grant your graces, gentlemen of the afterguard and gentlemen forward."*

With the sunrise prayers finished, the watch busied themselves hauling buckets of salt water over the side and scrubbing the decks with stiff brooms. For the next hour or so everyone was occupied in dressing the ship for the day. Then the *ampolleta* was turned up for the last time on that watch, and the gromet sang out:

> *"Good is that which passeth,*
> *better that which cometh,*
> *seven is past and eight floweth,*
> *more shall flow if God willeth,*
> *count and pass make voyages fast."*

When the eighth glass had run out, the boy cried:

> *"On deck, on deck, Mr. Mariners of the right side, on deck in good time, you of Mr. Pilot's watch, for it's already time; shake a leg!"*

The watch coming on duty stumbled across the deck, rubbing their eyes and chaffing each other. From oaken casks beside the large iron pots filled with sand where the cooking fires were built, each of the sailors picked a ship's biscuit, some cheese, a sardine, a clove of garlic, or whatever he wished for breakfast and drew a pannikin of water before moving aft to receive the morning instructions.

The helmsman gave the bearings to Eric Vallarte, who stooped over the compass card, checking the accuracy of the course that had been followed during the night. One of the crew took his position as lookout and the officer going off watch showed his reckoning of the night's run to Andrea and the shipmaster before entering it in the log book. This finished, the new gromet on duty wiped clean the slate upon which the notes for the log were kept and it was ready for the account of the next watch.

The carpenter next drew water over the rail and primed the pump. With two men operating it, the small amount of water taken into the bilges by the *Infante Henrique* during the night was quickly emptied over the side. The offgoing watch picked whatever they chose for breakfast and, locating a shady place on a convenient plank or bench, stretched out and were quickly sound asleep. While the sun climbed slowly toward the yardarm, the trim caravel raced along before the wind.

The watch on deck had the duty of setting the sails. But since in this particular latitude, with the wind constantly pushing them southwestward, that amounted to almost no duty at all, the men occupied themselves with scrubbing the rails, repairing chafing gear, or inspecting the rigging and tackle for any sign of wear which might develop into a weak spot and suddenly give way during a storm.

Eric Vallarte had assumed his station on the afterdeck, where he could watch the helmsman through a hatch. Two compasses were in use, one in front of the helmsman, the other where the master could watch it, so an unwary hand at the tiller could not let the ship stray off course.

Since there was a lady aboard, the crew hurried to take turns at the *jardines*, as the chairs slung over the after rail just above the water line were called. Suitably placed out of sight of the main part of the deck, they served for the satisfaction of nature's calls.

Shortly after the changing of the watch, Dom Bartholomeu appeared from the aftercastle and paused for a short

chat with Andrea and Eric Vallarte. He was not a particularly good sailor, but so smooth was the sea and so fine
the weather that even the veriest landlubber could enjoy it.

"When do you think we will first see the Canaries,
senhors?" he asked.

"Four or five days from now," Andrea said. "Our Viking friend here runs a good ship."

"When he has a fine ship to run." Eric cast an ap-
preciative eye aloft at the taut sails. "This is the best
ever built."

"You had better come on with us to the river Sanaga,
Senhor di Perestrello," Andrea said. "We can drop you at
Gomera on the way back."

Dom Bartholomeu smiled a little wistfully. "My
daughter would like that, but I have a job to do. If our
ships are to sail southward on a new route to the Indies,
we will need a base of operations in the Canaries capable
of furnishing supplies and timbers for repairs."

"The voyage home in these waters is no easy task,"
Andrea agreed. "Unless you sail toward the Açores, and
then head eastward, as we did in returning from Guinea."

"I still don't understand how you managed that," Fra
Mauro said.

"It is easy for a mapmaker to move us about on the
world as chess players move their pieces," Eric Vallarte
said caustically. "But it takes more than a fine map and
rash promises to bring a ship safely home."

Andrea was startled by the Norseman's tone, but he
held his temper. "If you follow the courses I will set, I
promise that you will come safely home again."

Eric flushed. "If I make no mistake, I am master of
this ship, senhor. As navigator you can advise, but the
final authority here is mine."

Before Andrea could speak and carry the near quarrel
any further, Leonor intervened. "The infante commissioned
Eric to sail the ship and Senhor Bianco to navigate it,"
she said. "Surely there is no conflict there."

"Not if this secret of his really does what he says," Eric
conceded. "After all I have not seen it."

"I have," she said, "and I can assure you it can do
everything Senhor Bianco claims."

Eric turned to Andrea, the anger in his eyes stronger
now than before. "How did this happen?"

"I described the use of the device to Madonna Leonor

and Fra Mauro before I left for Guinea," Andrea explained. "If I had not returned, they were to make it known to Prince Henry. And I intend to explain its use to you after we leave the Canaries, so both of us will know how to bring the ship back home."

"Keep your secrets to yourself," Eric said shortly. "I still know how to sail a ship."

On that strained note the group broke up. Afterward Andrea drew Fra Mauro aside. "What do you suppose is wrong with Eric?" he asked. "I never saw him act like this before."

The friar shrugged. "For an intelligent man you are not very observant, my friend. He is in love with Leonor and realizes that you are a rival."

"Has he spoken to her?"

"I doubt it. If he had, she would probably have told me. She wouldn't willingly make anyone unhappy."

"Then she does not love him?"

"As a brother, perhaps. Or an uncle."

Andrea could not help feeling happy with the answer, but it did not help solve his own problems. He loved Leonor—of that he was sure. And yet he could not shake off the tie that bound him to Angelita. In fact common sense warned him he would be a fool to do anything to make her angry at a time when she was willing to help him clear his name and regain the fortune Mattei had taken from him. Now his problem was further complicated by the fact that, should he win Leonor's love, he must at the same time hurt deeply a man of whom he was very fond.

"What are you going to do?" Fra Mauro asked.

Andrea threw up his hands in a gesture of futility. "What can I do?"

"As a man of honor, you should say nothing to her until the affair in Venice is cleared up. After that she must choose for herself. Meanwhile you and Eric have embarked upon a long voyage together. It will not help to have you at each other's throats."

"You lay a heavy burden on me, little brother."

"Only because I think you are strong enough to bear it, my son," the friar told him confidently. "Do not disappoint me."

VI

Day after day the *Infante Henrique* sped southwestward with hardly a break in the routine of a well-run ship. Each day, when the sun was nearing the zenith, Andrea set up the small gnomon above the compass, marking noon when the shadow fell exactly along the line of the needle. At this time the *ampolleta* was turned up and a new period of twenty-fours began. Each night he took observations of the North Star, setting down his records meticulously so they could be used by Mestre Jacomé and the mapmakers back at Villa do Infante, as well as serving, with the Al-Kemal, as a guide for the return voyage.

Eric Vallarte was a strict taskmaster and kept a well-run ship, so a regular routine was observed. Each day the cooper inspected the casks of water and wine stacked in the hold. In warm latitudes such as this, the wood could dry out, opening the seams and allowing some of the precious fluid to seep out. For food there was sea biscuit, not yet infected with weevils as it usually was toward the end of a long voyage. With it went wine, olive oil for cooking and soaking hard bread, dried or salted beef and salted pork, beans, onions, and garlic. Barrels of preserved sardines and anchovies also filled out the diet, plus vinegar, cheese, chick-peas, lentils, beans, honey, rice, almonds, and raisins.

The only hot meal of the day came at noon. For the officers and passengers it was heralded by another of the singsong announcements from the gromet on duty:

> *Table, table, sir captain and master and good company, table ready; meat ready; water as usual for sir captain and master and good company. Long life to the king and the Infante Henrique, our patron. Who says to him war, off with his head; who won't say amen, gets nothing to drink. Table is set; who doesn't come will not eat.*

Andrea and Eric Vallarte ate with Dom Bartholomeu, Leonor, and Fra Mauro at a table set for them on the afterdeck. The tough beef or pork, cooked over charcoal fires set in large pots of sand in the waist of the ship, was put on the table by the gromet in wooden trenchers and everyone attacked it as his appetite dictated. The meal finished, there was usually nothing for the navigator and the passengers to do but settle down for a nap or hunt other tasks.

Midafternoon brought the first dogwatch, and fishing lines were tossed over the rail, baited with whatever scraps of meat the gromets had left after the noonday meal. A bite caused much excitement and when a beautiful silvery fish was hauled over the rail to flop its few remaining moments of life away on the deck, both crew and passengers gathered around admiringly, anticipating the succulent dish that would grace the menu at the next meal.

Sunset brought evening prayers. Ordinarily presided over by the indefatigable gromets, in this instance they were read by Fra Mauro. The evening ritual began when a cabin boy lit the binnacle lamp over the steering compass at the moment when the sun dropped beneath the horizon to the west and sang in the same nasal monotone he used for all announcements:

> "*Amen and God give us a good night and a good sailing; May the ship make a good passage, sir captain and good master and good company.*"

As the quick velvet darkness of the tropics enveloped the ship, Fra Mauro led the company in La Doctrina Christina, with the Pater Noster, Ave Maria, and Credo. This finished, Leonor would lift her voice in the "Salve Regina" and the ship's company—as often off key as on—followed with the beautiful words of this lovely song of adoration:

> "*Salve Regina, Mater Misericordiae,*
> *Vita, Dulcedo, et spes nostra salve.*
> *Ad Te clamamus exsalves, Filii Hovae.*
> *Ad Te suspiramus Gementes et flentes*
> *In hac lacrimarum valle. Eia ergo*
> *Advocata nostra, illos tuos.*
> *Misericordes oculos ad nos converte.*
> *Et Jesum Benedictum fructum ventris tui,*
> *Nobis post hoc exsilium ostende. O clemens,*
> *O Pia, O Dulcis, Virgo Maria.*"

The boatswain doused the fires in the cooking pots and as the *ampolleta* was turned up for the first night watch, the gromet sang out:

> *"Blessed be the hour in which God was born*
> *St. Mary who bore Him*
> *St. John who baptised Him.*
> *The watch is called,*
> *the glass floweth;*
> *We shall make a good voyage,*
> *If God willeth."*

As the caravel sailed on southwestward into the night, only the soft rush of water from the prow and the murmured voices of the men on watch disturbed the warm silence.

It was the period of the day that Andrea loved best. Often he would sit alone in the secluded area of the foredeck where he made his nightly observations, listening to the stillness of the night. But when he went to this spot the evening before they expected to make a landfall on the island of Tenerife in the Canaries, he found it already occupied by Leonor di Perestrello.

Her manner toward him had been friendly but reserved since the morning when she had observed Polaris with his help. And after his talk with Fra Mauro about Eric's love for her, Andrea had not gone out of his way to seek her out. Now, seeing her there, he hesitated and was on the point of turning back when she said, "I did not mean to steal your place, Senhor Bianco. Since it is my last night at sea, I thought you would not mind."

"The place is not mine, madonna," he assured her, stooping to pass beneath the sail. They were shut off from the rest of the ship now in this triangle of deck, giving a sense of intimacy to the scene.

"What do you see up here every evening alone?"

"What any maker of maps sees, madonna—new lands beyond the horizon, new adventures and, perhaps, things of value to mankind."

"Do you expect to find these new lands?"

"Who can tell? Through losing my freedom a long time ago, I was privileged to journey to the edge of the Eastern world and witness things no white man besides myself has seen."

"What if you had no freedom?"

"I do not understand, madonna."

She turned to face him and he saw that her eyes were wet with tears. "A woman has no freedom in a man's world. I would go on with the *Infante Henrique* if it were my right to decide. But Father must get to work soon, so we will stay behind in the islands."

"They must be very beautiful," he pointed out. "Else they would not have been called the Fortunate Isles by the ancients."

"Don't you suppose a woman longs for something else besides cooking food and directing the household?"

"And bearing beautiful children?"

She stiffened. "Aren't you being impertinent, senhor?"

"It could not be impertinent to suggest that a beautiful girl will be the mother of fine sons and daughters, madonna. Especially when some of the finest blood of your country flows in her veins."

Behind them on the deck the gromet on watch piped up the inevitable tuneless song as he turned the glass:

> "One glass is gone
> And now the second floweth;
> More shall run down
> If my God willeth.
> To my God let us pray
> To give us a good voyage;
> And through His Blessed Mother,
> Our Advocate on high,
> Protect us from the water spout
> And send no tempest nigh."

Then his voice rose in a shout to the lookout: "Hey you, the lookout. Keep a good watch!"

The lookout growled an imprecation to show that he was awake and Dona Leonor laughed. "I wish I'd been a boy." Her good humor was apparently restored. "I'd sail as a gromet and one day be captain of a ship."

"Beauty and grace such as yours are all too infrequent in this world, madonna. We need them more than we need sea captains or mapmakers."

She shook her head. "Men like you and Eric are worth more than any woman."

"Why do you call him Eric and me always Senhor Bianco, madonna?"

"Why, I don't know. Eric is so different from my own people——"

"And very devoted to you; he loves you deeply."

She laughed then, a quick infectious laugh. "You jest, senhor. To him I am only a child."

"That is where you are wrong. He would give his life for you."

"Are you sure of—of what you are saying?"

"He told me himself." He did not add that Eric had not actually said it in so many words.

She turned back to the rail and Andrea could not help feeling a sudden shock of jealousy and pain. His revelation of the Norseman's love for her had obviously affected her deeply. Which could only mean that Fra Mauro was wrong about her not loving Eric, and equally wrong about her loving him.

"Eric is a fine man," he said and then, heaping coals of fire upon his own head, added, "a fine man and a good shipmaster. He will make you an excellent husband, madonna."

Her next act surprised him. She wheeled and for a moment he thought she was going to strike him. "No one employed you as a matchmaker, senhor. Please let me choose my own husband."

"But, madonna——"

"A man who loves me needs no other to plead his cause. As for you—go back to Venice; seek out your Angelita and marry her. It is no more than you deserve."

She was gone then and the slam of the aftercastle door shattered the stillness of the night. Eric Vallarte climbed from the waist of the ship to the foredeck.

"What happened up here?" the Viking demanded suspiciously. "Did you do anything to trouble Leonor?"

"I was pleading your cause, you great oaf," Andrea said in disgust. "I never saw her so angry."

"At me or you?"

"At me. But I did learn one thing. She is very fond of you; in fact, I think she loves you."

Eric changed the subject abruptly. "Have you looked at the sky lately?"

"No. Why?"

"From the looks of things we may be longer in seeing the peak of Tenerife than we planned."

Andrea looked up and what he saw sent a shiver of apprehension through him. He had noticed a slight haze in the sky when the sun was going down. Now it had spread and threatened to shut away the light of the moon. Along with these changes went a spiteful slap of the rising sea against the ship and a restless chafing of the rigging as the sails were pulled this way and that by the first portents of the most dangerous of companions for the sailor and his ship, a gale at sea.

"Why couldn't it have waited until we were beyond the Fortunate Isles?" Eric said bitterly. "Now we will have to make a landfall in the storm."

"Why not head for the open sea and ride it out?"

Eric looked up at the sky and back at the water. "It's only just beginning," he said. "The harbor at San Sebastián is supposed to be protected. Perhaps we can ride out the storm there."

"If we can find the roadstead and enter it," Andrea agreed. "The course we are on should let us make a landfall on Tenerife by morning. We can alter our plans then according to the way the land looks." He raised his eyes to the masthead. "But I'd feel better if we were heading for the open sea."

"Leonor and Dom Bartholomeu will be safer at San Sebastián," Eric said. "That's the most important thing."

VII

Morning showed the fiery peak of Tenerife on the horizon just where Andrea had expected it to be, well to the southwest. The gale which had been making up steadily during the night had turned the sea into an ugly world of foam-capped rollers. The wind was rising rather slowly, however, and there appeared to be some hope of being able to run before it to the safe anchorage afforded by the island of Gomera, the destination of Dom Bartholomeu and his household.

With the sail area reduced to only a square sail on the mainmast to keep her under control, the *Infante Henrique* was still driven hard by the rising force of the gale. The bright sunlight of yesterday was gone now and a dull glazing seemed to have been painted over the heavens, so that the world was lit only by a yellowish half-light, sure harbinger of even worse weather to come.

Andrea spent the day with the lookout watching steadily for a break in the coast line of Gomera as they approached it and the mouth of the river forming the harbor. There they could anchor and find security from the howling of the wind and the constant pounding of the seas as the ship rolled and wallowed in cross-currents that constantly beset it.

He had not seen Leonor since last night. Dom Bartholomeu was a poor sailor, and with the ship rolling until it shipped water over the low railing at the waist with every swing, the older man was prostrate and needed all her services. A little before sunset there was a slight lull in the storm, and Andrea made his way back along the deck to where a cask of biscuit and casks also of wine and water had been broached beside the mast so the crew could refresh themselves as they passed on their manifold duties of looking after the ship in a storm. No hot food would be served that night.

Leonor came out of the *toldilla* just then and he saw that her face was drawn and her shoulders drooped with weariness.

"Is the storm lessening?" she asked anxiously.

"Only gaining strength to become worse, I'm afraid, madonna. How is your father?"

"He will be all right as soon as we anchor in the harbor."

She looked about her at the clouds massing in the darkening sky and the oily surface of the huge swells that went sweeping by, lifting the ship as if it were a child's toy. After each rise the caravel raced down into the basin between it and the oncoming wave. For a moment the ship would be surrounded by a towering wall of water that threatened to spill over and deluge them; then its natural buoyancy lifted it on the breast of the wave to a new peak.

"Wouldn't it be safer to set the course for the open sea?" she asked.

"I was just going to speak to Eric about that," he told her. "We can't safely go any closer to the shore with darkness coming on and the storm increasing."

"Tell him not to trouble himself about us," she urged. "The important thing is the safety of the ship."

Just then the *Infante Henrique* struck.

Andrea had seen no sign of any obstacle in the water, and the lookout in the prow had reported none. But with the sea as troubled as it was, a rock or craggy outcrop just beneath the surface could easily have gone unseen.

The shock of the impact threw Leonor against Andrea and he put his arm around her to support her. A second crash thrust them against the wall of the *toldilla* as a torrent of water from a following sea surged in through the open port where the tiller was mortised into the top of the rudder post. It deluged them as it poured across the afterdeck and down into the waist of the ship and Andrea had to fight desperately to keep them both from being washed over the rail into the sea.

The *Infante Henrique,* shuddering in every timber as if trying to free itself from the clutches of a still unseen menace, staggered on. Andrea heard Eric shouting to the crew, but at the moment he had all he could do to keep himself and Leonor from being washed overboard when yet another surge of water poured through the opening around the tiller. The ship struck a third time and hung for a moment; then it seemed to slide slowly over some deep-lying obstruction.

The whole vessel gave a shudder, like the convulsion of a dying animal, and another surge of water poured through the open port beside the tiller and swept across the afterdeck. Andrea braced himself against the wall of the *toldilla,* pressing Leonor between it and the rail with his body.

"What did we hit?" she gasped.

"Probably a rock too far beneath the surface to be seen in the storm."

Again the stricken vessel was wracked by a giant shudder and from deep inside it came a harsh grating rasp as the keel slid across the obstruction. Then as the weight of the caravel, like a seesaw loaded more heavily on one side, swung the bow downward, a series of less intense rasping sounds shook the vessel and a final shudder appeared to set it free.

"Get inside and stay there with your father," Andrea said and helped Leonor reach the door of the *toldilla.*

"If we aren't foundering already, every hand will be needed at the pumps."

She nodded and let herself into the aftercastle, shutting the door behind her. As serious as their plight undoubtedly was, she showed no sign of hysteria. Andrea ran across the deck to where Eric Vallarte was laboring with the men, seeking to control the wildly slapping mainsail and regain at least partial control of the ship. But as he seized a line, Eric called to him.

"See about the damage to the hull, Andrea," he said. "We may have to run her on the shore to keep from sinking."

With the help of a sailor Andrea lifted the hatch cover amidships and let himself down into the hold. Water was sloshing about wildly with the rolling and pitching of the seemingly doomed caravel and everywhere was confusion as barrels and crates floated about, banging into each other and the sides of the ship. The water in the bilges was already up to his knees and, stumbling back to the hatch, Andrea pulled himself up level with the deck.

"Hand me a lantern," he called to one of the crew. "I need to inspect the damage further."

The tossing of the ship was somewhat less feverish now, by which Andrea judged that Eric had managed to swing her around to run before the wind with enough sail area filled to hold them on a steady course. When the lantern was handed down to him he lifted it high and began to wade through the water sloshing in the bilges.

He saw no great surge of water pouring in anywhere as it would have with a major break in the planking. Casks, boxes, and bales, freed by the battering the ship had taken, were now rolling about. It was a dangerous place to be, for they could crash against him or crumple him against the ribs of the ship as he stumbled along the length of the hold, in the half darkness, seeking to evaluate the damage more fully. And yet they had to know how much damage had been done by the submerged rock in order to act intelligently.

Andrea could discover no place where the planking had actually been broken through, however, and the water seemed to be rising more slowly, now that the ship was moving rapidly. Stumbling back to the open hatch, he handed up the lantern and was helped up to the deck.

Eric Vallarte's anxious face peered at him in the rapidly falling darkness as he came up out of the hold.

"We're taking water," he reported. "The rock must have opened some of the seams. But I believe the pumps can control it—for the time being at least."

"Flores!" Eric shouted for the carpenter. "Take all the men you need and man the pumps. Keep them going until you clear the hull of water." He looked down through the hatch at the casks and bales that were still crashing against the timbers with the pitching of the ship in the steadily rising gale. "Get those barrels and casks secured, too. We'll need all the water and supplies we have if the storm lasts very long."

Men surged past them on the way to man the pumps. Andrea clung to the mizzenmast for support and looked aloft. In the turmoil of the crash, the foresail had become loosened and was tearing itself to pieces. That could be replaced later, however; the important thing now was to keep the caravel afloat.

"What about the damage up here?" he asked. "Other than the hull?"

Eric's face was bleak. "Must have struck a rock just far enough beneath the water to let the keel slide over. The main part of the rudder was carried away."

There was no need to say more; both of them fully realized the seriousness of such a happening.

"Is any of it left?" Andrea asked finally.

The Norseman shook his head. "Not even enough to take a bite in the water. I've set the mainsail so she'll run before the wind, but we can only go one way—westward."

VIII

The storm continued to rise in fury as the hours passed, but the caravel was fairly stable with the square sail straining at the mast as the wind howled around them. Actually the *Infante Henrique* was making as much speed or more than with ordinary sailing, but every hour took them farther from the Canaries and the African coast.

With the pumps operating continuously and the ship moving rapidly, the level of water in the hull did not seem to rise perceptibly. Obviously the speed of the boat some-how helped to keep the water from flowing in, an observation they could not explain, but one well known to experienced mariners.

Eric Vallarte summed up their situation at a conference in the *toldilla* toward morning. Dom Bartholomeu was pale and there were dark circles under his eyes, but with the ship fleeing steadily westward before the wind, the wild pitching and yawing had given way to a far more rhythmic motion and he had recovered enough to be able to talk.

Leonor was pale, too. Her eyes were big and dark from lack of sleep, but she showed no sign of panic.

"Just what is our situation, Eric?" Dom Bartholomeu asked.

"We are afloat," the shipmaster said with a shrug. "For which we can only thank the gods, after my stupidity in going too close to the shore."

"You were seeking a safe harbor for all our sakes," Dom Bartholomeu said. "The important thing is, what can we do now?"

"As long as the ship keeps moving at this speed, the water doesn't seem to flow in any faster than the pumps can lift it out," Eric said. "With the wind at our backs we can sail westward and probably escape with our lives —until the storm ends."

"What then?"

"With calm weather we might rig a temporary rudder. But the water will come in faster when our speed slows, so there might not be time."

"You mean we can't stop sailing long enough to rig a new rudder?" Leonor asked.

"We won't know until we try," Eric said. "All we can do right now is run before the wind."

"Where could that take us?"

Eric shrugged. "You'd better ask the navigator that question."

"Is our position hopeless, Senhor Bianco?" Dom Bartholomeu asked.

"No position is hopeless, senhor, as long as we have a ship beneath our feet and sails to drive it."

"But without a rudder, how can you steer?" Leonor asked.

"At the moment we cannot," Andrea admitted. "So

long as the storm continues we can go only westward. When it finally blows itself out, though, we may be able to devise a substitute rudder as Eric says. Then we can sail northward to the Açores if the prevailing winds remain in the direction I think they are in that area."

"Could we possibly get back home?" Dom Bartholomeu asked.

"Perhaps," Andrea said. "The pirate *brigantino* I was on used long sweeps on each side of the stern for steering. Something like that might work with the *Infante Henrique*, once the storm lets up. Then if we can reach land and careen, our troubles will be over."

Eric looked bleakly around them at the storm-tossed sea. "Just where is this land you're speaking of?"

"The Açores perhaps."

"If we get there."

"Do you think we might reach them in our present condition?" Dom Bartholomeu asked Andrea.

It was a question that had been troubling him, and he did not know the answer. The most he could do was offer a little hope. "If my theories about wind directions are true," he told them, "the wind flow should turn toward the Açores as we go farther west and swing us in that direction."

"But how could we ever find such small islands in so large an ocean?" Dom Bartholomeu asked.

"I will find them for you," Andrea told him confidently.

The older man's face brightened. "Your navigational device. I'd forgotten it."

"It will guide us home from the other side of the earth, if necessary," Andrea assured him.

"Provided we keep a ship under our feet," Eric Vallarte said getting to his feet. "Since we can decide nothing now, it is back to the pumps for us, Andrea."

For two weeks the wind blew with almost undiminished fury at their backs and the caravel fled before it into the unknown seas to the west. Hour after hour, day after day, the men worked at the pumps, with Andrea and Eric taking turns beside the others.

When the wind slackened and the ship slowed, the water level inside the hull rose a little, only to fall again when the vessel increased its speed. Always, however, enough water continued to pour through the seams opened in the planking by their crash upon the rock to just about equal the amount pumped out in a day. Faces grew long, tempers short, and eyes bloodshot from staring into the mysterious west, where, hour after hour, only the big foam-topped rollers could be seen. Worst of all was the knowledge that if they stopped fleeing westward, the ship would soon sink.

Andrea had assured the members of the crew that he possessed a means of guiding them home, but even the veriest tyro of a seaman knew that a ship without a rudder could be steered on no course except the one way the wind blew. In this extremity, they could only fall back upon faith in God.

Fra Mauro was a tower of strength here. The pudgy Franciscan's girth lessened steadily as he took his turn with the others at the pumps, but he never lost his faith that God had saved them from the rocks for some purpose, which would soon be revealed. Taking heart from Fra Mauro's quiet confidence, the men pumped on, each unwilling to be the first to announce that he had abandoned hope.

Even with the storm, the sea and the air grew steadily warmer and on the occasions when Andrea was able to observe the North Star, he could see from its height in the sky that they were moving southward as well as westward.

Finally, as the storm began to blow itself out, the sun showed its face occasionally, and the rain squalls that had lashed them intermittently began to let up. Eric had rigged one of the sails as a rain catcher during the squalls and thus was able to replenish the water casks from time to time. Water was their most precious commodity now, since, with fish for the taking, they could always manage not to starve.

On the fifteenth night following the near disaster in the Canary Islands Andrea awoke for his turn at the pumps just before dawn to find the sky almost clear. A brisk wind still blew at their backs, but the ship was almost steady now, indicating that the tempest of the seas had subsided markedly. The night was still velvety black, but it was warm and the breeze seemed almost friendly. He could not see the surface of the water as he strained at the long handle of the pump, but he was sure that it, too, was smooth, compared to the turbulence of the past several weeks.

Although the wind still blew steadily toward the west, it had lessened in force and the ship was not moving nearly so rapidly as it had during the storm. The level of water in the hull had risen appreciably during the night, Andrea saw, and, worried by this increase, he went to awaken Eric Vallarte just as dawn was breaking. Exhausted from pumping as the men always were when they went off watch, the Norseman lay sleeping on the deck near the binnacle where he had dropped.

Eric rolled over when Andrea shook him by the shoulder and sat up rubbing his eyes. Then the realization that the skies were clear, and the wind steady and strong, struck him, and he jumped to his feet. "By the beard of Woden!" he cried. "The storm is over!"

Eric had shouted the words in his exultation. And as if this glad news was what they'd all been waiting for, the men at the pumps let up a sudden shout and those off watch who had been sleeping awakened and added their voices.

"God be praised! We are saved! *Salve Regina!*" sounded from all sides.

"Come here, little brother," Eric called to Fra Mauro, who had been sleeping on the afterdeck. "Lead us in a prayer of thanks for the ending of the storm."

The door of the *toldilla* opened and Dona Leonor came out. She was still fresh from sleep but fully dressed, for they had all slept in their clothes during these past two weeks. A glad smile broke over her face at the sight of the sun, and she turned to the open door of the cabin. "The storm is over, Father," she cried. "Fra Mauro is about to lead us in a prayer of thanksgiving."

Dom Bartholomeu emerged, with Leonor supporting him. Everyone, except the men wielding the pumps, knelt on the deck and Fra Mauro's voice rose in the prayer, competing only with the clank and creak of the pumps as they worked steadily to remove the water from the hull. When he finished the prayer, Leonor raised the "Salve Regina," her sweet clear voice floating over the ship and out across the sea. The others followed her lead, singing the noble hymn as they had never sung it before.

"I'm going to climb the mast and look around," Andrea told Eric Vallarte when the hymn was finished.

"You'd better take a look at the water in the hull. It rose some during the night when we were going slower."

"In my happiness over the end of the storm, I forgot everything else," Eric admitted sheepishly. "We are still in grave danger, of course."

Andrea clapped him on the back. "The world is a sphere, my friend. If we cannot go any way but west, then we will sail around it."

Seizing the shrouds, Andrea began to climb and was soon at the top of the mast, clinging to the strong wooden column that towered here above the surface of the sea. He could not have told what he expected to see; in fact, he did not know himself. But when the rays of the sun finally burst above the eastern horizon, he could hardly believe his own eyes.

As far as the eye could reach in every direction, the sea was blanketed with a layer of brownish green. It took only a second glance to tell him that the *Infante Henrique* was floating upon a vast ocean of seaweed.

IX

Those on deck noticed the weeds at the same time Andrea did and a sudden babble of fear broke out. "We are lost!" a seaman cried and one of the gromets started to bawl.

"Silence!" Eric Vallarte shouted. "A rope's end for the next one that snivels." Going to the rail he took one of the buckets with a line attached, dropped it over the side, and drew it up filled.

Andrea descended the shrouds to the deck and all on board gathered around as Eric lifted a stringy mass of brownish-green weed from the surface of the water in the bucket. Across the top of the weed were a number of small thin bladderlike structures which, when crushed, seemed to contain air, the means by which the growth was able to float upon the ocean.

"By Woden!" the Norseman exclaimed. "Whoever heard of anything like this?"

Fra Mauro spoke from the circle of men staring at the weed. "Mestre Jacomé once mentioned a legend concerning a sea of weeds somewhere in the western ocean."

A grizzled sailor spoke. "They say it can trap a ship and hold it forever."

"Weeds like this could not possibly hold back anything so great as a ship," Andrea pointed out.

Everyone wanted to believe him, but he saw little belief in their eyes and their faces. Only a deep hopelessness was in them now, hopelessness bred of a crippled ship many leagues from home and no certainty of ever getting back again.

"We'll put on more sail and see what happens," Eric decided and shouted orders to the crew. Glad of something to take their minds off their predicament, the men hurried to loose the reefed sail. As the canvas bellied out in the breeze that still blew constantly from the east, the caravel began to move more rapidly through the water.

"See, the weed does not hold us back!" Andrea cried. "We need not fear it."

"How do we get home?" One of the crewmen sounded the question that had been troubling them all. "If you can answer that, senhor, I will follow you anywhere."

"First we need to know how badly the ship is damaged and what sort of a rudder we can rig." Andrea looked up quickly for a strange sound had struck his ears, a sound he'd never expected to hear in the midst of a sea of weeds floating in the western ocean. It was the cry of birds swooping down to rest upon the blanket of seaweed and float there for a moment while they pecked at the green mass. The birds were white, with long tails that were as straight as reeds.

"Doesn't this—the seaweed and the birds—mean land is near?" Leonor asked.

Eric Vallarte shook his head. "Birds are often found far at sea, madonna."

"But not seaweed. That must mean we have drifted north toward the Açores." She turned to Andrea. "Don't you agree?"

Andrea hated to destroy whatever hope the presence of the birds and the vast fields of floating kelp had brought them. But to buoy up false hopes might make the ultimate reaction even worse. "I'm afraid not, madonna," he said. "My last observation put our position far to the south of the islands."

"Maybe the birds came from Antillia?" It was the first

time anyone had mentioned the fabled island since they had begun to sail westward, although the question of its location had been much on Andrea's mind.

"We might even be near one of the isles of St. Brendan," Fra Mauro added. Legend had it that years before a monk—later called St. Brendan—had led a group of people from Ireland to populate an island in the Atlantic. Here they were said to have prospered as a Christian community, but no one could swear to having seen either the island or its inhabitants.

"Most mapmakers believe the story of St. Brendan is only a legend," Andrea said. "But we could be near a land mentioned by the Zeno brothers of Venice."

Eric Vallarte looked at him sharply. "Is this a tale, to keep up our spirits?"

"Certainly not," Andrea said indignantly. "Antonio Zeno sailed westward about fifty years ago. He went to the Green Land in the service of Prince Zichmini of Thule and from there to another country lying to the southwest that he called Estotiland. Then his ship sailed still farther southwest to a land called Drogeo, where they found men dressed in the skins of animals and using only bows and arrows and spears for weapons."

"It could have been just another island," Leonor pointed out.

"Perhaps," Andrea admitted. "But in the account of the Zeno voyage Drogeo was said to be a very large country, like a new world. The people there told him that farther southwest the weather was warm even in winter and the inhabitants built cities and temples where they worshiped idols and even sacrificed men and ate them."

"Perhaps they meant the Indies," Leonor said. "Or the Island of Cipangu."

"Not if the world is as large as we believe it to be, madonna. All the evidence seems to indicate that a large body of land or at least a group of islands lie between Europe and the Indies."

"Beyond the island of Antillia?" Fra Mauro asked.

"Beyond it or nearby."

"What do you think we should do then?" Eric asked.

"The ship will only sail before the wind until we repair the rudder and stop the leaks in the hull," Andrea pointed out. "And for that we must find a shore where we can careen. Antillia must lie somewhere west of us in the direction we are going."

"Suppose we miss the island?"

"Then we may still come upon the shores of what Antonio Zeno called Drogeo," Andrea said.

"But we will be going farther away from home all the time," Leonor wailed.

"Sometimes it is best to sail away from home to get there, madonna," he told her gravely. "I hope it will be true here."

No one made objection since all of them recognized that there was no other choice.

"First we ought to examine the damage to the hull," Andrea continued. "If any of the rudder was left beneath the water level, we still might be able to bolt a tiller to it."

"You mean go under the ship?" Leonor cried.

"With a line attached to my belt," Andrea assured her. "Like the buckets we use to haul water from the sea."

"But the weeds."

"I don't think they're very deep. Eric fished me from the sea once, when I was weighted down with chains. He can do it again if I get into trouble."

She shivered. "Please be careful." Andrea knew by the stern set of Eric's face and the bleak look in his eyes that he had fully understood the implication of Leonor's concern. And fond of the Norseman as he was, the knowledge of his friend's unhappiness could only cause him concern.

Eric ordered the ship hove to briefly and, wearing only a loincloth such as had been his garb for so many years while a slave of the Moors, Andrea went over the stern of the ship with a strong line secured about his waist. Letting himself down along the splintered fragments of the huge rudder normally used to steer the ship, he entered the water. It was quite warm, and while the slimy touch of the seaweed upon his naked skin sent a shiver of revulsion through him, he found that he could push the thin surface layer aside without difficulty and clear a fairly large circle around him.

Taking a deep breath, he submerged, pulling himself down into the water by holding to the metal brackets which had attached the rudder to the stern planking before the rock had torn the steering gear away. The salt water burned his eyes a little when he first opened them, but this quickly passed. The blanket of seaweed shut off much of the light of the sun, but enough came through the cleared space he'd made at the surface for him to see fairly well.

The wooden part of the rudder, he discovered, had been ripped away by the rock they'd struck in the Canary Islands. Some of the metal fittings had held and the bolts were still in place, with fragments of board attached, though not enough wood remained to be of any use in steering. Fortunately the rudder had sheered away fairly cleanly and only a few of the metal fittings which had attached it to the hull here at the stern had been torn from the planking.

His initial investigation finished, Andrea pushed himself away from the ship and shot to the surface, Expelling his breath in a great "Woof," he looked up to see the rail lined with faces staring down at him anxiously.

"Whatever we struck in the Canaries sheared the rudder away cleanly," he reported. "Some of the iron fittings held, though. We can use them when we repair it."

"*If* we repair it," one of the seamen said, but nobody laughed. They all understood the seriousness of their situation.

"Let the line play out a little more, Eric," Andrea directed. "I'm going under the hull to examine it."

"Watch out for barnacles," the Norseman warned. Being new, the bottom of the *Infante Henrique* should not be very foul as yet, but the razor-sharp edges of the barnacles that grew on all ships could rip a man's flesh like a knife.

Drawing in a deep breath, Andrea pulled himself downward by clawing at the planking with his fingers. A few small barnacles were already growing on the hull and he felt a stab of pain as his finger tips were rasped by the sharp edges. Tiny streaks of blood from his lacerated fingers drifted through the water and he knew he must hurry before it drew the ever-present sharks. With his eyes open he studied the planking as he dived deeper. Long gouges in its surface showed where the cruel edges of the rock had attacked the wood, but none seemed deep enough to be in any immediate danger of giving way.

Beside the keel he discovered quickly the main trouble. The pounding that the *Infante Henrique* had taken as it slid over the submerged rock had opened the seams enough to loosen some of the calking and let the water through. Once the ship was careened, it would be a simple matter to hew thin strips of wood and pound them into the cracks along with fresh calking, before covering the whole bottom with pitch. Once these measures were taken, the *Infante Henrique* should be a dry ship again and practically as good as new.

In three dives Andrea was able to inspect the entire hull thoroughly, finding no danger more severe than the opening of the seams for the first several planks on either side of the keel. The main structure of the vessel seemed to be intact. None of the ribs had been caved in by the pounding they had taken and the keel was not broken at any point, although badly gouged by the rocky surface. He came up over the rail and changed into dry clothing while the sails were being hoisted again. Once more the caravel began to move through the thin layer of seaweed floating on the surface, her prow pointed slightly south of west as it had been for the past two weeks.

Leonor bound up the shallow cuts where Andrea's fingers had been rasped by the sharp barnacles. Afterward he stood beside the binnacle to make his report to the ship's company gathered on the deck before him.

"The ship is sound," he told them. "Only the seams beside the keel have opened a little. They can easily be calked when we careen the vessel and a new rudder can be hung at the same time. We have water for several weeks more of sailing and it is sure to rain before that in this locality. With the fish we can catch, there should be enough food, too."

"Do you know where we are now, senhor navigator?" one of the crew asked.

"Tonight I plan to take observations of the North Star," Andrea told him. "They should tell us how far south we have sailed."

"It is west I am interested in, not south," the sailor said. "How far west have we gone?"

"I have no way of knowing save by estimation." Andrea turned to Eric. "How far would you say, Captain?"

Eric shrugged. "Perhaps five hundred leagues. I cannot be sure."

The estimate was based on the Spanish league of roughly two and a half miles and put them farther west than anyone had ever recorded sailing. Before the enormity of the distance could exert its full disturbing effect upon the men, however, Andrea spoke again. "I believe we may not be far from the island of Antillia."

A grizzled seaman named Alonzo Sanchez spoke. "Has anybody really seen Antillia, senhor?"

"Someone must have seen it," Andrea assured him. "It has appeared on maps of the Western Sea for at least twenty years."

There were no more questions, so the crew went back to their duties. The blanket of floating seaweed was not solid here; sometimes an area perhaps a mile in width would appear where the water was clear. In these open spots baited lines were dropped overboard and fish quickly hauled up to add meat to their diet. From time to time they saw small crabs floating among the seaweed, but these did not seem large enough to be of any real value as food.

That afternoon a brisk tropic downpour helped fill the water casks and with a full meal in their bellies, the spirits of the ship's company were somewhat raised. The night was clear, and with a steady wind the ship plowed on southwestward, rising and falling only a little as it met the long, smooth rollers.

Andrea was able to make several observations upon Polaris that night with the Al-Kemal. Holding the string where it touched his nose, he studied the knots he had made during the voyage to Guinea.

"Our latitude is a little north of Cape Blanco on the African coast," he announced. "Ships of the infante have sailed much farther south than that."

"What of Antillia?" Leonor asked.

"We are a little north of where it is located on my own map of the world and the others," Andrea admitted. "I will ask Eric to change the course so it will take us to that parallel."

Leonor was alone when he came back to the foredeck after conferring with Eric Vallarte. She and Fra Mauro had been helping him study the North Star, but the Franciscan had gone to his own pallet on the main hatch where the crew slept.

"What will happen to us now, Andrea?" she asked as he settled on the narrow deck beside her. In the quiet intimacy of the secluded spot, it seemed perfectly natural for her to use his first name.

"I don't know, madonna," he admitted.

"Fra Mauro says most of the learned men at Villa do Infante don't believe Antillia really exists. They think it is probably a legend, like the Isle of St. Brendan."

"I'm willing to gamble that there is land somewhere to the west of us," he assured her. "A monk named Hoei-Sin claims to have discovered a fair country by sailing east from China nearly a thousand years ago. We know for sure of the place called the Wine Land by the Norse-men, and the area called Drogeo was plainly shown on the Zeno map. I saw it myself when I was a boy playing in Niccolò Zeno's attic in Venice. And Antonio Zeno was told by the people of Drogeo that there was a land to the southwest of them with temples and great riches."

"We're all in this gamble with you," she said simply. "Staking our lives on whether you're right or wrong."

"I know," he agreed soberly. "I don't mind risking my own life. It's yours I'm worrying about."

"Why—consider me any more than the others?"

"Because of the way I feel about you. That should be obvious to you."

"How could I know when you've never told me?"

Andrea drew in a deep breath. It still didn't seem possible that he had not misunderstood her and what her words seemed to imply. "I did not speak, because I love you in a way I've never loved before. And I don't want to hurt you in case a miracle ever happens, and you should one day come to love me."

She put out her hand and found his in the darkness. Her fingers were warm and very much alive as they closed about his in the nearest thing to an embrace or a caress since he had kissed her on the night of the fiesta back in Villa do Infante.

"The miracle has already happened, Andrea *mio*," she said softly.

Andrea steeled himself against the almost overpowering impulse to take her into his arms, because he knew he must be no less honest than she had been. Before he could speak, however, Leonor asked, "Are you silent be-cause you still love the girl in Venice, Andrea?" Her voice was carefully controlled, but he sensed how hard it was for her to speak the words.

He shook his head. "I know I could never love her as I do you. And yet——" He stopped, unable to explain just what was the lure, the hold, Angelita had over him —perhaps because he did not entirely understand it himself.

"And yet you cannot forget her? Is that it?"

"Something like that," he admitted. "If I could see Angelita again—meet her face to face—I'm sure that would be the end of the whole thing."

"How can you be so certain?"

"During the voyage to Guinea I forgot Angelita completely. And that day when I came back to Lagos and looked down from the deck to see you standing there on the quay, I realized suddenly how desperately I had longed for you all the while I was gone and how much I love you. I am sure I would have been perfectly happy never to see Angelita again, but——"

"But then you received the letter from her?"

He looked up in surprise. "How did you know?"

"Fra Mauro is my confessor. He didn't want me to break my heart over a man who loved another, so he warned me about her."

"She wants me to return to Venice," Andrea admitted. "She has even offered to help me regain control of the Bianco shipping firm."

She did not look at him when she spoke, but her voice was steady. "You must go, of course. No one could ask you to give up the chance to remove the stain of a conviction for murder from your name."

He took her gently by the shoulders and turned her so she faced him. Even in the darkness he could see that her eyes were wet with tears. "Will you be waiting for me, *carissima?*"

For answer she touched his cheeks with her fingers, before taking his face between her hands and kissing him. "You should know the answer to that by now," she said softly. "I am not one who gives her love lightly—or takes it away without good reason."

Andrea took a deep breath of sheer happiness. "Now I *must* guide us safely back to Lagos," he said. "All I want from Venice is a clear name. Mattei can keep the family fortune."

She smiled with the wisdom of women in love, whatever their years. "What greater fortune could any woman wish than to be loved by a man like you—Andrea *mio?*"

X

For ten more days the *Infante Henrique* plowed through warm seas, with a strong breeze filling the sails. Except for the constant rotations of the shifts at the pumps, there was little to occupy the members of the ship's company. Andrea was thankful for the constant pumping, since the work and the weariness that followed helped keep him and the others from wondering how much longer they could thus continue westward over what seemed to be a boundless ocean upon which few people—if in fact anyone—had ever sailed this far before.

And then, on the tenth day after they had entered the sea of weeds, something happened that buoyed up their hopes a little—a school of porpoises appeared. The frolicsome water beasts were not common in the Mediterranean, but Andrea had seen them in large schools along the route to Madeira and the Canary Islands and also on the run down the coast from Cape Blanco to the mouth of the river Sanaga. For this reason he dared hope that their appearance could mean the nearness of land. But they fulfilled another purpose, too, supplying a much-needed source of food.

What stores of dried and pickled pork and beef that had not been ruined by water were almost gone now, even though they had eked them out as long as they could. The day-to-day diet of fish was growing monotonous, especially since the dwindling supply of charcoal for the cooking pots made it necessary to eat the daily catch nearly raw.

By placing a skilled bowman forward at the prow, with a strong line attached to his arrow, they were able to shoot several of the porpoises and drag them to the deck, where they were swiftly cut up. And here they discovered another use for the catch; the heads contained a considerable amount of oil, and the blubbery flesh on the outside of the body just beneath the skin was also very oily. These formed a fine source of fuel and an excellent substitute for their dwindling supply of charcoal. Cut up into strips and placed on the fires built daily upon the sand of the cooking pots, the oil blubber burned with a hot flame.

That night they feasted on succulent red steaks of porpoise flesh and the next morning their spirits were buoyed up further by the sight of a log floating in the sea. The next day another log appeared. The end of this one was pointed, as if it had been chopped down by some sort of an implement. The finding aroused a certain amount of apprehension, for wherever there were men with tools capable of cutting down trees, there would possibly be enemies who could kill strangers landing on their shores. But they must chance it, having no other choice, and so sailed on while looking to their weapons.

With these portents of land to encourage them, Eric Vallarte ordered a rope sling attached near the top of the mainmast so a lookout could perch there continually above the bellying canvas of the mainsail and scan the sea ahead for any sight of land.

Three days later, just after dawn, the lookout shouted, "Land ho!" the cry they had all been waiting to hear for many weeks.

Andrea was first in the shrouds and quickly reached the masthead beside the lookout. There was no doubting that they had discovered land, for the low-lying dark outline of an island with palm trees showed almost dead ahead. It was small, hardly large enough, he estimated, to have a stream or a spring upon it, and certainly possessed no facilities for careening the ship. But it was land, something they had not seen now for almost exactly a month.

"An island lies dead ahead," Andrea called down to the deck where Eric Vallarte was looking up expectantly, along with the rest of the ship's company.

"Could it be Antillia?" Eric asked the question that was in all their minds.

"This one is much too small. It's probably one of the other islands that surrounds Antillia. We ought to be able to see more of them as soon as the sun rises well."

His prediction proved true, for as they came closer and the light brightened, several other islands could be seen ahead. None were very high and only a few had trees, but the fact did not depress the suddenly gay spirits of the travelers on the *Infante Henrique*. Where there were three islands or five, it seemed almost certain there would be more and larger ones. And certainly one of them would allow space for careening the vessel and repairing it, while they gathered food and water for the voyage to the Açores and hence to Lagos.

Andrea remained at the masthead, sweeping the sea ahead with his eyes for some sign of a large mass of land that could be the island of Antillia. On the maps it appeared to be some twenty or more leagues in length, so he had little fear of not recognizing it when it appeared.

No such mass of land took shape that day, however. Island after island appeared as the ship sailed on, but most were the same low-lying outlines of land as their first discovery, with here and there a few stunted trees. Some were surrounded by reefs, evidenced by the foaming crests of rollers breaking far out beyond the beaches. Before noon the longest line of land they had yet seen appeared to the northwest surrounded by a reef. And to the southeast another small group could be seen, with a passage between them.

With the green of deep water showing steadily ahead, the *Infante Henrique* sailed through what appeared to be a well-defined passage between two groups of islands visible on either side. A heavy current gripped the hull as they approached the broad pass, and Eric Vallarte shouted an order to take in sail. At the same time long steering sweeps were put over the stern on either side. Patterned after the steering oars used on the pirate brigantinos, these had been fashioned from the long oars still carried on all ships for moving in and out of harbors and to protect against going upon a lee shore in a calm. The makeshift rudders could not make it possible for a large vessel like the *Infante Henrique* to sail into the wind, but they did make the caravel much more maneuverable when sailing before it, as they were now.

Even with the sail area sharply reefed, the current swept the *Infante Henrique* through the passage at nearly breakneck speed. To strike a hidden rock here would have brought instant disaster, but they could do nothing except keep a sharp lookout and hope to see any obstruction in time to avoid it.

Andrea had remained at the masthead in order to be able to estimate the depth of the water and thus detect any obstruction before they came too close to avoid it. As the ship swept on through the channel, the two larger islands between which they had passed began to recede from the stern.

"What lies ahead?" Eric called up from the deck.

"I can see islands on either side of us," Andrea answered, "and what looks like a considerable shoal or bank to the northwest."

"Any sign of an anchorage?"

"None as yet."

"Come down for a conference," Eric called and Andrea slid quickly down the rigging to the deck. The whole company waited there, but with land on either side, their spirits were obviously improved. And since Andrea had guided the ship across a greater distance of ocean than anyone to their knowledge had ever sailed before, they naturally looked to him for leadership now. Even Eric seemed to agree in that.

"Are any of these islands Antillia?" Eric asked, while Andrea was unrolling his charts.

The mapmaker shook his head. "None are large enough according to these maps."

"Then where is it?"

"I don't know exactly," Andrea admitted. "This seems to be a group of islands and there is a fairly large one to the southeast. I can barely see the outline on the horizon. With a large bank such as you can see on the starboard side, there are sure to be others in that direction."

"Shall we change course and head that way?"

"We're only about a mile off the edge of the bank now by my estimate," Andrea pointed out. "I'd say the best thing to do would be to follow it and hope it will lead us to an anchorage and a larger body of land."

This was reasoning that seamen could understand, for shoal banks like this very often surrounded islands and larger bodies of land for some distance out at sea, cut in places by passages through which an entrance could be made into protected harbors.

"Suppose this is just an island chain and we sail through it?" Fra Mauro voiced the question troubling many of them.

"If we follow the edge of the bank we can hardly do that," Andrea assured him. "There were many banks like this on the coast of Africa, except where rivers emptied into the sea. Somewhere ahead there is sure to be a passage leading to a sheltered anchorage."

"As long as we can see islands, we're not likely to lose them," Eric Vallarte agreed, settling the matter of the course—for the moment at least.

Throughout most of the day the caravel sailed on in deep water at a varying distance from the edge of the great shoaling bank lying to the northwest. Sometimes the ship was barely half a mile from its edge and the bluish marl of the bottom was easily visible. At other times their course took them several miles away, but from the masthead the color of the bank could always be distinguished easily from the darker green of the deep water surrounding it. In places, small islands showed above the surface of the bank, sometimes barely awash and throughout the day the outlines of several others were visible on the horizon to the southeast.

Late in the afternoon came the cry they wanted most of all to hear. "Land ho!" floated down from the masthead. "A large island dead ahead."

Again Andrea went up the rigging to the masthead and this time a thrill of exultation went through him. As far as he could see in either direction stretched a long dark line, rising well above the surface of the sea and much too substantial to be a cloud. Some parts of the outline even seemed to be mountainous in character.

"It is a large island," he called down. "Or the mainland of a new continent."

"Could it be Antillia?" came the inevitable question from below.

"We'll have to wait until we get nearer," was all Andrea could say. "It may be morning before we can be sure."

The night was bright with moonlight and with a lookout at the masthead and another on the foredeck, they felt safe in sailing on with barely enough canvas aloft to keep the water level in the hull manageable while the pumps were kept in constant operation. By dawn everyone was on deck and as the rays of the sun burst over the horizon behind them, a shout of wonder and pleasure rose from the company of the *Infante Henrique*.

As far as one could see—and directly in their path—lay a great mass of land, still a number of miles away but plainly visible in the morning light. Cut with bays and river mouths, verdant and obviously fruitful, with hills towering several thousand feet into the warm morning air, no one could question that they were approaching either an island of considerable size or the mainland of a new continent lying here far to the west of Europe and Africa.

"Antillia!" A great shout went up. "We have reached Antillia!"

This time Andrea agreed, while his heart filled with pride. With luck—he was the first to admit—and a moderate amount of skill, they had brought the crippled *Infante Henrique* safely across the western sea to the fabled island. And with the Al-Kemal as a guide, future mariners should have no trouble at all in finding Antillia on other voyages. A new frontier of exploration had been reached and opened up, and perhaps a new way station identified upon what could one day be a sea route to the fabulous land of the Indies, the most sought-after path in the world.

Around him, when he descended to the deck, people were dancing and singing. As he stood feasting his eyes upon the verdant green mountains of the great island they had discovered, Leonor rushed up and, in the exuberance of her happiness, threw her arms around his neck and kissed him.

"You've done it, *carissimo mio*," she cried loud enough for all to hear. "You've brought us to Antillia—and saved our lives."

As he held her in his arms, there was only one discordant note for Andrea in this whole scene of unrestrained celebration. The accusing eyes of Eric Vallarte stared at him from the deck where the Viking stood beside the binnacle. His discovery of Antillia and Leonor's public announcement of their love, had cost him a friend, Andrea realized. For Eric could only think now that Andrea had gone behind his back to win the woman he loved.

BOOK FIVE
The Hand of Satan

I

WHEN THEY HAD SEEN ANTILLIA AND FOUND IT A large, well-wooded island, the next problem for the company of the *Infante Henrique* was to find a harbor suitable for careening the caravel and repairing the damage caused by the storm and the crash upon the rock at the Canary Islands. But having come so far around the world to discover the fabled island, it seemed that a perverse fate was now determined to keep them from landing on it.

Their passage through the sea of weeds and the channel between the island chain had been favored by good weather and a brisk wind at their backs. Now the wind perversely swung around to the north, tending to drive the *Infante Henrique* upon the wooded shore of Antillia. And since they had no previous knowledge of this coast, the dangers attendant upon entering a completely unknown harbor in the face of a rising storm made their situation more perilous than it had been at any time since the caravel had slid off the rock in the Canary Islands.

Complicating the problem, too, was the fact that the great bank they were skirting extended to within a few miles of the coast of Antillia in this area. Thus only a narrow tongue of deep water was left between the vast expanse of marl-bottomed shallows to the north and the jagged wooded coast line to the south. In this quandary the only sensible plan of action was to assign two strong men to each of the improvised steering sweeps and hold a course almost directly westward, paralleling the hilly coast line of Antillia while they searched for some sign of a safe harbor.

For two days they sailed thus by day, heaving to at night for an anxious nine or ten hours until the sun came up again and the lookout at the masthead could correctly judge the depth of the water once more. Only one thing kept their spirits hopeful in this impasse, the fact that the island of Antillia—if indeed it were an island and not part of some new continent—seemed to stretch endlessly westward. Also, the coast line was cut by numerous rivers and inlets, so there was good reason to suppose that, once the storm subsided, they would be able to find a safe harbor in which to careen the caravel, to repair it, and replenish the stores of food and water against the long voyage back to Portugal.

Meanwhile the routine of the ship went on, the endless pumping, the turning of the *ampolleta* each half hour, the nightly prayer and singing of the "Salve Regina."

The warm weather and the relative calmness of the seas had allowed Dom Bartholomeu to regain most of his strength. Although still pale from the ordeal of the two weeks when the *Infante Henrique* had been driven steadily westward over stormy seas, he was almost his normal self again and much concerned about their situation.

"Shouldn't we try to make an entrance into one of the inlets or river mouths here?" he asked Eric Vallarte as the second day of their enforced tour of Antillia was nearing an end.

Eric shook his head soberly. "After what happened in the Fortunate Isles I feel safer standing offshore until the wind lessens."

"What if we reach the western end of the island before the storm does subside?" Dom Bartholomeu asked. "Can we sail around it with only the sweeps as a rudder?"

"It would be hard to do," the Norseman admitted. "But we can always heave to in sight of the island, if the bank is not too close."

"So we are little better off than if we had not found Antillia," Dom Bartholomeu said.

"I disagree, senhor," Andrea said. "At the worst, the ship can be run upon the shore. From the looks of Antillia, we could always manage to live there."

"Do you think it is inhabited?" Leonor asked.

"The Zenos said the people of Drogeo spoke of others with cities to the southwest, so it does seem reasonable that there would be people on an island as large as this one."

"Could this possibly be a part of the Indies?" Fra Mauro inquired. "Or of Cipangu?"

Andrea shook his head. "If my calculations are correct, those places lie at least twice as far to the west of Antillia as we have already sailed, and probably even farther."

"But, can you be sure this is really Antillia?"

"Not entirely," Andrea admitted. "Plato wrote of an island in the Western Sea that he called Atlantis, four hundred years before the birth of our Blessed Lord. And a Greek named Theopompus mentioned about the same time an island of great extent lying west of Europe."

"Mestre Jacomé and the infante believe the Phoenicians may have sailed as far west as the Açores," Fra Mauro added.

Andrea nodded.

"Aristotle wrote of a calm sea filled with seaweed far out in the Atlantic, so someone must have sailed that far nearly two thousand years ago. The first map to use the name Antillia seems to have been drawn about 1424 by a countryman of mine named Zuane Pizzigano. He drew another island lying north of Antillia and called it Satanazes. One near Satanazes was called Saya, while another lying west of Antillia was named Ymana. Beccario gave Satanazes the name Salvagio when he drew his map about ten years ago. He also identified another island in this area called Reylla."

"Then both of you followed the Pizzigano maps," Leonor said.

"I thought Satanazes might be the same as the island called the Hand of Satan that some old geographers mentioned," Andrea admitted. "But it could be that whoever discovered Antillia and Satanazes originally might have called it that because the inhabitants were evil or very fierce."

"If we cannot land on Antillia we might still go ashore on one of the other islands," Eric suggested.

"Provided they are where Pizzigano drew them in 1424," Andrea agreed.

"I confess to considerable relief at what you have told us, Senhor Bianco," said Dom Bartholomeu gratefully. "I was beginning to think we would be forced to sail on forever."

Andrea had been alternating watches with Eric Vallarte, and as he stood on the afterdeck that evening near the binnacle where he could watch the compass, Leonor came out of the *toldilla*. She did not speak but looked out across the water toward the dark looming outline of Antillia to the south, plainly visible in the light of the rising moon.

"Doesn't it make you happy to be the first to discover land here in the west, Andrea?" she asked.

"I was not the first, *carissima*. Someone saw it before we did."

"But if you had not been so confident that it was here, we might never have had the courage to sail on."

"We didn't have much choice," he reminded her.

"I wonder who did see Antillia first. Do you suppose he was blown here by a storm as we were?"

"Who can say? But at least *he* came back to tell about it, so we can too."

"I wish I could be as confident as you are that we will return."

"All we need for careening is a shelving beach and a fair tide. Once the hull is calked and a new rudder in place, the *Infante Henrique* can easily sail back to Portugal by way of the Açores."

She had been looking toward the distant shore; now she stiffened and grasped his arm. "Look there, Andrea," she whispered, pointing toward the dark shadow on the shore line. "I was sure I saw a light just then."

"I have seen one several times."

"Then the island must be inhabited."

"Probably. I didn't mention it when we were talking just now, because I didn't want to alarm the others."

"Suppose the people of Antillia are like the Moors on the coast of Africa, the ones who tried to kill you at Arguim Island?"

"They only fought us when we attacked them," he reminded her. "And King Budomel received us well when we came peacefully to the land of Guinea. It was only when Dom Alfonso cheated him that he attacked the ship."

She shivered and moved close to him. It was dark and they were alone in the shelter of the aftercastle, so he drew her close for a long sweet moment. "I would not mind being cast on this shore forever, *carissima mia*," he told her, "so long as you were with me."

"I almost wish we could be," she admitted. "When I think of your returning to Venice—and her—sometimes I'm afraid."

"I will stay at Villa do Infante then," he offered.

"No," she said without hesitation. "You must go and claim what is rightfully yours. Besides, you must be sure of your love for me."

"I'm already sure of it."

"It might be different later," she insisted. "I wouldn't

blame you then for wondering whether you made a mistake in giving up what was rightfully yours. You must go back to see her—and be sure." She stood on her toes to kiss him quickly on the lips. "Good night, Andrea *mio*. I will pray God to find a safe harbor for us and set everything right."

II

On the third day of the coastwise cruise of Antillia the wind began to lessen somewhat, giving promise of subsiding to a point where the ship might be rowed with the sweeps to a safe harbor in the next inlet or river that showed itself. A particular kind of shore was needed for careening, particularly a broad, hard sand beach that did not shelve off too rapidly, yet was out of the water for much of the period between the daily high points of the tide.

Toward noon of the third day after they had first sighted Antillia, the edge of the apparently limitless bank of marly shallows which they had been skirting began to bear away toward the north. At the same time another bank of shallow water appeared to the south between them and the coast line.

The course had been a little north of west for the past two days. Faced now with the question of whether to seek open water between the two banks, or move closer to shore and risk the possibility of piling up on the broad expanse of shallows before them, Andrea called for Eric Vallarte, who was not on watch at the time. He had glimpsed the star Polaris the night before long enough to determine with the Al-Kemal that their position was still a little north of the latitude of Cape Blanco on the African coast. Other than that information—almost useless now to anyone except another navigator searching for Antillia—he had no real clue to their position.

Eric climbed the mast from which Andrea had been surveying the situation, and gazed over the wide expanse of ocean before them. When he came down his face was grave. "With that bank to the southeast of us, we're in danger of piling up on a shoal if we keep on this course," he said.

"Should we bear north then? Or south?"

"The new bank to the south of us may extend all the way to the shore," Eric pointed out. "A course to the northwest will take us farther away from Antillia, but it is the safer one."

"I vote to take it then," Andrea said promptly.

"And I," Eric agreed. "It is better to risk leaving Antillia and going on to some other island than to pile up on a bank so far from the shore that we would all drown before we could reach land."

And so the order of "West, one quarter of the northwest wind" was given and the sails were trimmed for the new course. As the coast line of Antillia began to recede, the spirits of the company were considerably dampened. There had been something comforting about the green-clad hills to the south, even when they could not land. To see the coast line of Antillia receding now and the open sea apparently before them again was a somewhat disconcerting thought.

Eric made an announcement to the crew to lessen their apprehension. "We will heave to around midnight, while still in sight of the coast," he promised. "By tomorrow the storm should subside enough for us to go in for a landing somewhere beyond the shoal to the south of us."

Hove to, the ship was strangely silent, the slap of loose canvas and the creak of blocks replacing the rush of wind through the rigging and the deep-throated humming of taut sails. With the vessel making hardly any way, work at the pumps had to be increased considerably and the watches were shortened to make the rest periods more frequent.

Once or twice in the early hours of the morning, Andrea felt that the ship was moving, but could not be certain. With the coming of the dawn, however, it was obvious that they had traveled a considerable distance during the night. The coast line of Antillia, which had been visible in the moonlight to the south when they had hove to a little before midnight, was gone now. Instead, the ship seemed to be pushed along by an invisible force, although no canvas was drawing. It was an eerie feeling, this sensation of riding a swift-moving current in the ocean itself, a thing that seemed quite impossible but nevertheless was actually happening.

One thing tended to make what was taking place a little less fear-inspiring. To the west a new chain of islands had arisen, extending as far as could be seen in a broken chain of irregularly shaped bits of land. Seaward of the islands a long reef was visible, broken at intervals by what appeared to be narrow passages leading to the calmer waters beyond. None of the islands were elevated very much, as Antillia had been, but many were well wooded and obviously capable of supporting life. One thing was certain, they effectively barred any further progress westward.

As soon as it was light enough to see, Andrea climbed the mast and surveyed the western horizon. Island after island stretched across the sea within his range of vision, some very small, others larger. At the moment he could detect no break in the barrier reef that appeared deep enough for the *Infante Henrique* to navigate.

From his post upon the mast, however, there could be no doubt that the ship was being borne along by a strong current. In fact, between the ship and the reef, a well-defined border in the sea was visible, separating the current itself from the ocean through which it poured. When he came down and reported his findings a troubled group of faces looked up at him from the waist of the ship.

"It is the devil himself!" one of the sailors cried. "His hand is pushing the ship to its doom."

"The current in the sea is plainly visible," Andrea objected. "It stretches as far to the north and south as I was able to see."

"Is it like the current you described between the Canary Islands and the African coast?" Fra Mauro asked.

"This is much stronger. It almost seems like a giant river in the sea itself."

"I still say it is the devil," the sailor grumbled. "We are doomed."

"Twice before, some of you said we were doomed," Andrea said sharply. "Once when we struck the rocks near Gomera, and again when we entered the sea of weeds. But we escaped death both times." He turned to the shipmaster. "Do you think we can break loose from the grip of this current, Eric?"

The Norseman went to the side and studied the water for a moment. "I am sure we can get free of the current," he said. "But are you saying I should pile the ship on that reef to the east there?"

"I'm counting on finding a pass through the reef somewhere ahead," Andrea explained. "We can go through it and let the ship drift ashore in sheltered waters at high tide if we have to. Later, after we've located a place for careening, with the longboat, we can pump her out at low tide and float her off when it comes back in."

Eric shrugged. "It's better than sinking. Get sail on," he shouted to the crew. "We'll cheat the devil of his due this time."

With both the mysterious current and the sails as motive power, the *Infante Henrique* plowed northward at a steady pace. In some places the rocky backbone of the protecting reef rose above the sea in the form of small sandspits or islands; at others it lay just awash. Sometimes the water showed blue and clear and only by looking sharply could Andrea see from his perch at the masthead the toothlike rocks still visible below the surface. At times it seemed as if the rocks lay deep enough for them to sail directly over the reef into quiet waters, but this was a desperate measure, which he did not want to take unless they had no other recourse. What he sought was a well-defined channel, and reason argued that it must be somewhere ahead.

The islands seemed to grow larger as they moved northward, although still interspersed with smaller ones. Once or twice Andrea dared hope he was seeing a real break in the reef, but each time closer inspection showed the reef below. As the day wore on and island after island appeared without any sign of a channel, he began to feel almost desperate. His head was aching from the strain of staring ahead in the bright sunlight and his body was covered with sweat from the hot sun beating down upon him in the unprotected position at the masthead.

Noon passed, with still no sign of a safe passage through the reef, and, in desperation, Andrea considered suggesting to Eric that they try to pick their way across the jagged rocks, risking the danger of ripping the bottom out of the caravel. Then, far ahead, he saw what looked like a more substantial shore line taking form, with a line of islands apparently between it and the protecting reef. He could also see what appeared to be a broad sandy beach and tall palms silhouetted against the sky, very much like the ones that had guided him to the mouth of the river Sanaga in the land of Guinea. And between two of the outlying islands he thought he glimpsed a major break in the reef.

"There may be a passage ahead," he called down to the deck.

Eric Vallarte came up the rigging with an agility surprising in so large a man. Hooking a leg around the mast he stared into the northwest toward the spot where Andrea had pointed.

"It's too early to be certain, but you may be right." The shipmaster looked at Andrea's sweating face and squinting eyes. "You should have asked for relief before now," he said. "Go down and rest a little, I will spell you for a while."

At the water cask, Andrea took a long drink. Going to the rail then, he drew a bucket of sea water and doused his head. The water was cool and refreshing and his head felt better immediately. The strange line of demarcation between the current bearing them and the sea through which it flowed was plainly visible now, for their course had brought them very close to the edge.

Leonor looked up from where she was mending canvas in the shadow of the mainsail. "You look like a boiled crab," she told him with a smile.

"It's like an inferno up there at the masthead. Speaking of crabs, maybe we'll be eating them ourselves before this time tomorrow."

"Do you think we'll find a passage through the reef soon?"

"That or a place where we can sail over the reef. We're going inside one way or another."

"I've seen no break in the shore for quite a while now. Do you suppose the large island ahead could be the one you called Satanazes?"

"It could be. And if it really is the Hand of Satan, it should be large enough to have a stream or two."

"And a break in the reef."

He nodded. "That's what I'm praying for, at least."

On the ship plowed for almost an hour, then Eric called down from aloft. "Come up here, Andrea. I want you to see something."

Andrea quickly ran up the shrouds to the masthead.

"Look there to the west," Eric directed. "Doesn't it look to you as though there's a break in the line of trees on the big island behind the smaller ones?"

Andrea could see what Eric meant, an apparent defect in the solid green wall forming the shore line of the largest island they'd seen since leaving Antillia. So large was it in fact that the northern end was not yet visible.

"It looks to me like the mouth of a river emptying into a bay inside the reef," Eric said.

"If it is, we should be able to see a break in the reef itself," Andrea said quickly. "And it ought to be somewhere nearby."

For a whole turn of the *ampolleta* they watched the coast line of the larger island take form. Then suddenly Eric pointed ahead. "It looks like the waves are breaking well out from the shore. That usually means a bar and a channel."

"Get down to the deck and set the course to break out of this current," Andrea told him. "When I see the channel I'll conn you through it from up here where I can judge the depth better."

Eric slid down the rigging, shouting orders as he went. The men at the long steering sweeps set their backs to them and the prow of the *Infante Henrique* slowly swung more to the northwest.

Sluggish and awkward from the water sloshing and gurgling in the hull, the caravel responded slowly to the steering sweeps. Almost it seemed as if the *Infante Henrique* were reluctant to leave the grip of the great north-flowing river that moved it along without effort.

Andrea found himself praying silently and was sure the others watching the battle on the deck below were doing the same as the caravel seemed to near, by no more than inches, the edge of the current, now sharply defined, both by the difference in color and by bits of foam and debris racing northward on the surface.

Then suddenly they were free of it and a cheer went up from the anxious watchers. The forward motion of the caravel slowed perceptibly, but no one was concerned, for Andrea was now able to see the bar plainly and describe a narrow channel leading through a break in the reef into the quiet waters of a sunlit bay. Beyond this the mouth of a river was also visible, breaking the solid green wall of vegetation back of the white beach.

"A quarter west," Andrea called down from the mast-head and the men at the steering sweeps tugged at the sweeps to swing the ship onto the new course.

The channel was clearly visible now, with waves breaking in jets of foam and spray over a bar at either side. Waterlogged as it was, the *Infante Henrique* rode much deeper in the water than it would normally have done, and Eric began to shorten sail as soon as they headed for the channel, leaving only enough to keep the ship under control. Thus, if they struck bottom here, it would be with the least possible force and there might be a chance for the caravel to float free when the tide was at its highest.

The water was clear and from his position high above the deck, Andrea watched the bottom shoaling up as they approached the spot where the reef was broken to form the narrow channel. He allowed himself an occasional glance to the west, enough to make out a narrow river mouth and broad hard beaches on either side—the sort of ground that was excellent for careening. Brilliant-colored fish swam in the warm clear water as the ship drove on, and once the dark shadow of a cruising shark rose swiftly from the depths to flash past the hull, as if examining this strange visitor to its sunlit water world.

"Is the channel open?" Eric called up anxiously from the deck.

"No sign of any obstruction yet." Andrea knew what was troubling Eric. If they failed to see it in time, the jagged formation that made up the reef could grind right through even the tough outer planking of the *Infante Henrique,* ripping her open beyond any possible repair save in a well-appointed shipyard such as the one at Lagos.

Beneath the keel the bottom continued to shelve up steadily as they approached the crucial test of the pass itself. But it was white sand, with none of the dark blobs on the surface to show where jagged crests of rock protruded through.

And then, so quickly that he hardly realized it had happened, the channel was deepening again, a sure sign that the reef had been crossed.

"We're over it!" Andrea shouted. "Praise God, we are over it!"

From the deck rose a shout of thanksgiving. The river mouth was plainly visible now, a dark hiatus between walls of green forming a welcoming harbor after their long weary weeks at sea.

Conning the ship toward the river mouth, Andrea studied the bottom, seeking the best section of beach for careening. The channel leading into the river mouth was fairly deep, and only when they were safely inside it did he call down to Eric to direct the prow of the vessel toward the shelving bottom near the shore. There, some tall palms that could be very useful in careening grew close to the water's edge.

The caravel was barely moving now, and by using the sweeps the crew was able to lay it up against the bank directly opposite the tall palms Andrea had selected. When finally the vessel touched bottom it settled upon the hard sand as easily and as comfortably as a wounded man resting on his pallet after a long and weary battle. Anchors were quickly dropped from bow and stern to hold her in place and Andrea scrambled down the rigging to join the others in their first act in this new land, a service of thanksgiving led by Fra Mauro for the Divine Providence that had brought them safely to shore.

III

The next few days were busy ones for the *Infante Henrique's* company. They had managed to beach the ship in an ideal position for careening, at the mouth of the narrow but deep river flowing swiftly from somewhere inside the vast expanse of vegetation to the west. When the tide was halfway out the bottom could be easily exposed by pulling the ship over with long lines run from the mast to the tall palms growing on the shore. Thus they had more than six hours twice a day in which to repair the damage to the hull.

The reason for their long stint at the pumps was clear now. On either side of the keel the seams had been opened wide when the ship had slid over the submerged rock at the Canary Islands. Much of the calking had been torn out then and more had worked loose on the long voyage westward.

The shore was sandy and covered with piny woods interspersed with swampy areas where rich green vegetation grew to form an almost impenetrable wall. Vines flourished in unbelievable profusion, interlacing in a thick network among the branches of the trees, and bright-colored flowers seemed to perch in the air, growing with no apparent roots. Streamers of a long, grayish-green plant hung from the limbs of many of the trees, swaying in the breeze like ancient graybeards.

Canvas was carried ashore and a tent shelter for Leonor and her father erected in the shade of the pines near the beach where the work of repairing the damage was going on. With other shelters of palm-leaf thatch for the rest of the company scattered about under the pine trees, the area quickly took on the appearance of a busy village.

Summer seemed to be the rainy season in this latitude. Although the weather was hot, a shower fell almost every afternoon to cool the air. An ample supply of water was furnished by a deep spring that flowed from the earth near the careening place, reaching the river by means of a short, swift-flowing brook.

Nor did they lack for food. The water was alive with fish and in the shallows flocks of wading birds stood, eyeing them trustingly, waiting to be knocked down by sticks wielded by the crew. Deer were plentiful in the woods and were easily killed by a crossbowman with one bolt. All in all, they seemed to have discovered a veritable earthly paradise at the end of their wanderings, a fit reward for their labors and their fears.

The fact that it was such a fair land did not lure the company of the *Infante Henrique*—like Ulysses and his men on the Island of the Sirens—into idleness. Anxious to start back home after the weary weeks at sea, they required little driving. As shipmaster, Eric directed the repairs while Andrea undertook the job of seeing that ample supplies were secured for the voyage home and the company kept well supplied with food.

With a bellows made from the hide of a deer, a blacksmith shop was quickly set up on the shore. Here one of the men who had gained some experience in that art hammered on red-hot metal from the stores they had been carrying for trade with the natives along the African coast and the supplies which Dom Bartholomeu had intended to land on Gomera in the Canary Islands.

The greatest problem was devising an anvil, for this pleasant land seemed to have no rocks. Finally they managed to bind several hammers together for that purpose. Brackets for the new rudder were fashioned first and spikes hammered out for putting it together. Wooden strips for blocking the large cracks in the hull were hewed from pine trees and secured with nails fashioned in the make-shift blacksmith shop. Rope ends were unraveled for calk-ing, and from the sap of the pine trees pitch was cooked with which to cover the freshly chinked and calked seams, making them watertight. One crew of men worked on the shore, cutting down trees and hewing timbers for the new rudder. This was fashioned by securing the freshly hewn planks together with iron spikes driven through and bent so they could not give way.

Altogether it was a scene of busy activity on land and on the ship itself, as the men swarmed over it, replacing chafed rigging with fresh cordage, repairing worn blocks, and scrubbing out the filth which had accumulated in the bilges during the long days when the hull had been partly filled with water.

Leonor busied herself sewing canvas to replace sails that had been split and blown to shreds during the storm which had driven them westward into the sea of weeds. She also helped with the cooking, freeing a man for more arduous duties with ax and calking hammer.

Andrea, with two of the most skilled among the cross-bowmen and several of the sailors, constituted the de-tail charged with procuring food for their daily needs and laying up a store against the long voyage back home. Fish were caught and preserved with salt made by letting sea water evaporate in the hot sun. Whatever meat was not needed from the daily kill of venison was also pickled in brine, and the hides of the deer carefully pegged down and scrubbed with sand and salt water so they could be used later for various purposes like patching sails and mending clothing. The plenitude of fowl furnished all the eggs they could eat and there was an abundance of fresh fruit. Most of this they had never seen before, but they judged it to be edible when they saw the animals of the forest eating without apparent harm.

Shellfish of all kinds, oysters, crabs, and a succulent tiny clamlike creature whose flesh made delicious broths were plentiful. Small octopi were easily caught, too, as were large snail-like creatures living in the large whorled shells that littered the shore. Huge crayfish, as big as the familiar *langosta* of the Mediterranean, scuttled about in the shallows.

Altogether it was a busy and happy group who worked

on the shores of the island called Satanazes—if that was really its name—and no one paused to wonder whether the savages for which it might be named did or did not exist. At the rate they were working, two weeks would see the *Infante Henrique* afloat once again, watertight and ready for the long voyage home.

Andrea came in from the hunt one day and stopped in the shade of a pine tree near the beach where Leonor was sitting, sewing on some of her father's shirts. Dom Bartholomeu had improved tremendously since their arrival on shore and was now helping with some of the work on the ship. Andrea carried over his shoulder a small animal somewhat resembling a fox but with alternating rings of black and white around the tail. They had already eaten several of these and had found them succulent and of a good flavor.

"If you don't stop getting so much food for us," Leonor said with a smile, "I will be getting too fat for my dresses. Then you'll have to add clothmaking to your many talents."

"We can hardly preserve this fellow." Andrea dropped to the ground beside her. "He will have to do for your father's supper and we'll pickle the fish that were caught today."

"You will soon have enough food for the voyage back, won't you?"

"At least as far as the Açores."

She shivered. "I hate to think of trying to find them out there in that wide expanse of ocean."

"I tied a knot for the Açores in the cord of the Al-Kemal before we left," he assured her. "But even if we should miss the islands, we ought to catch fish enough to keep us alive until we get to Lagos."

Leonor changed the subject. "Have you had the feeling of being watched lately, Andrea?"

"No. Why?"

"Once or twice I felt exactly as if someone were watching me from behind that wall of trees." She nodded toward a swampy area back of the beach where a dense network of green shut off all vision for more than a few feet.

"We've seen no signs of any savages while we were hunting," he told her, "except what might have been a path along the bank of the river. Things grow so quickly here that we couldn't get any idea how recently it had been used."

"Perhaps I'm just imagining things," she admitted. "This place is so beautiful, I suppose it is hard to believe something isn't wrong with it.'

Andrea looked out across the sparkling, sunlit bay and back along the shore with its teeming life. "In Europe millions of the poor are crowded together with hardly enough to eat to keep them alive, yet here on these islands things grow without even being planted. With the forests full of game and fish for the taking, this could be a paradise for them."

"But it takes such a long voyage to get here."

"Prince Henry is building finer ships all the time," he reminded her. "With the Al-Kemal to guide them, navigation would hardly be any problem at all."

"And think what riches that would mean for you, from the use of the Al-Kemal."

"Not any more," he said soberly. "After the African voyage I realized I could never profit from the sufferings of others. That's why I freed my share of the slaves. And now that I've known what it means to be adrift on the sea, I've decided to give the Al-Kemal freely to any mariner who wants to use it."

Leonor took his hand and drew it against her cheek. "I was hoping you would say that," she said softly. "It takes real courage to give up so much to save others."

Andrea grinned. "Don't think I will have to beg, so long as the infante needs a mapmaker."

"You will have your own fortune in Venice," she reminded him.

"I don't know about that either," he told her. "At Villa do Infante and again here on this island I have found so much peace that I wonder whether I want to go back to any sort of trade. Mestre Jacomé and the others at Villa do Infante are the richest people I know, because they can search for knowledge without being disturbed by anything else." Then he smiled. "But how selfish of me. You are the most important part of my life, *carissima,* and I haven't consulted you at all."

She squeezed his hand where it lay against her cheek. "My world will never be any larger than the circle of your arms, darling," she said happily. "And I need neither maps nor ships there."

IV

As the supply of game near the camp lessened, Andrea and his hunters were forced to range farther and farther afield to find meat. He was hunting a few days later, with the two crossbowmen who usually accompanied him, when he heard the sudden whirr of an arbalest bolt, a sound usually followed by the cry of triumph that told of a successful shot. This time, however, a scream of pain shattered the calm of the forest, followed by a thudding sound and the crash of bodies in the brush. Sensing that something out of the ordinary had happened, Andrea ran in the direction from which the sounds had come.

Seconds later he burst into a small open space and stopped, astonished by what he saw. The soldier who had fired the crossbow was wrestling on the ground with a wiry copper-skinned youth from whose wounded leg blood was flowing. Andrea needed only one glance at the boy to know that he did not belong to the company of the *Infante Henrique.*

The youth, although slenderer and younger than the soldier, was giving him quite a tussle. Andrea seized one arm of the struggling boy and helped the crossbowman to subdue him. Only then, when it was obvious that he was completely overpowered, did the copper-skinned savage stop struggling.

"Vediamo!" Andrea exclaimed, panting from the exertion. "Where did you find this kind of game?"

"I glimpsed what I thought was a large bird in a tree and fired a bolt at it," the crossbowman explained. "This devil screamed and fell out of the tree almost on top of me." He reached for his knife. "Shall I finish him off?"

"No. He may be of value to us. Hold him while I bandage his wound. Then we will tie him up."

With strips torn from his shirt, Andrea quickly bound up the shallow wound in the savage's leg. Then with the cords they carried to bind together the legs of the deer they shot, he tied the boy's hands behind him. This finished, he was able to get a good look at this totally unexpected prize.

The savage was only a youth, perhaps fifteen or sixteen

years old, Andrea estimated. But he was well muscled and tall. His skin was the color of burnished copper and his features were clean cut. Black, straight hair hung almost to his shoulders and his dark eyes had a look of intelligence.

"What are you going to do with him, senhor?" the soldier asked.

"We'll take him back to the camp. When he sees that we mean him no harm, perhaps we can get some information from him about where he came from."

The crossbowman shivered. "I never thought of it before, but a hundred of them could be within arrowshot of us right now and we wouldn't know it. The copper-skinned devils have probably been watching us all the time."

The word "devils" rang a bell in Andrea's mind. Beccario had called this the Isle of Savages, and Zuane Pizzigano, in his chart of 1424, had called it Satanazes. Perhaps, he realized, the soldier had spoken truer than he knew in calling the captured boy a devil. It was a disquieting thought, making it even more urgent that they get back to the camp at once.

A crowd gathered quickly when they reached the camp on the shore. Andrea saw the boy's eyes widen at the sight of the *Infante Henrique* and decided to see what effect a little kindness and friendliness would have on him. The boy ate and drank hungrily when they gave him roast meat and water. And when Andrea handed him a small applelike fruit, which they had found in profusion near the camp but had been afraid to eat because it might be poisonous, he seized it and crunched it with strong jaws and white teeth.

"I never saw a native of the Indies," Leonor said as she watched the boy eat. "Do they look like this?"

Andrea shook his head. "I've never seen a person exactly like him."

"Not even in Cipangu?"

"He doesn't look at all like the natives of Cipangu."

Andrea remembered a few words from some of the many tongues spoken by the people in India, words he had picked up at caravan stops while traveling as the slave-clerk of Ibn Iberanakh. They seemed to mean nothing to the boy, however, and finally he resorted to sign language, having had some experience with this while talking to the Azanegues and the subjects of King Budomel during the trip to Africa. Squatting before the boy he smiled and said, "friend."

The savage looked at him with bright intelligent eyes. "Friend," Andrea repeated and put his arm across the copper-colored boy's shoulder. For a moment the slender body was rigid; then suddenly it relaxed and a smile broke over the savage's face.

"Fren," he repeated in a reasonable imitation of Andrea's speech.

Standing up, Andrea pointed to the ground and made a small circle horizontally with his hand. "What place?" he asked.

The puzzled look in the boy's eyes did not change, but when Andrea repeated the action, they cleared suddenly and he smiled again. "*Cuchiyaga,*" he said eagerly and swung his hand to indicate the river and the forest behind him. "*Cuchiyaga.*"

"That could be the name of the river," Leonor suggested. "Or of this whole region."

With a stick Andrea next drew a rough sketch of the area, including the islands they had passed while coming to the anchorage. He sketched the place where they were now as an island and then to the southeast drew in another large island and pointed to it. "Antillia," he said. "Island."

The boy frowned and seemed not to understand.

"Antillia," Andrea said again, pointing to the larger island on his crude map in the sand.

"Maybe he knows it by another name," Eric Vallarte suggested.

"I think he does." Andrea put his finger on the island of Antillia. "What place?" he asked, making a question of it.

The boy leaned forward to touch the long outline of Antillia. "Acuba," he said, and repeated the word again, by which they judged that this was the name used by the savages for Antillia.

Then the savage did a curious thing, which they did not understand at the moment. Reaching only to the northern end of the rough outline Andrea had drawn for the island of Satan's Hand—or Satanazes—where he judged them to be, the boy erased the outlines of the island and traced two lines. One extended the eastern shore of the sketch northward and the other continued the western shore almost directly west.

By the end of the day, the boy—whom Andrea christened Salvagio, the name given to this island, if it were that, on the Beccario map—seemed perfectly at home in the camp. He was intelligent and quickly caught on to sign language. Andrea was able to learn that his people lived to the westward, apparently farther inland on the shores of a lake, which he identified as the source of the river upon whose banks they were camped.

It was a grave group who met around the campfire that night after the evening meal. For the first time since their arrival on these shores, guards were posted and additional weapons from the *Infante Henrique* had been brought ashore and placed where the men could reach them easily while at work, in case an attack should come.

Eric Vallarte sounded the opening note. "I think we ought to leave here as soon as possible," he said. "Before the savages attack us."

"They might be friendly," Leonor said, "like Salvagio."

"We cannot be sure of that, Leonor," Dom Bartholomeu objected. "I, too, vote for departure. What about you, Senhor Bianco?"

Andrea rubbed his chin thoughtfully. "Ever since we captured Salvagio, I've been trying to decide what effect his presence should have on our plans," he admitted. "It might be, as Madonna Leonor says, that the savages would be friendly and with Salvagio to help us we could learn a great deal about them."

"And lose our heads into the bargain," Eric said bluntly.

"You may be right," Andrea admitted gravely. "Now that we know there are savages on the island, we have even more reason to believe that whoever saw this place once before and named it Satanazes for the devil or devil men may have had good reason for calling it that. I would say leave here tomorrow if we could, except for one thing."

"What is that?" Dom Bartholomeu asked.

"An eclipse of the moon is scheduled to occur in five days according to the calendar. Mestre Jacomé and the infante knew it was coming and instructed me to determine the longitude of whatever place the ship was in at that time. They will be very much disappointed if I fail them."

"But they expected us to be on the coast of Guinea," Eric objected. "And here we are at least two thousand miles or more away."

"All the more reason why we should determine the longitude of this place," Andrea pointed out. "Think what it will mean to mapmakers and future navigators to know exactly where Antillia and the other islands we have seen are located."

"I will be happy just to get us safely off this shore," Eric grumbled. "But if the infante wants us to find the East-West height of this place, we must do it if we can."

"It will take several more days to float the ship," Andrea pointed out. "And we can be ready to sail as soon as the eclipse takes place, so there will not be much delay— if any."

"We'll sail sooner than that if the danger increases," Eric said. "The lives of the ship's company are worth more to me than any determination of longitude."

There was no trouble that night, however, nor on the succeeding days, during which the men worked doubly hard to get the *Infante Henrique* afloat. First the lines that had been carried out to the palm trees on the shore were removed, letting the hull which had been well calked and pitched settle into a deep trough Eric had ordered dug from where the keel had settled on the bottom into deep water. Next, the longboat, which they had carried on deck since leaving Lagos, was launched and a line carried from it to the top of the mainmast.

With these preparations for refloating completed, nothing remained except to wait for the tide to reach its peak. An hour before the flood the longboat moved into the stream, maintaining a tension on the rope attached to the mainmast. They planned to pull the ship upright when the sand showed signs of loosening its grip on the keel as the rising tide flowed around the hull where it rested upon its side in the shallows.

At the first attempt the vessel did not budge, even when the tide reached its peak and began to ebb. Eric was not discouraged by failure at the first try, however. This was work he understood, and no sooner was the keel clear of water again than he set the men to digging the trench deeper. "We'll make it on the flood in the morning," he assured them. "I've been marking the height of the tide with stakes along the shore and it's always higher then."

There was little sleep in the camp that night. If they failed this time, they might never be able to budge the caravel, for no sooner did they dig sand out from around it than the rising tide tended to fill up the trench again. This time, the men on shore did not wait for the boat to pull the vessel off. Instead they ranged themselves beside the hull, carrying long poles cut the previous day with which they hoped to help lever the caravel back into a floating position.

The tide moved in with maddening slowness, but it was definitely higher than before, as Eric had predicted. A half hour before the expected flood they felt the hull begin to stir as they pushed and pried with the long poles. Shouting to the men on the boat to lay their muscles against the oars and exert the strongest possible pressure on the mainmast to try and bring it upright into a floating position, those on shore set the poles in place, ready for the supreme effort.

Once again the hull shuddered as the rising force of the water sought to loosen the grip of the sandy bottom upon it. Then like a sleeping giant shaking himself as he awoke, the *Infante Henrique* began to rise in the water. Inch by inch it slid toward the deeper channel as the men wading in the shallows used the long poles as levers, and those in the longboat strained at the oars. The shouts of the men filled the warm tropic air, rising to a note of triumph when the caravel began to slide toward deeper water. The hull still lay over on the side, however, a dangerous position indeed for her to be in when deep water was reached.

The *Infante Henrique* had been built carefully, back in Lagos, and now that care began to show itself in her behavior. When the keel finally broke loose from the sand she tried valiantly to right herself. And as the water deepened, the top of the mast began to rise slowly, moving toward the vertical. Finally the whole ship broke free from the bottom and began to swing toward an even keel.

The caravel was afloat, but the force that had righted it was not yet spent. While the ecstatic cries of the company turned to groans, the mast swung far over toward the opposite side until the rail was almost awash. A little farther and water would come pouring over the deck, its weight tending to continue the rolling movement and possibly overturning the vessel completely, with mast and rigging buried in the water.

For a long tense moment the fate of the *Infante Henrique* seemed to hang in the balance. Then the skill which had gone into its construction began to outweigh the inertia that had sent it toppling toward the other side. The rail emerged from the welter of foam as the mast began to swing again toward the vertical. This time the degree of roll was not nearly so great and in a few moments the vessel had righted itself.

The line was quickly transferred from the masthead to the prow and the longboat towed her into the middle of the river channel, where she was anchored safely. Sound and ready, the *Infante Henrique* waited to carry them back home.

V

The next days were busy ones while the stores were transferred to the ship and the casks were filled with water from the spring. Salvagio's wound had healed rapidly, after Leonor bound it with a poultice of herbs which he showed her where to gather in the swamp, and Andrea was considering taking him back to Portugal. The boy identified many fruits about which they had been in doubt and even showed Leonor how his people made a kind of flour by grinding up a root that grew in the rich black earth, washing away the juices which he indicated as being poisonous, and drying the resulting paste in the sun. He and Leonor had quickly become friends and he followed her around all during the day.

In spite of the language difficulty, Andrea managed to gain a suprising amount of information from Salvagio. He learned that far to the west and south were many more tribes of the same sort of people as the boy, but much richer. These, Salvagio had been told, owned much gold and built great temples to their gods.

The boy did not know much about the remainder of this part of the world, although he had heard that a great mass of land extended far to the north and west. Now Andrea could understand why he had rubbed out the upper end of the island of Satanazes when he had drawn it in the sand. It had been his way of indicating that the land upon which they stood was not an island at all, but part of another continent, spanning at least a portion of the Western Sea.

Andrea could make but few preparations for determining the longitude of Satanazes until the night when—according to the calendar given him by Mestre Jacomé—the expected eclipse of the moon would be visible. Because it might be their last night on shore, the company celebrated with a great feast, roasting a whole deer on the coals and breaking out a cask of wine from the ship's stores. According to Andrea's estimates of the distance they had come, he could expect the eclipse to be visible in this part of the world sometime after midnight. But since he could not determine the exact time, he was on the beach at the mouth of the river before, studying the skies and the clear silvery circle of the moon which was shortly to be obscured by the eclipse shadow.

In order to be able to register the exact hour at which the eclipse began, he had carefully set up a gnomon on the sandy beach before noon that day and, using a compass, had determined the exact time when the shadow of the gnomon was the longest, indicating that the sun was at the zenith. At exactly this moment he had turned up two of the *ampolletas* from the ship. One had been placed in charge of Dona Leonor, with strict instructions to turn it each half hour when the last grains of sand had run through. The other Andrea took care of himself. Now the two half-hour glasses rested on the sand beside him.

Leonor and Fra Mauro accompanied him to the sand-spit at the mouth of the river where he planned to make his determinations of the exact hour of the eclipse in this part of the world. Eric Vallarte, scorning, like most ship-masters, any sort of navigation except the dead reckoning by which they sailed their vessels, would have none of what he obviously regarded as a form of the black art.

"How do you know just when to look for the eclipse?" Leonor asked while they waited.

"I don't," he admitted. "Since the time of the ancient Greeks, mathematicians have known how to calculate eclipses in advance. In fact Thales of Miletus once stopped a war between his city and another by predicting in advance an eclipse of the sun. But the time will be different here and I can only guess at that."

"Why is it different?"

"Did you notice that when we sailed westward from the Canary Islands the day seemed to follow with us?"

She laughed. "I was much too busy worrying about whether or not we were going to drown."

"I was pretty scared myself," Andrea admitted. "But if you had watched, you would have noted that as we sailed west, the day did actually seem to follow us, that is, almost seemed to slow down."

"But I still don't understand it."

"Determining the East-West height has never been very clear to anyone," he admitted. "The old Greeks knew how to find it the way we hope to do it here, but men forgot their methods for a long time. Mestre Jacomé and the others at Villa do Infante think they have it worked out again. This is actually to be something of a test. They know just when it is to occur at Villa do Infante and are keeping an accurate record. All I have to determine is the exact hour and the date when it happens here. Then when we get back home we can calculate how far west we went to get here."

"Won't you know until we get back to Portugal?"

"Not for sure. You see, every hour of difference between the time they see the eclipse at Villa do Infante and we see it here on Satanazes represents fifteen degrees of the earth's circumference."

"Then you can figure out from the number of hours just how many degrees we traveled," Leonor cried. "What could be simpler than that?"

Andrea laughed. "I wish it were that simple, *madonna mia*. Someone has to observe the eclipse in each particular area and determine the hour exactly, so our determination of the longitude can never be any more accurate than our method of keeping time. And you know by now how difficult it is to turn up the *ampolleta* always at exactly the right moment."

She nodded. "My eyes are hurting now from squinting to see the last grains of sand."

"Besides," Andrea continued, "until we know just how many leagues of distance are covered by fifteen degrees of the earth's circular measurement, our final result cannot be exact."

"Then why bother?"

"Discoveries, no matter what the field they are in, usually are not made by any one man. Each merely discovers some new thing for himself, adds what others have found, and comes up with an answer—if he is lucky. If I record the time of the eclipse exactly here on Satanazes and Mestre Jacomé does the same at Villa do Infante, we can calculate just how many degrees lie between us. Observers elsewhere in the world will also record their timing of this eclipse and also the next and the next. Someday astronomers will find two places whose distance can be measured accurately. Then we will know exactly what distance those fifteen degrees represent, and the correct distance around the world. And if we don't get busy," he added, "we'll miss what we're here for entirely."

While Andrea and Fra Mauro watched for the first sign of the eclipse, Leonor studied the half-hour glasses. "I can see it," Andrea said suddenly, and seconds later Fra Mauro confirmed his observation.

"The glasses have run through half the sand," Leonor reported. "Both are the same."

"Record it," Andrea directed. They had brought the ship's journal and pen and ink for making a permanent record.

Two more recordings of the time were made, one when the eclipse shadow was fully over the moon and again when it had completely passed across it.

"That's all we have to do," Andrea said with considerable satisfaction. "We have all the facts we need."

"And you have no idea what the distance is to Villa do Infante?" Leonor asked.

"My guess is a thousand leagues or slightly less," he told her, "but it is only a guess."

Leonor caught her breath. "We will never get back home! Never!"

"With the ship as good as new and the wind at our backs by way of the Açores, we'll fly like birds," he assured her. "Our troubles are behind us now."

VI

Andrea's optimism was justified when the morning dawned bright and clear. Preparations went on apace for loading the rest of the supplies and filling the last casks of water which would be stored in the hold of the *Infante Henrique*. As each cask was used up, it would be filled with sea water and replaced to maintain the ballast so the ship would not float dangerously high in the sea from lessening the weight in the hold.

The caravel made a brave show indeed, anchored in the brisk current of the river, with her decks freshly scrubbed, her canvas ready to be filled by the breeze, and the new rudder projecting from the stern. When he remembered how they had limped westward for nearly a thousand leagues with water sloshing inside the hull and the pumps going constantly, Andrea felt no fear of their being able to sail safely back to Portugal.

With signs and drawings in the sand, Andrea had made clear to Salvagio that they were leaving soon and would like to take him with them. The youth's wound was almost healed, and he agreed to go with all the eagerness of a child anxious to see a new thing. He and Leonor had been gathering fruits each day to add to the supplies being stored in the *Infante Henrique*. They left usually right after the morning meal before the weather became hot and, when they had not returned an hour before noon, Andrea became disturbed. Calling the crossbowmen who usually hunted with him, he set out to look for them.

He had no fear that Leonor would get lost with Salvagio to guide her, for the boy had shown himself to be as much at home in the forest as Andrea was on the deck of a ship. But when they had searched along the riverbank for some distance without finding any trace of either Leonor or Salvagio, Andrea's fears began to rise. One possibility he didn't even want to think about—that they had been captured by the savages of Salvagio's tribe—but he could not get it out of his mind nevertheless. When they went on another quarter of a mile or so without finding them—farther than Andrea and the soldiers had ever hunted before—he became definitely worried.

Stopping the others, Andrea listened for some sound that might give them a clue to Leonor's whereabouts, but could hear only the squawking of birds in the trees and the rush of the wind through the leaves. Not content, however, he climbed a tall oak with wide-spreading limbs until he was above the level of the surrounding vegetation.

At first he saw nothing but a sea of green, then to the westward he detected a plume of smoke rising into the sky. The sight of it sent a cold chill down his spine, for it must mean that the people of Salvagio's tribe had set up a camp only a few miles from the anchorage where the *Infante Henrique* floated at the river mouth. That Salvagio might have turned upon the girl and taken her prisoner, or played the traitor and led her into the hands of his fellows, Andrea did not believe for a moment. But with the savages camped as close as they appeared to be to the anchorage, it was quite possible that Leonor and the boy had been attacked while gathering fruit.

"Senhor Bianco," one of the soldiers called up from below him. "I think I hear voices ahead of us. Someone cried out. Perhaps it was Dona Leonor."

Andrea dropped rapidly down through the limbs of the tree to the ground. Cupping his hands to his mouth he called, "Leonor! Leonor! Do you hear me?"

Faintly from along the riverbank ahead of them he heard her answering call. "The savages have taken her," Andrea shouted. "Follow me along the riverbank."

The hunters had already discovered that a path of sorts wound along the bank of the river, possibly used by the savages in visiting the shore to obtain shellfish. Racing through the woods in the direction from which they had heard Leonor's cry, they followed this path.

Perhaps a few hundred paces farther along they came upon a scene that told them all too clearly what had happened to the two they sought. The underbrush was trampled down in a small area and a shred of Leonor's dress hung from one of the bushes. At the edge of the cleared space lay the body of Salvagio, a spear thrust through it and blood still oozing from around the wound.

Nothing could be done for Salvagio, so Andrea hurried on. He was hoping that Salvagio's defense had helped delay the capture of the girl long enough for him and the soldiers to catch up with them. Soon he caught a glimpse of Leonor's dress where the sunlight flashed through the trees ahead, and knew that they were closing in on their quarry. Moments later they came out in an open glade of piny woods where the underbrush did not grow so thickly and saw a tall savage dragging the girl along, while two others covered the retreat.

"Aim for the other two and drop them if you can," Andrea ordered the soldiers behind him. "I will take the one holding Dona Leonor."

The crossbowmen knelt and rested their weapons upon one knee for better aim. As he raced across the glade, Andrea heard the twang of the short, tough bows behind him and the whir of the bolts as they sped past. One of the savages pitched forward silently and the second stopped to stare at his fellow stupidly, apparently unable to comprehend an arrow which he could not see.

The other bolt missed its target, but neither of the copper-colored men seemed inclined to stand and fight. The one who held Leonor was lifting his spear to thrust it through her body before retreating—as he no doubt had done with Salvagio—when Andrea shouted at him, hoping to divert his attention.

Fortunately the first crossbowman had reloaded immediately. Even as the spear was descending to plunge into Leonor's body, the bolt thudded home and the savage went down with blood gurgling from his mouth, the weapon falling from his fingers. Startled by this seeming rain of death from the sky, the third man turned and ran, dodging from tree to tree so that neither of the crossbowmen could get a fair shot at him. Seconds later he disappeared into the green wall of the jungle growth.

Leonor threw herself into Andrea's arms when he reached her, clinging to him and shaking with relief at her near escape from death. A quick glance told him she was not hurt, save for a small cut on her lip where the savage had struck her in the face.

"Shall we go after him, senhor?" one of the crossbowmen asked.

"No," Andrea said. "We'd better get back to the ship as quickly as possible. I saw the smoke of a camp or village nearby when I was in the tree."

The soldiers needed no further urging to retreat. Leonor had recovered sufficiently now to be able to walk and, with Andrea supporting her, they made good time retracing their steps along the path following the riverbank. She was able to give a brief account of her adventure now.

"Salvagio knew of some trees with lots of fruit deeper in the forest," she said. "We were gathering it when the three savages appeared. Salvagio argued with them. I think he told them we are leaving, but they killed him just the same." She shuddered at the memory. "They were like devils."

"Whoever discovered this spot wasn't wrong when they called them devil men," Andrea agreed. "We must leave right away."

"Do you think they will attack us?"

"Probably; their camp isn't far away. But we may be able to embark before they do."

When they reached the open space around the anchorage, people ran excitedly to hear of Leonor's adventure and her near escape from death at the hands of the savages. Andrea called to Eric Vallarte and gave him a quick account of what had happened.

"We must embark at once," Eric said. "The tide is rising, so we should be able to cross the bar in a little while."

"How soon?"

"A few hours at most."

"We'd better prepare to defend ourselves then," Andrea said. "I am sure the savages have a camp only a short distance up the river. When the one who got away tells them we are leaving they may attack us at once to loot the ship."

With crisp orders Eric deployed the soldiers and the best bowmen among the crew in a perimeter around the camp and the loading place on the shore. Leonor and her father, with Fra Mauro, were hustled into the longboat with Eric in charge and started for the *Infante Henrique*. Meanwhile, Andrea made the rounds of the men assigned to defend the camp, instructing each to take whatever protection he could find behind trees and logs while they waited for the enemy to appear.

Andrea had expected Eric to remain on board the ship and carry out preparations for sailing, but the Norseman came back with the boat. He had put on his armor and helmet. The Viking short-sword hung at his belt, and the round shield was on his left arm.

"Why didn't you stay with the ship?" Andrea demanded. "The master's place is on board."

"Only you understand the secret of the device that can guide us to the Açores," the Norseman said. "If you are killed, we might never get back to Portugal."

"Then we will fight together."

Eric shook his head. "You're going on board the ship now—before the savages attack."

"But——"

"Leonor must be saved at all costs and you are the only man who can bring her safely home. I give orders here—remember."

There was no arguing with the shipmaster's logic. It was true that in an emergency Leonor and Fra Mauro might have been able to take accurate enough observations of Polaris to bring them back to Portugal. But the difficult task of guiding the ship to the tiny group of islands called the Açores across the vast expanse of the ocean would require all of Andrea's navigational skill, plus the Al-Kemal.

"They haven't attacked yet," Andrea reminded him. "I can at least stay here until it begins."

"Do I have to send you on board under arrest?" Eric demanded. "Or will you obey orders?"

Andrea shrugged. "I'll obey, of course. But I don't see why I can't stay on shore until the rest of the company has embarked."

"If anything happens to me, you are in command of the ship," Eric told him. "Be ready to sail at once." Then he smiled, and for a moment he was the old Eric, the jovial companion of the days at Villa do Infante and Lagos. "But don't think you can take my job away from me by sailing off and leaving me. Remember, we Norsemen can swim, too, and I'll be coming after you."

"I pray that no one of us will be left behind," Andrea told him sincerely and gripped his hand.

"If they give us time for two or three more loads," Eric said, "the devils can have this island for all I care."

Andrea ran down to the shore and stepped into the longboat, seizing one of the oars. With his powerful stroke pacing the rowers, the boat shot toward the *Infante Henrique* and quickly reached the boarding ladder.

"Put your backs to the oars," he told the four sailors who were rowing the boat back to the shore for the next load. "The sooner we're all aboard the quicker we can sail."

"Did you see anything of the savages?" Leonor asked anxiously as he came over the rail.

"Not yet. Eric ordered me to come aboard. He said if anything happened and only one of us could make the voyage, it should be me because I know how to use the Al-Kemal."

She looked shoreward to where the tall figure of Eric Vallarte could be seen, striding about the anchorage with the sun gleaming upon his helmet and shield. "He knows I love you," she said gently. "But he loves me enough to want my happiness first."

"Pray God the savages do not attack, then. Another hour and we'll have everyone on board, ready to sail."

Everything was in readiness, Andrea saw when he inspected the preparations Eric had ordered made for departure. Only one anchor held the *Infante Henrique* in the stream, with the prow pointing toward the channel through the reef leading to the open sea. In an emergency the cable could be slipped and the sails raised in minutes. Busy with his inspection, he did not have a chance to look shoreward until Dona Leonor's cry warned him that something was wrong there.

He went to the rail then, in time to see a wave of naked copper bodies rush into the open from the woods surrounding the campground, brandishing spears and shouting as they raced toward the little group of men defending the boat landing.

VII

Even from the distance of more than a hundred paces separating the *Infante Henrique* from the shore, Andrea could see that the men assigned to the defense of the landing were fighting coolly. Eric Vallarte, sword in hand, directed the crossbowmen as they knelt behind the impromptu barricade and poured a hail of metal bolts into the savages.

Leonor came up beside Andrea at the rail as one of the copper-skinned men lunged at Eric with his spear. The Norseman stepped easily aside and thrust the man through with his short-sword. Jerking it from the brown body as it fell, he waved the blade in the air and shouted encouragement to his men.

For a moment there was a vast confusion in the melee on the shore, with no way of telling how the battle was going. Standing safely on the ship, Andrea felt a little ashamed because he had no part in it, but could do nothing. Then his eye fell upon one of the bombards set up on the deck with its open mouth pointing toward the shore.

"You there, Perez," he called to one of the sailors. "Load the bombard. We'll drop a few balls on the shore."

Together Andrea and the sailor charged the squat iron cannon with powder and one of the round balls used as projectiles. Leonor had already run to bring a pan of coals from the fire which had been kindled in the cooking pots for preparing the midday meal. When Andrea applied a glowing coal to the touchhole of the cannon the powder exploded with a mighty crash, shaking the deck and enveloping them with acrid black smoke.

Watching the dark shadow of the ball hurtle shoreward, Andrea waited for it to strike. Even at best, aiming the clumsy bombards was a difficult business and one could never be sure of dropping the missile exactly upon a given target. But this time the ball went true, landing on the far edge of what had been the campground, smashing the trunk of a small tree and sending it crashing into the midst of the attacking savages.

Whether from surprise at the noise of the explosion, or from the sudden dropping of the ball in their midst, the attackers hesitated. Then, as yet another hail of arbalest bolts struck them, they turned and ran for the shelter of the trees surrounding the campground.

"The cannon drove them off," Leonor cried. "We've won the battle."

"They'll probably attack again," Andrea said grimly. "Load the bombard again, Perez," he directed. "Maybe we can discourage them a little more before they gain confidence."

Again the bombard thundered and another round shot went hurtling shoreward. This one landed in the woods back of the clearing, however, and did not appear to do much damage. While the sailor loaded the cannon once more, Andrea ran up the rigging and scanned the landing area from that elevation.

The longboat had reached the shore and he could hear Eric Vallarte calling the names of the men who were to go in the next load and urging them to push off. The other defenders, sharply decreased in number by those who made up the boatload, had retreated to the shore. They were feverishly engaged now in piling up logs and anything else they could get their hands on to build a rough barricade around the landing itself.

From his perch in the rigging Andrea could see the coppery bodies of the attackers beginning to form again at the edge of the wood and directed Perez to lower the mouth of the bombard a little. By shortening the range, he hoped to place the next shot nearer the shore with a better chance of landing among the savages now massing to attack.

Eric was striding up and down behind the barricade, where only about a dozen men now awaited the next move of the enemy, swinging his sword and encouraging them to keep their spirits up. The longboat with next to the last load of the company was almost to the *Infante Henrique* and the men on deck were dropping lines over the sides so those who were debarking could climb quickly up over the rail and let the boat return immediately for the remainder of those on shore.

For a moment Andrea dared hope the savages would delay their next attack long enough for the boat to reload and get back with the last group. But just as the prow of the longboat bumped against the side of the caravel, a yelling horde of copper-skinned bodies broke through the woods once more, racing down upon Eric and the pitifully small number of defenders behind the flimsy barricade.

"Fire the bombard," Andrea shouted. The concussion of the blast shook him as he clung to the mast. He heard a cry of pain from the deck and sensed that something was wrong but dared not take his eyes from the hurtling ball as it arched over the water to land hardly a dozen paces in front of the barricade in the midst of the yelling mass of savages. Terror-stricken by this mysterious death that dropped upon them from the skies with the sound of thunder, the red men turned and ran to the woods once more.

"It drove them off!" Andrea shouted down to the deck

jubilantly. "Load it again, Perez." There was no answer, however, and when he looked down he saw that the bombard would launch no more damage upon the enemy. The split in the barrel where it had exploded with the firing of the last charge was plainly visible and he saw Leonor bending over what was left of the body of Perez, the gunner. Part of the explosive force of the powder had evidently been expended in slamming Perez' body against the mainmast when the cannon had burst, breaking it like a doll crushed beneath the heel of a boot.

Andrea came down to the deck and ran to help Leonor, but a quick glance told him Perez was beyond any aid they could give. While she covered the sailor's body with a piece of canvas, he went to the rail to watch the progress of the boat now skimming over the water on its way to the shore for the last load.

As soon as the longboat grounded on the narrow beach the men from the barricade ran to it, piling over the gunwales and coming perilously close to swamping it there in the light surf that washed on the shore. Apparently realizing that this time they must make a successful attack or lose their prey, the savages, too, came pouring from the woods, converging upon the beach and the men seeking to embark.

No hail of arbalest bolts stopped the devil men this time; for those who had defended the barricade were busy scrambling into the longboat. The bombard, too, was out of action and nothing lay in the path of the howling men of Satanazes except the tall figure of Eric Vallarte, standing at the stern of the longboat in water up to his knees while he steadied it for the last of the defenders to climb aboard.

The attackers were already wading out into shallow water to try and stop the boat while those on board scrambled for the oars and sought to get it under way. Watching helplessly from the deck of the *Infante Henrique,* Andrea groaned as one of the savages lunged forward to try to seize the gunwale of the boat. Loaded as it was, there was barely room for the men to crowd in, and the gunwales were almost awash. If the boat were swamped now, all on board would be killed before it could be righted again.

"Climb in, Eric! Climb in!" Andrea heard a voice shouting and recognized it as his own. Only Eric remained outside the longboat now, but even from that distance Andrea could see that it would not hold even one other person and stay afloat.

Knowing that only one thing could save the boat now, Andrea still prayed that something else would happen. But Eric Vallarte, too, had recognized the truth of the situation. Bending to put his shoulder against the stern of the longboat just as the last of the men climbed aboard, he shoved it out into the deeper current where the attackers could not reach it. Then turning with his shield before him, he swung the short-sword and attacked the savages splashing through the surf in pursuit of the longboat.

Instantly the tall form in armor and helmet was the center of a boiling maelstrom of copper-skinned bodies as the men of Satanazes vented on the Viking their rage at being foiled in the attempt to capture the longboat and those in it. Numbly watching the heroic figure fighting in the shallows, Andrea felt Leonor's hand groping blindly for his as they stood beside the rail and put his arm around her.

"*Maria Sanctissima!*" she prayed softly. "Save him! Save him, Mother of God!" But even Eric's strength and courage could not withstand the mass of furious savages stabbing at him with spears. Once or twice the shield and the sword flashed in the sunlight before the brown flood finally engulfed him and he went down. Only when there was no longer any hope of Eric's escaping did Andrea give the order to haul up the anchor and hoist the foresail.

As the metal hook broke loose from the bottom and the sail filled smartly, the *Infante Henrique* began to move away from the shore. With two sailors manning the tiller and a lookout at the masthead to guide them through the channel that cut the reef outside the sheltered bay of Satanazes, the trim craft gained speed steadily. The new rudder swung easily to the touch of the steersmen at the long tiller and the ship responded like a spirited charger.

Watching the bottom of the channel from the foredeck, Andrea saw it shelving up to meet them at the pass and called for a reef in the sail. But even before the order could be executed, the sleek caravel was across the reef safely and surging through the channel traversing the sandy bar beyond, heading for the open sea.

A little while later they felt the strange current that had brought them to this spot grip the hull and send it surging northward. Andrea ordered all canvas broken out then, and with every sail drawing, the *Infante Henrique* fled from the land of the savages, seeking the winds and currents leading to the Açores and the home port of Lagos, a thousand leagues or more to the eastward.

VIII

The arrival at Lagos of the *Infante Henrique*—listed as lost at sea with all aboard when it did not make a landfall on Gomera—created almost as much of a sensation as the news that they had rediscovered the fabled island of Antillia over a thousand leagues west of the Canaries. Andrea's determination of the longitude on the night before their departure from Satanazes fixed the distance with fair accuracy, as did the dead-reckoning account of the return trip and the landfall on the Açores, where they had paused only for fresh water and supplies before sailing on to Portugal.

He had expected to appear before the assembly of scholars at Villa do Infante to make a report, as he had upon his return from Guinea, but it was a much smaller gathering that he faced the day after their arrival. Included were only Prince Henry and Mestre Jacomé, with Fra Mauro, Senhor Bartholomeu di Perestrello and, surprisingly enough, Leonor. She smiled when he came in and, as always, he felt a warm sense of pleasure flooding his soul at the sight of her fresh young beauty and the warmth in her eyes that was for him alone.

Eric's death had brought them even closer, and on the long voyage home Andrea had come to realize just how deep was his love for Leonor and how truly fortunate he was that her love for him was as great as his own. Only one thing marred their almost perfect communion of spirit, the shadow of Angelita and the lure she held out of regaining his name and fortune in Venice, with herself as the ultimate prize.

"You may be surprised that I have not asked you to address the full company here at Villa do Infante, Senhor Andrea," Prince Henry said.

"I am in your service, sire," Andrea said simply. "And therefore at your command."

"What Mestre Jacomé and I have heard of your adventure made us think we should listen first, before relating it to the full company."

Andrea gave a simple account of the voyage. When he described the near disaster at the Canary Islands he was careful not to intimate that any lack of care or good judgment on the part of Eric Vallarte had contributed to it. Both Prince Henry and Mestre Jacomé sat with rapt attention while he told of the flight westward before the storm. Neither spoke until he came to describe the sea of weeds.

"The Phoenicians must have sailed at least that far west," the old mapmaker interposed excitedly. "Aristotle speaks of this sea of weeds."

"I don't know who discovered it," Andrea said, "but I can vouch for its existence."

"And you say the weeds did not affect the sailing of the ship?"

"Not noticeably. Of course, the *Infante Henrique* was badly waterlogged; the hull was half filled much of the time."

"It is a miracle," the infante said, crossing himself quickly. "The Blessed Mother herself must have been watching over you."

"I am sure of that," Andrea agreed. "If the west wind had ceased to blow for as much as two days after the storm ended, the caravel would have sunk. All of our pumping could not have kept it afloat when it was not moving."

He took up his story once more, describing the island of Antillia and their good luck in finding a protected anchorage on what they thought to be Satanazes or the Hand of Satan. When he finished the account of their escape and the voyage homeward no one spoke for a moment; then Prince Henry spoke. "Eric Vallarte was a true knight. I will request that a Mass be said for his soul in the cathedral, even though he was not of our faith. But Eric did not die in vain," he continued. "He sailed his ship farther west than any man ever has, in our day at least—with the help of your skill as a navigator, of course, Senhor Andrea."

"The constancy of the winds did far more than any skill of mine, milord. Except for making a landfall on the Açores, everything happened largely by chance."

Dom Bartholomeu spoke. "Our friend Andrea is very modest," he said. "But for his conviction that land lay to the west of us, we might have tried to sail from the sea of weeds directly to the Açores and been trapped by changing winds while the caravel foundered."

"How could you be so sure land did lie ahead of you?" Mestre Jacomé asked.

Andrea grinned. "Perhaps because it had to be there, if any of us were to return home again. Actually I was sure that with so many mapmakers convinced of land in the west, some of them must be right."

"Do you believe what the boy Salvagio told you, that Satanazes is not really an island but part of a large mass of land, perhaps even a continent?"

"It fits the pattern," Andrea agreed. "His story of the people to the west and south of Satanazes is practically the same as that told the Zeno expedition by the people of Drogeo more than fifty years ago."

"If what we visited is not a continent," Dom Bartholomeu added, "I am convinced it is at least a large archipelago of islands extending both north and south."

Prince Henry toyed for a moment with the medallion that hung from a chain around his neck. "I believe in being honest," he said finally. "That is why we asked all of you to come here this morning. Besides yourselves, how many of the crew realized that you may have discovered a new continent—or at least a very large chain of islands?"

"None of them," Andrea said at once. "Leon—Dona Leonor and I extracted the information from Salvagio ourselves. We purposely did not make it known to the others for fear it might make them apprehensive."

"Then we six are the only ones who do know?"

"Yes," Andrea assured him. "I think we are."

"And you say this new group of islands—or continent, whichever it is—is very fertile?"

"More than any place I saw in the Canary Islands or on the coast of Africa, except perhaps in Guinea," Andrea assured him. "It would be a wonderful place to settle the poor from this part of the world."

"I have always thought of Africa for that purpose," Prince Henry said. "But this new land of yours might be suitable, too. After we have finished settling the Açores, we could move on to Antillia and the other area there." He turned to face Andrea directly. "I have a request to make of you, Senhor Andrea, and also of the others here. You may think it a strange one."

"Your wish is our law," Dom Bartholomeu assured him and Andrea added his own assurance.

"For reasons which Mestre Jacomé and I consider to be good ones," Prince Henry said, "I am going to ask you to be silent about your discovery."

IX

Andrea stared at the infante, unable to believe what he had heard. "May I ask your reasons, sire?" he said finally. "Or would that be presuming?"

"You have every right to know." Prince Henry got to his feet and went to a window. Through it the blue waters of the Western Sea were visible and, far in the distance, the darker shadow of the African coast line. He appeared to study it for a moment before he turned to face the others in the room.

"As all of you know, I have spent the greater part of my life fighting the Moors to the south of us," he said. "The Ceuta campaign was a glorious success, the others largely failures. Perhaps because of my own lack of skill in battle or courage—I don't know which—my beloved brother was killed by the Moors when we were forced to leave him in their hands as a hostage."

"I was with you in that campaign, sire," Dom Bartholomeu said warmly. "The defeat was not your fault! No one could have fought more bravely than you did."

"Thank you, my friend," the infante said sincerely. "I think the fault arose earlier, in the decision to attack. In any event I have let nothing deter me since from carrying out my avowed purpose of combating the forces of Islam. Somewhere to the east in Africa lies the kingdom of Prester John, a Christian prince. If the next river below the Sanaga proves to be the western Nile—or the next one after that—we may be able to reach his domain and join forces with him by that route. Or if our ships circumnavigate Africa and sail on to the Indies, the wealth we gain in that way will serve to advance the fight our faith is making against the Moslems."

He paused, then went on. "In either event I consider it

vitally important that nothing shall hamper this work to which I have devoted my life. Even now a fleet under the command of Senhor Denis Diaz is searching below the river Sanaga for the western Nile. I dare to hope they will reach the southern tip of Africa and find a way of linking up with the forces of Prester John. When that is done we will have forged a ring of steel around much of Islam and cut them off from valuable trade with the land of the blacks in Guinea. Nothing must interfere with this possibility, and because of this I am asking you to remain silent about what you have discovered, at least for a while."

Andrea could understand and even sympathize with Prince Henry's reasoning, knowing how he felt about the fight against Islam. And yet it was not easy to agree to hide a discovery of this magnitude, one that could quickly make him the most famous mapmaker and geographer in the world.

"I realize that I am asking much," Prince Henry continued, "particularly of Senhor Bianco, who could gain much by revealing the knowledge he possesses. But to announce the presence of a new land to the west as a possible source of gold and slaves, might only discourage those now searching for the water route around Africa to the Indies and for the kingdom of Prester John. I am determined that this should not happen."

This was a side of the infante Andrea had never seen, the stern ruler convinced of the rightness of his cause. And yet, knowing Prince Henry and his zeal for the propagation of the Catholic faith, he could sympathize with the viewpoint of the Portuguese leader. "I willingly give you a vow of silence, milord," he said simply and the others agreed.

Prince Henry smiled then and was once more his old self. "I was sure you would agree when you knew my reasons," he said warmly. "Believe me, Senhor Andrea, you will never regret your co-operation."

"There is still another reason why the discovery of a mass of land to the west between Europe and the Indies should be kept secret," Mestre Jacomé added. "A certain physician of Florence named Paolo Toscanelli openly claims that the Indies can be reached by sailing five thousand miles across the Western Sea. I have it upon good authority that the Medici family are very much interested in such a voyage, and as you know, Andrea, the Medici are always on the alert for new sources of trade and profit."

"Senhor Toscanelli is wrong," Andrea said positively. "Our voyage proves that. If the country Salvagio spoke of was India or China, I would have recognized it from his description. And besides, none of the savages we saw in any way resembled the Chinese or the inhabitants of India."

"What about Cipangu?" Prince Henry asked.

"I will take an oath that they are a different race entirely."

Mestre Jacomé smiled. "The point is, we *want* Senhor Toscanelli and the Medici to keep on being wrong. If they knew of a land barrier between here and the Indies—or that the distance is actually much greater than five thousand miles—they might try to sail around Africa, too, and search for that route to India and China."

"And perhaps get there before you," Andrea pointed out.

"Exactly," said Mestre Jacomé. "So why should we correct the errors of Toscanelli and the Florentines?"

"I can see your reasoning," Andrea admitted, albeit a little reluctantly.

"But you don't approve of it?" Prince Henry asked.

Andrea looked up, to see the thoughtful gaze of the infante fastened upon him. "I do not presume to approve or disapprove your actions and decisions, milord," he said. "Naturally I am disappointed that the discovery is not to be made known to the world, since I am sure that what this new land has to offer could mean much to the population of Europe now living under terrible conditions."

"You have discovered Antillia and so you shall be credited," Prince Henry assured him. "On your next map you may draw it in exactly as you found it, with Satanazes and the other islands as you remember them also. And as soon as we have discovered a way to link up with Prester John or the water route to the Indies by way of Africa, I promise that your discovery of what may be a whole new world in the West shall be made public."

"Meanwhile," Mestre Jacomé said with vast satisfaction, "the Florentines will be wasting their time seeking to tap the riches of China and India by sailing west. It is no more than they deserve for accepting the smaller world of Ptolemy without bothering to measure it for themselves."

The meeting broke up then. As the others were leaving, Mestre Jacomé took Andrea by the arm. "I have another matter to discuss with you," he said, "if you will wait a little while."

"Is it news from Venice?"

"Yes. I had a letter from there while you were gone. Your half brother, Mattei, disappeared before the owners of the galley you were captured on could have him brought to trial."

"Then he wasn't arrested?"

"Not according to my information. Whoever wrote you must have been expecting him to be, but the letter could have been written before he was actually taken."

"It was his wife—Signora Angelita."

"So? That may be the reason she came to Lisbon then."

"Angelita in Lisbon!" Andrea could hardly believe his own ears.

"So it is reported to me. She traveled there on the galley commanded by Signor Cadamosto."

This was startling news indeed. Angelita in Venice had been far away, almost a shadow in his memory since he'd declared his love for Leonor. He had easily persuaded himself to delay going there to see her. But in Lisbon she was only a two days' ride away and he could not put off very long meeting her and settling the whole question of their relationship.

The full meaning of Mestre Jacomé's news was beginning to strike him now. If Mattei had indeed flown Venice before the *polizia* could arrest him, leaving Angelita behind—as seemed to be the case—she could easily get an annulment of her marriage, leaving her free to marry anyone she chose.

"I am sorry to be the bearer of bad tidings," Mestre Jacomé continued. "According to my information your brother was able to sell the Bianco shipping business to the Medici, before his departure, for a large amount—all of which he took with him."

"But leaving Angelita behind?"

Mestre Jacomé shrugged. "She is in Lisbon. As for Mattei Bianco, he may have set himself up in Trebizond or Constantinople. Many Venetian merchants trade in those lands and he would be familiar with the region."

Trust Mattei to land on his feet like a cat when dropped, Andrea thought. He was not so much disturbed by the loss of the money; that had always seemed far away. But the idea of Mattei swindling him and going unpunished was a different matter—plus the fact that as long as his half brother was alive his own life would always be in danger.

"I will never be able to clear my name in Venice now," Andrea said morosely.

"That, I am happy to say, has already been done," Mestre Jacomé assured him. "Your brother's actions were a confession of guilt in themselves. When the *Infante Henrique* was reported lost Prince Henry petitioned the Pope on your behalf to clear your memory as a tribute to you. He sent all the evidence to his representatives in Venice, with the petition approved by His Holiness. That, plus additional evidence which my friends there were able to provide, quickly established your innocence before the Venetian courts. The Council of Ten cleared you and would have ordered your property reinstated—but your half brother had already flown with the money."

"What about the Palazzo Bianco?"

"I am told that the courts awarded it to you, since the sale had not been completed." Mestre Jacomé shot him a keen glance. "You don't seem overjoyed at your good fortune."

"Overcome is the word," Andrea assured him. "How can I ever thank you for what you have done?"

The old mapmaker smiled. "First you can marry Dona Leonor. Then you can settle down here at Villa do Infante and draw fine maps for our shipmasters and help us seek a simple way of measuring the longitude. Perhaps you might even navigate the ship that finally does reach the ports of the Indies."

"I can think of nothing I would rather do," Andrea assured him sincerely.

"Did your navigational device prove satisfactory?"

"Entirely. I determined that Antillia lies on the same parallel of latitude as Cape Blanco on the African coast. The river where we careened on the shore of Satanazes is on roughly the parallel of Cape Bojador."

"And you are sure it would take you back to these places?"

"As easy as going from Lagos to Villa do Infante," Andrea assured him. "I had never been to the Açores, but because I knew the islands were on a circle of latitude that cut the coast here between Lisbon and Sagres, I was able to sail directly to them from Satanazes."

"I know how disappointed you must be, not being able to announce your discovery," Mestre Jacomé said as the two were parting. "But the infante's reasons are sound ones. And your navigational device will still bring you riches and fame."

Andrea shook his head. "Being as near death for so long, as we were, I had time to think about the predicament of seafarers who are far from home. If I sell the secret of this device to others, some will not possess it and so will be lost. When certain things are settled Leonor and I hope to be married. I know how he feels about the Al— about the device and I plan to give it to her as a wedding present. Then together we will reveal the secret as our gift to mariners everywhere."

"No man would have a right to ask such a sacrifice of you."

"That is why Leonor and I must do it together," Andrea explained. "Only she, Fra Mauro, and I know the secret, and the good friar will not reveal it until I free him of a vow. Once before, I made a sacrifice—when I freed the slaves—and it brought me a thousandfold reward in Leonor's love and the opportunity to go on the voyage to Antillia and Satanazes."

"Perhaps this one will still bring you a greater reward," Mestre Jacomé suggested.

"You have only to be a thousand leagues from home on a trackless ocean to know what it means to be certain of the route back home. Just to know others have that assurance, too, will be reward enough."

X

Even though he knew Angelita was in Lisbon, Andrea found ways of putting off the time when he must go to her. One day was taken up with an appearance before the assembly of scholars at Villa do Infante, where he gave an account in detail of the voyage westward and the discovery of Antillia, omitting only the things he had learned from Salvagio concerning a possible new continent of which Satanazes might be a part. Another day was required for the inevitable fiesta in honor of their return. He and Leonor left the gay festival early and walked hand in hand across the dunes to the promontory of Sagres, where he had shown her and Fra Mauro how to use the Al-Kemal the night before he had sailed for the river Sanaga with Dom Alfonso Lancarote.

The path ended on the promontory overlooking the ocean, and now they stood with the surf breaking on the shore below them, looking out across the seemingly endless expanse of the Western Sea. The moon was just rising and its light made a silvery path across the water, like a road leading westward.

Neither had spoken since they had left the festival and Leonor did not resist now when he took her in his arms. Her lips were soft and fragrant beneath his own when he kissed her hungrily, as if afraid he might lose her.

After a long sweet moment they drew apart. "Is anything wrong, darling?" she asked. "You act almost as if you were afraid."

He tried to keep his voice light. "It must be the natural reluctance of a bachelor to give up his freedom. Mestre Jacomé wants us to marry and settle down so I can draw maps and navigate some of the voyages southward."

She caught her breath and moved into his embrace again, putting her arms around him and holding him tightly. "You can draw all the maps you wish, *carissimo*, but you've done enough sailing. A married man should stay at home."

"You'll not have to argue very hard to convince me of that," he promised. "At least not for a long time."

But even as he held her in his arms, the fear he refused as yet to give a name came back. And his arm tightened about her until she cried out in pain. Instantly contrite, he released her, but she did not move away. Instead she took him by the shoulders and looked up into his eyes. "Something *is* wrong, Andrea," she said. "I knew it just now."

There was no point in keeping the cause of his fears from her—or from himself—any longer. "It's Angelita," he told her. "Mattei has left her and she is in Lisbon."

"Lisbon! Why would she go there?"

"I remember her saying once that she had an uncle in Spain, so she must be staying with his family. Mestre Jacomé learned from friends in Venice that Mattei sold the shipping business and fled with the money."

"You must go to Lisbon and see her, Andrea."

"I suppose you are right," he admitted. "But I was afraid to hurt you."

"Knowing you still loved her would hurt me more," Leonor said quietly. "A part of you still remembers Angelita and until you see her again, you will never be certain whether you love her or not."

"I will go to Lisbon and settle it," he promised. "There doesn't seem to be any other way."

Several days later a note arrived for Andrea by messenger from Angelita. It left no doubt concerning her feelings toward him:

> *Andrea, carissimo* (she had written),
> *My heart was broken when Captain Cadamosto brought me word from Lagos that you had been lost at sea. But now the good news has come that you are safe, and I cannot wait to see you.*
> *Mattei treacherously deserted me, and I had no choice but to leave Venice. My Uncle Piero has for a long time been the head of the Medici bank in Lisbon and when he insisted that I come and stay with him, I was overjoyed because it brought me nearer to you. The messenger who carries this has instructions to bring you back with him. Hurry to Lisbon and into my arms. They have been empty for so long,*
>
> > *Your beloved,*
> > *Angelita*

The messenger, a page wearing the Medici livery, waited while Andrea finished reading the note. "Will the Senhor leave for Lisbon today?" he asked respectfully.

"Tomorrow morning," Andrea told him. "Can we make it in two days?"

"If we ride hard and change horses several times. I brought a horse for you from the inn of Lagos."

"You can rest here," Andrea told him. "We will leave at dawn."

Leonor had gone to Lagos to visit a friend, and the household of Dom Bartholomeu was still asleep when Andrea rose in the chill of the early winter morning and dressed quickly. He stopped by the kitchen for a crust of bread and a gulp of wine. The page who had brought Angelita's message was already in the courtyard holding the horses, but as Andrea started out, he saw the pudgy form of Fra Mauro emerge from another part of the house.

"I am glad you are awake, little brother," Andrea told him. "Tell Leonor good-by for me when she returns. I should be back from Lisbon in less than a week."

Normally a jolly man, the Franciscan's round face was grave this morning. "You are only a man, even though a fine one, Andrea," he said. "Be sure you do not let a man's desires and lusts betray you. Even great wealth is not so precious as the love of a girl like Leonor."

"I am going to Lisbon only to exorcise an old demon that will not let me rest," Andrea assured him. "But exorcise it I shall. That you can depend upon."

"Go with God then," the friar said. "My soul is much lighter."

The morning fog was rolling in from the sea as they galloped through the sleeping town and headed north on the road to Lisbon.

XI

True to the page's promise, Andrea rode through the streets of Lisbon late in the afternoon of the following day. He was tired, but glad he had finally taken this step along the road to renunciation of his old love for Angelita. In addition, he was sure now that the warmer and far more spiritual feeling he cherished for Leonor would remain after he had exorcised the demon of his old purely physical desire for Angelita, and anxious to be about the job of ridding himself of it.

As always since he had sailed on the voyage to Guinea, Andrea carried the A1-Kemal strapped about his waist in a canvas belt. Without even looking at the string he could identify in his mind the knots that led to the Canaries, to Cape Blanco and the river Sanaga, and to Antillia and Satanazes in the west, as well as to the Açores. That cord was actually a map of the known world south and west of Europe, much of which he had discovered himself, and the thought of all the things he had accomplished in less than a year since he'd faced seemingly certain death in Venice filled him with a sense of pride.

Venice held nothing for him any more, he had decided on the long ride to Lisbon. If Angelita wanted the Palazzo Bianco, he would give it to her. That in itself would relieve him of any further obligation as far as she was concerned. His real ties were with this part of the world, with Lagos and Villa do Infante, the verdant coast of Guinea, and the exciting new land that lay to the west, waiting for men of courage and strength to explore it and wrest away its secrets and its wealth. The center of his existence from now on would be the home he would make with Leonor, the quiet days at the drafting board while he drew maps of this rapidly expanding world, and the happy voices of their children playing in the garden.

"Here we are, senhor." The page's voice broke into Andrea's reverie and he saw that the horses had halted before a lovely small house at the edge of a spacious estate.

"Does Signora Bianco live here alone?"

"Senhor Piero's home is nearby," the page assured him. "This is part of the grounds." Darkness was falling already, but Andrea could see a much larger house some distance away.

He dismounted stiffly and slung his saddlebag over his shoulder while the page took the horses away to stable them. The door of the cottage was opened to his knock by a dour-faced elderly woman. "I am Senhor Andrea Bianco," he said. "Senhora Bianco is expecting me."

"The Senhora is at her uncle's house," the servant said. "I will send word to her that you are here. Your chamber is ready."

Andrea followed the woman to a sumptuously furnished bedchamber. It was decidedly not what one would expect in the house of a woman whose husband had run away and left her penniless, he thought. Then he remembered that, as a member of the Medici banking and commercial firm which controlled a sizable portion of the gold in Europe, Angelita's Uncle Piero was undoubtedly rich.

Water was brought for Andrea to wash away the grime of travel and wine with spiced cakes for him to refresh himself. Angelita had not returned when he finished drinking a glass of wine, so he stretched out on a broad, soft couch. Weary as he was from two days of riding he fell asleep immediately.

He was awakened by a knock on the door; the dour-faced servant stood outside. "Senhora Bianco has returned," she announced. "She waits in her chamber to welcome you."

On the way to Lisbon Andrea had decided that the simplest procedure would be to meet Angelita formally, tell her of his decision to turn the Palazzo Bianco over to her and of his coming marriage to Leonor, then leave as soon as possible. Concerning her feeling for him, the letter he had received a few days before left no doubt, but he was resolved not to mislead her. The question of their future relationship must be settled once and for all, and the sooner he got it over with, the better it would be for everyone. Realizing that he did not love her any longer, Angelita would surely cast aside her infatuation for him.

And yet, in spite of his stern intentions, Andrea could not quell a rising sense of excitement as he followed the servant through the house. At the moment, he found himself wishing he could be more certain of his own strength to resist Angelita's beauty and the memory of what they had been to each other. But he'd come this far, he reminded himself sternly, and there was no going back. Besides, he was a man of the world now, not a callow youth ready to succumb to the first woman who came near him.

The servant paused before a closed door and knocked upon it. *"Entrino,"* a well-remembered throaty voice said, and Andrea felt his heart take a sudden leap. The servant opened the door and as he stepped through, closed it behind him. He faced the woman who turned from the mirror of her dressing table to greet him and realized that where he had left a lovely girl back in Venice, a beautiful and utterly desirable woman had taken her place.

"Andrea," she said, rising and coming to him with extended hands and a warm smile. "Andrea *carissimo.*"

"Buon giorno, Angelita." He took her hands and wondered why his voice sounded a little hoarse.

"Aren't you even going to kiss me?" she asked. "It was different the last time we were together. Or have you forgotten?"

He could do nothing then but kiss her, as a brother should. There was nothing sisterly about the softness of her mouth beneath his, however, and he forced himself to draw away before the quick response of his own body made him go farther.

Angelita pulled away, too, but did not let go his hands.

"Why so stiff, *carissimo?*" she asked reproachfully. "Are you angry at me because I did not come to the prison in Venice?"

As lovely as she was now, it was difficult to be angry at her about anything.

"Mattei told me the man in prison was an impostor, trying to extort money from us," she assured him. "After all, you had been reported as dead years before, Andrea. How could I know it was really you?"

"It doesn't matter now," he said. She was still holding his hands and they were only a step apart. She wore a frilled dressing sack tied about her waist with a gold-embroidered cord and—he guessed from the way it clung to her—little else.

"Come sit beside me." She drew him over to the dressing table and indicated a cushion beside it. "I hurried from Uncle Piero's house to bathe and dress for dinner but I couldn't wait to see you." She reached for her comb and the silk of her dressing sack pulled aside a little, half revealing one lovely full breast, which she made no move to cover up again.

"The years have been kind to you, Andrea," she said, smiling at him from the mirror. "You are far handsomer than before."

"And you are much more beautiful, Angelita."

She wrinkled her nose at him. "We are old friends—and more—so you can be truthful. I am nearly ten years older, remember?" She started brushing her dark lustrous hair again. "And what about you, *carissimo?* It must have been awful on the galleys."

"I stayed alive and was lucky enough to travel very widely—so it wasn't an entire loss."

"Where did you learn about the navigational device?" she asked casually.

Andrea looked at her sharply. "How did you know of it?"

"Captain Cadamosto brought me here from Venice. He talked of nothing else except what it can do—and the money it will make for you."

"I am going to reveal the secret to all mariners in a few weeks."

She turned quickly to face him. "But that would be foolish, darling. With it you can easily become one of the richest men in the world—that is if it can do everything Signor Cadamosto says it can."

"Being nearly lost at sea on this last voyage taught me I could never profit from something that could conceivably cause men to lose their lives because it was denied them. Leonor and I——"

She frowned. "Leonor?"

"Dom Bartholomeu di Perestrello's daughter. She came to see you at Chioggia on my behalf."

"I remember her now. She is very pretty."

"We are going to be married, Angelita—I hope with your blessing."

She got up suddenly and went to the fireplace, in which a brisk pile of coals was burning against the chill of the night. He could not help noticing how the outlines of her body were revealed through the thin stuff of the dressing sack, or fail to be stirred by her loveliness.

"This is a shock, Andrea," she said finally. "I'd thought we two——" Then she turned to face him once more. "But I should have known that after eight years . . ."

"I carried your memory enshrined in my heart for most of that time," he told her. "Even after I learned that you had married Mattei."

"How could I know you were still alive, Andrea?" Then with an effort she seemed to get control of herself. "But we won't let what might have been spoil our being together again. I raided Uncle Piero's wine cellar especially for you. After dinner we can sit here by the fire and talk about your adventures."

Andrea took a long breath. The problem of breaking to her the news that he loved another had proved easier than he had expected. And she had taken it well, which made him feel a warm sense of gratitude toward her. There was no reason at all, he told himself, why he and his brother's widow should not be friends. The fact that they had once been lovers need not come between them now.

"We'll dine here where it is warm," Angelita decided. "Do you mind if I don't dress any more formally than this?"

"Of course not," he told her gallantly. "You're lovely as you are."

"Dear, sweet Andrea," she said softly. "Actually you haven't changed at all, except to grow more handsome."

While Angelita was arranging for the meal to be served there, Andrea moved about the room, examining the furnishings. They were quite luxurious, as were the fittings of the dressing table, the silver frame of her mirror, and the exquisitely carved boxes that held her cosmetics. The room was filled with her perfume and everything in it, even the broad couch with its pile of soft pillows, was utterly feminine. With the Medici fortune behind her, plus her own loveliness, he decided, Angelita would not remain unmarried long.

Dinner was as delightful as his companion. They were very gay and the wineglasses were filled often. Uncle Piero's wine was indeed powerful, Andrea decided, when his head began to whirl a little and the flames in the fireplace took on an unusual brightness. Angelita, however, seemed not to be affected particularly.

When the dinner dishes had been taken away by the servants they sat together on the broad couch, sipping wine and talking of the old days in Venice when they had been courting and of his travels over the world. Andrea would have been less than human not to feel a comfortable sense of admiration and affection for the lovely woman beside him who had once meant so much to him.

"Have you heard from Mattei . . . since he went away?" he asked once, but she quickly turned the conversation to another vein, by which he judged that the memory of his half brother's faithlessness and treachery brought her pain. Finally Andrea pushed away the wineglass and got to his feet. "I should be getting to bed, Angelita," he said. "It is a long ride back to Lagos and Villa do Infante. Besides"—he grinned—"if I don't go now, the servants may have to carry me." Already the room was beginning to sway a little and he grasped a chair to steady himself.

"They're gone," she told him with a warm smile. "I sent them to Uncle Piero's."

Even in his somewhat befuddled condition the import of her words set a sudden fire burning inside him. Nor was there much question about the light in her eyes when she stood up and came close to him. "But don't worry," she said. "I'll see that you get safely to bed."

He knew he should go now; prudence demanded it. But there was no prudence in the warm tide surging up within him, or the eager flood of desire that almost set him trembling with its urgency. It had been like this in the summerhouse back at Venice that night, he remembered. Both were flushed with wine, and Angelita had not resisted when he'd taken her in his arms—just as he was sure she would not resist now.

Yet something held him back, the memory of Leonor and of Fra Mauro's round troubled face, reminding him that he was not free to take what was so obviously being offered.

"I'll let you go to bed," Angelita said softly. "But only after you kiss me good night."

He could never be certain just how she got into his arms, whether he reached out for her or she came into them of her own accord. He only knew that her body was soft and yielding against his and her lips parted and eager beneath his mouth when he kissed her. She made no move to hinder him while his hands were fumbling at the cord of her dressing gown. And when he cupped her breasts in his two hands, her arms only strained his body to hers all the harder.

Even through the haze of the wine that threatened to engulf his consciousness completely, Andrea heard the door open and tried to draw away, thankful for the interruption that had brought him to his senses again. But Angelita's arms around him were suddenly like iron bands, pressing his own against his body, so that for the moment he could make no move to see who had entered the room.

Then rough hands seized him by the shoulder, jerking him away. Already unsteady from the wine—which he realized in a moment of clarity now must have been drugged—he toppled over against the couch and rolled to the floor, while booted feet kicked at him savagely again and again. He heard a shrill voice that was vaguely familiar cursing viciously, but only when he finally managed to roll far enough to escape the kicking was he able to see who had so rudely interrupted the tryst.

The distorted face mouthing obscenities at him was that of his half brother, Mattei!

XII

As Andrea staggered to his feet, the sword in his half brother's hand came up and the point touched his chest.

"Get dressed, you slut," Mattei snapped at Angelita, who was calmly straightening her dressing gown about her body. "If I hadn't come in when I did, I suppose you would have given yourself to him as you have to others."

Angelita turned back to the mirror with a shrug. "He's a better man than you," she said contemptuously. "I should have some reward for betraying him."

The shock of Mattei's appearance and the threat of the sword in his hand was clearing Andrea's head rapidly, even of the drugged wine. "What do you want with me, Mattei?" he asked.

The smaller man turned on him fiercely, pressing forward with the sword point until it touched Andrea's throat and he had to step back to keep from being thrust through then and there. "I want your life," Mattei spat at him. "Your life for setting the Jews on me and making me flee from Venice like a common thief—and for this."

"Nothing happened here."

"It was not your fault—or hers. With my wife naked in your arms when I found you, no court in the world would hold me liable for killing you."

"You and Angelita planned this," Andrea accused him, the whole pattern of tonight's happenings beginning to fall into place now.

"*I* planned it," Mattei corrected him. "When Gil Vicente was fool enough to let you get the best of him I had to be rid of you somehow. And what better way than this?"

"Mattei and I understand each other, Andrea," Angelita said from the dressing table. "He needs my family connections with the Medici and I tolerate him for the money he gives me. It's a profitable arrangement."

"What about me?" he asked, remembering how she had responded to his kiss and his embrace.

She shrugged. "You should have returned from your voyage before Mattei got to Lisbon."

"Then he intended coming here all the time?"

"Of course. You were nearby, and with you out of the way our fortunes will be clear."

He didn't like the casual way in which she disposed of him as being as good as dead. But then he couldn't blame her, he supposed. Certainly he had never been in a situation where the outlook seemed more hopeless. And yet, the fact that Mattei had not killed him outright when he burst into the room lent to the situation some small element of hope. He turned to face Mattei now, wondering if he dared pit his great strength against the sword in the smaller man's hand.

"Don't consider trying to overcome me, Andrea," Mattei warned grimly. "Two of my own men are outside the door."

It could be a bluff, but Andrea didn't think it was. Still, he needed to know for sure. "I don't believe it," he said.

"Dominic! Angelo!" Mattei spoke without turning his head. Two lackeys appeared in the doorway at once, each with a long knife in his hand.

"Why not kill me now?" Andrea asked.

"I would do it—willingly," Mattei told him. "But we did have the same father, so I'm going to be generous and give you your life in exchange for the secret navigational device you possess."

It was as simple as that, Andrea saw, and cursed himself for a fool in not expecting all along that Mattei would plan some such strategy to get control of the Al-Kemal, whose value he could well understand because of his knowledge of shipping and trade. After all, Mattei had sent an assassin to follow him once, even as far as Arguim Island, which should have been warning enough. The fact that his half brother wanted the secret badly enough not to kill him at once added a further sinister note to a situation that was already too grave for comfort.

"What do you say?" Mattei demanded. Angelita was calmly brushing her hair.

"What will happen to me if I reveal it to you?" Andrea asked.

"I told you the terms," Mattei said impatiently. "Your life in return for the secret of the device."

"How do I know you will carry out your part of the bargain?"

Mattei shrugged. "You have my word. That should be enough."

"Very well," Andrea said. "I will give you the device." He started to unbutton his tunic to get the belt, but Mattei pressed him with the sword point and he was forced to step back against the wall.

"Try no tricks!" the smaller man warned. "I will be only too happy to kill you."

Andrea was careful not to anger his half brother more. Many a time, as a boy, he'd seen Mattei kill living pets in a fit of fury over some trifling happening.

"What you seek is in a canvas belt around my waist," Andrea explained. "I have no weapon."

Mattei stepped back warily and watched while Andrea loosened the canvas belt. From it he took the Al-Kemal and handed it to his half brother.

"I was going to turn this over to Prince Henry so all mariners could use it," he explained. "Now it is yours."

"That thing!" Anger blazed in Mattei's eyes as he jerked the Al-Kemal from Andrea's hand. "Do you take me for a fool, to hand me a thing like this?" In a fit of insane fury at what he evidently considered an attempt to dupe him, he whirled and tossed the Al-Kemal into the flames burning in the fireplace. Then he turned upon Andrea again, pressing with the sword until the point pushed him back against the wall.

"Now, give me the real instrument and don't think I'm fool enough to be taken in by a block of wood and a piece of string," Mattei shouted, trembling with rage.

"What you just destroyed is called an Al-Kemal," Andrea told him. "Arab sea captains make it from glass or porcelain or even from a piece of horn; I made that one out of wood."

Mattei glanced toward the fire. The block was already practically consumed by the flames. "You are lying," he accused, but there was no conviction in his voice.

"That worthless block of wood, as you call it, led me from Guinea back to Lagos," Andrea said. "And it guided us to the Açores from the island of Antillia."

Mattei looked at the fire, where the Al-Kemal was already only a charred mass, and Angelita spoke, her voice cold with contempt for her husband. "Andrea wouldn't have kept the thing hidden in a special belt around his body if it wasn't valuable, you fool," she snapped. "That vile temper of yours has betrayed us again, Mattei."

"Keep silent, slut!" He spat at her like a cat, holding Andrea still pinned to the wall with the point of his sword. "If you made that one, Andrea, you can make another— and show me how to use it?"

"I can," Andrea said. "If the reward is great enough."

"You were quick enough to give it to me just now to save your life," Mattei sneered. "You will make another for the same reason."

Angelita spoke again. "Do you think he is fool enough

not to realize that by killing him you would lose any chance you might have of getting the device now?"

"Angelita is right, Mattei," Andrea seized the lead she had given him. "You have to keep me alive because that's the only way you can ever get it."

For a moment he thought that in his fury Mattei was going to split him with the sword anyway. But in the end the smaller man's love for money prevailed. "Bind him and throw him in the cellar," he ordered the lackeys. "We'll see how much he resists after a few days of persuasion."

"I'll make you all the Al-Kemals you want," Andrea promised, "when you can guarantee that I will not be killed. But I'll need something more dependable than your word."

"Put him in the cellar," Mattei repeated. "And bind his hands to his feet—no, bring me the cords, I'll bind him myself."

The two men brought strong cords and Mattei made Andrea lie down on the floor. Then, giving his sword to the man called Angelo, he deftly bound Andrea's wrists together.

Andrea tried an old trick of the slave markets, tensing his muscles so that when he relaxed the cords would be loose, but Mattei was alert to this sort of thing, too, and tightened the cords until they bit into the flesh. Even when Andrea released the tension of his muscles he could hardly move his wrists, and there appeared to be no possibility at all of working his hands through the loops of the cords.

Mattei next tied Andrea's ankles tightly together. Then, taking a longer piece of cord, he looped it through the circles formed by Andrea's bound wrists and ankles, pulling the cords tight until they were drawn behind his back, touching each other. It was a diabolical way to pinion a man with both his arms and legs behind him and his back arched, a position that would soon become practically unbearable.

When Mattei rolled him over, Andrea saw Angelita looking at him from the bench before her dressing table. Her eyes were wide and he wondered whether there could be at least a small measure of compassion for him in them.

Obeying a sudden impulse, he spoke directly to her.

"My friends in Lagos know I came here to see you, Angelita," he said. "When I do not return Prince Henry will send the police to arrest you. Mattei has earned the gallows, but I'd still hate to see the rope around your neck."

Mattei leaned over and struck him in the mouth, cutting his lip, but Andrea spat out the blood and kept on speaking to Angelita. "Both of you will be hounded from one city to another until you're arrested," he told her. "You would have been better off casting your lot with me."

Mattei struck him again. "Save your breath for screaming," he snarled. "And be sure to leave enough so you can call me when you're ready to make another of the navigational devices."

The two lackeys lifted Andrea and carried him from the room.

XIII

The cellar of the cottage was damp and without any kind of heat. Straw was scattered here and there and a pile of rags occupied one corner. By lying on his side Andrea was able to inch his body along until he could work some of these between himself and the cold stones of the floor, but that was all he could do for his own comfort.

He quickly gave up any idea of getting his wrists loose, since every motion only made the cords dig into his flesh. Nor did it help to work his feet together and try to free them. In fact he soon decided that he would live longer in this predicament with less pain if he relaxed as much as possible while he tried to devise some other means of escape—if there was any such possibility, which hardly seemed likely.

As the hours wore on, Andrea managed to get a little sleep by lying on his face on the pile of sacking and letting his stiff muscles relax. He could sleep for only a few moments, however, before the cords cut off the circulation to his hands and feet and the pain brought him abruptly awake. A few moments of cautious and restrained exercise would establish the circulation again, and then he could drop off to sleep once more for a short while.

His prison had been dark when they thrust him unceremoniously into it, so he'd had no chance to discover any details about it. These would come with the dawn, but he did not doubt that Mattei would arrive then with some more ingenious method of torture to help accomplish his purpose. This would logically be to break Andrea down to where the prospect of death, after he revealed the secret of the Al-Kemal to Mattei, would seem no worse than the torture he was undergoing. Once he had made one of the navigational devices and explained its use, he was sure Mattei would destroy him. Nor would Mattei be punished —once Angelita testified that Andrea had sought to seduce her.

His attempt to sway her in his favor by pointing out that she and Mattei would inevitably be punished for his death had been a forlorn hope, Andrea decided now. Angelita was obviously what Mattei had called her, a slut. In fact, he was sure now that the two of them must have been in league to deprive him of his birthright when Mattei had taken the initial step of having him captured by the Turkish corsair so long ago.

His one hope, Andrea decided—and a faint one it was indeed—lay in the possibility that he had sowed some small seed of doubt in her mind, or at least started her to wondering whether in the end he might be a better one to back than Mattei. As to what he would do if she did decide to help him against his half brother, Andrea had no idea at the moment.

And so the long hours of the night passed. It was just after dawn when a key turned in the lock and Andrea prepared himself for the torture that he was sure would come with Mattei's appearance. But it was Angelita who came into the cellar. She carried a lighted candle and a small flagon of wine.

"Speak only in a whisper," she cautioned as she put the candle on the floor and opened the flagon. He accepted the mouth of the bottle when she put it to his lips and gulped the wine thirstily until the flagon was empty. That it might be poisoned or drugged did not cross his mind. Dead he was worth nothing to his captors, alive he could still furnish them with the secret of the Al-Kemal.

"What did you mean yesterday when you said I would be better off casting my lot with you?" she asked.

"I am now chief navigator in the service of Prince

Henry," he explained. "He is certain to send someone to look for me when I do not return."

"Does he reward you well? I mean with riches and a fine house?"

"The prince lives simply and so do those who serve him. But if you will release me, I will deed to you the Palazzo Bianco in Venice."

"If I let you go, Mattei will kill me," she said matter-of-factly. "So we have to kill him first. Is what Cadamosto says true—that the person who controls your secret can name his own price for it?"

The reason for her coming was in the open now. She had seen the chance, as he had hoped, to get more money through him than with Mattei. "Is Cadamosto in this thing with you?" he asked.

She shook her head. "He and I were friendly on the voyage from Venice." Andrea could guess what she meant by that. "But after we got to Lisbon he learned somehow that Mattei had come here to meet me. We are pretty sure he suspected that we planned to get the device and then kill you and that he went to Lagos to warn you. That's why I sent the page in such a hurry to bring you here before you saw Cadamosto."

"What is your price for setting me free?" he asked.

She studied him for a moment, evidently weighing both sides of the situation, the future with him against the same prospect with Mattei. "Half of what we receive for your device goes to me," she said finally. "Plus the Palazzo Bianco in Venice."

The terms were better than Andrea had expected—if he could trust her. As to that, he was not yet decided. Of one thing he could be sure. Whether she had him murdered later and took everything for herself would depend, not on any love she might have for him, but on what seemed to promise most for her.

"Of course you will have to kill Mattei first," she added.

"And be executed for murder?"

"I will testify that you came to visit me on family business," she said. "And that Mattei was lurking outside and tried to kill you."

"What about you?"

She seemed to measure him with her eyes, like a man buying a horse. Then she smiled, evidently liking what she saw. "I go with the agreement," she said frankly, "at least until I tire of your embrace. Then we can make other arrangements."

"Like the one that you and Mattei have?" he could not help asking.

She shrugged. "Tonight you had at least a promise of what life with me can mean. Why ask questions—especially with your life at stake?"

"What is your plan?" he asked, without agreeing at all to undertake it.

As he had hoped, she took it for granted that no man could renounce the promise of her favor. "Tonight only Dominic will be on guard," she said quickly. "He has—reasons—to be anxious to please me, so he will not object when I visit you—apparently to talk you into doing what Mattei wants. I will cut your bonds and give you a dagger. Later you can call Dominic in and——" She made an expressive gesture that left no doubt of her ex-lover's fate. "He's been troublesome lately anyway with his demands."

"And Mattei?"

"He will be asleep in our chamber; I will see to that, too. You can take care of him with one thrust. Then I will set up a clamor, and when the authorities come I will swear that Mattei followed me from Venice to kill us both and that you fought with him after he had killed poor Dominic, who tried to defend me. With Mattei out of the way we can sell your device. Florence, Genoa, and Venice will all bid for it, so we will undoubtedly be rich."

"It's a clever plan," he admitted.

She got to her feet. "Naturally. I am good at such things. Be ready when I come; it will be a little before midnight."

Andrea had given her no promise, but Angelita's vanity and confidence in her own power over men had led her to assume that he would follow her plan. And follow he would, he vowed, at least to the point of overcoming Mattei and turning them both over to the authorities of Libson before he started back to Lagos—and Leonor.

XIV

Mattei visited Andrea during the midmorning, with the bulky Angelo beside him. He had exchanged his sword for a long whip coiled over his arm. "Have you decided to do as I wish?" he demanded peremptorily.

"Release me first," Andrea told him. "I will return to Lagos at once and send you a new Al-Kemal."

"Do you take me for a fool?" Mattei slashed him with the whip, putting the full strength of his slight body into it. He lashed Andrea again and again while he lay helpless on the floor of the cellar and, in the end, it was Mattei's lack of strength, rather than his own fortitude, that saved Andrea.

"This is just the beginning," Mattei promised as he left the underground chamber. "I'll be back to give you more later. By then maybe you'll be ready to do what I ask."

Andrea's pain was so great that he didn't bother to answer. His face and neck were crisscrossed with welts and his body burned like fire where the whip had cut through the material of his tunic. He had no way of knowing how many hours passed while he lay on the floor of the cellar, half conscious from pain, hunger, and thirst. Sometime later in the afternoon he was awakened when a beam of light struck his eyes. Thinking that Angelita had come to release him and that he had slept through the sound of the key turning in the lock, he rolled over quickly, but saw at once that he was still alone. The room had only one small leaded window, and when he raised his eyes to it he could see the shaft of sunlight that had awakened him. It came through a small opening in one of the leaded panes, perhaps as wide and as long as a man's thumb.

The glass had been broken, he could see now, possibly by small boys with a stone. It would be at about ground level outside, he judged, but inside the cellar the window was well above a man's height from the floor. The heavy leaded panes admitted only a little of the afternoon sunlight, but the defect where the sliver of glass had been knocked out had allowed the single ray to enter the room

and strike his face. Rolling around again, he was able to
detect the spot of brightness where the ray of light struck
the opposite wall.

Suddenly an idea seized Andrea, an idea so bright with
hope that it penetrated the haze of agony which had blanketed his mind since the whipping by Mattei. If the
sliver of glass had fallen inward at all recently, he
thought, it must be still on the floor beneath the window,
for the cellar showed no sign of having been cleaned for
a long time. And a sliver of glass could, conceivably, cut
the cords that bound his wrists and ankles.

Ignoring his own discomfort, Andrea inched, rolled,
and crawled across the room toward the side containing
the single window. From the angle made by the shaft of
light through the opening he judged that he had little more
than an hour of daylight left, which meant that he must
be very fast indeed if he were to carry out the plan rapidly taking form in his mind. First, however, he must find
the triangular-shaped piece of glass broken from the
windowpane—if it really existed.

Rocking himself on his stomach, Andrea moved slowly
back and forth across the space just beneath the window,
often bumping his chin and even his nose against the
floor when he rocked too far. Sharp twinges of pain from
impaired circulation in his hands and feet as the cords
were stretched made all motion agonizing, but he did not
dare stop. His one chance of life, he was sure now, lay in
finding that sliver of glass, if it still remained on the floor.

Beneath the window where the wall and floor met,
the light was very poor and as he burrowed with his face
in the dust, he had to fight back a cough whenever he
sucked it into his lungs. At all costs, he knew, he must do
nothing to warn the lackey on guard at the head of the
steps leading to the cellar.

Again and again Andrea worked his way across the
dust-covered floor beneath the window, moving a little
farther away from the wall each time he traversed a space
only a little wider than the window itself. And as the light
gradually failed without revealing the presence of the
sliver of glass he sought, his spirits began to sink in defeat.
He had been a fool even to hope, he told himself dismally
now, for it might have been years since the pane had
been broken and the fragments of glass long since swept
out.

And then, just as he was about to give up from pain and disappointment, something pricked his chin through the dust on the floor. The pain was like a tiny spot of fire and, hardly daring to hope he might have found what he sought, Andrea arched his neck to raise his head high enough to look at it.

A tiny sliver of glass lay there in the dust. Hardly bigger than a small needle, it was much too small for his purpose, but the discovery filled him with a quick surge of hope. For if this tiny sliver still lay on the floor, then the larger one he needed must almost certainly be there, too. Unless—the thought struck him with chilling abruptness—the entire fragment had slivered into tiny pieces like this one.

Just then his chin struck another sharp point and, raising his head again to look at it, he saw with a sudden thrill of joy that this was the larger fragment he had been seeking. It was roughly the size he had estimated, perhaps as wide as a man's thumb and somewhat longer. The leaded pane from which it had been broken was fairly thick and the edge of the fragment looked sharp and strong enough to cut through the cords binding his wrists—if he could ever bring them into contact with it.

Unwilling to risk feeling for the glass fragment with his bound hands in the semidarkness of the corner where the light was rapidly growing more obscure, and perhaps knock it farther away, Andrea concentrated upon trying to pick it up with his mouth. The sharp edges several times pricked his lips before he finally managed to get the sliver between them. Then, holding it in his mouth, he began to work his way back across the floor toward the center of the cell where the light was better.

Now he must solve the problem of how to use the piece of broken glass. The ideal way, of course, would be to fix it somehow in a crack in the stone floor of the cellar and saw the bonds binding his wrists against it until they' were severed. But there wouldn't be time for this before darkness fell, he decided, and he could not risk losing the glass in the darkness.

In desperation, for time was running out, he seized the fragment in his fingers and, rocking back and forth on his face—an agonizing position—began to saw through the cord that bound his ankles. The whole thing had to be accomplished completely out of sight, since both his hands and his ankles were behind him, a difficult task indeed. But he was spurred on by the knowledge that with his feet free he could almost surely find some method of using the glass to cut the bonds securing his wrists.

Intermittently as he worked, Andrea had been half conscious of activity outside, the muted rumble of carriage wheels and an occasional sound of voices. But nothing further had happened to give promise of rescue and he had been too busy with the glass to think much about it. He was just beginning to make some progress, judging by the pressure which he was able to maintain against the cord by holding the triangular fragment of glass between his fingers, when he heard voices outside and the grating of a key being thrust into the lock. He barely had time to hide the glass by clutching it in his hands and turning over on his side before the door opened.

Mattei came in, followed by Angelo who bore a lighted candle against the darkness which was falling rapidly now. Andrea felt a surge of relief when he saw that his half brother was not carrying the whip he'd used that morning.

Mattei held up the candle and in its flickering light, Andrea saw that his face was grim. "Did you hear anything just now?" he demanded.

"Maybe a carriage. Why?"

"Your friend Cadamosto developed scruples, it seems, as we suspected. He saw me here in Lisbon and went to Lagos to warn you."

"Was that Cadamosto just now?"

"With your patron, Senhor di Perestrello, and his daughter. They didn't see me, and Angelita assured them you had been here and had started back to Lagos."

Andrea decided to play the prisoner who has lost all hope; it wouldn't do to let Mattei suspect that he had his own plan for escaping now. "I could have shouted to them," he groaned, "if I'd only known."

"I doubt if they would have heard you." Mattei was recovering his good humor. "But I'm not taking any chances. Cadamosto is no fool and he may still suspect that we have you a prisoner here. Tonight you will be moved by carriage to a farmhouse in the country belonging to Angelita's aunt. If your friends come looking for you again in the morning, she will let them search the house. Then they will go back to Lagos."

From the doorway Mattei added, "And don't expect Angelita to help you. She told me of her talk with you this morning, but I convinced her that I'll get a higher price for your secret than you ever would. Besides, I'm already rich, after selling our business in Venice. Gold is a language in which Angelita and I understand each other perfectly."

Waiting only until the steps of the visitors had died away, Andrea resumed work on the cords with the fragment of glass. The sudden release of the bonds about his ankles almost made him drop the piece of glass. That, in the darkness which now filled the cellar, could have been disastrous, but he managed to hang onto it.

For a moment or two he allowed himself the exquisite pleasure of stretching his legs, but the intense pain when the blood rushed into them after the cramped position in which he had lain for a whole day and most of the night almost made him cry out. Setting his teeth into his lips to keep back the cry, he attacked the problem of getting at his wrists.

This seemed impossible, until he remembered a game he had played as a boy, swinging from the limb of a tree and passing his body back and forth through the circle thus made by his arms. The feat was infinitely more difficult of course, with his hands tied behind his back, and a precious half hour—it seemed—of patient squirming was used up before he felt his arms slip around his hips and along his thighs. A moment of further working brought his legs and feet through. His arms were now in front of him, although his wrists were still bound together. The glass fragment was tightly gripped in one of his palms.

The only way to cut the cords that bound his wrists seemed to be to hold the piece of glass in his teeth and Andrea quickly transferred it there, hoping silently that it would not shatter before he was finished. Should the glass fail him, he would have no choice except to sever the cords with his teeth—provided of course there was time before Mattei returned to take him into the country.

He was not able to put much pressure on the sharp edge while holding the fragment of glass in his mouth, but he worked rapidly and soon severed the last strands of the cord. The pain in his wrists and arms as the blood flowed freely again was exquisite, but so was his joy at being free again. He might die here in the cellar in the next few hours, he told himself grimly as he spat out the sliver of glass along with a few drops of blood where it had cut into his lips. But he could face that prospect almost cheerfully, now that he had at least a chance to defend himself.

As he flexed his powerful muscles, Andrea could feel a great surge of joy in their strength well up inside him. It was comforting to know that if he were lucky enough to kill Mattei with his bare hands tonight—as he fervently hoped to do—the strength he used would in no small degree be a result of Mattei's having betrayed him to the corsairs in the Mediterranean. Thus, through a macabre twist of fate, his treacherous half brother would be responsible for forging the very weapon that would destroy him.

The sound of voices outside warned Andrea that Mattei must be coming to take him away. Quickly he went to stand behind the door, ready to attack whoever came through it. He was counting on the suddenness and unexpectedness of the attack to give him the advantage, before whoever entered the cell could bring either sword or dagger into use.

The key crunched in the lock and the door swung open slowly. The candle in the hand of the visitor cast a circle of light into the room, but Andrea was crouching behind the open door where he could not be seen immediately. As the visitor moved into the room, he was tensing himself for the spring that would bear them both to the floor when he realized the identity of the slender figure in the dark cloak.

It was Angelita!

XV

"Andrea," she called in a low voice as she stepped farther into the room and lifted the candle above her head. "Andrea, where are you?"

He did not answer the call. Even if by some chance Angelita had come to free him—in spite of what Mattei had said a few hours ago—it would do no good to let her know he was free before he knew the full import of the situation and was ready to take immediate advantage of any opportunity that presented itself. And the best thing at the moment seemed to be to allow her to reveal her purpose.

Not finding him in the cell, Angelita turned quickly to the door. "Dominic!" she called. "Come here! He's gone!"

Heavy feet crunched on the stone floor outside the door and Andrea saw the hulking form of the lackey lunge through the frame, knife in hand. Only then did he launch his own attack, savagely determined to gain the advantage he needed in one move.

Head down and charging like an enraged bull, Andrea struck the lackey in the side and carried him across the room to crash against the wall. Momentarily stunned by the savage attack, the man dropped the knife, but Andrea wasted no time grappling for it on the dusty floor. Dominic recovered quickly and tried to fight back, but his strength was nothing against muscles that had pulled the oars of a slave galley for five years. Seizing the lackey by the shoulders, Andrea battered his head savagely against the stone wall again and again.

He heard Angelita scream behind him, but he was so filled with the savage joy of combat that he ignored her. Only when the body in his hands went suddenly limp did he drop it like one of the sacks on the floor and stoop to pick up the dagger which had fallen from Dominic's nerveless grip. Armed now, he turned to face Angelita, who stared at him, her mouth already open to scream again as he moved to the door. He heard feet charging down the stairs and had barely time to raise his fist with the knife gripped in it when Mattei lunged into the room, sword ready in his hand, and moving so swiftly that Andrea was not able to strike him.

Angelo was right behind his master, however, and as the lackey hesitated in the doorway for a moment, Andrea rose on his toes and chopped down with his fist clenched around the handle of the dagger, using it like a hammer to strike the man's neck just below where it joined the skull. It was a brutal blow, intended as such, with all the pent-up anger from Andrea's long hours of torture here in the cellar behind it. Angelo went down without even so much as a groan.

For what happened next, Andrea found no explanation at the moment. Later he was able to visualize the scene as it must have appeared to Mattei when he rushed into the room. Angelita stood almost in the middle of it, the candle still upheld, as if to afford light for someone else. Dominic's inert body was on the floor and Andrea was poised beside the door, ready to attack whoever entered with the knife in his hand. For Mattei, who had never trusted anyone, there could be but one answer—betrayal.

"Slut," he spat at Angelita. "You freed him."

"No——" The word died on Angelita's lips as Mattei lunged, insane with rage at what he thought was her betrayal of him by releasing Andrea.

Andrea, too, cried out in protest, but his voice was drowned by Angelita's scream of terror and pain when the sword penetrated her breast. The scream broke off with a horrible gurgling of death as her body started to fall. Overcome with horror, Andrea failed to take advantage of the moment when Mattei's sword was buried in his wife's body and so gave the madman time to jerk it out and turn upon him.

The candle had fallen from Angelita's dying grasp and the soft wax guttered for a moment on the floor before the flames caught in the dry straw and flared up. In the light of the flames, Andrea saw Mattei rushing at him, holding the naked sword still dripping with Angelita's blood. Somehow he managed to leap aside and evade the thrust. Vaguely he was conscious of the tramp of feet upon the stairs and of shouting voices, but had no time to wonder what they meant, being far too busy at the moment escaping Mattei's mad lunges at him with the sword.

Once, twice, and a third time, Mattei thrust and Andrea leaped aside, too intent upon avoiding the rushes even to try and deliver a blow himself. On the third pass Andrea was not able to twist away quickly enough and the blade entered his right shoulder. He felt a stabbing pain, but that small victory proved Mattei's undoing.

Momentarily the sword was embedded in Andrea's flesh and Mattei was within reach of Andrea's left hand. The right was useless, even the dagger had dropped from his fingers at the impact of the sword through the muscles of his shoulder. But there was more than enough strength in Andrea's left arm to seize Mattei by the collar and lift him from the floor, shaking him as a cat does a mouse, before tossing him against the stone wall.

Mattei's body struck the wall with a crash, went limp from the force of the blow, and slid to the floor. The sword, which he had held tightly in his grasp, was drawn from Andrea's shoulder, but it, too, fell free of Mattei's unconscious hand.

Andrea was staggering toward his half brother, determined to end this lightning-swift melee, when a hand dropped upon his shoulder and gently drew him back. He turned then and saw that the door of the room was jammed with people, one of whom was Dom Bartholomeu di Perestrello. The man who held him was Cadamosto.

"Let Mattei Bianco live to pay for his crimes, Senhor Andrea," the Venetian captain said. "He cannot harm you any more now."

"Andrea!" Leonor rushed into the room and seized him in her arms. Then, feeling the blood from his shoulder on her fingers, she drew back. "You are bleeding," she cried. "Where is the wound?"

"Only a prick in the shoulder." He managed to grin as he put his good arm around her and drew her close again. "I didn't jump fast enough."

Men wearing the uniform of the Lisbon police were crowding into the room now, stamping out the burning straw and applying manacles to the unconscious forms of Mattei and his two lackeys.

"See about Angelita," Andrea called to Cadamosto. "Mattei thought she had freed me and stabbed her."

"She is dead," the Venetian said. "It was a merciful thrust; now only he will die on the gallows."

XVI

Much later, when Andrea's wound had been effectively bandaged by a physician at the home of some friends of Dom Bartholomeu's, he was able to ask a question that had been troubling him. "How did you manage to arrive at exactly the right moment?" he inquired of Cadamosto.

"We didn't," the Venetian captain said. "The action was finished when we came through the door." He shook his head. "Three armed men against one without arms. The odds were formidable, my friend, but to you they were nothing."

Andrea grinned. "It still seems to me that you dropped from the skies."

"When we talked to Signora Angelita earlier I suspected she was not telling the truth," Cadamosto explained. "We could not prove that either you or Signor Mattei were in the house, so we pretended to leave. Then Dona Leonor thought of finding the page who had brought you from Lagos. He told us no horse had been brought to the cottage for you, so we knew you were still in Lisbon and probably in that house. Dom Bartholomeu explained our predicament to the *polizia* and they agreed to cooperate with us in watching it."

"Signor Piero de' Medici is a man of some influence here in Lisbon," Dom Bartholomeu explained. "The police would not enter the house without more evidence, but Signor Cadamosto figured that if you were a prisoner inside, they would try to take you away during the night, in case we should decide to come back later."

"They were going to do just that," Andrea confirmed.

"When Donna Angelita screamed," Leonor added, "Signor Cadamosto rushed in with the guards."

The Venetian smiled, showing white teeth in his dark-skinned face. "But too late to help," he said. "As would be expected, Senhor Andrea had the situation well under control."

"You came soon enough to keep me from killing Mattei," Andrea said gratefully. "I'll not have that on my conscience at least."

"For a man of peace, Senhor Andrea, you are very efficient in battle," Cadamosto said, admiringly. "I hope you will always be on my side."

When the door had closed behind Dom Bartholomeu and the Venetian Andrea put his good arm around Leonor's waist. "My battling days are over, for a while at least, *carissima mia*," he told her. "And I can't say that I'm sorry."

"They're over forever," she corrected, lifting her face to his. "It's time you returned to your regular trade of mapmaker."

"Why not a new one," he asked her at the end of a long kiss. "That of husband and father."

"I'm afraid you'll have to prove yourself there," she said demurely. "But then I have yet to see something that Andrea Bianco cannot do well."

Beloved Biblical Novels by

FRANK SLAUGHTER

"Always a consummate storyteller"
—Chicago Tribune

Rousing Historical Novels by

FRANK SLAUGHTER

"A whale of a spinner of tales"
—Chicago Tribune